UNMASKING MISS APPLEBY

OTHER WORKS

THE BALEFUL GODMOTHER SERIES

THE FEY QUARTET (SERIES PREQUEL)

MAYTHORN'S WISH
HAZEL'S PROMISE
IVY'S CHOICE
LARKSPUR'S QUEST

ORIGINAL SERIES

UNMASKING MISS APPLEBY
RESISTING MISS MERRYWEATHER
TRUSTING MISS TRENTHAM
CLAIMING MISTER KEMP
RUINING MISS WROTHAM
DISCOVERING MISS DALRYMPLE

OTHER HISTORICAL ROMANCES

THE COUNTESS'S GROOM
THE SPINSTER'S SECRET

FANTASY NOVELS (WRITTEN AS EMILY GEE)

THIEF WITH NO SHADOW
THE LAURENTINE SPY

THE CURSED KINGDOMS TRILOGY
THE SENTINEL MAGE ~ *THE FIRE PRINCE* ~ *THE BLOOD CURSE*

UNMASKING
MISS APPLEBY

Emily Larkin

A Baleful Godmother

Novel

www.emilylarkin.com

Book Layout © 2014 BookDesignTemplates.com

Cover Design: The Killion Group, Inc

Unmasking Miss Appleby / Emily Larkin -- 1st ed.

ISBN 978-0-9941384-1-5

Dear Reader

Unmasking Miss Appleby is the first novel in the Baleful God-mother historical romance series. A full list of the books in the series can be found at www.emilylarkin.com/books.

Those of you who like to start a series at the very, very, very beginning may wish to read the Fey Quartet novellas, where any questions you might have about *how* and *why* this particular family of women have a Faerie godmother are answered.

I'm currently giving a free digital copy of *The Fey Quartet* to anyone who joins my Readers' Group. If you'd like a copy, please visit www.emilylarkin.com/starter-library.

Happy reading,

Emily Larkin

It is a truth universally acknowledged,

that Faerie godmothers do not exist.

CHAPTER ONE

October 10th, 1805
London

MARCUS LANGFORD, NINTH Earl of Cosgrove, strode down the steps of Westminster Palace. Clouds streamed across the face of the moon.

"Excellent speech, sir," his secretary, Lionel, said.

Marcus didn't reply. His mind wasn't on the address he'd made to the Upper House, it was on the sniggers he'd heard as the debating chamber emptied, the whispers that followed him down the corridor. *Cuckold Cosgrove.*

A black tide of rage swept through him. "We'll walk back," he said abruptly, and lengthened his stride. The icy wind gusted, making the torches flare in their brackets, almost snatching his hat from his head, filling his mouth with the stink of the Thames.

Lionel tucked the satchel of papers more firmly under one arm and trotted to keep up. "Did you see Hyde's face, sir? He was so angry, he went purple. I thought he'd have apoplexy, right there in the chamber!"

"I wish he would." St. James's Park loomed dark on their left. "We'll cut through here."

The clatter of carriage wheels faded behind them. The fetid smell of the Thames receded, overlain by the scents of dank soil and dead leaves. Gravel crunched beneath their boots.

"You're correct, sir," Lionel said, puffing faintly alongside him. "It's the best course. Abolition of the trade, not of slavery itself. Slavery will disappear as a natural consequence."

Marcus grunted. He spread his hands wide, clenched them. He needed an outlet for his anger. A bout with Jackson or—

"Did you hear that?" Lionel swung back the way they'd come. "Sir . . . I think someone's following us."

Marcus half-turned. He saw leafless branches whipping in the wind, saw shadow and moonlight patterning the ground. "There's no one—"

His ears caught the faint crunch of gravel.

There. Not half a dozen yards distant, in the deepest shadows: three men, mufflers hiding their faces.

Footpads.

His pulse kicked, and sped up.

"Run, sir!" Lionel cried.

Marcus ignored him. He stepped forward, hands clenched, teeth bared in a snarl. This was exactly what he needed. A fight.

The footpads abandoned their stealth and rushed from the shadows.

Marcus threw a punch at the nearest man, connected solidly, and followed with a left hook that brought the footpad to the ground.

A second man aimed a sloppy blow at him. Marcus grabbed his attacker's wrist and twisted, tossing him over his hip. A perfect cross-buttock throw. *Pity Jackson didn't see that.*

"Sir!" Lionel cried, his voice high with panic. "Run!"

Marcus swung again, striking the third man in the mouth. Lips split beneath his knuckles. The satisfaction of drawing blood made him laugh, a harsh sound that echoed in the night.

The first footpad scrambled to his feet. Marcus sank his fist into the man's belly. The footpad collapsed with a *whoosh* of gin-scented breath.

Out of the corner of his eye he saw the second footpad lurch upright. Lionel hit him over the head with the satchel.

Marcus ripped off his torn gloves and gulped a breath, gulped a laugh. He'd rarely felt so alive—the cold air in his throat, the sting of broken skin on his knuckles, the savage exhilaration in his blood.

He whirled to face the third footpad. The man ducked his punch and grabbed him in a bear hug that smelled of sour sweat and ale. They grappled for a moment, muscles straining. The footpad slammed his forehead against Marcus's.

The night dissolved into stars—then snapped back into focus: the moon, the scurrying clouds, the skeleton shapes of the trees. A knee jabbed into Marcus's stomach. "Cuckold Cosgrove," the footpad growled.

Marcus tore free of the man's grip, stumbling back, almost winded. *He knows who I am?*

The footpad struck at him with both fists.

Marcus brushed aside the first blow and caught the second on his brow, threw an uppercut that snapped the man's head back, grabbed the footpad and buried his knee in the man's groin.

The footpad doubled over with a choked cry. He collapsed when Marcus shoved him away. Two yards away, the first footpad was on hands and knees, retching.

Marcus gulped a breath of icy air. He tasted blood on his tongue, felt it trickle down his brow and cheek. His exhilaration hardened into anger. The footpads knew his name; this wasn't a random attack.

From behind came the crack of bone breaking and a cut-off cry of agony.

He spun around.

Lionel lay sprawled on the gravel path. The last footpad stood over him. Sheets of paper spilled from the satchel, scurrying across the ground, spinning in the wind like large white moths.

Marcus uttered a roar. He charged at the footpad, knocked him down. "You son of a whore!" He grabbed the man's hair and smashed his fist into the upturned face, battering him until he sagged senseless.

Marcus shoved the footpad aside. "Lionel?" He fell to his knees alongside his secretary. The anger snuffed out. In its place was a deep, sucking fear. "Are you hurt?" Blood trickled into his eyes. He blinked it back and shook his head, spraying droplets. "Lionel! Answer me!"

CHAPTER TWO

October 13th, 1805
Westcote Hall, Essex

CHARLOTTE APPLEBY LAID down her needle and flexed her fingers. The handkerchief was almost finished: her uncle's initials intertwined, and beneath them a tiny red hand, the symbol of a baronet. *As if it helps Uncle Neville blow his nose better to know he's a baronet.* She snorted under her breath.

The back of her neck prickled, as if someone had moved noiselessly to stand behind her.

Charlotte turned her head sharply.

No one stood behind her. The corner of the parlor was empty.

Charlotte rubbed her nape, where the skin still prickled faintly. *A draft, that's all it was.* She flicked a glance at her aunt and cousin, seated beside the fireplace.

Lady Westcote thumbed through the *Lady's Monthly Museum*, barely glancing at the pages, her lips pursed. Anthea was bent over the dish of sugarplums, choosing the plumpest.

Charlotte rethreaded her needle and started on the border around her uncle's monogram.

Lady Westcote tossed the magazine aside. "Charity."

Charlotte lifted her head. "Yes, Aunt?"

"Fetch my shawl. The cashmere with the pink border."

Charlotte obediently laid down her sewing. She let herself out of the parlor and climbed the sweeping oak staircase. *Calm,* she told herself. *Calm.* But her resentment was sharp today—she almost tasted it on her tongue, as bitter as bile—and the tight knot of anger in her chest only seemed to grow larger with each step she took.

She knew why: Today was her birthday. Her twenty-fifth. *And instead of everything I dreamed of, I have life at Westcote Hall.*

Charlotte pushed her spectacles firmly up her nose. What she had was better than many others had—a roof over her head, food in her stomach. She was lucky.

Lady Westcote's maid, Litton, was laying out evening clothes in her aunt's dressing room: a gown of puce silk, a turban crowned with curling ostrich plumes, satin slippers. Beneath the cloying scent of Lady Westcote's perfume was the sour undertone of her perspiration.

"My aunt would like her cashmere shawl, Litton. The one with the pink border."

Litton nodded and turned to the clothes press.

For a moment they were both framed in the cheval mirror: Litton dressed in a gown of kerseymere that was in the latest fashion; herself in one of Anthea's castoffs, taken in at the waist and let down at the hem. Alongside the maid, she looked shabby, her wrists protruding from cuffs that were slightly too short.

I look more like a servant than Litton does.

"Here you are, Miss Charity."

Charlotte took the proffered shawl. "Thank you."

She let herself out of the dressing room. *I could run away and become a lady's maid.* At least she'd be paid for her drudgery. And no one would call her Charity.

Charlotte tried to imagine what it would be like. *Appleby, this petticoat is ripped. Darn it. Appleby, my hair needs to be curled again. Make sure you do a better job this time. Fetch my tooth powder, Appleby—and be quick about it!*

She pulled a face. No, Litton's job wasn't to be envied.

Charlotte went back downstairs, her hand gliding over the cool oak balustrade. As she stepped onto the half-landing, the hairs on the back of her neck stood upright.

She jerked a glance behind her. The staircase rose in empty, curving flights.

Charlotte rubbed her neck. *Idiot.* She walked briskly down the last half-flight, pushed her spectacles up her nose again, and opened the door to the parlor. "Your shawl, Aunt."

Lady Westcote took the shawl without a word of thanks.

Charlotte gritted her teeth. *I am grateful to my aunt and uncle for giving me a home,* she told herself. *Grateful.* She took her seat in the corner of the parlor and bent her head over Uncle Neville's handkerchief, trying to find a calm place in her mind.

"Only five months until I make my début." Anthea clapped her hands in delight. "Oh, I can't wait, Mama!"

Charlotte halted mid-stitch. She lifted her head and stared across the parlor at her aunt. *And what of my début? What of the promise you made my father on his deathbed?*

"I shall do better than Eliza," Anthea declared. "I shall catch a husband in my *first* Season."

"Your sister did extremely well." Lady Westcote arranged her shawl around her shoulders. "Tunbridge is a wealthy man. And well-connected."

Charlotte snorted silently. *And as stout as a pig that's been fattened for the Christmas spit.*

Anthea pouted. Her gaze slid to Charlotte. "Even if it does take me two Seasons, at least I shan't be an old maid."

Charlotte pretended the barb hadn't struck home. She curved her mouth into a smile—cheerful, unruffled.

Anthea tossed her ringlets and looked away.

Charlotte returned her attention to the handkerchief. She tried to concentrate on her sewing, tried to make each stitch as small and even as possible, but her cousin's voice kept intruding. "For my coming-out ball, I want spider-gauze sewn all over with pearls, and a white satin gown underneath. And white satin dancing slippers tied with ribbons."

Resentful anger mounted in Charlotte's chest. It was a dangerous, reckless emotion. It made her want to throw down her sewing. It made her want to tell her aunt and cousin exactly what she thought of them. Made her want to storm out of the parlor and slam the door.

Made her want to risk being turned out of Westcote Hall.

Charlotte stabbed the needle into the handkerchief. *Gratitude.* She had a roof over her head. Clothes on her back. Food in her belly. Those were all things the Westcotes gave her. All things she was grateful for.

"Charity, pour me another cup of tea."

The pressure in her chest increased. *My name is Charlotte.* "Of course, Cousin."

Anthea curled a ringlet around one plump finger. "I shall catch myself a duke. You will all have to call me Your Grace."

Charlotte walked to the tea service. She picked up the teapot and poured. In her mind's eye, she saw herself throw the pot across the room, saw it shatter against the silk-covered wall, spraying tea and shards of porcelain.

"Your Grace," Anthea repeated, with a self-satisfied giggle.

Charlotte glanced at the door, wishing she was on the other side of it. A few hours of silence, of privacy—

If you want that, you know what you have to do.

Charlotte took a deep breath. She placed the teacup and saucer on the table alongside Anthea. "Your tea, Cousin," she said, and flicked the cup with a finger as she stepped back.

The cup fell over in its saucer with a delicate *clang.* The porcelain handle broke off. Tea flooded the saucer, spilling onto the tabletop, trickling to the floor.

"Look what you've done!" Anthea cried, pulling her skirts out of the way.

Lady Westcote surged to her feet with all the majesty of a walrus. "You clumsy creature!"

Charlotte turned to face her aunt. She felt marvelously calm. *Send me to my room for the rest of the day. Please, Aunt.*

"Broken!" Lady Westcote's face suffused with color. She advanced, one hand upraised. "One of my best Staffordshire teacups!"

The slap almost dislodged Charlotte's spectacles.

"Go to your room! I don't want to see you until tomorrow."

Thank you. Charlotte straightened her spectacles. Heat rushed to her cheek, but beneath the heat was a cool, serene calmness.

"And don't think you can ask one of the servants for food!" Lady Westcote cried shrilly. "You can starve until tomorrow morning! Do you hear me?"

"I do, Aunt." Charlotte curtsied and let herself out of the parlor.

She closed the door with a quiet *snick* and stood for a moment in the corridor. She felt light, as if she'd grown wings and was hovering a foot off the ground. *A whole evening to myself.* No aunt and uncle. No cousin.

Relief filled her lungs and spread across her face as a smile.

A whole evening alone.

HER BEDCHAMBER WAS next to the schoolroom, a small room that had once been the governess's. Charlotte closed the door and let the silence sink into her skin. The rug was threadbare and the furniture had seen better days, but this room was hers. No one else came here.

She touched her cheek, feeling the heat, the stinging residue of pain. It had been worth breaking the teacup for this: silence and solitude.

Across the room, her reflection stared at her from the mirror. Brown hair, brown eyes, a face that was neither pretty nor plain.

Charlotte grimaced at herself. *Happy birthday.*

She curled up on the bed, hugging a blanket around her, enjoying the silence. Daylight drained from the sky. When the room was dark, Charlotte lit a candle and closed the shutters. The clock on the narrow mantelpiece told her it was dinnertime.

Hunger stirred in her belly. Charlotte ignored it.

She took the candle next door to the schoolroom. Here, she'd tutored the Westcote boys until their entry to Rugby. Here, she'd taught Eliza and Anthea until their seventeenth birthdays. No words had been spoken in the schoolroom for months, no fires lit in the grate. The air was inert. Cold had soaked into the floorboards, into the walls.

At the back of the schoolroom was the old pianoforte.

Charlotte pulled out the stool and sat, resting her fingers on the keys, feeling their smooth coolness.

She visualized the score, heard the music in her ears, and played the first notes. Quiet. Beautiful. The last of her resentment and anger evaporated. Joy flowered inside her like a rose unfurling its petals. The world receded. Westcote Hall was gone. Her aunt and uncle and cousin were gone.

The hairs stood up on the back of her neck.

Charlotte jerked around, lifting her hands from the keys. The schoolroom was empty except for shadows, and so was the doorway.

The echoes of music died away. She held her breath and heard only silence. No creaking floorboards, no furtive footsteps.

Stop this foolishness! Charlotte placed her fingers firmly on the piano keys and filled the room with sound. A jaunty, cheerful tune that begged to be danced to—

"Miss Charity?"

Charlotte jerked around on the stool. The piano strings vibrated with a discordant hum.

A housemaid stood in the doorway. "Mrs. Heslop said to give you this. Venison pie. And a newspaper that were in Sir's fireplace."

"Oh, Lizzie." Foolish tears rushed to her eyes. Charlotte blinked them back and stood. Her footsteps echoed hollowly on the floorboards. "Please thank Mrs. Heslop from me." The newspaper was charred at the edges, the linen-wrapped pie warm and fragrant.

Back in her bedroom, she slipped off her shoes, climbed up on the bed, and unfolded the newspaper. A warm glow of happiness spread through her. What a perfect evening: the precious solitude, the music, the kindness of the housekeeper.

Charlotte ate hungrily, read hungrily. A rich and varied world existed beyond the walls of Westcote Hall and the newspaper brought it vividly to life: the war with France, political debates and criminal trials, the doings of the Prince Regent and the *ton*, concerts and exhibitions and theatrical performances.

When she'd finished the pie, Charlotte gave a deep sigh of contentment. This was the best birthday she'd had since her father had died.

The thought was sobering. She frowned down at the columns of closely typeset print. Her eyes fastened on an advertisement.

Wanted by a Gentleman's Family in the county of Hertfordshire, a GOVERNESS competent to instruct two young girls in Music, Geography, and English. A thorough knowledge of the French language is required.

Charlotte reread the advertisement. She could do that.

Her gaze skipped down the page. *Wanted immediately, a single YOUNG MAN to act as a Gentleman's secretary. A strict*

Character required. Good wages will be given.

She could do that, too. Hadn't she been her father's secretary until his death? And a secretary would earn more than a governess.

But she wasn't a man.

Charlotte pulled a face and read further.

A position exists for a JUNIOR SCHOOLMISTRESS well-qualified to teach English, French, and Latin grammatically. Applications to Mrs. Bolton, of Mrs. Bolton's Ladies' Boarding School, near Basingstoke. Testimonials of Character will be required.

Charlotte read the advertisement again. If she worked at a school, she'd have colleagues, other teachers she could become friends with.

Friends.

Charlotte raised her head and stared across the bedchamber, not seeing the stiff wooden chair in the corner. *I should like a friend.* Someone she could talk with, share confidences with, laugh with.

But who was to say that she'd find a friend at Mrs. Bolton's Boarding School?

And did she really want to be a junior schoolmistress?

It couldn't possibly be any worse than life at Westcote Hall and quite likely much better—at the very least, she'd be paid for her labor—and yet . . .

She recognized the uneasy, twisting sensation beneath her breastbone: fear.

The Westcotes were her only family. They might treat her little better than a servant, but they gave her a home, gave her safety and security. If she left, there'd be no coming back; her uncle had made that quite clear.

Charlotte frowned at the wooden chair in the corner. What was more important?

Family? Security?

Or independence?

If I leave, will I regret it? Or will I regret it more if I stay? Without foresight, there was no way of knowing—

The wooden chair was no longer empty. A woman sat there.

A scream choked in Charlotte's throat. She jerked backwards on the bed. The hairs on the back of her neck, on her scalp, stood upright.

The woman snapped her fingers. A fire flared alight in the fireplace, flames filling the narrow grate and roaring up the chimney. Four blazing beeswax candles appeared on the mantelpiece.

"That's better." The woman folded her pale hands on her lap. She was dressed in a gown that had been fashionable hundreds of years ago, blood-red velvet trimmed with gold. A high white lace ruff framed her throat and head. Her face was as pale as wax, her eyes as black as obsidian, not reflecting the candlelight, but swallowing it. "Charlotte Christina Albinia Appleby?"

CHAPTER THREE

CHARLOTTE OPENED HER mouth, but no sound emerged. Her heart thundered against her ribcage. Where had the woman come from? How had she made the fire roar to life and burning candles appear on the mantelpiece?

"Charlotte Christina Albinia Appleby?" the woman repeated.

Charlotte found her voice. "Who are you?" It came out too high, her voice squeaking on the last word. "What are you doing in my room?"

Thin black eyebrows arched in a movement that was both amused and mocking. "Has your mother not told you?"

"My mother is dead."

The woman's lips tilted in a faint smile. "Careless of her."

"Who are you?" Charlotte demanded again.

"My name is not for you to know."

"Then leave." Charlotte scrambled off the bed and stood. She was taller than the woman now. She pointed at the door, trying to make her voice loud and commanding. "Get out of my room!"

The woman didn't move. "Are you certain that's what you wish?" The faint, mocking smile touched her lips again. "You haven't taken your gift."

"What gift?"

"The gift I owe you."

The words made no sense. "Who *are* you?"

The woman's smile widened, showing her teeth. They were as white and even and pointed as a cat's.

Charlotte took an involuntary step back.

"You call my kind Faeries."

Instinctively, Charlotte shook her head—there was no such thing as Faeries. But the evidence was before her: Those black eyes and sharp white teeth were clearly not human.

The prickling on her scalp, on the nape of her neck, intensified. It felt as if every hair stretched itself on end. "Have . . . have you been watching me today?"

The woman's smile seemed to widen fractionally, her teeth to grow infinitesimally sharper. "What do you choose? Levitation? Metamorphosis? Translocation?"

Charlotte swallowed. She clutched her hands tightly together. "Why are you offering me a gift?"

"Because I owe it to you."

"You owe *me*?"

"One of your ancestors did me a service. As payment, she demanded a wish for each of her daughters." The woman's mouth twisted, as if she tasted something sour. "And their daughters in turn."

Charlotte turned this answer over in her mind, trying to make sense of it. "You gave my mother a gift?"

"On her twenty-fifth birthday, yes."

Charlotte shook her head again. *No. Not possible.* But her mouth was already forming words: "What did she choose?"

"Levitation."

Charlotte blinked. "My mother could . . . fly?"

The woman ignored this question. She leaned forward, her eyes fixed on Charlotte. Dark eyes. Predatory eyes. "Make your choice."

Charlotte tried not to recoil. She moistened her lips. "How

long do I have?"

"Until midnight."

Charlotte's gaze jumped to the clock—half past seven—then back to the woman's face. "Why tonight?"

"Because the women in your line receive their wishes on their twenty-fifth birthdays."

Line? Her mind fastened on the word. "There are other lines?" Other women who'd had been offered this choice?

"That is not relevant to you." The woman's gaze became sharper, blacker, skewering her like a moth pinned to paper. "Choose your gift."

Fear shivered up the back of Charlotte's neck. She rubbed the skin, trying to force the sensation away. She sat carefully on the end of the bed. Thoughts churned in her head, possibilities spilling over one another. A Faerie gift. She could be free of her aunt and uncle's charity. Free of Westcote Hall. Free to live a life of her own choosing.

What gift should I take? Not levitation. Something that gave her independence.

"Money," Charlotte said. "Can you give me money?"

The woman's pale upper lip curled in scorn. "Money? No, that is not within my power." Her eyelids lowered for a moment, then lifted again. She smiled, showing her teeth. "But I can give you the golden touch. If that's what you wish?"

"No!" Charlotte jerked back on the bed. "Not that!" To be Midas? To turn everyone she touched into gold?

The woman's lips folded together. Spite glittered in her eyes.

Charlotte's heart began to beat even faster. *She'll trick me if she can, give me a gift that will harm me. I must choose wisely.* "What are the gifts I may choose from?"

"You wish me to list them all? We haven't time. You must choose quickly."

Charlotte pushed her spectacles up her nose and tried to look as if she weren't terrified. "There's plenty of time." Her voice was firm, with no squeak to betray her. "Midnight is several hours away." Fear trembled inside her, but alongside the fear was determination. *You won't rush me into a mistake.* "The other gifts. What are they?"

The woman's face seemed to narrow, her eyes to grow larger and darker, to swallow more of the candlelight. "Levitation," she said, in a voice that was as thin and sharp as a knife blade. "The ability to tell truth from lies. Translocation. Longevity—"

"What's translocation?"

"The ability to transfer yourself from one place to another."

Charlotte frowned, considering this. *I could translocate to London. I could...* What? Rob a bank? She shook her head. "Please continue."

"Control of fire. Metamorphosis—"

"What's that?"

"The ability to change shape."

Charlotte turned this over in her head. "Could I be another person?"

"A person, an animal."

"Is it permanent?"

"I can make it permanent, if that's what you want." The pale eyelids lowered and lifted, the black eyes gleamed. The woman seemed to lean forward fractionally on the wooden chair, like a hunting dog that had scented prey yet dared not move from its place at its master's feet.

"And if I don't want that?" Charlotte said hastily.

The terrible eagerness dissipated. "You may change back when you choose."

Charlotte glanced down at the newspaper, with its singed pages and columns of type. "So . . . I could be a man?"

"If you wish."

Is that what I want? To be a man? To be able to obtain better employment than I can as a woman? "What else?" Charlotte asked, looking back at her guest. "What are the other gifts?"

"The ability to communicate with animals. Augmented physical strength. The ability to hear others' thoughts." The woman paused. "Are you certain you don't wish for that?" Her voice was honeyed, sweet, persuasive. "It's a powerful gift."

The tone was warning enough. Charlotte shook her head.

Malice flickered across the woman's face, making the pale skin stretch more tightly over the bones. "Invisibility," she said. "Enhanced hearing. The ability to see in the dark. The ability to find things. Foresight."

"Please stop," Charlotte said. "I need to think." She closed her eyes. *What do I want most?*

The answer was easy. She wanted to earn her way in life. To be independent. To never need the Westcotes' charity again.

Invisibility, translocation, levitation . . . they wouldn't give her that. They were nothing more than showy tricks, useless unless she wanted employment as a freak at a fair. Or to steal money instead of earn it.

Charlotte opened her eyes. She stared down at the newspaper. *Wanted immediately, a single YOUNG MAN to act as a Gentleman's secretary.*

If she chose metamorphosis, she could apply for that position—or any other that she liked. Tutor. Secretary. Schoolmaster. She could study at Oxford. She could enter the church and take orders. She could be a solicitor or merchant or diplomat's aide. She could travel the world.

Charlotte pressed her fingertips to her mouth. *Is this what I truly want? To be a man?* She lifted her head and stared across the brightly lit room at her guest.

The woman stared back, her eyes not reflecting the candlelight.

Charlotte lowered her hands. "Tell me about metamorphosis,

please. How does it work?"

Impatience flickered across that pale, inhuman face. "You think of who or what you want to become, wish yourself to change—and it happens."

"What about my clothes?"

"They don't change."

Charlotte nodded. "And when I want to change back to myself? Do I simply wish it?"

"Yes."

"I can do it as often as I like?"

"Yes."

"And I can take as many shapes as I like? I can be a bird and fly? And then a fish and swim in the sea?"

"You may be any animal that exists in this realm. Creatures that exist in *our* realm are forbidden."

Images of what those creatures might be flashed into Charlotte's mind. Gryphons. Unicorns. Basilisks. She pushed them aside and studied the woman. "What are the dangers?"

The woman's eyelids lowered. She said nothing.

"What are the dangers?" Charlotte repeated.

The pale eyelids rose. The eyes staring at her were ink-black with malevolence.

Charlotte's mouth was suddenly dry. The hair lifted on her scalp again. It was like being in a cage with a leashed lion, knowing the creature would harm her if it could. She pushed her spectacles up her nose and raised her chin. *I will not let you intimidate me into making a mistake.* "What are the dangers?"

The woman's lips parted to show sharp, glinting teeth. "If you're pregnant, you will lose the babe."

Charlotte almost recoiled from the gleeful malice in that smile, the gleeful malice in that voice. She controlled her flinch, and considered this answer. *What is the chance of my marrying? Having children?* "Are there any other dangers?"

"No."

Charlotte eyed her guest. "Could I forget who I am and become an animal in truth?"

The woman uttered a snakelike hiss of impatience. "No. Only your outward form changes. Inside, you remain yourself."

"Could I change form without meaning to? If I'm tired or distracted or . . . or asleep?"

"You only change if you deliberately wish it." The woman's lips parted in another glinting, gleeful, sharp-toothed smile. "Or if you die. Then, you return to your true form."

Charlotte shivered. What other possible dangers were there? "Could someone make me change shape without my wishing it?"

"No."

Charlotte stared down at the newspaper advertisements. Her heart beat fast and staccato beneath her breastbone. Emotions churned in her stomach: fear, excitement. She was aware of the woman watching her, aware of the flames roaring in the fireplace, aware of the clock ticking away the minutes until midnight.

Charlotte took a deep breath. She raised her head and met the woman's eyes. "I choose metamorphosis."

CHAPTER FOUR

THE BOOKCASE IN the schoolroom held texts on geometry and algebra, geography and the use of globes, a battered collection of lexicons—English, French, Latin, Greek—and all six volumes of Swiffen's *Cyclopaedia*.

Charlotte chose a volume of the *Cyclopaedia* at random and returned to her bedchamber. She turned the pages hastily, looking at the illustrations. "Too old," she muttered under her breath, at a sketch of a bearded Menelaus. "Too young," to a youthful Narcissus. "Too fat." Nero.

She found the ideal illustration in the *O*s.

Orpheus, the sketch was titled, and the man depicted was young without being boyish, fair of face, and appeared to be in good physical shape beneath his toga. He stared from the page, his gaze steady and direct. He looked personable and intelligent, and most of all, dependable.

"Perfect," Charlotte said. Who wouldn't hire a man who looked like that?

She latched her door and undressed, neatly folding her clothes. Her palms were damp, her breath short, her pulse gathering speed.

Charlotte laid the *Cyclopaedia* on her dresser and studied the sketch again.

She inhaled a shallow breath, blew it out, rubbed her sweaty hands together, glanced at herself in the mirror—brown hair, brown eyes, bare breasts—and fixed her gaze on the sketch and said, "I wish to look like this man, Orpheus."

An itching sensation crawled over her skin, as if a thousand millipedes marched there. The itching intensified, digging into her bones—Charlotte felt a flicker of panic—and then the itching stopped as abruptly as it had started.

She lifted her gaze from the *Cyclopaedia* to the mirror.

A bare-chested man stared back at her.

Shock almost made her recoil a step. Charlotte caught herself, made herself stand still, made herself meet the man's eyes. *My eyes.* She touched her face in wonder, poked her cheek, felt that square chin—and saw the man in the mirror imitate her movements.

This is real. This is me.

Incredulity swelled in her chest. Incredulity, disbelief—and mounting excitement. She stepped as close as she could to the mirror and peered intently at herself. Hazel eyes. Blond hair curling back from her brow. White, even teeth. Strong throat. Adam's apple.

Charlotte rubbed her chest. How odd to have no breasts. How odd to have blond hair growing there.

Blond hair grew at her groin, too.

Charlotte tentatively touched the unfamiliar appendage dangling there. It was soft and warm and spongy, like a finger without any bones in it. She searched for a name for the appendage, and came up with a word she'd once overheard: *pego.*

Charlotte turned the pego this way and that, looked underneath it and examined the plump testicles. How did one urinate?

I guess I shall find out, she thought, and sudden laughter climbed her throat.

She released the pego and surveyed herself in the mirror again, hands on hips. A fine fellow, Mister Orpheus. Taller than

Miss Appleby, broad in the shoulder and chest. A strong, robust man.

This is my body now. My face.

And with the alteration to her face and body, the world had altered, too. Charlotte had a strange, unsettling sense that her boundaries had expanded a thousandfold. She felt almost dizzy, as if the floorboards had moved beneath her feet and the walls of her room pushed outwards.

No, the world hasn't changed; I have.

She could do things she'd never been able to do, go places that had been forbidden, grab opportunities no one would ever offer a woman. How large the world was! How full of possibility.

But first, I need clothes. Breeches and shirts, waistcoats, tailcoat, boots.

Those were things she could purchase as a woman—provided she had the correct measurements.

Charlotte turned away from the dresser and rummaged in her darning basket for the tape measure.

And she didn't just need clothes; she needed a name.

What shall I call myself?

She pondered that question while she unraveled the tape measure. Charlotte Christina Albinia Appleby becomes . . .

She glanced at the mirror, met the hazel eyes there.

Hello, Christopher Albin.

CHAPTER FIVE

October 16th, 1805
London

MARCUS READ THE character reference again, his eyes skimming over the words—*honesty, sobriety, good head for figures*—to fasten on the signature at the bottom. *Mr. Charles Appleby, Esq.* He glanced at the young man seated across the desk from him. "And you say that Mr. Appleby is dead?"

"Yes, sir."

Christopher Albin had an open, honest face, with a scholar's broad brow and child's wide gaze. His coloring was fair—blond hair, hazel eyes.

"How old are you, Mr. Albin?"

"Twenty-five, sir."

Marcus rubbed his face. Scabs were rough on his brow and cheek. *When did I start feeling so tired?* He felt decades older than Albin, not a mere half dozen years.

Marcus glanced at the character reference again, at the scrawled signature of a man who was dead. "You were Mr. Appleby's secretary for five years?"

"Yes, sir. Until his death, sir."

In my experience, Charles Appleby had written, *Mr. Albin is a competent, reliable, and efficient Secretary.*

There was no way of checking the character reference; he'd

have to take Albin at face value. Marcus put down the sheet of paper, steepled his hands, and studied the young man. Albin's neckcloth was atrociously tied. It added to his appearance of youthfulness.

"What are your views on the slave trade, Mr. Albin?"

"I believe it's wrong, sir."

Marcus grunted. *Damned right.* "Can you fight?"

Albin blinked. "Fight?" He glanced down at his hands. "I guess so, sir. I've never tried. Why?"

Marcus tapped his steepled fingers against his chin, studying Albin. *Do I want this lad as my secretary?* Wouldn't it be better to hire someone older? Tougher? Better able to defend himself in a fight?

But for all his fresh-faced youth, Albin's shoulders and height were encouraging. He'd have a better chance in a fight than poor Lionel.

Marcus sighed and lowered his hands. "I've been having some . . . trouble lately, Mr. Albin."

"What sort of trouble, sir?"

"Windows broken. Nightsoil left on the doorstep. Last week, I was attacked in St. James's Park. It wasn't random; the foot-pads called me by name." Memory gave him the sound of Lionel's wheezing, agonized breaths. His stomach tightened. "My secretary was injured. He's at my Kent estate, recuperating, but it's doubtful he'll be able to write again. Among his injuries, his right arm was badly broken."

Albin was silent for a moment, his eyes on Marcus's face, examining the bruising, the healing cuts. "Do you think it will happen again, sir?"

"There's a risk it will, yes."

Albin nodded. A faint frown creased his brow. Cogs were almost visibly turning in his head.

A mood of gray fatalism descended on Marcus. This was

where the last three applicants had balked. Albin was going to balk, too. *And how can I blame him?*

He looked down at his hands, at the bruising, the scabs across his knuckles. He flexed his fingers, feeling the scabs pull. *I should have run, as Lionel wanted me to.*

"Why are you being targeted, sir?"

Marcus looked up. "I don't know. It could be political. Or personal." The admission brought a sour taste to his mouth. *Do I have so many enemies?* "One of your tasks will be to help me find who's responsible."

Albin nodded, but said nothing. His gaze turned to the carpet. His frown deepened, furrowing between blond eyebrows. He was thinking, weighing things up. *Deciding he doesn't want to risk his neck for me.*

Albin looked up and met Marcus's eyes. "I'll take the position."

Surprise held Marcus stunned for a second, and then optimism surged through him. "You will?" He found that he was smiling, that he was leaning forward across his desk. He held out his hand to Albin. "You won't regret it."

CHARLOTTE RETURNED THE handshake. She tried to squeeze back with a grip as strong and manly as the earl's.

Cosgrove released her hand and sat back in his chair. The fleeting smile vanished, leaving his face grim once more.

Charlotte stared at him. Her employer.

Cosgrove was a tall man, with a face that was almost harsh— strong jaw, strong cheekbones, strong blade of a nose. His hair was coal-black, his eyes dark gray. A striking man, despite the signs of violence on his face: half-healed cuts veering across his brow and right cheek, bruises dark around one eye.

Charlotte gave herself a mental shake. *You're a man now,*

and a man wouldn't think about what Cosgrove looks like.

"Let's start with a list of my enemies." The earl pushed a sheet of paper towards her, and his inkwell and quill.

Charlotte pulled her chair closer to the desk, dipped the quill in ink, and sat with her hand poised over the paper. For a brief, dizzying moment, her fingers were too large, too long, wrong. She shook her head fractionally, dispelling the notion. "How many are there, sir?"

Cosgrove gave a humorless laugh. "How many? Half a dozen that I can think of."

Half a dozen enemies? Charlotte kept her face carefully neutral. "Who are they, sir?"

"Lord Brashdon and his set. Sir Roderick Hyde. Keynes."

The names were vaguely familiar. Hadn't her uncle spoken of them? "Anti-abolitionists?"

"Yes." She heard contempt in Cosgrove's voice, saw it in the curl of his upper lip. "Men who place profit above human life."

"And you are an abolitionist, sir." It was a statement, not a question.

"Yes."

Charlotte wrote down the first name. *Lord Brashdon.* She watched her fingers wield the quill—large, blunt-tipped, male—and the dizzying sense of wrongness came again: her hand was too large, the quill too small.

The letters came out lopsided and awkward, like a child learning to write.

Charlotte exhaled sharply through her nose. *Don't think about it.*

She wrote the next two names without watching her hand. *Sir Roderick Hyde. Keynes.*

There. That was much better.

Alongside the names, she wrote: *Political enemies. Anti-abolitionists.* "Who else, sir?"

"My heir. Phillip Langford."

He counted his heir among his enemies? Charlotte tried to keep her eyebrows from lifting. *Phillip Langford,* she wrote. *Heir.* "Yes, sir?"

"Gerald Monkwood. The brother of my late wife."

Charlotte glanced up.

"I'm a widower." Cosgrove said the words stiffly, as if they fitted uncomfortably in his mouth. "Monkwood blames me for Lavinia's death."

"I'm sorry, sir."

Cosgrove made a twisting movement of his lips, silent negation of her sympathy. Charlotte looked down at the paper again. *Gerald Monkwood,* she wrote. *Brother-in-law.* Had the marriage been an unhappy one? Was that what that brief grimace implied? She glanced up. "Anyone else, sir?"

Cosgrove didn't immediately answer. He looked down at his hands, as if studying the fading bruises. He spread his fingers, clenched them, looked up. "Sir Barnaby Ware."

"And he is?"

Hard lines pinched on either side of Cosgrove's mouth. "He was a friend of mine—until he had an affair with my wife."

Charlotte wrote the name silently. *Sir Barnaby Ware. Ex-friend. Adulterer.* She glanced at the earl. He looked like a man who had everything: wealth, a title, an attractive face, a strong body. A man in his prime. A man who led a charmed and privileged life.

Except that perhaps his life wasn't as charmed as it appeared from the outside.

She glanced back at the list, reading the six names. Brashdon and Hyde and Keynes. Langford. Monkwood. Ware. "Where would you like to start, sir?"

"With Monkwood. Tomorrow."

She looked up. "Because you think he's the most obvious,

sir?"

"He's been the most vocal of my detractors." Cosgrove rubbed his brow. He looked weary and battered, slumped in the chair, his right eye shadowed by bruises, his forehead and cheek scored by half-healed cuts. A man who'd been beaten too many times. And then—as if to prove how wrong her imaginings were—the earl pushed vigorously to his feet and strode across to a mahogany bookcase. "You'll also help me with my speeches. I'll write them, but I shall expect you to check them for me."

"Speeches?"

"To the Upper House." Cosgrove opened the bookcase's glazed doors. "About abolition of the slave trade."

Charlotte glanced around the room. Uncle Neville described abolitionists as mean little men trying to drag the nation down into ruin. *They resent our wealth,* he liked to proclaim, his face flushed with brandy. *They want to bring us all down to their level of destitution.* Cosgrove clearly wasn't destitute. The study was spacious, the furnishings handsome: the thick Aubusson carpet, the two desks with their cabriole legs and gleaming marquetry, the winged leather armchairs beside the fire, the cabinets and bookcases lining the walls, the heavy brocade curtains.

Her gaze returned to Cosgrove. His clothes had the austere elegance that spoke of a master tailor.

No. Not destitute.

"We lost the last vote—but by God we'll win the next one."

Charlotte believed him. The determination on Cosgrove's face, in his voice, was the sort that won wars. Agamemnon would have looked thus—grim, implacable—when he contemplated the walls of Troy.

"Here." Cosgrove held a sheaf of handwritten papers out to her. Behind him, tall windows framed a view of Grosvenor Square, now fading into dusk.

Charlotte stood and took them. "What are they, sir?"

"My last three speeches. And this." A book was thrust at her. "An essay on the slave trade."

"By you, sir?"

"No." Cosgrove closed the bookcase. "Take them back to your lodgings. Read them. It will give you a better understanding of the issue."

CHARLOTTE READ THE speeches huddled in bed in a nest of musty blankets. She'd pawned her mother's jet necklace and brooch in Halstead, but the fare to London and clothes for Christopher Albin had consumed most of those shillings. There'd been barely enough left for a few nights' accommodation in one of the poorer lodging houses.

But once I'm paid, I'll be able to afford a room with a fireplace.

Excitement stirred in her belly. She was making her own way in the world now, she was independent, she was earning good money.

Charlotte wriggled numb toes and glanced around the bedroom. It was scarcely larger than a cupboard, with a bare wooden floor and one grimy, cracked window. Mold and water stains crept down the walls, the bedding reeked of tallow candles and fried onions, the horsehair mattress was lumpy and sagging, but she wouldn't swap this bedroom for her old one at Westcote Hall. Or swap her old life for this one.

Excitement twisted in her stomach again, like a snake tying itself in knots. She was no longer Charlotte Appleby. She had a new face, a new body, a new name—and a career that was better than any she could have as a woman. No poorly paid governess or schoolmistress, but secretary to an earl!

Memory gave her a glimpse of Lord Cosgrove—the strong-boned face, the gray eyes, the cuts and bruises. His admission echoed in her head: *Last week I was attacked in St. James's Park. My secretary was injured.*

Charlotte put the speeches aside. Working for Cosgrove might not be the wisest choice, but the wages he offered were astonishingly generous. Far more than she'd dared hope to earn. A few years in his service and she'd have a comfortable sum saved.

She shrugged inwardly. If she was attacked, she could use her Faerie gift. Turn into a bird and fly away.

Charlotte scratched the prickly stubble on her cheeks, and picked up the book Cosgrove had given her, a slender volume with the title and author's name stamped into the calfskin cover: *An Essay on the Slavery and Commerce of the Human Species, Particularly the African, translated from a Latin dissertation, by Thomas Clarkson.*

She opened it and began to read. The pages were dog-eared. Cosgrove had underlined passages and made extensive notes in the margins.

It was almost midnight by the time she finished. Charlotte closed the book and looked at it, rubbing her thumb over the cover. A better understanding of the issue—yes, she had that . . . but did the earl realize how much of himself he exposed to her?

The speeches revealed his public face—articulate, championing an end to slavery—but the notes he'd written in the margins of the essay were more personal, more private. This was the man uncensored. Each jotted word, each underlined sentence, gave her a glimpse of who he was. His thoughts, his opinions, his values—all were laid out for her to see.

I like him.

Charlotte put the book aside and shrugged out of the blankets. She pulled the chamber pot from under the bed—and hesitated. Every time she urinated using her pego, she ended up with splashes on the floor.

She stood for several seconds with the nightshift half-raised, then let the hem fall and wished herself back into her own shape. Her skin itched intensely, as if a thousand ants crawled over her, and then the sensation vanished.

The room became blurry.

Charlotte groped for her spectacles. The room came into focus. The nightshift hung voluminously, pooling on the floor around her feet.

She peed quickly, and with a strong sense that she was cheating. If she was going to live as a man, she needed to learn how to handle her pego.

She wished Swiffen's *Cyclopaedia* had an entry on the pego, explaining its peculiarities. Why was it so stiff when she woke in the mornings? How could something so soft become so hard? And what did one do to control it? Using her Faerie gift to wish it limp again worked, but she'd never seen a man walking around with his pego tenting his breeches, so there must be a way of controlling it that didn't involve magic.

Unless there was something wrong with hers?

There was no one she could ask. She would have to figure out the answers for herself.

But not tonight.

Shivering, she looked at the drawing she'd pinned to the wall, concentrating on the young man's face. Broad brow. Wide-set eyes. Curling hair.

Clean-shaven cheeks, she reminded herself. *And perfect vision.*

Charlotte took off the spectacles, closed her eyes, and wished herself back into Christopher Albin's shape. One thousand invisible ants crawled over her skin again. When she opened her eyes, the nightshift no longer puddled on the floor; instead she saw large feet wearing thick woolen socks.

She touched her face. The shape of cheekbone and jaw was

Christopher Albin's. The prickly stubble was gone.

How interesting it was to be a man, she thought, climbing in-to the sagging bed. People spoke to her more bluntly and met her eyes more directly. They treated her with a different kind of respect from what she was used to. *As if I am somehow more than I was.*

Charlotte curled up in the cocoon of blankets and blew out the smoking tallow candle. Anticipation fizzed in her blood, like the bubbles in a glass of champagne. She was a man. She was independent. She had a career.

I'm glad I chose this path.

CHAPTER SIX

October 17th, 1805

London

"THAT'S MONKWOOD'S HOUSE."

Charlotte followed the direction of the earl's gaze. A gray, unfriendly sky hung over Hanover Square. The buildings were rigid in their uniformity, mirroring each other across the square: tall façades, rows of staring windows, frowning roofs. The sound of a church bell ringing three o'clock drifted in the air.

"What would you like me to do, sir?"

"Watch him. See whether you can tell if he's lying."

They crossed Hanover Square briskly and climbed the steps to Monkwood's door. The earl rapped the knocker. Charlotte resisted the urge to peel off her gloves and wipe her sweating palms. *How will I know if Monkwood is lying? What if I make a mistake?* Behind them, a carriage rattled across the square, splashing water from the puddles.

The door opened. A dour-faced butler stood there.

"Afternoon, Sprott," the earl said. "Is Monkwood in?"

"I shall see if he's at home to guests, sir."

Charlotte glanced around the entrance hall while they waited. The gilt-topped marble tables and massive mirror with its gilded frame shouted Monkwood's wealth. Blue and gold Sèvres vases preened in front of the mirror.

The butler returned. "Mr. Monkwood will see you, sir."

Gerald Monkwood was in his library, seated beside the fire. The fireplace was in keeping with the entrance hall, an ornate marble confection with nymphs and gilded acanthus leaves. The man was in keeping with it, too. Monkwood's blond hair was pomaded and curled, his waistcoat embroidered in rich blues and greens and purples like the plumage of a peacock, his neck-cloth intricately folded and pinned with a single, massive emerald. Even his Hessian boots were a work of art—the golden tassels, the mirrorlike finish.

Charlotte halted one step behind Cosgrove, in the middle of the library.

For a long moment there was silence, broken only by the quiet *snick* of the door as the butler closed it, then Monkwood spoke: "Cosgrove." His gaze flicked over Charlotte, before resting on the earl again. He rose to his feet, his slowness an insult.

Monkwood was two inches shorter than the earl and a good thirty pounds heavier. The elaborate neckcloth and high, starched collar-points, the exaggerated shoulders and nipped-in waist of his coat, made him look almost effeminate.

An overgrown Cupid. The thought flashed into Charlotte's mind and stayed there. The plump cheeks and shining golden hair, the full, soft mouth with its pouting lower lip—they were Cupid's cheeks and hair and mouth.

"Monkwood." Cosgrove inclined his head slightly in greeting.

Monkwood didn't offer them a seat. He turned to Charlotte. "And this is . . .?"

"Mr. Albin. My new secretary."

"Ah, yes . . ." The soft, girlish mouth turned up at the corners. "I heard your secretary had a most unfortunate accident." His gaze returned to Cosgrove, lingering on the bruises.

"No accident," Cosgrove said. "It was deliberate."

The tiny smile became a smirk. "Surely not?"

"Were you behind it, Monkwood?"

For a heartbeat, Monkwood didn't react. He stood as stiffly as a wax figure, the smirk frozen on his face, and then he laughed loudly. "What? You think *I* attacked you in St. James's Park?"

"Did you hire the men who attacked me?" Cosgrove's voice was perfectly expressionless. There was no warmth in it, no animosity. "Did you hire whoever it is who breaks my windows and piles shit on my doorstep?"

"Shit on your doorstep . . ." Monkwood said the words slowly, as if savoring them on his tongue. His lips tilted upwards in another smirk. "How distasteful for you."

"Are you responsible?"

Monkwood blinked, widened his eyes, placed a hand over his heart, like an actor feigning surprise. "Me?"

He's baiting Cosgrove.

"Yes, you."

Monkwood lowered his hand. "Why would I do that?" The affected surprise was gone. His voice was flat with hostility.

"You know why."

Monkwood's mouth twisted. "You didn't deserve Lavinia."

"Did you do it?" Cosgrove asked.

"She should never have married you. You never appreciated her. You never saw she was an angel!"

"She wasn't an angel. She was an adulteress."

Fury flooded Monkwood's face, flushing his cheeks, flaring his nostrils, pulling his lips back from his teeth in a snarl. The transformation was startling. The softness, the effeminacy, the likeness to Cupid, were gone. Monkwood looked as savage as Cerberus.

He raised a fist and took two stiff-legged steps towards the earl.

Charlotte's heart kicked in her chest and sped up. *He's going to attack him.* She stepped forward until she was shoulder to shoulder with Cosgrove.

Monkwood didn't so much as glance at her. His attention was fixed on the earl. "She's dead because of you." Rage thickened his voice. "You drove her to it! It's your fault!"

"Lavinia's death was her own fault." Cosgrove turned his back on Monkwood, dismissive, unintimidated. "Come, Albin."

Charlotte followed hastily. At the door she glanced back, seeing blazing fury in Monkwood's blue eyes, stark hatred on his plump face. *He hates Cosgrove. He'd like to see him dead.*

THEY STRODE BACK to Grosvenor Square at a pace that almost made Charlotte short of breath. She glanced at Cosgrove once, then kept her eyes on the pavement. The earl's silent anger was as alarming as Monkwood's snarling, thick-voiced rage. It made his face more angular, as if jawbone and cheekbones were trying to push through his skin.

Cosgrove's butler took one look at his employer and kept his greeting to a simple "Sir" as he took the earl's hat and gloves.

Cosgrove strode down the corridor to his study.

Charlotte followed.

A fire crackled in the grate, devouring lumps of coal. Cosgrove went to stand before it. He stared down at the flames.

Charlotte silently closed the door. She dared not speak.

A minute passed, ticked away by the ebony and gold clock on the mantelpiece. Cosgrove turned to her. The angularity was gone from his face. He looked merely weary. "Well?" He walked to a leather armchair and sat. "What did you think?"

Charlotte relaxed fractionally. "I think he could be responsible for the windows and the shit, sir." *Shit.* A word she would never have uttered as a woman, and yet it came easily off Albin's tongue. "But I'm not sure about the attack. His reaction, the hesitation . . . it could have been a sign of guilt, but equally it could have been outrage."

Cosgrove studied her face for a moment, a perusal so intense that she thought he saw down to bone and ligament, and then he nodded. "I agree. The shit could be him. The attack . . ." He shrugged, then pushed to his feet and crossed to the decanters lined up on the sideboard. "What would you like? Brandy? Whiskey? Madeira?"

"Uh . . ." For a moment her wits deserted her. Which one should she ask for? "Brandy," Charlotte said at random.

She heard the gurgle of liquid as Cosgrove poured. He turned, a crystal glass in each hand. "Here."

"Thank you, sir."

Cosgrove sat again. He gestured to the second leather arm-chair.

Charlotte obediently sat, copying the earl, cupping the glass in both hands.

"My wife killed herself," Cosgrove said.

Charlotte's mouth fell open. She hurriedly closed it. What should she say in response to such a revelation? What *could* she say?

Fortunately Cosgrove didn't appear to expect an answer. He turned his head and stared into the fire, a frown pulling his eye-brows together.

Charlotte studied his face. The earl didn't look like a man ca-pable of driving his wife to suicide. His expression was dauntingly bleak right now, but the laughter lines at the corners of his eyes and mouth told her he wasn't always so grim.

The earl turned his head and looked at her. "Take my advice, Albin. Never marry a beautiful woman."

Charlotte's heart seemed to miss a beat—not the impact of the words, but the impact of his gaze, the intensity of his gray eyes. "No, sir," she said, automatically, and then her brain caught up with her ears. *What?*

Cosgrove must have seen the confusion on her face. "My wife married me for my earldom and my money. Beauty, in exchange for wealth." His mouth twisted into an ironic, humorless smile. "I was fool enough to believe it was a love match."

"Oh." How should she respond to an admission like that? "I'm sorry, sir."

Cosgrove shrugged, dismissing her sympathy, and stretched out his legs towards the fire, still cradling the brandy glass in his hands. "I learned a valuable lesson. Believe me, I shan't make the same mistake again."

"No, sir." After a moment she stretched her legs out, too.

Cosgrove swirled his glass and then raised it to his nose, inhaling the smell.

Charlotte copied him. The brandy fumes stung her nose, bringing tears to her eyes. She blinked them back.

"Monkwood was right about one thing: Lavinia looked like an angel. Golden hair, blue eyes." Cosgrove swallowed his brandy in one long gulp. "The face of an angel and the heart of a whore; that was my wife." He pushed to his feet and poured himself another brandy.

While his back was turned, Charlotte took a cautious sip of brandy. It filled her mouth with heat, burning her tongue, scorching down her throat. Her nose stung again.

"Lavinia committed suicide by mistake," Cosgrove said, returning to his chair. "The coroner ruled it an accident."

"Sir," Charlotte said awkwardly. "You don't need to tell me—"

"You need to know what happened if you're to be any help to me figuring out who's behind the attack."

"Yes, sir," Charlotte said, abashed. So this wasn't a baring of Cosgrove's soul; it was a presentation of facts.

The earl stretched his legs out towards the fire again. "Lavinia grew up under her brother's guardianship. You saw how much he adored her?"

Charlotte nodded.

"Monkwood indulged her. Anything she wanted was hers for the asking. For the first year of our marriage, I was as open-handed as Monkwood—until I realized she was manipulating me." He caught Charlotte's blank look and said bluntly: "Sex. She was using sex to get me to do what she wanted."

"Oh." Heat filled her cheeks. Charlotte took a hasty sip of brandy, almost choking as it burned down her throat.

"She tried temper tantrums next," Cosgrove said. "But those didn't work. After that we were at a stalemate for several months. Until she began the suicide attempts." He grimaced. "She got what she wanted the first couple of times. I thought they were genuine. It took me a while to realize they were as much an act as the sex had been."

"The first *couple* of times, sir?"

Cosgrove's smile held a glimmer of black humor. "Lavinia made five attempts that I recall. Six if you count the time she actually managed to kill herself." The gleam of humor vanished. He looked away from Charlotte, at the fire. His frown returned.

Silence stretched. Ten seconds. Twenty. A minute.

He's remembering.

Cosgrove stirred and rubbed his brow, as if the frown had given him a headache. "Most of our arguments were about money. I made Lavinia an allowance of one thousand guineas a quarter, but she always wanted more."

Charlotte's eyes widened. One thousand guineas a quarter? Four thousand a year? *I could live the rest of my life on such a sum.*

"But the last time—the time she died . . . I'd found out about the affair with Barnaby. I told her I was divorcing her. Lavinia ran up to the widow's walk and climbed over the parapet and threatened to throw herself off."

Divorce. Cosgrove must have felt very strongly about his wife's adultery to take such an extreme step. The scandal—

"The stone she was standing on was loose. She fell." Cosgrove's voice was no longer quite so matter-of-fact, so emotionless. "She tried to grab the railing, but she missed. The look on her face . . ."

He may have no longer loved his wife, but her death hurt him.

Charlotte took another sip of brandy. This time it went down more easily.

Cosgrove turned his head and met Charlotte's gaze squarely. "My wife didn't intend to kill herself. It was just another attempt to make me do what she wanted." His lips twisted into a humorless smile. "You could say that it failed. Quite spectacularly."

Charlotte studied the earl's face, the laughter lines at the corners of his eyes, the skewed smile. What had he been like before his marriage?

Happier. He was much happier.

"I'm sorry, sir."

Cosgrove shrugged. He swallowed another mouthful of brandy. "So you understand why my wife died? And why Monkwood hates me? Why he might be behind the attack?"

"Yes, sir. And I understand why he might want to kill you."

Cosgrove choked on his brandy. He coughed several times before catching his breath. "Kill me?"

"If he loved his sister that much, if he holds you responsible for her death . . . why not, sir?" She remembered the fury suffusing Monkwood's face, the anger blazing in his eyes. "It must enrage him to see you alive while she's in her grave."

"Thank you, Albin," Cosgrove said dryly. "I hadn't thought of that."

His tone made Charlotte grin. "You're welcome, sir."

An answering smile lit the earl's eyes.

Charlotte's throat tightened. For a moment she couldn't breathe. Cosgrove was disturbingly attractive—the strong bones of his face, those smiling gray eyes.

She took a hasty mouthful of brandy. It burned all the way down to her belly. "When did the vandalism start, sir?"

"Start?" The smile vanished from Cosgrove's eyes. "About six months ago."

"And when did your wife die?"

"Last year. October twenty-eighth."

Nearly a year ago. Charlotte frowned. "So . . . maybe the vandalism isn't related to her death?"

Cosgrove frowned, too. "Perhaps not."

"Did you make a note of the dates, sir? When the windows were broken and the, er . . . the shit left on the doorstep." This time the word stuck on her tongue.

"No. But the glazier's charges will be in the account books." Cosgrove made as if to stand.

Charlotte got hurriedly to her feet. "I'll get them, sir." It must be the brandy that was making her so conscious of the earl— aware of his maleness, aware of how attractive he was, aware that only a few feet of carpet separated them. She hadn't been so intensely conscious of him earlier today, when they'd sat across the desk from one another and he'd explained what he wanted her to do with the accounts for each of his estates, with his correspondence and appointments, his speeches.

Charlotte selected the most recent ledgers for the London residence and brought them back to the fireplace. She left her glass, with the dangerous brandy in it, sitting on the bookshelf.

CHAPTER SEVEN

THE FIRST WINDOW had been broken in April, the last just the previous week. On May 15th, the earl's birthday, a total of twelve windows had been smashed, but most weeks only three or four windows were broken.

Charlotte listed each date and, alongside it, the number of windows smashed. At the bottom, she tallied both columns. The totals were sobering. She looked up at Cosgrove. "Someone hates you, sir."

"I know." The earl's face was grim.

"When were you attacked, sir?"

"Last week. The tenth."

She added it to the list. "And the nightsoil?"

"That started in May. The fifteenth."

"Your birthday."

"Yes. It was the most noteworthy gift I received this year."

"And the other times, sir? Was the, er, shit always left on the same nights windows were broken?"

"Sometimes." Cosgrove shrugged. "At least, I think so. I wasn't in London for all of it."

"Would your housekeeper remember?"

"Perhaps." The earl rang the bellpull. "Fetch Mrs. Maby," he told the footman who answered the summons. "And tell Guillaume that Mr. Albin and I will dine in an hour."

"Yes, sir." The footman bowed and withdrew.

Cosgrove turned to Charlotte. "After dinner we'll visit my heir."

SHE'D EATEN LUNCH with the earl, but it had been daylight then. Dinner was a different matter entirely. The closed curtains and the candlelight made the meal seem much more intimate.

Charlotte swallowed a mouthful of veal and chased it down with some claret. The wine was smooth, expensive, all too drinkable. *I must not have too much of this.* She put the glass down. "Your heir, sir . . . how is he related to you?"

"Phillip? He's my cousin's son."

"And why do you think he might be behind the attack?"

"Because he once told me he'd like to kill me."

"He *what*?"

"Said he'd like to kill me." The earl leaned back in his chair, wine glass held casually in one hand. "Said it to my face. In this very house. Not a twelvemonth ago." He lifted the glass, as if in a toast, and drank.

"Why, sir?"

"Because I'd told him I wouldn't pay any more of his debts."

"Are you his guardian?"

"Thank God, no." Cosgrove gave an expressive grimace. "His maternal uncles had that pleasure until he came of age."

"He's of age? Then why would he ask you to pay his debts?"

"Because he's my heir." Cosgrove put down the glass and pushed it away. "And unless I marry again, he will inherit the earldom. The estates, this house, everything. And that prospect, let me tell you, is the only reason I intend to remarry." His mouth tightened. "I will not allow the earldom to pass to a spineless, drunken profligate."

Charlotte laid her knife and fork on her plate. "Is he that, sir?"

Cosgrove nodded. "Phillip was still in swaddling clothes when my cousin died. He was indulged by his mother, cosseted, spoiled, allowed to do whatever he pleased. It ruined him." He picked up his glass and frowned at the claret. "Phillip came down from Oxford last year. Since then he has distinguished himself by his drinking, his gambling, and his whoring."

Cosgrove drained the glass in one swallow, poured himself another, and offered the decanter to Charlotte. She shook her head.

"The first time Phillip found himself in dun territory, he applied to me for funds. I extended him a loan. He is my cousin's son, after all." The earl picked up his glass, but didn't drink. He turned the stem between his fingers. His frown deepened. "Edmund wouldn't like the man his son has become."

Charlotte met his eyes. She didn't say anything.

"I told Phillip that when he applied to me for more money. Thought it might make him change his behavior. More fool me."

"It would have made me change, sir." Her father's respect was something she'd treasured.

"Perhaps." Cosgrove shrugged. "But you're a different person from Phillip. And you knew your father. Phillip didn't."

Charlotte accepted this with a silent nod. She folded her linen napkin and laid it beside her plate. "Can you remember what date Phillip told you he wished you were dead, sir?"

"The exact date?" Cosgrove shook his head. "March, I think. I know it wasn't long after we'd lost the slavery vote. I wasn't in the best of moods." He grimaced. "I don't blame Phillip for hating me. No man likes to be told he's a bloodsucking leech."

"You told him that, sir?"

"That, and that he didn't need my money; he needed to grow a backbone and take responsibility for himself. It was ill done of me." He placed his wine glass on the table, undrunk from, and pushed it away. "He'll break his shins against Covent Garden's rails, if he's not careful. In fact, I'm astonished he hasn't done so already."

Charlotte blinked. "I beg your pardon, sir?"

"The Covent Garden ague."

Charlotte shook her head to show her lack of comprehension.

"French gout."

She shook her head again.

Cosgrove's expression became bemused. "You truly don't know?"

"No, sir."

The earl leaned back in his chair and stared at her for a long moment before enlightening her: "Venereal disease."

"Oh." Charlotte felt her cheeks flush scarlet.

Cosgrove's mouth twitched, but he was too polite to laugh aloud.

Charlotte fumbled to speak through her embarrassment. "So Mr. Langford is . . . er, he's . . . a . . . a . . . ."

"Phillip is a beard splitter, to put it crudely. And he's none too careful where he finds his entertainment."

Beard splitter. It was another term she'd never heard, but she could guess its meaning.

Charlotte fixed her eyes on her plate. Her knife and fork lay side by side. They were silver, with the Cosgrove crest stamped on them. She moved the knife handle a quarter of an inch, so that it was precisely parallel to the fork. She took a deep breath, mastered her embarrassment, and raised her head. "Mr. Langford is given to wenching, sir?"

"Addicted, would be more accurate." Cosgrove glanced at her plate. "Are you finished?"

Charlotte nodded.

Cosgrove placed his hands palm-down on the table. "Let's find Phillip. If I know anything of him, he'll be in a bawdy house." He pushed to his feet.

A bawdy house. *That* was a term she'd heard before. It meant a house where whores plied their trade.

Dread clenched in Charlotte's chest. She pushed back her chair slowly.

Cosgrove strode to the door.

You chose this path, Charlotte told herself. *This was what you wanted: to have a man's career.* She raised her chin and followed the earl from the dining room.

PHILLIP LANGFORD'S MANSERVANT gave them the name of the brothel his master had been frequenting recently. "This will be an education for you, lad," the earl said, as they clattered back down the stairs to the street.

He hailed a hackney and gave the jarvey an address.

"Is it in Covent Garden, sir?" Charlotte asked, as they climbed in.

"Worse."

"Wouldn't it be better to wait until tomorrow morning, sir? When Mr. Langford is . . . isn't occupied?"

"By tomorrow morning, Phillip will be too drunk to string two words together." Cosgrove stretched out his legs and crossed them at the ankle.

"But wouldn't that be the perfect time to question him, sir? When he's unable to prevaricate?" Apprehension churned in her belly. She wished she hadn't eaten so much for dinner.

"Chin up, lad. I won't let Mrs. Henshaw's girls debauch you."

Charlotte's cheeks burned in the dimness of the hackney carriage. "I am not afraid of whores," she said stiffly.

CHAPTER EIGHT

MARCUS GLANCED UP at the shabby façade of Mrs. Henshaw's establishment. A torch flared in a bracket, throwing light over the cracked doorstep. "Ready, Albin?"

His secretary swallowed audibly. "Yes, sir."

"Good lad." Marcus rapped loudly on the warped wooden door panels.

"Have you ever been here before, sir?" Albin asked in an undertone.

Marcus turned his head and stared at him. Albin stared back, his blatant naivety taking the insult out of the question.

"I shall pretend you didn't ask me that," Marcus told him.

"Oh." Albin blushed fierily and looked down at his top boots. "Forgive me, sir. I didn't mean—"

The opening door cut short his apology. Raucous laughter and the stench of sweat and cheap gin rolled out at them.

One of Mrs. Henshaw's bullyboys stepped into the doorway, a burly man with shoulders as broad as the door was wide. He assessed the cost of Marcus's clothing and stepped back without saying a word.

Marcus entered, his secretary at his heels.

The short hallway opened into a large salon. Marcus strolled into it and looked around, searching for his heir.

A boisterous crowd filled the room: half-dressed whores and

the men who sought their services. The clientele were mainly working men—Thames River boatmen, coalmen, shopmen—but a red-coated soldier was disappearing up the staircase with a whore, and in the far corner two young bucks in tailcoats and knee breeches were haggling with a blowsy blonde.

Albin pressed close. "Do you see Mr. Langford, sir?" His voice was higher than usual.

"No." The air was over-warm, heavy, sour. It filled Marcus's mouth and nose, almost rancid on his tongue. "If he's here, he must already be upstairs."

"Up . . . upstairs, sir?"

Marcus nodded at the staircase. Another bullyboy lounged at the foot of it.

"But sir, if Mr. Langford is upstairs—"

"Then we go up."

"But—"

Marcus pushed his way through the crowd, heading for the staircase and its guardian. The floorboards were sticky with spilled alcohol; his boots adhered slightly with each step.

A woman took hold of his arm. "Wot you be wantin', luv?"

Marcus glanced at her.

She was young, no more than eighteen, her bodice open to expose lush breasts. Despite her ripe figure, there was nothing tantalizing about her; her skin was grubby and marked with bruises. Gin fumes wafted from her.

"Wotever you wan', Sal can do it." She pressed her naked breasts against his arm, rubbed her nipples across the blue superfine, and slid her free hand down to cup his groin intimately.

Marcus shrugged her off. "No thank you, madam." He stepped aside and pressed on into the crowd. Albin scurried after him, almost treading on his heels. He had the impression the lad was barely restraining himself from clutching his sleeve.

The man guarding the foot of the stairs looked as if he'd

spent time in the ring. His nose sat crookedly on his face.

"I'm looking for Phillip Langford." Marcus gave the man a glimpse of a silver shilling. "He's twenty-two, running to fat, dark hair—"

"Upstairs," the man said, holding out his hand for the coin. "Room at the end."

"Thank you." Marcus set his foot on the first stair. The carpet was frayed and stained. "Come along, Albin."

The bullyboy slid the shilling into his pocket. "We don't want no trouble 'ere."

"Trouble?" Marcus showed his teeth in a smile. "Us?"

The man shrugged and stepped aside.

Marcus climbed the stairs. At the top was a corridor with doors on either side. Most of them were closed.

He walked down the corridor. The smell of sweat and cheap gin was pervasive here, too. Noises came from behind several of the doors—squeals of feminine laughter, the rhythmic banging of a headboard against a wall. At the end were two doors, one on each side. Marcus glanced at his secretary. "Well? Which one shall it be?"

"Sir, are you certain we should—"

"Not thinking of quitting on me, are you, Albin?"

The lad flushed. "No, sir, of course not! But . . . but what if he's busy—"

"Then we interrupt him."

"But isn't it rude—"

"Extremely rude. But don't worry, lad, he might invite you to join in. I hear he likes *ménages*." He almost laughed at Albin's appalled expression. "Left or right?"

Albin swallowed. He lifted his chin. "Right, sir."

Marcus gave a quick rap on the right-hand door and opened it without waiting for a response. Heaving buttocks met his eyes.

The whore and her client were on hands and knees, rutting

like sheep in a paddock. They were too involved to notice their loss of privacy. The man's buttocks quaked and jiggled with each thrust. They looked like large white blancmanges.

Marcus took a step into the room to see if the man was Phillip. He was plump enough, dark-haired enough—

The man's head jerked around. He wasn't Phillip.

His rhythm faltered. His mouth began to form a question.

"I beg your pardon," Marcus said, bowing. "My mistake." He shut the door and turned to Albin with a grin. "Wrong choice, lad."

Albin didn't reply. He looked as startled as the man they'd interrupted, his mouth half-open in shock.

"Which means that Phillip must be in here . . ." Marcus opened the left-hand door, not bothering to knock.

Three people were inside. One was indeed Phillip. He sprawled on a sagging bed, naked, his shoulders propped against the headboard, his legs spread to accommodate the whore who had his cock in her mouth.

Marcus stepped into the room. Phillip didn't notice. His attention was on the second whore. Her gown was down to her waist, her ample breasts bared to Phillip's groping hands.

Marcus glanced back at Albin. The lad hadn't moved. He stood rooted in the corridor, his expression appalled. "Come in, lad," Marcus said. "Meet my heir."

Phillip turned his head. "Wha'?"

"Ladies, if you don't mind, I'd like a word with your client." Marcus dug in his pocket and pulled out two shillings.

The woman kneeling between Phillip's legs lifted her head. Her eyes fastened on the coins.

"I'll ask you to wait outside, please," Marcus said.

The woman scrambled off the bed. Her companion extricated herself from Phillip's grasp and followed, not bothering to cover her breasts.

"Thank you, ladies." Marcus handed them each a silver coin. "We won't be long."

He shut the door after them and turned back to his heir.

Phillip pushed himself up to sit. His cock was at half-mast. "What the devil are you doing here? Can't send 'em away. I *paid* for 'em. Paid for 'em both!"

"I came to talk to you," Marcus said, strolling to the bed.

"Me?" Phillip scowled. "Why?"

"I was attacked last week. In St. James's Park."

The scowl vanished. Phillip sniggered. "I heard."

"Did you hire the men who attacked me?"

Phillip squinted up, blinking owlishly as he tried to focus on Marcus's face. "Huh?"

"Did you hire the men who attacked me?"

Phillip thought this through for several seconds, then shook his head. "Wish I'd thought o' it, though." He sniggered again. "You've got a black eye."

Marcus stepped closer until he loomed over Phillip. "What about the broken windows? The shit on my doorstep? Was that you?"

"Shit?" Phillip said. "What shit?"

"The shit on my doorstep."

"Shit." Phillip repeated. "Shit on your doorstep." He flopped back on the bed, giggling, his arms wide, his belly heaving. "Shit."

Lying back on the bed, his groin was prominently displayed. His cock had wilted and lay flaccid in a nest of dark hair.

"Did you do it?"

"Shit," Phillip repeated, giggling. "Cuckold Cosgrove has shit on his doorstep."

Marcus reached down and shook Phillip's shoulder, digging his fingers into the soft flesh. "Did you do it?"

Phillip blinked blearily up at him. "Do what?"

"Put the shit on my doorstep."

Phillip went off in a peal of giggles that ended with a hiccup.

Marcus shook him again. "Did you do it?"

Phillip batted at his hand. "Stop that."

"Did. You. Do. It?"

Phillip glowered up at him. "Wish I had," he said, between hiccups. "You deserve it."

Marcus released his heir's shoulder. He straightened and turned to Albin. His secretary was staring at Phillip, utter revulsion on his face. "Let's go."

Albin tore his gaze away from Phillip. He fumbled for the door handle, jerked the door open, and hurried out into the corridor.

The two whores were waiting outside. Marcus nodded to them. "Thank you for your patience, ladies."

He walked down the corridor to where his secretary stood at the head of the stairs. Albin's face was chalk-white. He looked as if he was about to be ill.

"Well?" Marcus asked. "What do you think of my heir?"

"I don't like him, sir," Albin blurted.

"Neither do I." Marcus straightened his cuffs and headed downstairs.

AT THE FOOT of the staircase, the crowd engulfed them. Charlotte curled her fingers into her palms to stop herself grabbing the earl's coat. *I am a man,* she told herself. *I must act like one.*

She set her jaw and followed the earl, her gaze resolutely on his back. In another minute they'd be outside, away from the stench and the heat and the press of unwashed bodies and the hubbub of voices—

Someone grabbed her arm.

Charlotte spun around, trying to pull free. "Let go of me!"

"Where you orf to in such an 'urry, luv?" It was the same whore who'd stopped Cosgrove earlier, her gown open to show her breasts. They were as large as melons.

The whore's lips were rouged. And her nipples.

"Sal can give you wot you wan', luv."

"No, thank you." Charlotte tried to twist her arm free.

"Oh, but I can, luv." The whore leaned close. "Anything you wan'. I does it all."

Charlotte recoiled from the pressure of the girl's breasts against her arm.

"Jus' tell me wot it is an' I'll do it." The whore's other hand groped for Charlotte's groin.

Charlotte swallowed a yelp. She wrenched her arm free, stumbling backward, almost falling over her own feet. "No!" She raised her chin and groped for her composure. "Thank you, madam, but no."

She turned and hurried forward, pushing through the crowd, looking for Cosgrove.

He was nowhere in sight.

Panic lurched in her chest. If he left her here—

Control yourself. She wasn't a woman alone amid drunken, rowdy men and whores; she was Christopher Albin. She was a man. She was in no danger.

Charlotte gulped a deep breath and headed for the door. Her gaze skidded off stubbled faces, off florid faces glistening with sweat, off whores' painted faces—

There he is.

The height was unmistakable, the strong shoulders, the black hair beneath the elegant beaver hat.

He was almost at the other side of the salon. *Don't leave me here, sir!* Charlotte scrambled after him, using her elbows, not caring if she trod on people's feet.

She caught up with the earl just as he reached the corridor.

He glanced back at her. "You may stay if you wish, Albin—although I don't recommend it."

It was a joke—she could tell from the way his eyes creased at the corners—but she couldn't joke back. She was tense, trembling. "I don't want to stay, sir."

Cosgrove shrugged lightly. He strolled down the short corridor to the front door, completely unfazed by his surroundings.

The man guarding the door opened it for them.

"Thank you." Cosgrove inclined his head politely, as if he were leaving an exclusive soirée, not a bawdy house on the edge of London's slums.

Charlotte followed him down the steps, stepping over the open gutter. The air was cold after the fug of the brothel. Her breath plumed in front of her face.

The trembling eased as they walked down the street. *I did it.* She'd entered a brothel, been touched by a whore, seen people engaged in the sexual act—and she'd not betrayed herself.

"Well?" Cosgrove asked. "What do you think?"

Charlotte forced her mind back to the matter at hand. "I think . . . he had nothing to do with the attack, sir. But he would have liked to."

She caught a glimpse of Cosgrove grimacing as they passed a flaring torch outside a tavern. "Yes. That was my impression, too."

"He doesn't like you, sir."

"The feeling is mutual." They turned into another street. "What about the broken windows? The shit?"

Charlotte shook her head. "Not him. Although he liked the idea of it."

"He did, didn't he?" Cosgrove grunted. "He'll probably drop a few turds on my doorstep tonight."

The crudeness of his language shocked Charlotte speechless for several seconds, and then she shook herself. *He thinks I'm a man. He'd never talk like that to a woman.*

How would a man respond? "I think he'll be too drunk, sir."

"With any luck."

They stepped to one side of the street as a hackney trotted past. "Shall you take Phillip off the list, sir?"

"Not off it, but at the bottom."

They walked in silence for another street.

Cosgrove made a choking noise. It sounded like—but couldn't be—laughter.

Charlotte glanced at him enquiringly.

Cosgrove halted. "That first bedroom," he said, in a strangled voice. "His expression—"

Memory supplied her with the image: a gaping mouth, eyes stretching wide with astonishment.

Cosgrove uttered a whoop of laughter.

Charlotte stared at him. He thought it was funny?

Perhaps it was male behavior, to be amused by such things?

She gave a half-hearted, unconvincing laugh.

Cosgrove doubled over, leaning against the nearest wall. His laughter rang in the street.

Charlotte shifted her weight from foot to foot, waiting. If that was what sex was, she was relieved she would never experience it. She'd not realized it was so grotesque, so ugly.

She glanced down the street. They were alone apart from a slinking dog.

Cosgrove pushed away from the wall, wiping his eyes. Footsteps approached from behind them. Charlotte stepped to one side to let whoever it was past.

Someone buffeted her shoulder, knocking her to one knee.

"Look out!" Cosgrove shouted.

A fist swung at her out of the darkness.

CHAPTER NINE

CHARLOTTE DUCKED, CHOKING back a scream. She scrambled backwards on hands and knees until she slammed against the wall. Her hat tumbled from her head.

For a terrifying moment it seemed that a dozen men were attacking them, huge, faceless shadow-figures—and then the half-seen shapes resolved into three men: the earl and two strangers, fighting in the middle of the street.

Someone hit the ground with a thud, and scrambled to his feet cursing.

Charlotte cowered against the wall, trying to make herself as small as possible. Instinct howled at her to run, to hide—

A yelp of pain echoed in the street.

Was that the earl who'd cried out? Charlotte pushed hesitantly to her feet. Were they hurting him? Killing him?

Her heart galloped in her chest. That noise filled her ears, drowning out the sounds of violence—scuffle of boots, harsh grunts, muffled curses. All she heard was the deafening *thud-thud-thud* of her heart.

Charlotte took a deep breath and clenched her hands. She ran towards the struggling figures. For a moment she couldn't distinguish friend from foe—which was the earl?—and then her eyes fastened on a man wearing a bulky frieze coat, a muffler concealing his face.

She hit him as hard as she could in the side of the head.

The man swung around to confront her.

Run! a voice shrieked in her head.

Charlotte ignored it. She launched herself at the man, flailing with her fists, kicking with her feet. Sanity and reason fled. There was a roaring in her ears, a roaring in her blood, a primitive ferocity that made her hit the man again and again and again, until he staggered back and fled at a stumbling run.

Someone grabbed Charlotte's arm. She spun around, swinging her fists.

It was the earl. He evaded her punches easily. "Easy. They're gone."

Charlotte lowered her hands, panting, trembling.

Cosgrove clapped her on the shoulder. The street was empty behind him. "Well done, lad. We scared them off."

Charlotte gulped a breath. She barely heard the earl's words. Her heart was beating faster, louder, now that the danger was past.

Remember you're Christopher Albin. Don't let the earl see you're upset. She gulped another breath. "Were they the men who attacked you last week, sir?" Her voice was breathless, too high.

"No. They were just footpads."

The trembling grew worse; her whole body was shaking. Bile rose in her throat. Charlotte clenched her teeth shut to stop herself vomiting. A man would take something like this in his stride. A man would shrug it off, maybe even laugh about it. She looked around for her hat. It lay against the wall. She walked over to it on unsteady legs, picked it up, placed it on her head.

She tried to laugh as she turned back to Cosgrove. The sound came out with a slight wobble in it. "I'd heard London streets were dangerous."

"Never doubt it," Cosgrove said. "Come along, lad. Let's get home. I need a drink."

IT WASN'T UNTIL they reached the safety of the earl's house that
Charlotte remembered she could have changed shape when they
were attacked. She could have become a lion. One roar, and the
footpads would have run for their lives.

It doesn't matter, she told herself as they climbed the steps to
the towering front door. What mattered was that they'd scared
their attackers off. And she hadn't revealed her magic. Hadn't
lost her job.

She handed her hat to the butler. But what if there had been
five footpads, not two? What then? Would she and the earl have
been injured? Perhaps even killed?

Charlotte somberly followed Cosgrove into his study. It was
one thing to choose not to use her Faerie gift; it was another
thing entirely to forget to use it.

"Your first mill, Albin."

"Yes, sir."

"You acquitted yourself well."

You didn't see me cowering against the wall. Her hands still
trembled faintly. She clasped them behind her back so the earl
wouldn't notice.

Cosgrove strolled across to the decanters. "Brandy?"

Charlotte hesitated. Perhaps it would stop her hands shaking?
Uncle Neville always said brandy cured all ailments. "Thank
you, sir."

Cosgrove poured two glasses and held one out to her.

This time she didn't sip cautiously; she took a reckless
mouthful. The brandy scorched her tongue, stung her nose, filled
her mouth with heat. Charlotte swallowed. The heat burned
down her throat into her belly.

"If you will forgive me for saying so, Albin . . . you would benefit from some instruction in the science of boxing."

"There's a science to it, sir?" She drank another mouthful. The heat expanded through her body.

Cosgrove paused, his glass halfway to his mouth. For a moment he stared at her, his eyebrows raised in disbelief, and then he said, "Of course there's a science to it."

Charlotte grimaced inwardly. Clearly she'd made a blunder.

She swallowed another mouthful of brandy. Uncle Neville had been right: brandy did cure ailments. Her hands were no longer shaking and the slightly nauseous feeling in her belly was easing.

"Show me what you did back there."

Charlotte obediently put down the glass. She clenched her hands and raised them.

"No." Cosgrove winced. "Never—*never*—do that." He put down his own glass, reached out, and took one of her fists. "Never have your thumb inside. You'll break it." He opened her hand and rearranged her fingers and thumb, forming a fist again. "Like this. Thumb out."

"Oh." The touch of his hands—large, strong, sure—was unnerving. Charlotte's cheeks flamed with heat. Hastily she reclenched her other fist, thumb on the outside.

Cosgrove stepped back, picked up his glass again, and surveyed her curiously over the rim. "Did your father never teach you how to make a fist?"

Charlotte shook her head. She hesitated, choosing her words carefully; she didn't want to lie to him. "My father was a scholar. He was uninterested in blood sports."

"But surely you milled with your brothers, with your friends?"

She shook her head again, searching for words that were truthful. "I was an only child and we lived rather isolated. It was miles to the nearest village."

"But at school—"

"I was tutored at home, sir."

Cosgrove regarded her silently for a moment. Did he suspect she was lying, even though she'd spoken the absolute truth?

No. It was pity in his eyes, not suspicion.

Charlotte bit her lip. She looked down at the floor.

"Very well," Cosgrove said. "Let's have a lesson."

She glanced up, startled. "What?"

Cosgrove put down his brandy. "A lesson."

"Now, sir?"

"Why not?" Cosgrove raised his fists.

Charlotte swallowed the nervous lump in her throat. She obediently mimicked him, clenching her hands as he'd shown her, thumbs on the outside.

"Good. Now try to hit my hand." Cosgrove opened one hand and held it at shoulder height, palm out.

"But what if I hurt you, sir?"

Amusement lit Cosgrove's face. "I doubt you will."

"But—"

"I've been boxing for years. Who do you think is most at danger here?"

Charlotte flushed again. He was laughing at her—in a kind way, but still laughing. She clenched her fists more tightly, focused on his palm, and cautiously punched.

Cosgrove batted her fist away. "Harder."

"But, sir—"

"Harder."

Charlotte took a deep breath and punched as hard as she could. Her fist sank into Cosgrove's palm, his fingers curling around her knuckles as he absorbed the force of the blow. "Good." He released her hand. "But this time, put your shoulder behind it."

Charlotte punched him again.

"Better. Do it again."

She did.

"Excellent. Now try with your other hand."

Charlotte punched with her left hand. It felt awkward.

"Harder."

She gritted her teeth and obeyed.

"Again."

With each punch it became a little easier. After several more, Cosgrove nodded. "Good. Now put the two together. Jab with the left; cross with the right." He demonstrated. "You try."

Charlotte frowned in concentration. *Jab with the left. Cross with the right.* There was far more power behind her punches than if she'd been in her own body. Albin had weight, had strength.

"Excellent," Cosgrove said, fielding her punches.

She grinned at him.

"Again."

Charlotte did as he bid. Left, then right. Left, then right.

"Now move your feet. Don't stand in one spot. You don't want to be an easy target."

CHARLOTTE WAS PANTING by the time the lesson was over. They'd both stripped out of their tailcoats and neckcloths.

"Excellent." Cosgrove clapped her on the shoulder. "You're a natural."

She lowered her fists. Pride warmed her cheeks. "Thank you, sir."

"I have a punching bag in the cellar. You may use it, if you wish." Cosgrove picked up his brandy again. "And we'll get you some lessons at Jackson's."

"Jackson's?"

"Gentleman Jack." Cosgrove sipped the brandy. "Surely

you've heard of him?"

Charlotte shook her head.

Cosgrove's expression became bemused. "Beat Mendoza in '95. Won the title of English Champion."

"I was living in the country, sir," Charlotte offered as an excuse. She reached for her brandy glass.

Cosgrove shook his head. "Lad, you weren't *living* in the country, you were *buried* there." He sat in one of the armchairs beside the fire. "I'll take you to one of Cribb's fights."

Charlotte sat, too. She dared not ask who Cribb was. She mimicked the earl, crossing her legs, cupping the brandy glass between her hands.

Cosgrove must have read her ignorance on her face. "He's shaping up to rival Jackson at his best."

"Oh," Charlotte said.

Cosgrove shook his head. "What am I going to do with you, Albin?"

"I'm sorry, sir."

"Don't be." He smiled at her, a surprisingly friendly expression.

Charlotte felt heat rise in her cheeks again. She stared down at her brandy. Cosgrove had a stern face—that forbidding nose, that uncompromising jaw, those black eyebrows and dark gray eyes—but when he smiled he was more attractive than any man had a right to be. She gulped another mouthful of brandy.

His affability was because they'd fought off the footpads together. Somehow, those few chaotic seconds had changed their relationship. *We're almost friends.*

"You should learn some wrestling throws, too."

Charlotte's heart seemed to stop beating for an instant. Didn't wrestlers strip to their waists? Didn't they put their arms around each other? Her head jerked up. "That won't be necessary, sir."

"Nonsense," Cosgrove said. "Good skill to have. Saved my

neck last week." He lightly stroked the fading bruise around his right eye.

"Sir . . . what happened to the men who attacked you?"

Cosgrove shrugged. "Dragged themselves off. I wasn't paying much attention; Lionel was in bad shape." His eyebrows drew together. "Which is why you need lessons, lad."

When Cosgrove frowned like that, he was quite intimidating. "Yes, sir." She gulped another mouthful of brandy.

Cosgrove's frown deepened. "Perhaps a sword stick would be best, until you're more proficient . . ."

"A sword stick? But I could kill someone!"

"Better them than you." He pushed to his feet and walked across to the sideboard. "More brandy?"

Charlotte shook her head. She felt warm and slightly light-headed. She put down her glass. "I should go, sir." She stood and reached for her neckcloth, winding it around her neck, twisting it into a knot.

Cosgrove winced. "You need a lesson in that, too." He held out an imperative hand. "Give it to me."

"But, sir—"

"Give it to me."

Charlotte bit her lip. She unwound the limp, wrinkled neckcloth and handed it to him.

The earl shook it out with a snap. He stepped close and placed the neckcloth around her neck. "Chin up."

Obediently she lifted her chin higher.

"Keep it taut—" Cosgrove's knuckles brushed her throat.

"Yes, sir." Heat shivered across Charlotte's skin. She was excruciatingly aware of Cosgrove's proximity—his large, lean body radiating warmth, the vee of skin exposed at his throat, the heady scent of brandy on his breath.

"Not a lot you can do with a neckcloth as wrinkled as this," the earl said, ruthlessly knotting it. "But at least it can be tight.

And neat."

He had a beautiful mouth.

What would it be like to kiss him?

Charlotte felt a flush of warmth in her groin and a faint stirring, as if her pego moved slightly. Alarm surged through her. Was it going to stiffen, the way it did first thing in the morning? Would Cosgrove be offended if it did?

"There," the earl said. He stepped back and surveyed her. "Much better."

"Thank you, sir." Charlotte turned hastily away from him, reaching for her tailcoat, glancing down at her groin. No, there was nothing to see.

She dragged on the coat, shoving her arms into the sleeves.

"I'll give you a proper lesson tomorrow," the earl said, resuming his seat beside the fireplace.

"It's not necessary—"

"A gentleman is judged by his neckcloths, Albin. Surely you know that?" Cosgrove stretched his legs out towards the fire. "And your neckcloths—if you don't mind me saying so—are execrable." His face was straight, solemn even, but the gleam in his eyes told her he was teasing.

Charlotte flushed—not with embarrassment, but with awareness of him.

"Away with you, lad," Cosgrove said, picking up his brandy glass. "You did well tonight."

Charlotte let herself out of the study. In the cool, shadowy darkness of the corridor she pressed her hands to her hot cheeks. *You did well tonight.* Cosgrove had said it with approval, as if he were her father.

But he's not my father. He was only half a dozen years older than she was.

And she liked him far too much.

CHAPTER TEN

October 18ᵗʰ, 1805
London

THE EARL WAS out riding when Charlotte presented herself at Grosvenor Square in the morning. A footman showed her to the study, brought a teapot and sweet rolls warm from the oven, and left her to her work. Charlotte ate hungrily, chewing as she examined the bills, sipping tea while she tallied the columns and wrote the totals neatly.

Contentment hummed beneath her skin. *Look at me! I'm a secretary. Earning my own money.* The quill between her fingers, the ledger open on the desk, Christopher Albin's clothes, the neckcloth she'd labored over this morning—all were part of her new life. *I am a man. I am earning my living. I am independent.*

But would a man sit like this? With his knees demurely together? Weren't men less prim, more relaxed?

Charlotte shuffled in the chair, trying to take up more space, moving her elbows and knees, planting her feet several inches apart on the floor.

She poured herself another cup of tea, began tallying a fresh column.

Would a man hum beneath his breath as he worked?

She stopped humming and bent her attention to the accounts

from Cosgrove's Dorset estate. Coal and spermaceti oil and candles ... Her concentration wavered, giving her an image from the brothel, the candlelit room they'd barged into. What had the woman kneeling between Phillip Langford's legs been doing?

Charlotte hissed between her teeth. *Don't think about it.* But the image intruded again, the question butting against the inside of her skull, persistent. What had the woman been doing?

Could she ask Cosgrove?

Charlotte tapped the quill against her chin, remembering the conversations she'd had with the earl. He'd been surprisingly frank about many subjects, sex included. *Men must talk about such things openly and without embarrassment.*

She tapped the quill twice more against her chin and came to a decision: if the opportunity arose, she would ask the earl what the whore had been doing.

Charlotte bent her attention to her work again, adding up the amounts Cosgrove had spent on reroofing his tenants' cottages, the wages of the household servants, the bills for peppercorns and India tea and sugar. It was past noon by the time the earl strolled into the study. "Afternoon, Albin."

"Good afternoon, sir." Charlotte put down her quill and stood. "I brought back your speeches, and the essay."

"Read them?"

"Twice, sir."

"Good lad." But Cosgrove didn't walk across to his desk; he looked at his watch. "I want to talk to Brashdon today. Have you had lunch?"

"Yes, sir."

"Good. Let's go."

Charlotte closed the ledger she was working on and hurried after him down the corridor. She crammed her hat on her head, grabbed her gloves, and followed the earl outside. The sky was low and gray, pressing down on the rooftops.

Charlotte shivered as she pulled on her gloves. The garden in the middle of Grosvenor Square looked like a cemetery behind its wrought iron fence, the trees leafless, the bare flowerbeds laid out like rows of graves. "Sir?" she asked, as they crossed the square. "Can you tell me a little about Lord Brashdon?"

"Brashdon? He's Mammon. Money is his god—although he'd claim to be Christian."

Charlotte digested this statement. "And Hyde? Keynes?"

"They're of the same ilk. Ruled by self-interest and greed." They turned into Charles Street. The street was narrow, funneling the cold wind. "Brashdon's the worst of them. He's been to the West Indies. Seen it."

"Keynes and Hyde haven't?"

Cosgrove shook his head. "They own property there, but they haven't sailed out."

"Have you seen it, sir?"

"Yes. I have." The words were curt, clipped, with hard edges.

Charlotte bit her lip. *Don't ask any more questions.*

They walked in silence until Berkeley Square. It was as bleak as Grosvenor Square, the tall buildings hunched against the cold. "My grandfather purchased a plantation in the West Indies," Cosgrove said. His voice was matter-of-fact, the hard edge gone. "Nearly fifty years ago. My father sent me out to see it after I came down from Oxford."

Charlotte glanced at him. Dare she ask a question? His profile was encouraging—grave, but not grim. "Were there slaves, sir?"

"Oh, yes." Cosgrove's smile was a thin stretching of his lips over his teeth. "There were slaves."

They walked briskly across the square and down Berkeley Street. Charlotte hunched her shoulders, wishing she had a muffler and greatcoat. *As soon as I'm paid, I'll buy more clothes for*

Christopher Albin.

"My father was like Brashdon. He saw nothing wrong with slavery. Not if it brought wealth into the family." They halted for a carriage to pass. "I saw women whipped until they could no longer stand. I saw men burned alive in punishment for crimes I doubt they committed." The earl turned to face her, his eyebrows winging together, his nostrils flared. "Slavery is *wrong*. Africans are human beings. They should not be treated as less than animals."

"Yes, sir. I know."

Cosgrove inhaled a long breath through his nose. He resumed walking. "I resolved to sell the plantation as soon as my father died." The sound of his footsteps was flat and emphatic. "Five years ago, he did—and I realized that my solution was no solution at all." They halted at Piccadilly. "If I sold the plantation, someone else would buy it. And continue to use slaves."

"So what did you do, sir?"

"I kept the plantation, but freed the slaves—which wasn't as simple as it sounds—the damned roundaboutation with the officials, all the manumission deeds, the fees. But I managed it in the end. And however much money it cost, it was worth it. A hundred times over." Cosgrove stepped over a steaming pile of horse droppings. "Once the slaves were free, I employed them. I took the best of my bailiffs with me, a man I trust. He manages the plantation for me."

Charlotte hurried to keep pace with him as he crossed Piccadilly.

"When I got back to England, I joined with Wilberforce and Grenville and Fox, to see that slavery is abolished. And it *will* be, Albin. Mark my words: It *will* be."

"Yes, sir." She had no doubt that Cosgrove would achieve whatever he set his mind to.

Where did the earl get his confidence from? His certainty?

His belief in himself? Was it because of his title and wealth, or was it because he was male?

Charlotte turned those questions over in her head. "Sir?" she said, when they reached St. James's Street. "What will you do when the slave trade is abolished?"

Cosgrove glanced at her, his eyebrows angling upwards. "Do?"

"With your time, I mean."

He shrugged. "Why should I do anything?"

Charlotte pondered this answer. She couldn't imagine Lord Cosgrove settling into a life of leisure. He was no Uncle Neville, content to tax his mind with nothing more strenuous than which waistcoat to wear next and what wine to drink at dinner. Cosgrove had too much fierce intelligence. If he didn't have something to strive for, he'd be bored. But that wasn't an observation a humble secretary could make to one's aristocratic employer.

Cosgrove halted. "Out with it, lad."

"Sir?"

Cosgrove made a *tell me* gesture with his hand.

Charlotte bit her lip, and then blurted: "Won't you be bored if you have nothing to strive for?"

Cosgrove's eyebrows lifted again. He eyed her, his expression faintly bemused. "You think I would?"

"Yes, sir."

Cosgrove shrugged. "Probably." He started walking again. "But that's a long way off. One thing at a time, Albin. One thing at a time."

Charlotte fell into step with him again. A long way off, perhaps, but it *would* happen. With men like Cosgrove leading the cause, it was inevitable.

And whatever goal the earl chose after that, she had no doubt he'd achieve it, too.

I can also be that confident. She knew what she wanted: independence. And she'd taken the first steps to achieving it. She had a career.

Charlotte lifted her chin. *I, too, am indomitable.*

Cosgrove halted two blocks down St. James's Street. He nodded at the building across the street. "We'll likely find all three of them here. If we do, I want you to watch Brashdon. Don't be distracted by Hyde."

"Brashdon, sir? Why?"

"Because Keynes is nothing more than a smile, and Hyde is all hot air and noise. Brashdon's the dangerous one."

"Dangerous? In what way, sir?"

"He's more intelligent than the other two."

Cosgrove waited for a carriage to pass, then crossed the street. Charlotte followed him up the shallow steps to the entrance. "What does Lord Brashdon look like, sir?"

"Nondescript. Easy to overlook. But Hyde is bald and Keynes will be smiling."

The door opened and a servant bowed. "Good afternoon, Lord Cosgrove."

"Is Lord Brashdon here?"

"Yes, sir."

"Excellent." Cosgrove handed over his hat and cane. "I wish to see him."

Charlotte took off her hat and held it out to the servant. The man looked her up and down. "And this is . . . ?"

Charlotte glanced at Cosgrove. Was she going to be barred entry?

"My secretary," Cosgrove said, boredom in his voice. He wasn't challenging the doorman to admit her; he was telling the man he expected it to be done.

"Very good, sir." The servant took Charlotte's hat.

"Are you a member here, sir?" Charlotte whispered. The air

was scented with furniture polish and camphor and an aroma of prudence and respectability. The narrow wainscoting had a dark patina, as if centuries of tradition had soaked into the wood.

"Yes, but I prefer Brooks. It's less conservative." Cosgrove's glance took in the heavy oil paintings on the walls and the rigid formality of the silver vases lined up on the mantel. "My father used to like it here."

The servant led them along a corridor, knocked on a door, opened it. "Lord Cosgrove," he said, and stepped aside.

Charlotte followed Cosgrove into the room. It was a private dining room. Three men sat around the remains of a luncheon. Plates had been pushed aside and napkins discarded.

"Good day, gentlemen," Cosgrove said.

There was a long moment of silence.

Charlotte closed the door and stood with her back to it. She surveyed the three men, putting names to faces. Sir Roderick Hyde would be the man with the bare, domed skull and square face. He looked like a bulldog, squat and aggressive. "Cosgrove," he said, shoving his half-filled wine glass away, as if he'd like to do the same with the earl.

The man next to Hyde smiled, a genial expression that sat on his face without reaching his eyes. "Lord Cosgrove. To what do we owe this pleasure?" He would be Keynes.

Charlotte fastened her attention on the third man. He was older than the other two, with a long face and small pursed mouth. His graying hair and pale skin made him look as if he were fading, ghostlike, into the dark paneling behind him.

"A question I'd like answered." Cosgrove strolled further into the room. Charlotte stayed at the door, her gaze fixed on Brashdon.

"A question?" Keynes said, smiling. "Of me? Or Sir Roderick here, or—"

"All of you."

"How intriguing." Keynes gave a little chuckle and reached for his glass. "You perceive us all ears, Lord Cosgrove."

Cosgrove halted in front of the table. He looked down at the three men. "Did you hire the footpads who attacked me in St. James's Park?"

Lord Brashdon blinked.

"What?" The word was almost a bellow.

Charlotte glanced involuntarily at Sir Roderick and saw him push up from his chair, his face flushed with anger.

"How dare you—"

She dragged her attention back to Brashdon. He had moved, too, leaning back in his chair, a faint smile on his thin lips.

"I should call you out for this, my lord!"

Lord Brashdon touched two fingertips to his mouth, as if trying to hide his smile.

"Gentlemen, gentlemen," Keynes said. "Let's not lose our tempers."

Brashdon turned his head, as if he'd felt Charlotte's gaze. The smile vanished from his face. He lowered his hand. His expression seemed to congeal.

Charlotte found herself unable to meet that stare. Too rude, too discourteous. She looked away.

"A damned insult, that's what it is!" Hyde's face was ruddy with anger, his hands fisted on the table.

"An ill-judged question, certainly," Keynes said, soothingly. "But I'm certain his lordship meant no offense."

Hyde snorted.

Charlotte glanced back at Brashdon. He was still staring at her.

She looked away again and shifted her weight. Would a man meet that stare? Be boldly ill-mannered? Or—

"As you can see, my lord, we had nothing to do with that unfortunate attack." Keynes's smile was conciliating.

Hyde sat. "Get out." He muttered something beneath his breath. To Charlotte's ears it sounded like *Cuckold Cosgrove*.

"I beg your pardon?" The earl's voice was quiet, but her skin prickled with the recognition of danger. Hyde's belligerence had been loud and blustering, but this—Cosgrove's quietness—was something to be afraid of.

Hyde seemed to recognize it, too. He closed his mouth on whatever he'd been about to say.

Keynes hurried to fill the silence. "I'm sure it was nothing, my lord." He gave an awkward laugh and rose to his feet. "We've detained you long enough."

The earl didn't move. "No. Sir Roderick has something he wishes to say." His voice was light, but Charlotte heard the un-spoken challenge in it.

Hyde heard it, too. His face swelled, becoming even more ruddy.

Cosgrove waited, while the clock ticked the seconds away. The dark oil paintings on the wall were holding their breath, the silver platters on the table, even the candles in the heavy candelabra. Ten seconds, twenty, thirty.

The earl gave a slight, contemptuous bow. "Gentlemen." He turned on his heel.

Charlotte opened the door and followed him out. She glanced back—Keynes, standing, an uncomfortable smile on his face, Hyde sitting in red-faced, humiliated rage, and Brashdon, his mouth pursed so tightly it had almost vanished, his gaze venomous as he watched the earl depart.

CHAPTER ELEVEN

"WELL?" COSGROVE SAID, as they went down the steps to the street. "What did you think of Brashdon?"

"He hates you, sir."

"They all do. They're afraid of what will happen to their fortunes once the slave trade's abolished." The earl began to stride along St. James's Street. "What else did you notice? Hyde rather captured my attention."

Charlotte hurried to catch up. "Brashdon was amused by your question, sir."

"Amused?" Cosgrove halted and swung round to face her.

"Yes, sir."

Cosgrove's jaw tightened, as if he gritted his teeth. He exhaled a sharp breath through his nose. "Do you think he had anything to do with the attack?"

"I don't know, sir. He seemed surprised, and amused, and then he caught me looking at him and . . . I looked away. I'm sorry, sir."

She braced herself for Cosgrove's anger, but the earl merely grunted and started walking again. At the corner, while a ragged youth swept the roadway clear of horse droppings, she looked at him out of the corner of her eye. He was still frowning, but he seemed thoughtful, not angry. "Sir . . . were you trying to make Hyde call you out?"

Cosgrove glanced at her. "Yes."

"He was afraid of you."

"He was." The earl stepped onto the street and tossed the street sweeper a coin.

Charlotte wrestled with her curiosity as they retraced their route, crossing Piccadilly, walking the length of Berkeley Street, cutting across Berkeley Square. When they turned into Mount Street, she asked: "Sir . . . have you fought duels before?"

"No."

"Then why was Hyde afraid of you?"

"Because I'm good with a sword, and even better with a pistol." It wasn't a boast, just a matter-of-fact statement.

"Better than Hyde?"

"Yes." They strode down Charles Street. Grosvenor Square opened out in front of them.

The earl halted.

Charlotte halted, too. She followed the direction of his gaze. Cosgrove's townhouse was one of the larger edifices, its chimney stacks towering above the square. She couldn't see anything to warrant the frown on his face. The steps were clean of refuse. The rows of elegant sash windows were unbroken. "Sir?"

"I have no wish to be penniless, Albin. I like my house, and my estates."

She glanced at him, surprised by the harsh note in his voice.

"But I would give it all away and live in a peasant's hovel before I'd have slaves."

It was an extravagant statement, but the flatness of Cosgrove's voice, the matching grimness of his face, made it believable.

Charlotte nodded, unsure what to say.

Cosgrove seemed to shake off his dark mood. He crossed the square briskly and climbed the steps two at a time. "Forget the accounts," he said, as they entered, their footsteps ringing on the polished marble floor. "We'll pay Barnaby a visit. I'll be down in fifteen minutes. You may wait for me in the library."

The butler, Fellowes, showed Charlotte where the library was. Unlike Monkwood's butler, he smiled as he opened the door for her, an affable expression.

"Thank you."

Monkwood's library had been showy; Cosgrove's was comfortable, with leather armchairs and scattered Turkish rugs. A large globe stood on one of the tables. Charlotte touched it with a finger, making it spin slowly, watching the continents come into view and then vanish. As the earl's secretary, would she travel with him? Perhaps to the West Indies?

Do I really want to see slaves being flogged?

Charlotte grimaced, and turned away from the globe. An open door caught her eye. She crossed to it, her boots sinking silently in the thick rugs, and peered inside.

MARCUS STRODE INTO the library. "Albin—" The sound issuing from the music room froze his words on his tongue.

The world seemed to lurch sideways.

Lavinia was alive. She was in the music room. She was playing the pianoforte.

Marcus shook his head sharply, breaking the spell. He crossed the library, halted in the doorway to the music room, and stared.

I'll be damned.

Albin sat at the pianoforte. His hands moved over the keys, fluent, assured, effortless. He didn't notice that he had an audience; he was focused utterly on the sheets of music in front of him.

Marcus leaned against the doorframe and listened. The piece was one he'd heard before; Lavinia had practiced it from time to time. Under her hands it had been pretty enough. It wasn't pretty now. It filled the room, vibrating with life, with passion, with joy.

The music halted abruptly.

"I'm sorry, sir." Albin scrambled up from the piano stool, a blush blooming on his face. "I should have asked your permission—"

"Nonsense. Play as often as you like."

"Sir?" A footman entered the library. "The carriage is here."

"Excellent. Come along, lad. Let's be off."

Albin obediently followed him. "Where does Sir Barnaby live?"

"Surrey."

"Surrey? But—"

"We'll stop at your lodgings on the way. Ah, Fellowes." Marcus accepted his hat and gloves from the butler. "I expect to be gone no more than two days."

"Very good, sir."

Marcus stepped outside. His traveling chaise was drawn up at the foot of the steps, the Cosgrove crest gleaming on the door panels. He took a deep breath. *Surrey.*

He hated Surrey. Hated the memories.

Marcus forced himself to stride down the steps. "Where do you live?" he asked Albin.

"Uh . . . Montock Street, sir."

"Montock Street," Marcus told the coachman.

He climbed into the carriage. Albin scrambled in after him. The door swung shut.

The traveling chaise swayed gently as the footmen clambered into the rumble seat, then lurched forward. Towards Surrey. Where Barnaby had cuckolded him. Where Lavinia had killed herself—

"Is your valet not coming, sir?"

Marcus wrenched his attention back to Albin. "We'll only be gone a night or two." He settled back in his seat, stretching his legs out, crossing them at the ankle. "Leggatt likes to believe that I can't function without him, but I am perfectly capable of dressing myself." His gaze fell on Albin's neckcloth, lopsided and somewhat wrinkled. "Unlike some of us."

Albin raised a hand and fumbled with his neckcloth.

"Don't. You're making it worse."

Albin flushed. He folded his hands on his lap. "I beg your pardon, sir."

He looked so abashed that Marcus laughed. "Lad, what am I going to do with you?"

"You don't have to do anything, sir," Albin said earnestly.

No. He didn't. And yet he felt a sense of responsibility towards the lad, an odd protectiveness.

Marcus pondered this as the carriage traversed Mayfair and entered the narrow warren of streets near the Thames. For all his twenty-five years, Albin was as green as an unbreeched babe. He needed someone to look out for him until he acquired some town bronze. A friend. Someone his own age. Did the lad know anyone in London? *Am I his sole acquaintance?*

The carriage halted. A moment later, the door opened. "Montock Street, sir," one of his liveried footman said.

Albin scrambled down from the carriage. "I shan't be more than five minutes, sir."

Marcus climbed leisurely down and looked around. Montock Street was as shabby as a man down on his luck. The buildings were tattered and patched. Shutters hung askew and rubbish overflowed in the gutters.

Marcus frowned. Why on earth was Albin lodging in such a ramshackle neighborhood?

He crossed the street, avoiding the worst of the puddles, and followed Albin into his lodgings. The building reeked of onions and tallow and urine.

Albin's room was halfway down the corridor. Marcus surveyed it from the doorway. The room was scarcely larger than a closet, with a bare wooden floor and a broken-paned window. Water stains and mold decorated the ceiling and walls. Albin knelt beside the narrow bed, stuffing a shirt into a valise.

Albin's head jerked around. "Sir!" He stood hurriedly, his face reddening. "I didn't expect— Uh . . . wouldn't you prefer to wait in the carriage, sir?"

Marcus examined the room again, noting the flaking gray whitewash on the walls, the broken floorboard in the corner, the threadbare blankets and sagging mattress. A three-legged stool was crammed into the narrow space between the bed and the wall. On it were a pair of spectacles and the stub of a tallow candle. The only other furniture was a lopsided wooden chair on which Albin's clothes were stacked. Several hooks had been hammered into the walls. From these a shirt, a wrinkled neckcloth, and a pair of stockings hung drying.

There was no fireplace. How did the lad keep warm?

I told him I'd rather live in a hovel than own slaves—and he's actually living in one. "Why the devil are you lodging here?" Marcus demanded.

"It's all I can afford, sir."

"That's easily remedied." Marcus dug in his pocket and pulled out several folded banknotes. He peeled off two notes and held them out. "Here."

Albin put his hands behind his back. "I haven't earned—"

"Consider this an advance on your wages. You may update the ledger when we get back."

Albin hesitated, and then took the banknotes. "Thank you, sir."

"Bring everything with you." The thought of Albin returning to this cramped, dismal little room was abhorrent. "You may stay at Grosvenor Square until you find better lodgings."

"With you, sir?" Albin looked taken aback. "I couldn't possibly—"

"Nonsense. You can't wish to remain here."

Albin opened his mouth as if to disagree, and then shut it.

Stop mollycoddling him, Marcus told himself. "Lionel had good rooms in Chandlers Street," he said briskly. "They may still be available."

"Yes, sir. Thank you, sir."

"Hurry up, lad. I'd like to reach Hazelbrook by nightfall."

"Yes, sir." Albin hauled a portmanteau from under the sagging bed. He grabbed the pile of clothes on the chair and crammed them into the portmanteau.

A piece of paper pinned to the wall caught Marcus's attention. He stepped into the room for a closer look. It was a page ripped from a book, a drawing of a young man wearing a toga and holding a lyre. Beneath it was written: *Orpheus.*

"Good Lord." He bent to examine it more closely. "What an extraordinary resemblance."

"What? Oh!" Albin snatched the paper from the wall and crumpled it in his hands. "It's nothing, sir."

"May I see it?" Marcus held out his hand.

Albin hesitated, and then gave him the drawing.

Marcus smoothed the creases and studied it. Orpheus didn't just resemble Albin, he looked *exactly* like Albin—the shape of his face, the arrangement of jaw and cheekbones and nose, the wide-set eyes. "Extraordinary. Where's it from?"

"Swiffen's *Cyclopaedia.*" Albin's fingers made tiny plucking movements, as if he wanted to snatch the page from Marcus's grip, but didn't quite dare.

Marcus ignored his secretary and examined the drawing. The likeness was uncanny. Even the way Orpheus's hair curled back from his brow was the same as Albin's. He'd swear the lad had been the model for the drawing—but Swiffen's *Cyclopaedia* had been published a good fifty years ago. "Extraordinary," he said again, and relinquished the drawing to Albin.

Albin shoved the page into the portmanteau. He stripped the drying clothes from the hooks and thrust them in on top, closed it, and fastened the buckles.

"Ready?"

"Yes, sir."

Marcus picked up the valise.

Albin's expression became horrified. "You can't carry that, sir! You're an earl!"

"My earldom does not make me incapable of carrying luggage."

"But, sir—"

Marcus turned on his heel. He strode back down the malodorous corridor. Behind him, he heard Albin hurrying to catch up, puffing as he lugged the heavy portmanteau.

CHAPTER TWELVE

MARCUS STARED OUT the carriage window. Dusk gathered behind the stands of yews and box trees. The village of Betchworth was behind them; another couple of miles and they'd be at Hazelbrook Hall. Where Lavinia had destroyed his marriage, where she'd ruined his oldest friendship, and where she'd managed to kill herself.

He felt a familiar clenching in his chest. He wanted to rap on the carriage roof and tell the coachman to stop, to turn the carriage around and go back to London.

Marcus glanced across the carriage. Albin wasn't watching the Surrey landscape unfold. A deep frown furrowed his brow.

"A penny for your thoughts, lad."

"What? Oh . . ." Albin blushed. "I was just . . . I was thinking about last night, sir, at Mrs. Henshaw's."

"Mrs. Henshaw's? What about it?" Marcus stretched his legs out, clasped his hands behind his head, and prepared to be amused.

Albin hesitated, while the carriage lurched and swayed, then took a deep breath and said: "Sir, what was that woman doing to Mr. Langford?"

Marcus's thought processes seemed to freeze for an instant, like a pendulum clock whose weights were jammed. "What?"

"The woman kneeling between Mr. Langford's legs. What

was she doing?"

Marcus lowered his hands and sat up straight. "Uh . . . she was . . . er, she was playing his pipe."

Albin's face creased with confusion. "What?"

"Playing his pipe. His silent flute." And then, since the lad clearly didn't understand, he gestured to his own groin. "His virile member."

"Oh." Understanding dawned on Albin's face. He reddened. "I beg your pardon, sir. I haven't heard it called those names before."

Marcus bit the inside of his cheek. "There are lots of different words for it," he said, once he'd quelled the urge to laugh.

"There are, sir?" Curiosity was bright in Albin's eyes. "What are they?"

The carriage slowed to a halt. Outside came the sound of voices as the last tollgate before Hazelbrook was negotiated.

Marcus pretended an interest in the proceedings. He turned his head and watched the gatekeeper exchange civilities with the coachman. Albin's question rang in his ears.

He could snub the lad—but he had invited Albin's confidence. *This is your own fault,* he told himself ruefully. *You asked what was bothering him.*

The carriage lurched forward again. Marcus turned back to Albin. "Other names? Let's see . . . There's prick and cock and Man Thomas and . . ." He racked his brain. "Hair splitter and arbor vitae."

Albin nodded, his expression serious. His lips moved slightly, as if he was repeating the words.

"Which one do you use, sir?

I should have snubbed him. "Cock," Marcus said, trying not to feel embarrassed.

Albin gave another serious nod.

Marcus crossed his legs and looked out the window, signaling the conversation was over, but Albin said: "So what was she doing, sir? The whore? Was she trying to play music on Langford's cock?"

His brain gave him a ludicrous image of the whore blowing on Phillip's penis and producing a tune. Marcus blinked. Albin didn't *really* think—

He turned his head and stared at Albin.

Albin stared earnestly back at him.

He *did* think it.

Laughter bubbled up from Marcus's chest and spilled out of his mouth. He tried to gulp it back, but it was unstoppable.

Albin flushed scarlet, not just his cheeks, but his forehead and throat and even his ears.

It was a full minute before Marcus mastered his amusement. "I beg your pardon," he said, when he finally caught his breath. He pulled out his handkerchief and wiped his eyes. "That was extremely ill-mannered of me."

Albin shook his head. His cheeks were still deep pink with embarrassment.

"To answer your question, no, she was not trying to play music. She was . . . er, she was . . ." The last of his amusement drained away. How to explain this?

Marcus folded the handkerchief and put it back in his pocket. He cleared his throat. "She was using her mouth and tongue to induce a pleasurable spasm."

"Oh," Albin said. From his blank expression, he clearly had no idea what a pleasurable spasm was.

Marcus scrutinized the lad for a moment. "Albin . . . have you ever been with a woman?"

Albin shook his head.

Marcus blinked. His twenty-five-year-old secretary was a virgin? *We'll have to do something about that,* he started to say—and then shut his mouth, catching the words on the tip of his tongue. Perhaps Albin wanted to be a virgin? Perhaps he intended to enter marriage as unsullied as his eventual bride?

Marcus winced inwardly. What a terrible thought. "Albin, er . . . in my experience, it is helpful if a man has some skill in sexual matters before he marries."

"It is, sir? Why?"

"Because otherwise the wedding night can be unpleasant for one's bride."

Albin's brow creased. "Why, sir?"

Marcus tugged at his neckcloth. It felt rather tight. "Because women experience a degree of pain when they lose their virginity. A man skilled in sexual matters can ensure that she also feels some pleasure." Lavinia had uttered mewing cries and wept in his arms, but her distress had quickly turned to passion and she'd reciprocated his lovemaking with an innocent enthusiasm that had made him love her all the more.

Or perhaps even that had been pretense. *It wasn't my skill at lovemaking; it was her skill at simulating pleasure.*

"Oh," Albin said, frowning. "I didn't know it hurt. For women, I mean."

Marcus nodded and prepared to change the subject.

"But only the first time? After that it's pleasurable?"

"Er . . . no, I believe it's not always pleasurable for women. Unless the man knows what he's doing. And cares enough to do it."

Albin's head tilted sideways. "What do you mean, sir?"

"When one is with a professional, one naturally does not bother to, er . . ." Marcus tugged at his neckcloth again. "One has paid to *receive* pleasure, not to give it. Although, of course, a gentleman never hurts a woman he's bedding, even if she is a whore."

"But men try to give their wives pleasure?"

Marcus shrugged. "That depends upon the marriage."

"How, sir?"

"With a love match, a husband naturally wishes to give his wife pleasure."

"And if it's not a love match, he doesn't?"

Marcus shrugged again. "An intelligent man would endeavor to. A wife who enjoys the pleasures of the bed can greatly enhance a marriage." In the early days of his marriage, with Lavinia eager in his bed, he'd thought himself the luckiest man in England.

Albin's eyebrows lifted slightly. "It can, sir? Why?"

"Because sex is the greatest physical pleasure one experiences in life."

Albin considered this answer, his lips pursed slightly in a frown. "Only for men? Or for women, too?"

"If the man knows what he's doing, then yes, I believe it is extremely pleasurable for women, too."

Albin nodded seriously.

"If you ever contemplate marriage, I suggest you gain some experience before the event." *Or your wedding night is likely to be a disaster.*

"Experience? You mean with a prostitute?" Albin grimaced, an expression of revulsion.

"One from a respectable establishment," Marcus hastened to say. "*Not* like Mrs. Henshaw's. One that has clean girls."

"Is that what you did, sir?"

Marcus stared at his secretary, torn between amusement and offense. *I really should tell him it's none of his business.* But Albin was gazing at him with such earnest seriousness that he couldn't. "Yes," he said. "But they'd be above your touch, lad. Very expensive."

As rebuffs went, it was very mild, but Albin blushed and subsided into silence.

Marcus turned his attention to the scenery. Dusk crept across the horizon. He felt a surge of bitterness. Every woman he'd ever slept with had done so because of his money—the high-class courtesans who'd warmed his bed until his marriage, the wife he'd thought had married him for love.

"Sir, is playing on her husband's pipe something a wife does—"

Marcus jerked his head around. "No! Good God, no! Don't *ever* ask your wife to do that!"

Albin flinched from his vehemence. Bewilderment furrowed his brow. "Why not, sir?"

"Because it's not something a respectable woman would do."

"Oh."

"One pays a prostitute to do it, one hopes one's *chère-amie* will do it, but one *never* asks one's wife to do it."

Albin nodded, his expression serious. "Thank you, sir."

"You're welcome." Marcus returned his attention to the window. The trees were vanishing into pools of shadow.

"So you recommend that . . . that someone such as myself visit a respectable establishment and ask for a lesson, sir?"

Marcus's eyes winced shut at the image that conjured up in his head. "No," he said, turning to look at Albin. "I recommend that you visit a respectable establishment and discover the pleasures of sex. And then, after a while, you might think about asking one of the girls to show you some of the things that please women."

Albin nodded. "I see."

"Good." Marcus stared out the window again. The line of the horizon was blending into the sky. A thought struck him. Albin was unusually gullible . . . He turned back to his secretary. "And Albin, don't *ever* tip a whore's velvet. Even if she tells you women enjoy it."

"Tip a whore's velvet?" Albin's brow wrinkled. "What's that, sir?"

"It's, er . . ." Marcus pulled at the knot of his neckcloth. It really was uncomfortably tight. "To tip velvet is to . . . er, to . . . to tongue a woman."

"Tongue?" Albin shook his head to show he didn't understand.

Marcus cleared his throat. To his annoyance, he felt himself blush. "By licking her private parts."

Albin recoiled slightly. An expression of disgust crossed his face.

"I believe it's very pleasurable for a woman." Marcus's voice didn't come out quite as he'd intended; there was a defensive note in it.

Albin's eyebrows rose up his forehead. "It is?"

Marcus nodded.

"Is it something a husband does—" Albin broke off at Marcus's headshake. "Not respectable, sir?"

"Definitely not respectable."

Albin's expression became perplexed. "But if one shouldn't do it with a whore and one shouldn't do it with one's wife, with whom does one do it?"

"One's *chère-amie,* if one wishes." Marcus shrugged. "If one knows she's not diseased."

"Have you ever—?"

"No," he said, cutting off the sentence. *I don't want to snub you, lad, but if you ask me one more question—*

The carriage slowed and made a left-hand turn. Marcus glanced out the window. To his relief he saw a familiar gatehouse. "We've arrived."

CHAPTER THIRTEEN

October 19th, 1805

Hazelbrook, Surrey

MARCUS STRODE DOWN the marble staircase, grim momentum building with each step. *It's like having a tooth pulled. The faster one does it, the easier it is.* "Mr. Albin?" he asked the footman on the landing.

"In the long gallery, sir."

His grip on the riding crop tightened. "Thank you."

Marcus's boots slapped the floor, each stride taking him closer to Barnaby. Face to face. For the first time since Lavinia's death.

The long gallery was hung with paintings, but Albin wasn't looking at scenes from Holland or Italy. He was gazing at the portrait of Lavinia, his mouth half-open, awestruck.

Marcus's jaw clenched. Paris must have looked just as foolish when he first set eyes on Helen of Troy. *As must I have, the first time I saw Lavinia.*

Albin's head turned. "Sir. Good morning." He blinked, frowned, turned back to the portrait. "Was she truly that beautiful, sir?"

Marcus crossed the gallery. He stared at the portrait. Golden hair. Sky-blue eyes. "She was."

"She did look like an angel."

"Yes." Sir Thomas Lawrence had perfectly captured Lavinia's delicate beauty, the expression of sweetness on her face.

Marcus's mouth tightened. Sweetness. It had snared his heart as much as Lavinia's slender, golden beauty had. He had wanted to cherish, to protect, to love.

But Lavinia's sweetness had gone no deeper than her smooth, petal-soft skin.

Marcus slapped the riding crop against his thigh, a sharp sound, and turned on his heel. "Let's go."

MARCUS'S MOOD DIDN'T improve once they emerged from the house. Everything brought back memories of Lavinia. He'd strolled with her down the slope of the lawn to the reed-fringed lake, almost dizzy with disbelief in his good luck. *My wife.* He'd picnicked with her in the Grecian folly on the far side, had kissed her beneath the cool, marble shade of its portico, had thought himself the most fortunate man in the Empire.

Lord, what a fool I was. Marcus turned away from the vista of lawn and lake, trees, hills. "We'll ride over."

"Ride?" Albin looked dismayed.

"You do ride, don't you?"

"Of course. It's just . . . it's been a long time, sir."

Marcus grunted. He strode in the direction of the stables, his boots crunching sharply in the gravel. "Hurry along, lad. I'd like to leave as soon as possible."

It was a lie. He didn't want to visit Barnaby. Didn't want to see his face. Didn't want to speak with him.

Like pulling a tooth. The faster one does it, the easier it is.

Their arrival in the stableyard sparked a bustle of activity. Two mounts were brought out. Marcus's stomach tightened as he swung up into the saddle, as he found the stirrup with his right boot, as he settled his weight. *Like pulling a tooth,* he told himself again.

He watched Albin heave himself up, fail to get his leg over the horse's back, and lurch back to the ground.

The lad tried again, launching himself so vigorously that he almost pitched over the other side of his mount. He clutched the saddle, barely keeping his seat.

Marcus snorted. A drunken sailor could have mounted with more finesse. "Would you prefer we took the carriage?"

Albin flushed scarlet. "No, sir."

Marcus shrugged. He pressed his heels to his horse's flanks and trotted from the stableyard. He didn't look back. No thud came from behind him, so presumably Albin managed to keep his seat.

Marcus followed the curve of the carriage sweep. At the edge of the trees, he waited for Albin. The lad held the reins in a death grip, as if he expected to fall off at any moment.

"How are you at jumping?"

Albin hesitated. "Not very good, sir."

Marcus grunted. At least the lad was honest.

He chose an easy route through the woods, avoiding such challenges as fording the river and jumping the high yew hedge that marked the boundary between his land and Barnaby's. The woods were bleak, wintry. Trees reached skeleton arms to the sky, the bare bones of their fingers outstretched. Dead leaves lay like sloughed skin at their feet.

The knot in Marcus's belly grew tighter the further they rode. Here was the old oak he'd fallen from, breaking his collarbone, knocking himself senseless. Barnaby had run for help as fast as his six-year-old legs could carry him to fetch help. Here was the stream he and Barnaby had dammed, hauling rocks and branches, making themselves as filthy as two children could possibly be. And here was the glade where bluebells bloomed. Where he'd kissed Lavinia. Where perhaps Barnaby had kissed her, too.

The knot in his belly twisted even tighter, as if a fist squeezed his innards.

They came out of the woods. Mead Hall was visible ahead—gray stone and tall Tudor chimneys. Marcus halted. Nausea rose in his throat. He clenched his teeth together.

"Is that where Sir Barnaby lives, sir?"

"Yes."

The mare caught Marcus's tension. She tossed her head. Her muscles bunched; she wanted to gallop. Marcus held her back.

Rage chased away the nausea as they trotted across the last field. He and Barnaby had played together as children, endured Eton together, gone up to Oxford together, had lived almost in each other's pockets, as close as brothers. *And then he had an affair with my wife.*

The rage was a hot, fermenting pressure in his chest by the time they reached the stableyard. Marcus dismounted and strode around to the front door, not looking back to see whether Albin followed. He rang the bell with a loud peal.

Albin hurried up, puffing slightly.

The door opened. "Lord Cosgrove." Surprise showed on the butler's face.

"Good morning, Yardley." It took effort to be civil, to not elbow the man aside and barge into Mead Hall. "Is Sir Barnaby in?"

"Yes, sir."

Marcus stepped into the stone-flagged entrance hall. He paid no attention to the tapestries on the walls, the crossed battle-axes above the doorway, the suits of armor flanking the oak staircase. "Breakfast parlor? Study?"

The butler hesitated. For more than twenty years Marcus had run tame in this house, entering without ceremony, needing no servant to announce him. "Study, sir."

"Very good, Yardley." He strode across the entrance hall, underneath the crossed axes, and down the corridor to the right.

Albin followed.

Marcus rapped once on the door to Barnaby's study, a peremptory sound, and opened it without waiting. Rage seethed in his belly.

Time seemed to swing backwards. How many times had he entered this room? How many times seen Barnaby seated at that desk, papers strewn messily around him and a painting of Agincourt, the battle that had won the Wares their baronetcy, hanging behind him on the wall?

Barnaby looked up. His face was so familiar—the curling red-brown hair, the freckles, the hazel eyes—that Marcus felt a moment of disorientation, as if the clock had turned back and the events of last year been erased—betrayal, death—and he could step up to the desk with a cheerful greeting and Barnaby would once again be his closest friend.

It seemed Barnaby experienced the same disorientation. For a split second, a grin lit his face—and then died. There was a moment of silence, of stillness. Barnaby laid down his quill and pushed aside the sheet of paper he was writing on. His movements were jerky, as if he had a marionette's wooden joints. "Marcus. Good morning."

Marcus didn't return the greeting. He clenched his hands, furious with himself for almost returning that grin, for wanting—if even for a second—to be friends with Barnaby again. "Did you send men to attack me?"

Barnaby stiffened. "What?"

Marcus walked towards the desk, fury building with each step. "I was attacked last week. Was it your doing?"

Barnaby stood, shoving his chair back so hard it struck the wall. "No, it was not." Behind him, the painting of Agincourt trembled, the turmoil of knights and pennants and horses momentarily alive. "The devil take you, Marcus!" He came around the desk. "How dare you think I'd do such a thing!"

"Why not?" He had control of his anger now; his voice was cold and contemptuous. "You fucked my wife."

Barnaby's head jerked back, as if he'd been slapped.

"I take it the vandalism wasn't you either?" There was a sneer in his voice. He couldn't help it. He wanted to hurt Barnaby, wanted to wound him as deeply as Barnaby had wounded him.

"Of course not!"

Instinctively, he believed Barnaby. Instinctively, he trusted him. But he'd trusted Barnaby before, and Barnaby had betrayed him. Marcus's upper lip curled. "On your word of honor? We both know how much *that* means."

Anger flared in Barnaby's face. "Damn you, Marcus! She came to me in tears! Said you were treating her cruelly, beating her—"

"Beating her?" The accusation took Marcus's breath away. He stood with his mouth open for a moment, incredulous. "How could you think—?" Rage choked his throat. He swallowed, found his voice. "I never raised my hand against Lavinia. Not once." He swung around abruptly and headed for the door, almost ramming into Albin. He'd forgotten his secretary's existence.

"Marcus, don't go. Please."

Marcus halted. He stood motionless for a moment, trembling, tense, then turned back to face Barnaby.

He knew Barnaby almost as well as he knew himself, could tell his moods at a glance, could see whether he was bored or amused or angry. Right now, it wasn't anger that was stamped on Barnaby's face.

He hates himself as much as I do.

"I'm sorry, Marcus. I never meant to . . . to . . ." Barnaby's hands moved, a beseeching gesture. "If I could take back that afternoon, I would. If . . . if I could undo it . . ."

Marcus's fury drained away. In its place was a weight of sadness. How could he blame Barnaby for falling prey to the same pretty face, the same caressing wiles, that he had? *He made the same fall I did, and just as disastrously.*

"Marcus, please . . . can't we . . . can't we—"

He knew what Barnaby was going to ask: *Can't we start again? Can't we be friends?* And he knew the answer. "No."

Barnaby's face tightened, the muscles around his mouth and eyes pinching in.

"I forgive you," Marcus said, and—astonishingly—that statement was true. Two minutes ago he'd have sworn forgiveness was impossible, but somehow it had happened. In his heart, he had forgiven Barnaby. "But I no longer trust you."

Barnaby swallowed. He gave a short, jerky nod.

"Good day," Marcus said, and he turned on his heel again and walked from the room.

Albin followed.

Marcus let himself out through a side door. He walked slowly around to the stables. The rage that had propelled him into Mead Hall was gone. Silently he swung up into his saddle and rode out.

He left the road, cantering across the fallow fields, jumping the hedges. It wasn't until he was halfway across the third field that he remembered Albin. He hauled on the reins, halting his horse.

Albin was only a dozen yards behind.

"I'm sorry," Marcus said, as the lad stopped alongside him. "I forgot you're not—"

Albin grinned, and shook his head. "It's fun, sir."

Fun? Marcus grunted. He felt a thousand years older than Albin.

He urged his horse into a slow canter, watching as Albin took the next hedge, if not with flair, then at least with competence.

They forded the river and rode back through the woods, climbing a low hill. The trees pulled back for a moment. Mead Hall was visible, nestled in the valley, a gray stone building amid gray, leafless trees. Marcus gazed at it. He felt as gray as the landscape, tired and drained, almost elderly. He was aware of an ache in his chest, of sadness, of regret. "Barnaby didn't do it."

"No." Albin shifted his weight in the saddle, and asked hesitantly: "Sir . . . why didn't you duel with Sir Barnaby? After you found out?"

"Because I would have killed him. And that would have ended my political career."

He'd wanted to kill Barnaby, had wanted quite *fiercely* to kill him. That desire was gone now, snuffed out. In its place was a hollow ache.

THEY RODE SLOWLY back through the woods. Dank drifts of leaves muffled the horses' hooves. The village church bell tolled eleven o'clock as they emerged from the trees. On the other side of the lake, Hazelbrook sat smugly.

Marcus halted and gazed at it.

If it could walk, Hazelbrook would strut like the Prince of Wales, full of self-importance. It would pick up the wide marble skirts of its terrace and mince down to the lake and preen, admiring its reflection—the tall spears of the paladin columns, the glittering tiers of windows, the delicate tiara of its widow's walk.

"Is that where your wife died, sir?"

"It is." His stomach clenched in memory. He saw Lavinia's face for a moment, the shock when she'd realized she was falling, the way her mouth had opened in a cry, the desperate grab she'd made for the railing, fingers outstretched. His ears almost heard the sound she'd made, shriek more than scream, full of rage.

"What's that, sir?"

Marcus shook his head, dragging himself back to the present. He followed the direction of Albin's finger. "The conservatory. My mother had it built. It's one of the finest examples in England." He frowned at the building. How absurd it looked, a turreted pavilion from the Far East perched on a hillside in Surrey.

"Sir . . . do you *like* Hazelbrook?"

Marcus uttered an uncomfortable laugh. The lad was far too perceptive. "No. If I could, I'd sell it."

Albin gave a nod of understanding. "It's entailed."

"No. But my mother . . . she said the conservatory was her gift to her descendants. To my children and their children."

"Oh," Albin said. He looked slightly daunted.

Yes. I'm stuck with it.

"Up to a few more hours in the saddle, lad? I'll show you round the estate, introduce you to the bailiff. You'll be coming down here as part of your duties." *And I won't be with you. Not if I can help it.*

CHAPTER FOURTEEN

BY THE TIME they'd ridden around the boundary of the estate, lunched in the village, visited the tenants' cottages, and gone over the farm with the bailiff, deep shadows were pooling in the hollows. The first gray-pink shades of dusk tinted the sky.

Marcus blew out a breath. There was one final thing to show Albin.

He swung down from the saddle and watched Albin achieve a creditable dismount. The lad was improving.

The conservatory soared above their heads—domed roof and delicate turrets. Inside, shadows moved: the gardeners finishing their work for the day.

Marcus knocked on the nearest pane of glass and beckoned. A gardener hurried out. "Sir?"

"Noake, isn't it? Take the horses back to the stables, please. And tell Mrs. Kerr to draw baths for us. We'll be in in half an hour." He turned his attention back to Albin. His secretary was gazing upwards, his expression awed.

"What's it made of, sir? Marble?"

"Wood." Marcus rapped his knuckles against the slender joinery. "Painted to look like stone. Come inside before it gets dark." He entered the conservatory, Albin at his heels.

Warm, damp air enveloped them, pushing into Marcus's nose and mouth. He held his breath for a moment, then forced himself to inhale. The smell was heavy, organic, with an undertone of decay. He suppressed a grimace. It was like being in an over-crowded ballroom—the heat of too many people in too small a space, each breath filled with a hundred different scents, not all of them pleasant. He glanced at his secretary.

Albin's eyes were wide, his lips parted in wonder.

Marcus tried to see it as the lad did: the orderly jungle of flowers and ferns, the vast expanse of glass, the high, vaulted roof, the thousands of delicate white and blue tiles that covered the floor. He scuffed one with the toe of his boot. "The tiles are from Constantinople."

Albin closed his mouth. He glanced down at the floor and then up at the ceiling again. Words burst from him: "It's enor-mous, sir!"

And the cost of heating it was enormous, too—as Albin would discover when he did the Hazelbrook accounts. "Covers more than an acre." Marcus walked further into the conservato-ry, following an artificial stream in a bed of blue tiles. Albin trailed behind, craning his neck from side to side, gazing at the banks of narcissi, the exotic lilies, the orchids.

Marcus halted beneath the dome. Here, beside the bubbling fountain, he'd proposed to Lavinia. Here, she'd accepted his of-fer. Here, he'd declared himself the happiest man in the world.

What a blind, besotted fool I was.

"What do you think? Do you like it?"

"How could one not?"

Marcus shrugged. "There's a lily pond at the end." He led the lad past the fern-filled grotto, down shallow steps where water descended in graceful cascades on either side, to a pond in which water lilies bloomed. "We hold public days twice a year."

"I imagine they're very popular, sir."

"Yes."

The wilderness was a pretense. Each plant was carefully positioned, carefully maintained, carefully clipped and trained.

He looked around. There, glimpsed between a riot of orchids and luxuriant fern fronds, the three Graces poured water from urns, their marble limbs pale and graceful. And there, beside the bank of massed crocuses, was the seat where his mother had liked to sit and take her tea in the afternoons.

Seven years she'd been dead, but memory gave him her image clearly: the rigid posture, the crisp lines of her gown, the tightly pursed mouth.

The words he had for his mother—reserved, distant, cold—seemed to have no connection with the conservatory. One couldn't help sweating in this close, damp heat. It was alive, decaying as it bloomed, blooming as it decayed.

Marcus turned on one heel. *How little I knew her. How little she allowed me to know her.*

"Are there any orange trees, sir?"

He shook his head, and brought his attention back to Albin. "No. Or fruit trees of any kind. My mother didn't judge them beautiful enough."

Albin considered this, his brow slightly wrinkled.

"You disapprove?"

"It isn't my place to approve or disapprove, sir."

Marcus grunted at this neutral answer. "The Kent estate has an orangery and large succession houses. All our fruit is grown there out of season." The succession houses were more to his liking than this monument to beauty and frivolity. Those plants fed hundreds of mouths. These . . . they were like Hazelbrook itself: for show.

The jasmine bower caught his eye. He'd picked one of those luxuriant sprays of flowers for Lavinia once, had woven it into her golden hair. She'd laughed and stood on tiptoe and kissed him, and they'd gone back to the house and made love, even though it was only afternoon and sunlight had streamed in through the windows.

Had she been as eager for his lovemaking as she'd seemed, or had it been pretense?

Pretense, a cynical voice whispered in his ear. *She was softening you up. Don't you remember? She asked for a diamond and sapphire diadem, and you gave her one.*

Marcus turned abruptly away from the lily pond. Beneath the perfume of flowers—jasmine, narcissus—was a strong smell of decomposing vegetation. "Come along."

He strode back through the conservatory. Outside, the air was cold, crisp, clean. Marcus dragged a deep breath into his lungs. Above him, the thousands of panes of glass were tinted pale pink in the sunset. The conservatory was a fairy castle, beautiful.

He turned his back to it.

Marcus crossed the lawn at a tangent and climbed the steps to the terrace two at time. Memories filled his head: Lavinia's hand tucked warmly in his, the fragrance of the jasmine he'd woven into her hair, her smiling upward glance. *Let's go upstairs, Marcus.*

Marcus wrenched open the door to the library and strode inside. It was cool and dark, smelling of calfskin book covers and aging paper—but even in here there were memories. On that sofa, Lavinia had coaxed him into buying a new carriage lined with pale-blue silk. And, later in their marriage, she'd stood in the doorway shrieking at him like a fishwife.

"Sir?"

Marcus realized he'd halted in the middle of the room. He shook himself. "Upstairs with you, lad. Mrs. Kerr should have a bath ready for you. Dinner in an hour."

AFTER THEY'D DINED, they moved to the library. The earl poured two generous glasses of port, gave her one, and sat down with the newspaper.

Charlotte picked up the latest *Gazette* and flicked through it. The list of advertisements caught her eye. Memories unfolded in her head: her bedroom at Westcote Hall, the woman appearing out of nowhere, the old-fashioned gown, the sharp cat's teeth, the malice glittering in her black eyes.

Charlotte shivered. She put down the newspaper, gulped a mouthful of port, and stretched her legs out towards the fire. Her muscles ached from the hours spent in the saddle.

She felt warm and sleepy, light-headed. The armchair seemed to float an inch or two above the floor. *Is this what being foxed feels like?* Memories of her birthday drifted like leaf-boats caught in an eddy of water. Black eyes. Sharp teeth. A blood-red gown.

The evening of her birthday seemed like a fantastical dream—preposterous, unbelievable—and yet it had been real. *Look where I am now. Earning my living.*

Her gaze shifted to the earl.

He'd put aside his newspaper. He slouched in the embrace of his armchair, one booted leg slung over the arm, his neckcloth loosened, a glass of port in one hand. His face was in profile, showing her the jut of nose and jaw, the strong cheekbones.

Charlotte's pulse gave a queer little kick and sped up. Cosgrove wasn't classically handsome, but he was striking, arresting. Those gray eyes . . .

She wrenched her gaze away and stared at the fire. How could the countess have chosen Sir Barnaby over Cosgrove?

Charlotte frowned at the flames, trying to answer the question. Perhaps Lady Cosgrove had wanted to be worshipped? Perhaps she'd turned to Sir Barnaby because he was susceptible to her charms, as the earl had no longer been?

Or perhaps she'd wanted to wound Cosgrove deeply and had chosen destruction of his closest friendship as her method.

If that had been the countess's goal, she'd succeeded. It had been blindingly obvious this morning how deep each man's emotions were. How much they were hurting.

"That's a fearsome frown you're wearing, lad." The earl pushed to his feet and placed another log on the fire. "You're not still thinking about Mrs. Henshaw's, are you? I'd advise you to put it out of your mind."

"Oh, no, sir. I was thinking about . . ." *You.* Heat filled her face, scorching. The skin on her throat, her cheeks, even her scalp, seemed to burn. "Someone," Charlotte finished lamely. She put down the glass of port. *I must not drink any more.*

Cosgrove's eyebrows pulled together in a frown. "In love are you, lad?"

Charlotte shook her head vigorously. "No, sir."

His frown deepened, as if he disbelieved her. "A word of advice—don't confuse love with lust." He crossed to the decanters. "More port?"

"No, thank you, sir."

"Lust addles your brain," Cosgrove said, choosing a decanter and pouring. "Makes you make bad decisions. If you have an itch to scratch, choose a clean whore—don't go imagining yourself in love."

"An itch? You mean . . . sex?"

"I do." Cosgrove sat again. "The best thing you can do right now, lad, is to lose your virginity to an expert. Scratch the itch and it usually goes away."

Charlotte picked up her glass and gulped a mouthful of port. *Lose my virginity to an expert?* She choked back a giggle. *He'd never offer such advice to a female.* "Thank you, sir. I shall consider it."

Cosgrove yawned. "But mind you use protection."

"Protection?" The burning blush had faded. Her cheeks felt merely warm.

"A sheath."

"Sheath?"

"A piece of dried sheep's intestine that fits over one's cock."

Charlotte blinked. "Oh." She tried to visualize Christopher Albin's pego with dried intestine wrapped around it, and repressed a shudder. "What does the sheath protect against, sir?"

"French gout. And pregnancy."

"Oh," Charlotte said again, more thoughtfully. "It sounds uncomfortable."

The earl shrugged. "It's better than burning one's poker. Or siring by-blows." He yawned again. "A lot of whores use sea sponges, of course. But that won't stop you getting burnt."

"Sea sponges?" Charlotte said, utterly lost. "What for?"

"Preventing pregnancy."

Charlotte turned this answer over in her head. Whatever way she looked at it, it made no sense. "How?" she asked, finally.

Cosgrove glanced sideways at her. "What if I said she ate it?"

Charlotte frowned. "I don't see how—"

Cosgrove whooped with laughter.

Charlotte closed her mouth, feeling her cheeks grow hot again.

"Forgive me," Cosgrove said, when he'd caught his breath. "I couldn't resist."

Her heartbeat became jerky. *That grin. Those eyes.*

"She inserts the sponge inside herself," Cosgrove explained. "To stop the mettle reaching her womb."

"Oh." Mettle was another word Charlotte didn't know, but she could guess its meaning: a man's seed.

Cosgrove's grin changed into another yawn. He loosened his neckcloth further, ran a hand through his hair, tousling it, and leaned his head back in the chair, his eyes half-closed. He looked tired and rumpled and even more attractive than he had before.

Charlotte felt a surge of protectiveness. *He needs to go to bed.*

Her imagination took flight. If she were Cosgrove's wife, she could walk across to him, smooth back that disheveled hair, and say: *You're tired. Time for bed.*

Charlotte put down her glass. She'd definitely drunk too much port. She pushed to her feet. "Excuse me, sir. I shall retire, with your leave."

IT WAS PAST three o'clock in the morning when Charlotte jerked awake. *Something's wrong.*

She caught hold of the bed curtain and yanked it back.

Silence. Darkness.

Charlotte sat for a long moment, listening. Was that the sound of running feet? Were those shouts?

She scrambled out of bed and groped along the wall until she found the door. Cautiously, she opened it.

Silence. Darkness.

Charlotte leaned against the door jam, her head aching. Had she dreamed the noises? Was she still foxed?

No. She heard the *slapslapslap* of someone running. A bobbing gleam of light grew on the wall, as if from a lantern.

Charlotte tensed, but the person who appeared around the corner was the earl. He looked as if he'd scrambled out of bed— hair uncombed, jaw unshaven—and thrust on yesterday's clothes. The lantern cast grim, spiky shadows across his face.

"What's wrong, sir?"

"The conservatory's on fire." Cosgrove passed her and disappeared down the corridor at a run.

CHAPTER FIFTEEN

THE CONSERVATORY LOOKED as if it was made of fire. Flames leapt into the sky, their reflections writhing across the panes of glass. Men ran, shouted, threw buckets of water, tiny against the towering blaze.

Charlotte hurried to join them. The air was furnace-hot, the night loud with the sound of glass shattering, loud with the roar of flames.

Someone caught her arm, jerking her almost off her feet. "Get back." It was the earl. His grip was hard, painful. He shoved her backwards and turned to yell at the men. "Get back! Everyone get back!"

In the chaos, it took several minutes before his order was obeyed. One of the gardeners, almost sobbing, refused to lay down his bucket.

"Is it worth your life, man?" Cosgrove shouted. "Get *back.*"

They clustered some distance from the conservatory, gardeners and stablemen and servants from the house, some in nightshirts, others half-dressed, faces red in the firelight, silent, like mourners at a funeral.

Cosgrove came to stand beside her. "It can't be saved."

"No, sir. Do you think the house, the woods—?"

"There's no danger unless the wind picks up." The last word was swallowed by a huge *woomph* of sound as the dome of the conservatory collapsed. Shards of glass and flaming splinters of wood sprayed outwards.

"How was it heated, sir?"

"By stoves."

"It weren't the stoves, sir," one of the men standing nearby said. "This started outside."

Cosgrove turned swiftly to look at him. "Are you certain, Cray?"

"As certain as I am of anything, sir. The fire started in more than one place. And it started outside."

"Arson."

"Without doubt, sir."

Cosgrove scowled, one cheek flame-red, the other lost in shadow. "Barnaby." The word was low, savage.

"Maybe not, sir," Charlotte ventured. "It could be—" she glanced at the man, Cray, and spoke obliquely, "—one of the others."

Cosgrove considered this for a moment, his face fierce in the firelight, then turned abruptly away. "Where's Sugden? Sugden! Do you still have that bitch? The one that can smell rabbits half a county away?"

"She died, sir." One of the men, a stableman by his garb, turned away from watching the fire. "But I have one of her last litter."

"Fetch it," Cosgrove ordered. "Let's see if it can pick up a scent."

But the dog, when it was brought, was little more than a pup. It was delighted to greet Cosgrove, delighted to jump up and lick his face, but confused by its master's commands. When brought closer to the fire, it cowered from the flames.

"It's no good," Sugden said. "Sorry, sir."

"Not your fault, man." The earl turned and gave rapid orders to the assembled servants, some to watch the fire, others to search the woods.

Charlotte watched as men scattered, to dress, to fetch lanterns. She chewed on her lower lip. A dog had more chance of finding any tracks than a man.

She backed away from the fire. When she was no longer illuminated by the flames she ran round to the front of the house. The back, with the stableyard and the sleeping quarters for gardeners and grooms was busy, but here, looking down towards the lake, all was silent.

In a little shrubbery beneath the looming cliff of the terrace she found what she needed. Here, shielded by topiary, she could hide. There was even an empty urn in which to conceal her clothes.

Charlotte stripped out of the clothing she'd thrown on less than fifteen minutes ago. Her breath plumed in front of her face, silver in the moonlight. Pieces of gravel were like lumps of ice beneath her bare feet.

She hopped from foot to foot, shivering. She'd never tried being an animal before. What if something went wrong? What if—

If she thought about it too much, she'd be too afraid.

Charlotte squeezed her eyes resolutely shut. "I want to be Bess," she said under her breath, building an image in her mind of her father's dog, brown and long-legged.

The itching came—as if a legion of insects crawled over her skin, under her skin, inside her bones—and then was gone.

Charlotte opened her eyes.

Disorientation washed over her. Night didn't look like this. The color was wrong. The shapes of the shrubs were wrong, towering over her. She inhaled. Smells filled her mouth and nose: the stink of smoke, the scents of grass and soil and dead leaves, the whiff of a dead animal decaying.

Charlotte gagged.

She pressed herself into the gravel, eyes squeezed shut, trying to anchor herself, trying not to vomit.

Gradually the smells became less overwhelming. The urge to vomit faded.

Charlotte lay panting, her heart racing in her chest. Cautiously she opened her eyes. Shrubbery loomed above her, bushes as tall as trees. Her nose told her they were yew, and it told her that a dead creature, a mouse perhaps, was rotting at their base.

She half-rose at the sound of running feet, so loud the runner must be upon her—and then her eyes caught movement near the woods. Two of the gardeners, lanterns in hand.

She crouched while noises rushed at her. Shouts. The crackle of flames. Breaking glass. The hooting of an owl. The clamor of night insects. Sounds blended together in a cacophony; she heard people moving in the woods, crashing through the undergrowth, heard them running across the silvery expanse of lawn, their boots crunching the frost. And then a voice jumped out at her from all the other sounds, unmistakably Cosgrove's—the deep timbre, the note of authority.

Charlotte stood. She shook herself. The movement felt odd as it traveled down her body. She was too long, too low. She had four feet planted on the ground and a tail.

Charlotte walked from the shrubbery, placing each paw with care. Right, left, right, left. Her progress was slow and awkward. After a few paces her legs tangled. She overbalanced and fell over.

She lay on the cold gravel, shivering. Men shouted in the woods. Glass cracked in the fire. A full moon hung overhead, almost as bright as the sun. What was wrong with her? Dogs walked on four legs without any difficulty.

But she wasn't a dog. She was a human in a body that was the wrong shape.

I can do this.

Charlotte huffed a breath and pushed up onto all four paws.

She fastened her gaze on a point several yards distant. *Don't think about how many legs I've got, just walk.*

She reached the spot without tangling her legs. It took a moment to realize that the strange sensation coming from her hindquarters was her tail wagging.

Charlotte headed back to the fire. Her legs moved of their own accord, a natural rhythm—fast, faster—until she was trotting, her paws making soft crunching sounds on the gravel.

Two men watched the blaze, the rest had dispersed.

The fire looked quite different through her dog's eyes. The flames were no less fierce, but they were an odd color, the intense reds and oranges gone.

Charlotte circled the conservatory, a slow and slinking path that kept her in the shadows. Dozens of smells overlaid each other. Burning timber and charred vegetation. The horse smell of the stablemen and earthy smell of the gardeners. Lord Cosgrove's scent, faint but distinct, and a scent that she recognized, to her surprise, as Christopher Albin's. There were other smells, too—rich, damp soil and layer upon layer of flower scents—and a smell that was oddly out of place, yet familiar . . .

Whale oil. She smelled it on the ground.

Someone had used it to fuel the fire.

Charlotte trotted away from the fire, casting in a wide arc, sniffing, trying to catch the scent of whale oil.

There. Faint but distinct. Heading towards the driveway.

Charlotte lengthened her stride. She was running as fast as a man. Faster. As fast as a horse. It was exhilarating. Her muscles bunched and stretched, bunched and stretched, the frosty ground flashing beneath her paws.

The scent of whale oil led down the driveway. Before the gatehouse, it swung into the woods. Two horses had waited here, concealed in the trees. A pile of droppings steamed gently, the scent rich and sweet. None of Cosgrove's men had found it yet. Would their human noses smell it, or would they continue blindly past?

The two horses had ridden through the woods, squeezed through a gap in the high yew hedge, and headed east along the road.

Charlotte followed, stretching her legs into a long, ground-covering gallop.

She didn't know how long she ran for. Perhaps twenty minutes, perhaps half an hour. She passed Sir Barnaby's manor, with its tall Tudor chimneys, passed farmhouses, passed cottages. Her pace slowed from headlong gallop to steady lope. Above her, the moon hung, heavy and full. Milestones gleamed whitely. Was this the sixth she'd passed? The seventh?

The scent of horses, of men, of whale oil, grew stronger. How far was she behind now? A few minutes?

A village came into sight. She smelled woodsmoke, heard voices and the clatter of horses' hooves.

Charlotte slowed to a cautious trot. Light spilled onto the road ahead of her—an inn, with an ostler leading away two horses, and a coach-and-four standing ready to depart, a postilion astride one of the wheelers and another mounted on the outside leader.

Her nose told her that the two men standing beside the coach had lit the conservatory fire. They smelled of sweat and smoke and whale oil, of horse, of leather and wool, but each had a distinct odor; one was sourer, the other had a musty, sweeter scent.

She halted. She couldn't follow a coach-and-four.

Lamplight lit each man's face as he climbed aboard. Charlotte stared intently, trying to memorize their features. Perhaps it was because she had dog's eyes, but the two men seemed unremarkable. She couldn't even tell what color their hair was.

The carriage door slammed shut, the horses moved forward, and the whole equipage swept out of the village.

Charlotte sat down, panting, her tongue hanging from her mouth.

The innkeeper carried his lamp inside and closed the door, shooting the bolts. Sounds came from the stableyard, but all was dark and silent in front of the inn.

Charlotte slunk across the street and plunged her muzzle into the horse trough, drinking greedily. Her long dog's tongue got in the way. She choked and fell into a fit of coughing.

The ostler came round from the stableyard. "Away with you!" He shied a stone at her.

THE ROAD STRETCHED endlessly in the moonlight. Running was beyond her; the most Charlotte could manage was a weary trot.

When Sir Barnaby's manor came into sight she stopped and lay down on the road, legs trembling, laboring for breath.

Not much further now.

Charlotte closed her eyes. Exhaustion pressed her into the dirt. It would be so easy to lie here, to sleep . . .

An owl hooted. Charlotte jerked her eyes open and staggered upright. Her pace this time was little more than walking. When she reached the Hazelbrook woods she left the road, squeezing through the hedge.

It was darker between the trees. Thick layers of dead leaves were soft beneath her paws. Water burbled—the river she'd forded that morning with Lord Cosgrove. Thirst spurred her into a slow, lumbering run. She charged into the water and lay down, too tired to stand.

"CAN'T SEE NOTHING that looks like tracks, sir."

Marcus raised his lantern and looked around. Trees loomed out of the darkness. This was futile. Far better that he return to

Hazelbrook, saddle one of the horses, and ride over to confront Barnaby.

Movement caught his eye. He swung around.

A dog came through the trees, walking slowly. Even at this distance he saw its ribcage heaving.

"Whose is that?"

"Never seen it afore, sir."

The dog halted and stared at him, its eyes gleaming in the lamplight. It was dark brown and short-coated, with a long muzzle and legs.

Marcus walked over to it. The dog didn't cower from him, didn't snarl, just stood there panting.

He reached down and patted it. Its coat was wet. Its body trembled beneath his hand. "You're exhausted, poor creature."

The dog gave a deep sigh, as if it understood his words and agreed, then nudged his leg and walked away between the trees.

Marcus stared after it. That nudge had been like a wordless good-bye. *How strange.*

He turned back to the gardener. "Tell the others to stop looking. We won't find anything in this dark."

"Yes, sir."

Marcus made a cast through the woods, repeating the order, and then plowed uphill through the trees. No point searching when he knew who'd lit the fire.

With each step, his rage grew. It was the same sick fury that had consumed him after he'd learned of Lavinia's affair. How could a man he'd grown up with, a man he'd counted as his brother, do this?

He'd just broken out of the trees—full moon, red glow of the fire—when he heard his name being called. "Lord Cosgrove! Sir!"

"Here!" He raised his lantern.

Gravel crunched as someone came towards him, half-running. "Sir . . ." It was Albin.

"What is it, lad?"

Albin halted and gulped for breath. "I followed them, sir."

"What?" Excitement surged in his chest. "Who? Tell me, lad. Quickly!"

"Don't know who they were, sir." Albin bent over, braced his hands on his knees, panted. "Two men. They had horses in the wood."

"You ran after two men on *horseback*?"

"Yes, sir." Albin sat down on the ground. His hair was wet with sweat, plastered to his brow. "They weren't that far ahead. I thought—I didn't want to lose them."

Marcus crouched alongside him. "Where did they go? Mead Hall?"

"No, sir. They rode to the next village."

"Betchworth?"

"Don't know what it's called, sir. The one past Mead Hall."

"East? That's Tewkes Hollow." Marcus stared at his secretary in disbelief. "You ran all the way to Tewkes Hollow?" He put his lantern on the ground. "Impossible."

"It's true, sir."

Marcus gripped Albin's shoulder. "I don't doubt you, lad. But . . . Good God! That's all of seven miles!" The lad was trembling with exhaustion.

"They took a coach-and-four, sir. From the inn. It left just as I got there."

"Where were they headed?"

"I don't know, sir. I . . . I thought you'd want to question the innkeeper yourself."

"By Jove, yes!" Marcus stood. "Come on, lad. Let's find out who they were—and where they went!"

He hauled Albin to his feet, but it took only a few seconds to realize that the lad wasn't going anywhere tonight. He shivered convulsively, close to collapse.

Marcus slung Albin's arm over his shoulder and helped him back to the house. "What would you like most?" he asked, as he half-carried Albin up the steps to the front door. "A bed, or food?"

"Something to drink, sir."

Candles blazed in the entrance hall. Marcus gave rapid orders to his housekeeper. "Mrs. Kerr, blankets for Mr. Albin, and a tankard of ale and some hot food." He steered the lad into the library. "And see that the fire is built up in here." He eased Albin into the armchair closest to the fireplace and turned to his butler. The man's face was anxious and unshaven. "Gough, send round to the stables. I want a horse saddled for me. Now!"

CHAPTER SIXTEEN

ALBIN WAS ASLEEP, cocooned in blankets in the armchair, when Marcus returned. An empty tankard and the remains of a substantial repast were on the table alongside. A fire filled the grate, throwing out heat. The lad's hair was dry, curling up from his brow.

"Excellent, Mrs. Kerr." Marcus stripped off his riding gloves. "You've looked after him well."

"The conservatory, sir—"

"The fire wasn't lit by anyone local. Mr. Albin discovered a clue that leads us back to London. I'm leaving as soon as the carriage is brought round." He glanced at his watch. Seven o'clock. Dawn soon. "A tankard of ale, please, Mrs. Kerr. And a basket of food for the journey." As if to reinforce this order, his stomach gave a low growl. "Bread and cheese is fine."

"I should hope I can do better than bread and cheese, sir!" Mrs. Kerr hurried down the corridor in a flurry of skirts.

Marcus turned to his butler. "Gough, please see that my valise is packed and brought down."

"I'll attend to it myself, sir."

Marcus stroked his jaw. Stubble rasped beneath his fingers. There was no time to shave. He crossed to the chair where his secretary slept. "Wake up, lad." Albin was so deeply asleep that he had to shake him.

For a moment the lad seemed not to know where he was—confusion and alarm crossed his face—then he blinked. "Sir." He struggled to free himself from the blankets.

"I'm leaving for London in fifteen minutes. You may stay here if you wish and travel back later by post—"

"The two men?"

"Went to London."

Albin stumbled slightly as he stood. "I'll come with you, sir."

"Good lad." Marcus gripped Albin's shoulder briefly. "Gough is upstairs. He'll help you pack."

He strode around to the smoldering ruins of the conservatory, whistling under his breath. A dozen men stood watching flames gnaw the embers. Marcus beckoned to the bailiff and the head gardener. "Whoever lit the fire wasn't local. The trail leads back to London. I'm leaving immediately. Clear the debris once it's cooled. Take it right back to bare earth."

"Will you be rebuilding, sir?"

"No." He saw the flash of anxiety on the head gardener's face, and understood it. "You may assure the men they won't be turned off. There'll be employment for all of you—if not here, then on another of my estates. You have my word."

FIFTEEN MINUTES LATER, as the carriage lurched and swayed down the driveway, Albin asked him the same question: "Will you build another conservatory, sir?"

"No. I shall sell Hazelbrook." With the conservatory razed, the obligation to his mother was gone.

"It . . . it has an unhappy history," Albin said, clearly trying to show that he understood.

"Yes." But it wasn't only Lavinia's memory that tainted Hazelbrook. "My grandfather purchased it from the profits of the plantation in the West Indies. Slave labor." Marcus opened the basket Mrs. Kerr had provided. He took out a meat pie wrapped in a linen napkin. His stomach clenched in anticipation. "The conservatory was built from those profits, too." The thousands of pretty blue and white tiles, imported at great expense from Constantinople, had been paid for by the sweat and blood of slaves in the tropics, as had each pane of glass, each exotic plant, each statue and fountain.

Marcus bit into the pie. He'd sell Hazelbrook, buy another plantation, give the slaves their freedom. The money would go full circle.

Across from him, Albin yawned. "Sir, what did you discover at the village?"

Marcus chewed and swallowed. "The two men arrived yesterday, by post-chaise from London. They hired horses from the inn and went out twice—in the afternoon, and at midnight. They arranged for the post-chaise to convey them back to London at an unspecified time this morning." Five o'clock, as it had turned out. "They paid well, so the landlord asked no questions."

Albin nodded and smothered another yawn.

"The post-chaise was from the Bull and Mouth in London. With any luck, we'll find them there, or information that will lead us to them."

"What were their names, sir?"

"Smith. Clearly false." Marcus bit into the pie again.

Albin asked no further questions. By the time Marcus finished the pie, he'd fallen asleep.

Marcus covered the lad with a blanket and settled back in his own corner. He rummaged in the basket, whistling softly. He was rid of Hazelbrook, and in a few hours he'd know who was behind the arson, and perhaps the attack and the vandalism, too.

He took out a second pie and sank his teeth into it. Outside, wisps of pink and gold lit the sky.

THEY REACHED THE Bull and Mouth just on midday. Albin was so deeply asleep that Marcus hadn't the heart to wake him. He leapt down from the carriage and crossed the courtyard, anticipation humming in his veins. The clamor of the posting-inn engulfed him—shouts, the clatter of hooves and coach wheels, a baby's wail. He sidestepped a pile of trunks and skirted an argument between two postilions and a red-faced country squire. The taproom was crowded, the din of voices pushing out through the door.

Marcus stood in the doorway and scanned faces. Were the men he wanted in here? In the coffee room? Upstairs asleep?

He halted a waiter carrying a tray piled with plates of roast meat. "The post-chaise-and-four that arrived from Tewkes Hollow this morning, where would I find the passengers?"

The waiter shrugged and continued on his way.

Marcus plunged further into the bustle of the hostelry in search of the innkeeper. "The post-chaise-and-four from Tewkes Hollow this morning," he repeated, when he found the man. "Where would I find the passengers?"

As the waiter had done, the innkeeper took in his appearance with a glance—hair unbrushed, face unshaven, wearing the clothes he'd thrown on in the middle of the night, no waistcoat or neckcloth, everything filthy and stinking of smoke—and dismissed him with a shrug.

Marcus gritted his teeth. *I'm an earl, not a vagabond.* He resisted the urge to comb his hair with his fingers and instead dug into his pocket for a guinea. "The passengers who arrived from Tewkes Hollow in one of your post-chaises. Where would I find them?"

The innkeeper was most apologetic. The chaise had arrived half an hour previously and the passengers had immediately departed, not pausing to dine or slake their thirst. No, he had never

seen them before. No, he didn't feel he could describe them—
they had been a most ordinary pair. No, he couldn't remember
their names, but he had a record . . . ah, there it was . . . Smith.

"The postilions? May I speak with them?"

"Joseph's gone home to bed, but Samuel may still be here,"
the innkeeper said, his eyes on the golden coin.

"I'd like to speak with him."

The postilion was in the stables, chatting with a stableman
and nursing a tankard of ale. At the sight of his employer, the
stableman remembered the broom he was leaning on and began
sweeping up scraps of straw.

"Samuel," the innkeeper called curtly. "Here!"

The postilion drained his tankard and obeyed. "Sir?"

"Answer this gentleman's questions, then off to bed with
you." The innkeeper took the empty tankard, cast a glance of
disapprobation at the stableman, and hurried back into the inn.

The postilion huffed a scornful breath through his nose. "An
old woman, 'e is."

Marcus fished in his pocket for a half-crown. "The passengers you took to Tewkes Hollow and back. Tell me about them."

The postilion's eyes fastened on the coin. "What d' you want
to know?"

"Their names."

"Smith," the postilion said promptly.

"What did they look like?"

The postilion scratched his head. He had a weather-beaten
face beneath ginger hair. "They was big men, like you."

Marcus waited, but Samuel seemed to have nothing more to
say. "That's it? That's all you can remember about them?"

The postilion shrugged. "They wasn't men as stood out, sir. I
don't rightly know I'd reco'nize 'em if I saw 'em again."

Marcus kept his patience with effort. "You'd never seen them
before?"

"Not so's I remember, sir."

"Your employer says they didn't stop to dine here. Is that correct?"

"Yes, sir. They left as soon as we got 'ere. In an 'urry, like."

"Did you hear anything they said? Either today or yesterday?"

"I was riding the leader," the postilion said regretfully, looking at the half-crown as if he expected it to be withdrawn. "I didn't hear but one word they said."

"Your colleague, Joseph, do you think he might have?"

The postilion shrugged. "I couldn't rightly say, sir."

"Where would I find him?"

"He's got hisself a new girl. Dunno where she lives."

Marcus clenched his jaw. "When is he due back here?" Some of his frustration leaked into his voice, but the postilion didn't appear to hear it.

"We's booked for a ride to Watford at five o'clock."

"Then I shall return later this afternoon." Marcus gave him the coin.

"Thank you, sir." The postilion tugged his forelock and headed in the direction of the taproom.

Marcus strode back to the street. The anticipation that had hummed in his veins was gone. Half an hour. He'd missed them by half an hour.

He wanted to snarl at the elderly lady who stepped unwittingly into his path, wanted to yell at the footman who held the carriage door open for him. Marcus took a deep breath and released it with a slow hiss.

He climbed into the carriage. Albin still slept in the far corner.

MARCUS SHOOK ALBIN awake as the carriage entered Grosvenor

Square. "We've arrived, lad."

Albin sat up groggily. He peered out the window. "What about the Bull and Mouth?"

"I've been there." Frustration leaked into his voice again. The postilion hadn't noticed it; Albin did.

"What happened, sir?"

"They'd gone. I spoke to the innkeeper and one of the postilions and learned nothing." The carriage slowed. "I'll return this afternoon to speak to the second postil—" Marcus gave a snarl of rage and wrenched the carriage door open, jumping down before the vehicle had fully halted.

Albin scrambled down after him.

Eight windows. Broken.

"Does today's date have any significance, sir?" Albin asked. A cold wind blew through the square, sending dead leaves scurrying. "The fire and now this—"

"And there was shit left." The steps leading up to the front door were damp. The smell of scrubbing soap was strong.

Impotent rage swelled in Marcus's chest. He felt like picking up a cobblestone and smashing what was left of the windows himself.

The door opened. His butler hurried down the steps, wringing his hands. "Sir, I'd hoped that by the time you arrived—"

Marcus forced a smile to his mouth. "It's of no matter, Fellowes." Two glaziers were at work installing new panes of glass. "What time did it happen?"

"Between two and three this morning, sir. The night watchman was good enough to knock on the door and let us know. The back door, I should say, sir. The front steps were . . . er—"

"Piled high. Yes, I can see." Marcus turned back to the carriage. The coachman and two footmen were dusty from the journey, their faces unshaven, weary. The coachman had a smear of soot across his brow. "Thank you for your service at

Hazelbrook last night," Marcus said. "You may have the rest of the day off."

The coach clattered around to the mews. Within minutes the tale of the conservatory burning down would be circulating among the servants.

"Mr. Albin will be staying for a few days, Fellowes. He may have the Blue Room."

"Very good, sir."

He climbed the damp steps. Fellowes closed the door, shutting out the scent of scrubbing soap. Marcus could smell beeswax polish, his own sweat, the stink of smoke. "Tell Mrs. Maby we shall both want baths."

"Yes, sir."

"I'm going to bed," he told Albin. "I suggest you do the same. I'll be leaving for the Bull and Mouth at four o'clock, if you wish to accompany me."

CHAPTER SEVENTEEN

THE SECOND POSTILION, Joseph Timms, reminded Marcus of a cockerel—cocky, confident, a strut in his step. He was flirting with a chambermaid at the back of the Bull and Mouth, but abandoned this activity when he saw them. "Sam told me you come round asking questions." His manner was expectant.

Marcus extracted a half-crown from his pocket. "Your passengers to and from Tewkes Hollow. I'd like to know everything you can tell me about them."

Joseph was happy to comply, but he had little to tell: he'd never seen the two men before and doubted he'd recognize either of them again. "They was ordinary, sir."

"How old were they?"

Joseph shrugged. "Older than 'im—" he jerked his thumb at Albin, "—but younger 'n you."

"Tall? Short?"

"About as tall as you, but heavier, like."

"And Smith was the name they gave?"

"Yes, sir."

"Did they call each other any other names that you heard?"

"No, sir."

"When they reached London, what happened?"

"Nothin', sir. They paid up and left." He reached for the half-crown.

Marcus kept hold of the coin. "Did you hear them say anything? Anything at all?"

Joseph gave another shrug. "One of 'em wanted to stop for a glass of daffy. To celebrate their success, 'e said. But the other 'un said no. Someone was waitin' for 'em and 'e'd be cross if they weren't there as fast as could be."

"Someone?" Excitement flared in his chest. "Was the name Monkwood?"

The postilion shook his head. "No, sir."

"Langford?"

Another shake of the postilion's head.

"Brashdon? Hyde? Keynes?"

"No, sir, none of them." Joseph's brow wrinkled in an effort of concentration. "It weren't a real name . . . I misremember exactly, but it were something like 'is 'ighness, or 'is lordship or . . . or . . . 'is nibs. That were it! They called 'im 'is nibs." He held out his hand again.

"His nibs?" Marcus frowned. "And other than that they said nothing that you heard?"

Joseph gave a cocky grin. "One of 'em said he needed a piss, when we got to Clapham."

"Did they leave here on foot?" Albin asked. "Or by hackney?"

The postilion shrugged. "How'd I know?"

"Might someone have noticed?"

"Doubt it. It were right busy 'ere this mornin'."

Marcus gave him the coin. "Thank you."

"What kind of accents did they have?" Albin asked, as the postilion turned to go. "Were they Londoners?"

"They was from Lunnon. Whitechapel, I'd say." He put the coin in his pocket and headed for the stables, whistling.

"We could ask the hackney drivers," Albin suggested. "See if one of them remembers—"

"Do you know how many hackneys there are in London?" Marcus kicked a stone savagely across the yard. "Hundreds!" His promising lead had evaporated. He wanted to tip back his head and howl his frustration at the darkening sky like a child.

"If only I'd run faster," Albin said, his face miserable. "If I'd seen them more clearly—"

"The innkeeper in Tewkes Hollow couldn't describe them, and he saw more of them than anyone. They must be singularly unremarkable men." Marcus strode back to the street and climbed into his town carriage.

Albin followed silently.

Church bells were ringing when they reached Grosvenor Square, calling worshippers to evening service. Marcus didn't want to go to church; he wanted to go to Jackson's Saloon and hit something.

But it was Sunday, and Jackson wouldn't be at his saloon.

All the smashed windows had been replaced. The blank, unbroken panes of glass didn't improve his mood. Marcus scowled, and climbed the steps to his front door. Albin, normally at his heels, lagged behind. His gait had a slight limp.

"Stiff?"

"A little," Albin admitted.

"Have a hot bath. That's an order!"

"Yes, sir," Albin said meekly.

Marcus strode past his study, strode past the library, and took the stairs two at a time down to the cellar where his punching bag hung. He stripped out of his tailcoat and waistcoat and tossed them aside, pulled off his neckcloth, rolled up his shirtsleeves.

THEY DINED TOGETHER, the two of them at the long polished mahogany table in the dining room. The earl no longer vibrated with suppressed rage. He ate silently, a deep frown on his brow.

"At least we know it wasn't Sir Barnaby, sir," Charlotte ventured, after the second course had been placed on the table and the footmen had retreated from the room.

Cosgrove lifted his eyes from his plate. "I wish I knew the significance of today's date."

"Perhaps there is none."

"Perhaps." Cosgrove returned to frowning contemplation of his food.

Charlotte chewed slowly. *I could go back to the Bull and Mouth tonight. If the men didn't leave by hackney, I might find a scent to follow.*

A scent to follow.

She looked up. "Sir . . . are the windows always broken at the same time each night?"

Cosgrove pushed his plate away and leaned back in his chair. "Between one and four." He picked up his wine glass. "Are you suggesting we mount watch? Try to catch him in the act? It's been done, lad. Myself and several of the servants kept watch, back in September. We saw him, but he was faster than Hermes. Gone—" he snapped his fingers, "—like that. And if you think you're a fast runner, so is one of the grooms. He couldn't get close to him."

"What did he look like?"

Cosgrove shrugged. "Too dark to tell."

Charlotte laid down her cutlery. "What if I didn't try to catch him, sir? What if I just followed him? To see where he went?"

"I think you'll lose sight of him." Cosgrove shrugged, sipped his wine. "You may try if you wish. Rudkin can go with you. He's the fast runner."

Charlotte hesitated. How to turn this request down? She lined the knife and fork up on her plate, precisely parallel. "He's less likely to notice one person following than two, sir."

"And you're more likely to get into trouble if you're alone." Cosgrove shook his head. "No, you'll take Rudkin."

Charlotte bit her lip against further arguments.

"You may start tomorrow night, if you wish. Tonight, I think you're too tired."

Charlotte ducked her head. When the earl looked at her like that, with kindness in his eyes—

She turned the knife and fork over on her plate, lined them up again. "You think it's a waste of time, sir?"

"I do. But if you prove me wrong, lad, I'll be delighted."

CHARLOTTE LOCKED HER bedroom door, stripped out of Albin's clothes, sat on the edge of the bed, and closed her eyes. "I wish to be a sparrow." The familiar insect-itch of magic prickled over her skin and through her bones.

She opened her eyes. The bed had become a precipice, terrifyingly high, terrifyingly sheer.

Charlotte flinched back. The hands she put out instinctively to catch her balance were wings.

Panic surged inside her. Charlotte squeezed her eyes shut, battling the urge to change back into herself. She took a deep breath. Exhaled it. Took another breath. Waited for her heart to beat a little less loudly, a little less fast. Inhaled again. Cautiously opened her eyes.

The room was a vast cavern filled with looming furniture. Bed hangings towered above her like cliffs. The ceiling was as high as the sky.

Charlotte's heartbeat became louder again. It was deeply wrong to be this small. Deeply wrong to have wings instead of arms.

No. Not wrong. This is right for a sparrow.

Charlotte sat for several minutes, finding her balance in this new, strange body—the tail projecting behind her, the beak jutting from her face, the wings. The sense of wrongness slowly faded. The sound of her heartbeat quietened.

I'm a bird.

She flapped her wings tentatively, a tiny movement, not enough to lift herself off the bed, but enough to give her a momentary sense of weightlessness. It felt . . . odd.

Charlotte folded her wings and peered over the edge of the bed. It was a long way to the floor. Jumping off felt like an extremely dangerous thing to do.

Birds do it all the time.

She blew out a breath and resolutely spread her wings. *One. Two. Three.*

Charlotte jumped.

Her heart seemed to stop in fear—and then her wings caught the air. She glided across the bedchamber, as light as a windblown leaf.

I'm flying!

The dresser reared at her, colossal, with hard, sharp edges.

Charlotte veered away in a wild swoop, losing height. The floor lunged up at her.

She cheeped in terror, clawed at the air with her wings, found herself plunging upwards.

It took two lurching circuits of the bedchamber before she found her balance in the air. Dip of wing, flap of wing, became natural and effortless.

The wild racing of her heart steadied. *See, it's easy when you know how.*

CHARLOTTE PRACTICED FOR an hour. Taking off and landing from the bed, the floor, the dresser, the pelmet above the window. Hopping up and down from the windowsill. Using her claws to cling to the curtains. Flying between the bedposts. Gliding. Swooping up and down. Flying in circles. In figure eights.

When she felt confident, she landed on the bed, shook her feathers, and changed back into Christopher Albin.

She dressed in Albin's night clothes, took up the bedside candle and a blanket, and let herself out of the bedchamber. The house was dark and silent; Lord Cosgrove and the servants were abed.

Charlotte tiptoed down to the drawing room. She pulled aside the corner of one curtain and peered out, seeing moonlight and shadows and the fenced garden in the middle of Grosvenor Square. Nothing moved.

She settled herself on a sofa, wrapped the blanket snugly around her, and blew out the candle.

CHARLOTTE JERKED AWAKE to the sound of splintering glass. Cold air gusted into the drawing room. The sound came a second time. A third.

She threw aside the blanket and ran to the nearest window. Glass crunched beneath her slippers. She drew the edge of a curtain slightly back. A dark figure stood in the square. She saw an arm raised to throw, heard glass break in the next room along.

She hurried back to the sofa, stripped off the dressing gown and nightshirt, and stuffed them behind the cushions. Two more muffled crashes sounded. She kicked off her slippers and pushed them under the sofa, shoved the blanket under, too.

Charlotte changed into a sparrow. She flew up to the windowsill and hopped carefully through the broken pane of glass.

The person was still in the square, still hurling stones. She heard the sharp *crack* of glass shattering—and from inside the house, the sound of running feet.

The door to Lord Cosgrove's house slammed open. Lamp-light spilled out onto the steps. A shout echoed in the square.

CHAPTER EIGHTEEN

THE DARK FIGURE took off into the mews behind Grosvenor Square. Charlotte followed. Her sparrow's eyes were confused by the gloom, the shadows. Where was he?

There. Ducking down a narrow alley.

Charlotte followed, trying to keep him in sight. *I should have been an owl.* Where had he gone? He'd disappeared—

There.

They emerged into a wider street. The runner vanished into the shadows on the other side. His footfalls dimmed; he'd plunged into another alleyway.

Charlotte landed. *I want to be Bess!*

The night changed around her, became easier to see, less confusing. The runner was gone from sight, but she heard his boots slapping on the ground, caught his scent: sweat, ale, fried onions.

Charlotte loped after him.

After several minutes, the runner's pace slowed from sprint to steady trot. The route he chose was circuitous—along alleyways, across sleeping squares, through mews—but he never hesitated, never lost his way.

They traversed London, heading east, past sleeping houses, past rows of shuttered shops, past dark churches and noisy taverns. She saw the occasional carriage, the occasional pedestrian, and once a night watchman doing his rounds. The streets became dirtier, the air foul with smells she couldn't identify. More people were abroad. Drunken revelers staggered home. Women she took to be whores waited in doorways, smelling of gin and sweat. Once she passed a man and woman copulating in an alley.

Finally the runner slowed to a walk. He glanced back over his shoulder, climbed the steps to a tavern, and pushed the door open.

Light fell on him for a second before the door closed.

Charlotte stood, panting, trying to fix his appearance in her memory. Thin face, lank hair falling over a narrow forehead. He was young; the faintest down had shown on his cheeks, glinting in the lamplight.

She looked around, taking note of her surroundings—gutters overflowing with waste, stinking puddles of stagnant water. Something moved, rustling: rats.

Abruptly, the tavern door opened. Charlotte flinched from the roar of noise, the stink of fetid air.

A man came out and urinated, clutching the wall with one hand to steady himself, and staggered back into the tavern.

Charlotte hesitated. Should she wait to see if the runner emerged?

The door slammed open again and disgorged half a dozen men, unshaven and unwashed, reeling with drink. She backed away as one vomited noisily into the gutter. The others seemed inclined to brawl, shoving each other, throwing punches. Metal glinted in the moonlight: a knife blade.

Charlotte fled back down the street. Behind her, someone bellowed, an animal sound, full of rage.

BREAKFAST WAS IN the back parlor, a housemaid apologetically informed her, because the windows in the breakfast parlor were broken again. Charlotte thanked the girl and went downstairs.

Lord Cosgrove was already there. His plate held a sirloin and several poached eggs. He glanced up from the newspaper he was reading. "Good morning."

"Good morning, sir." Charlotte crossed to the serving dishes lined up on the sideboard. The mingled smells made her mouth water. She spurned the kippers, piled her plate high with sausages, bacon, sirloin, and eggs, and sat opposite the earl. Christopher Albin had a significantly larger appetite than Charlotte Appleby.

They ate in silence, the earl reading his newspaper, Charlotte turning the events of the past night over in her head. When she'd finished eating, she laid down her knife and fork. "Sir?"

Cosgrove looked up.

"Last night . . ." She straightened the knife and fork on her plate, lining them up with one another. "Last night more windows were broken."

"I had noticed," the earl said, dryly.

"Well, sir, I . . . uh, I followed him."

Cosgrove observed her over the top of the newspaper for several long seconds, then folded the paper and laid it aside. "I thought I told you not to do so alone."

Charlotte flushed. "You did, sir, but . . . but I woke up when I heard the glass break and I saw him in the square and I couldn't *not* follow!"

Cosgrove stroked the bridge of his nose, as if deciding what his response would be. The ticking of the clock on the mantelpiece was loud.

Charlotte held her breath.

Cosgrove lowered his hand. He picked up his teacup and leaned back in his chair. "Where did he go?"

She released the breath she was holding. "I don't precisely

know, sir. I didn't recognize the streets. But it was east of here."

"How far?"

"We ran for close to an hour."

"An *hour*?"

"Almost, sir."

Cosgrove glanced at her plate. "No wonder you had such a healthy appetite." He sipped from his cup. "Very well, tell me."

Charlotte obediently related her tale, finishing with a description of the window-breaker.

"And he didn't see you?"

"No, sir. I kept well back." It wasn't a lie, but it felt like one. Charlotte straightened her unused cutlery on the tablecloth.

"He went into a tavern? "

"Yes, sir. But I couldn't see the name. It was too dark."

Cosgrove put down his teacup. "Did you go in?"

"No, sir. It . . . it looked a very rough place." Again, it wasn't a lie, but it had the shape of one in her mouth. She reached out and moved her butter knife a quarter of an inch to the right, so that it was precisely parallel to its companions on the tablecloth.

"At least you showed *some* sense."

She glanced up in time to see Cosgrove close his eyes for a moment. He looked as if he was in pain.

Charlotte decided that it was best not to reply to this comment. She bit her lip and moved the fish knife she hadn't used, lining it up with the butter knife.

"Almost an hour's running east of here, you say?"

She glanced up again and nodded.

"Could you smell tanneries?"

"Oh, is that what it was?"

Cosgrove rubbed his brow, as if her tale had made his head hurt. "Lad, I think you were in Whitechapel."

The name meant nothing to her.

"Of all the places in London!" The fierceness of his voice

made her flinch in the chair. "You should be lying in a gutter with your throat slit!"

Charlotte bit her lip again and looked down at her table setting. Everything was neatly lined up. She reached out and aligned the silver salt and pepper shakers.

"Will you stop doing that!"

Charlotte jerked her hand back. She risked a glance at him.

The earl's gaze pinned her to her chair, fierce. "I absolutely forbid you to go back there! Do you understand me?"

"Yes, sir."

The earl released a long breath. His anger seemed to die, like a candle being snuffed. "Could you find it on a map?"

Charlotte nodded. "But . . . but you won't go there yourself, will you, sir?" Memory of the men spilling from the tavern was vivid in her mind. Cosgrove might spar regularly with Gentleman Jack, but what good were fists against knives?

Cosgrove's eyebrows quirked up. "Would you refuse to show me the way if I said yes?"

"You said yourself that it's dangerous."

His expression became amused, as if her concern was a joke. "I'll take a couple of footmen with me."

"But, sir . . ." She stared at him, remembering the glint of the knife blade in moonlight. "But . . . but your appearance is striking. Unlike the Smiths, you *are* memorable. If you ask questions, how long do you think it will take for news of it to reach the lad who broke your windows—and the person who hired him?"

Cosgrove's smile faded.

"We have an advantage, sir. A very slight one. If you go to the tavern, we lose it."

Cosgrove's eyebrows drew together. He pinched his lower lip between forefinger and thumb, tugged, thought.

Charlotte held herself motionless, almost not breathing.

"You've made your point, lad." Cosgrove pushed to his feet. "But I still want to know where that tavern is. Wait here."

He returned carrying a map. "Show me." He swept aside her neatly arranged cutlery.

"Where are we?"

The earl planted his finger on the map. "Here."

Charlotte traced her route, acutely aware of the earl leaning over her, acutely aware of the warmth of his body, the smells of soap and freshly washed linen. The map told her the names of the streets she'd run along last night: High Holborn, Cornhill, Leadenhall Street, Rosemary Lane. "Sir . . . you promise you won't go there, if I tell you?"

"Lad," Cosgrove's voice was startlingly close to her ear. "You do remember that I'm paying you, don't you?"

Charlotte bit her lip and kept silent, her gaze fixed on the map.

After a moment, Cosgrove laughed. She felt his breath ruffle her hair. "Very well, you have my word. I won't go there."

"The tavern was on this street, sir." Charlotte pointed. "Cripple Lane."

The earl grunted. He pushed away from the table and walked to the window, stared down at the mews, his brow creased in a frown.

"It doesn't help much, sir, does it?"

He turned to face her, leaning against the windowsill. "It may be possible to hire someone to patronize the tavern. Someone familiar with Whitechapel. Someone who won't stand out."

"How does one locate such a person, sir?"

"A good question, lad. I wonder if Gentleman Jack would know a likely fellow?" His frown deepened, he seemed to gaze through her, and then his gray eyes focused. His expression grew pained. "Albin, if you're going to sleep under my roof, then I must insist—I really *must* insist—that you learn to tie a respectable neckcloth."

Charlotte touched the knot of muslin at her throat. "What's wrong with it, sir?"

"An organ-grinder's monkey could tie a neater neckcloth." Cosgrove pushed away from the windowsill. "Upstairs with you. It's time you had a lesson."

CHAPTER NINETEEN

THE EARL'S BEDCHAMBER was a spacious room decorated in brown and gold. His valet was there, folding Cosgrove's night-clothes. "Leggatt, half a dozen neckcloths, please."

"Of course, sir." Leggatt withdrew to the dressing room.

Cosgrove untied his neckcloth and tossed it on the bed. "Take that thing off." He gestured at Charlotte's neckcloth.

The earl's bed was a commanding piece of furniture, as wide as it was long, with four posts of turned mahogany. The counterpane and hangings were a rich, earthy brown. Gold threads sparkled like gleams of sunshine.

Charlotte jerked her attention away from the bed. She fastened her gaze on the earl's dressing table, with its silver-backed brushes, and unwound the neckcloth from her throat.

The valet emerged with six starched neckcloths hung over his arm.

"On the back of the chair, Leggatt."

The valet did as he was bid, laying each neckcloth out tenderly.

"Come here, lad." Cosgrove stood in front of a tall cheval mirror.

Charlotte obeyed.

The earl took the crumpled strip of muslin from her hand and tossed it on the floor. He surveyed her for a moment, eyes narrow. "Something simple . . ." He took two neckcloths from the back of the chair and handed one to her. "A Barrel Knot. Watch carefully. Around the collar thus, so that the right end is longer than the left . . ."

Charlotte copied him.

"Make a loop, then pass the cloth over a second time . . . No, no—" Cosgrove released his own neckcloth. "Like this." His hands guided hers, his fingers warm and strong and confident. "See?"

Charlotte felt a blush rise in her cheeks. "Yes."

"Try again."

She did, acutely aware of him watching. The blush refused to fade; she felt it heating her face.

"Good. Now pull the left end through. Yes, like that. And tighten it. No, lad, watch what you're doing in the mirror. The knot should be horizontal."

Charlotte stepped closer to the mirror, wrestling the knot into place across her Adam's apple. "Like that, sir?" she asked, turning to him.

Cosgrove reached out and tugged the knot, straightening it, tightening it. His knuckles brushed the underside of her chin. The blush flamed hotter in Charlotte's cheeks. Her pego stirred.

Alarm lurched through her. Was it going to stiffen? Now, of all times? *I wish to have a soft pego,* she said frantically in her head.

Magic itched at her groin. Her pego stopped stirring.

Cosgrove stepped back, examined her, shook his head. "No."

"Maybe I should just purchase a stock—"

"Stocks are for country parsons." Cosgrove held out another neckcloth to her. "Watch me, then try again."

She labored over the Barrel Knot for half an hour, her face hot, her fingers clumsy. They weren't alone—the valet was quietly setting the room to rights—but it felt alarmingly intimate to be standing at the mirror alongside Cosgrove, with the bed just behind them. She was acutely aware of the earl's proximity, his clean scent, the timbre of his voice. Her chin and fingers tingled where he'd touched her. Her pego kept wanting to stiffen. *I wish to have a soft pego,* she chanted silently.

Charlotte threaded the left end of the neckcloth through the loop and pulled it tight. She peered at her reflection. Was the knot straight enough? Tight enough?

She turned to Cosgrove. "There, sir."

Cosgrove surveyed her.

Charlotte wanted to reach out and touch his face, to stroke her fingertips from cheekbone to jaw, to feel the grain of his skin. The urge was sudden and shocking and intense. Her pego gave a strong twitch.

She clenched her hands at her sides. *I wish to have a soft pego.*

"Leggatt? What do you think?"

The valet stopped straightening items on the dressing table. He crossed to the mirror and stood with his head tilted to one side, his lips pursed. "Adequate," he said finally.

Cosgrove grinned. "Rare praise, lad."

"It's all right?" She reached up to touch the neckcloth.

Cosgrove caught her hand. "Leave it alone."

Heat surged in her face again. *I wish to have a soft pego.* "Yes, sir."

Cosgrove released her hand. He took the last neckcloth from the back of the chair, placed it around his throat, and tied it swiftly. "A Mail Coach," he said, when he was finished. The knot was obscured by a fall of starched muslin. "I'll teach you it next." He glanced in the mirror, made a minuscule adjustment, straightened his cuffs, and headed for the door. "Come along, lad."

Charlotte followed him from the bedchamber. In the coolness

of the corridor she pressed her hands to her face, as if she could push the blood from her cheeks by force.

She had to conquer her partiality for Cosgrove. *Had* to. The blushes were bad enough, but now it was affecting her pego, too.

Cosgrove strode along the corridor. Charlotte soberly trailed him. She'd learned something about the male body this morning. A man's pego stiffened when its owner felt physical desire. That's why Phillip Langford's pego had been sticking up at the brothel. It had been responding to the whores.

And my pego is responding to Lord Cosgrove.

Today, the earl had mistaken her blushes for embarrassment, but tomorrow she might not be so lucky. If he noticed that she blushed when he stood close, if he noticed her pego moved when he touched her, if he realized she was attracted to him—

He'll dismiss me.

Scratch the itch and it usually goes away, Cosgrove had said. But this was one itch she couldn't scratch. Not with Lord Cosgrove. She had to master her response to him, wrestle it under control, expunge it.

"Sir . . . you said your last secretary had rooms nearby."

"In Chandlers Street. Three minutes' walk from here." Cosgrove started down the stairs.

"May I have the address please?"

"Anxious to leave?"

"I'm your employee, sir, not your guest."

Cosgrove glanced back, his eyes creased in amusement. "So you are, lad. So you are. Twelve Chandlers Street, I think it was."

"Thank you, sir." The sooner she was gone from his house, the less chance she had of betraying herself.

THE EARL INSISTED on accompanying her—*You'll find me use-ful, lad*—and in the event, he was correct. The landlady, Mrs. Stitchbury, was flattered to receive a visit of inspection from an earl. She allowed herself to be persuaded to rent her best set of rooms—larger, sunnier, and quieter than poor Mr. Lionel's rooms—at the same price.

The earl smiled charmingly as he thanked her.

Color mottled Mrs. Stitchbury's face.

I must look like that, always blushing. "I can move in today, sir."

"Tomorrow's soon enough, lad. I'm sure Mrs. Stitchbury would like the opportunity to air it."

"Oh, yes, your lordship. Of course! I'll have the maids turn the mattress for the young gentleman and air the bedding and—"

"Thank you, Mrs. Stitchbury." The earl made an elegant bow.

Mrs. Stitchbury's face reddened again. She curtsied low, as if in the presence of royalty.

Charlotte saw the earl's lips twitch, but his face was perfectly straight when Mrs. Stitchbury rose again.

"What did I tell you?" Cosgrove said, as they strolled back to Grosvenor Square. He glanced sideways at her. "Useful."

"You were making up to her, sir!"

"Me?" Cosgrove placed a hand over his heart. "Lad, you wound me."

Any answer she could make dried on her tongue. *How am I to conquer my partiality when he looks at me like that, with laughter in his eyes?*

"Lionel said she was a pompous, silly woman. Just the sort to be flattered by a visit from an earl."

They turned into Grosvenor Square. The laughter extinguished in Cosgrove's eyes. His face hardened. He seemed to age ten years in the space of one second.

Charlotte followed the direction of his gaze. The house

looked pained, the shattered windows wounds in its façade. "He broke fewer windows last night."

Cosgrove grunted.

They crossed the square. Charlotte hid a yawn behind her hand as they climbed the steps to the front door.

"Tired?" Cosgrove said. "I'm not surprised. Have the rest of the day off."

"Me? But sir, you pay me to work, not to sleep!" Charlotte hurried into the house after him. "And besides, you had forbidden me to follow him!"

"Now he remembers," the earl said, to no one in particular.

Charlotte bit her lip. Another yawn crept up on her. She tried to swallow it.

The earl noticed. "Off to bed with you." The note of finality in his voice was unmistakable. "Now!"

CHAPTER TWENTY

CHARLOTTE CLIMBED THE stairs to the Blue Bedchamber, but she didn't go to bed. She stripped out of her clothes, opened her window several inches, and changed into a bird. Not a sparrow this time, but a swift-winged pigeon.

Cosgrove had forbidden her to return to Whitechapel, but he hadn't asked her to pledge her word. *And besides, I'm going as an animal, not Christopher Albin.*

She followed the route she'd run last night—London's roof-tops flashing beneath her wings—and landed in an alley off Cripple Lane and changed into a dog. The air was even fouler than she remembered.

Cautiously, she left the alley. Her nose told her that three men had spilled blood here last night. A dark puddle lay in a hollow, swarming with flies. To her dog's eyes the blood wasn't red, but dull brown.

Charlotte crept to the tavern doorstep and sniffed. The smell of fresh blood obscured fainter scents but . . . yes, there was the scent she'd followed last night. The window-breaker.

She followed his trail down Cripple Lane, around the corner, and into a busier thoroughfare. An open gutter ran down the middle of the street. Women sat on doorsteps, nursing babies, drinking from bottles of gin. Unshaven men stood in groups, watching the passersby.

Charlotte trotted fast. A prickling down her spine told her that her hackles were raised. A man spat at her as she passed and aimed a kick.

She was practically running now, following the window-breaker's trail, her ears pricked for danger. *I can change into a lion if I have to.* No, something even bigger. A bear. With claws six inches long.

Three streets later, the trail she was following turned into a doorway. The door was unpainted and firmly shut.

Charlotte sniffed the doorstep. The window-breaker's scent was strong, as if he'd entered this door hundreds of times. His home, she guessed—and then her attention was arrested by another familiar scent.

Her heart kicked in her chest and sped up. One of the men from Tewkes Hollow had been here recently.

The man's scent led up the street and around the corner, headed west for two blocks, then swung north. Charlotte followed, excitement spurring her faster. How pleased Cosgrove would be if—

Charlotte came to a cringing halt.

A dog stood in her path, barrel-chested, with hackles bristling down its spine.

Charlotte wagged her tail tentatively.

The dog growled. Lips peeled back from sharp teeth.

Charlotte took a step backwards, her body low, cowering. A second step. A third. *There's no need to fight. See, I'm leaving—*

The dog advanced, stiff-legged.

Charlotte tucked her tail between her legs and fled back the way she'd come. She raced down the street, hurtled around the corner, and bolted into the nearest alley.

The alley ended in a brick wall.

She spun to face her pursuer. Her heart was trying to batter its way out of her ribcage. *A bear!* a voice shrieked in her head.

Change into a bear!

The change happened so fast it felt as if her bones were bursting from her skin. One instant she was a dog, cowering; the next she was a bear.

She heard a high-pitched yelp from her attacker's throat, heard claws scrabble on dirty cobblestones, and then—silence.

Charlotte blinked and looked around. The alley was much smaller than it had been a moment earlier. *No, I'm much bigger.*

She changed back into a dog. A strange, rank odor filled the alley. *That's what I smelled like as a bear.* She slunk to the mouth of the alley and peered out. Her attacker was nowhere in sight.

Charlotte trotted cautiously north again, following the man's scent. At the end of the street, the trail turned west. The scent was stronger now; he'd passed along here many times. And alongside it was another scent she recognized: the second man from Tewkes Hollow.

The streets grew busier. Carriage wheels scythed past on the roadway. Pedestrians trampled the scent trail. Street vendors sold produce from baskets, from stalls, from carts, crying out their wares, swearing at her as she passed, shying stones at her.

The trail divided, splitting into several strands—one heading north, one west, one turning into the doorway of a tavern.

Charlotte sniffed the tavern's doorstep. The scents of both men were strong. She sat down, panting. The trails continued past the tavern, invisible threads that might lead her to where the men lived, but she shrank from following them. These streets might be safe for a man to walk on, but not a dog.

Keep going or come back later?

It felt like an admission of defeat to stop now. The men's lodgings could be less than half a block away.

Or three miles. And she still had half of London to fly back across.

Charlotte squinted up at the tavern's sign. The Pig and Whistle.

The door opened. A woman wearing a dirty apron emerged and emptied a bucket into the gutter. "Get out of here, y' mongrel!"

Charlotte backed away. Later. She'd come back later as a man and ask questions.

BACK AT GROSVENOR Square, she climbed into bed, yawning so hard her jaw cracked, and fell immediately asleep. It was late afternoon when she woke. Half past four! Lord Cosgrove must think her the greatest slugabed in the Empire!

But when she went downstairs, dressed in Albin's clothes and with a Barrel Knot tied around her throat, the earl wasn't home.

She went into his study, to see if he'd left any work out for her, but her desk was bare.

He did give me the rest of the day off . . .

"A pot of tea, Mr. Albin?" a footman inquired behind her.

"Uh . . . yes, please. In the music room."

She was deep in a new sonata, the tea cold in its pot, when someone entered the room. She glanced up. Cosgrove's butler stood alongside the pianoforte. Something in his face halted her fingers on the keys. "Is something wrong, Fellowes?"

"Mr. Langford is here." She heard a note of perturbation in Fellowes' voice, the same perturbation she saw on his face. "He said he would wait for the earl in his study. I suggested the library, but he was most insistent that it be his lordship's study."

Charlotte pushed back the music stool. "I have work I can do in the study."

The frown cleared from the butler's forehead. "Thank you, Mr. Albin."

Charlotte trod quietly down the corridor and opened the door to Cosgrove's study. Phillip Langford was at the earl's desk, opening drawers.

"Can I help you, sir?"

Langford jerked upright. "No." He slammed a drawer shut. "Go away."

"I regret that I'm unable to do that." Charlotte crossed to the shelves of leather-bound ledgers, extracted one, and placed it on the earl's desk with a loud thump. "Lord Cosgrove has requested that I check these accounts." She drew out the chair, forcing Langford to step back.

"Do it later."

"Lord Cosgrove was most insistent that I do it today." She opened the ledger.

"Then use the other desk!" The smell of alcohol wafted from Langford. "That's what it's for, isn't it? Your petty little counting of pennies."

"Lord Cosgrove said that I might use his desk."

"I was here first!"

He sounded so much like a petulant child that Charlotte couldn't prevent her upper lip curling.

Langford saw it. "Don't sneer at me! You're nothing but a servant."

Charlotte ignored the insult. She turned her attention to the open ledger, running a finger down a column as if checking the figures.

"Damn your impudence!" Out of the corner of her eye she saw Langford's hands clench. "Which drawer does he keep his money in? I need five hundred guineas."

Charlotte turned a page in the ledger. "I suggest you wait until Lord Cosgrove returns." Her voice was bored, polite.

Langford reached down and opened a drawer.

Charlotte closed it with a snap. "I said, *wait*."

"How dare you! I'm the earl's heir. He'd give me that money

in an instant!"

Charlotte kept her hand on the drawer. *I doubt it.*

"I order you to open that drawer!"

Charlotte gazed at him blankly, as if she were deaf.

Langford knocked her hand aside and wrenched the drawer open, jerking it out of the desk. It tumbled to the floor, its contents spilling over the carpet.

Charlotte pushed to her feet, her hands clenched as Cosgrove had taught her.

"Boys, boys . . . no fighting." The voice was the earl's. He stood in the doorway, still wearing his hat and gloves.

Charlotte flushed and lowered her hands.

Langford swung around, swaying slightly. "I want some money."

"Do you?" The earl removed his hat and advanced into the room. "How much?" His tone was mild, but there was nothing soft in his face; it was all angles and planes. He was angry, holding his temper in check.

"Five hundred guineas. Chicken feed!"

Chicken feed? It was more than she'd earn in two years. Charlotte kept her face impassive with difficulty.

The earl placed his hat on the desk. "Do you recall what I said the last time you made such a request, Phillip?"

Langford's face reddened.

"I thought you might." Cosgrove removed one glove, and then the other. "My answer remains the same."

"Damn you! What does five hundred guineas mean to you? You're as rich as Croesus!"

"Be that as it may, I will not finance your drinking and whoring." Cosgrove's voice was almost bored.

Langford's face swelled in fury. He crossed to the nearest bookcase and swung his fist at the glazed doors. "Cuckold!"

Cosgrove made no reaction to the sound of breaking glass, no reaction to the insult thrown at him. He stood calm and aloof.

Langford strode to the door. "I hope you die!" he said savagely from the doorway.

There was a long moment of silence after he'd gone. Cosgrove met her eyes. He smiled, a humorless stretching of his lips. "I really must get myself a wife and start producing children." His voice was light, but Charlotte could almost taste his anger on her tongue. "The alternative is too horrible to contemplate, is it not?"

Charlotte didn't answer. It seemed to her that it was nothing to joke about.

Cosgrove seemed to shake himself, to slough off his anger. His face became less angular, his eyes less hard. He strolled around the desk and looked at the drawer on the floor. "And what's your role in this, lad? Were you defending my property?"

"He was going through your desk, sir!" Charlotte knelt and began to gather the scattered contents.

"Then I must thank you for your intervention." The earl picked up the drawer and fitted it back into its slot. "But I keep my money under lock and key; Lavinia taught me that. Which reminds me, I must give you a key."

"Me, sir?"

"You may need to make payments from time to time. Fellowes and Mrs. Maby hold money, but some expenses are outside their purview." Cosgrove picked up the open ledger on his desk. "What's this? I thought I gave you the rest of the day off."

"It was a prop, sir." Charlotte refilled the drawer: sealing wax, wafers, two bottles of ink, a handful of unused quills. "It didn't seem wise to leave Mr. Langford in here alone."

"No, not wise." The earl returned the ledger to its place on the shelf, then produced a small key from his pocket, held it out to her. "Here, you may have this."

Charlotte took the key. It was warm from the heat of his body. "Won't you need it, sir?"

"I have another one upstairs." Cosgrove walked to a tall, solid mahogany cabinet, opened the door, tapped one of the drawers. "It fits this."

"Are you certain—?"

"I don't believe you'll steal from me, will you, lad?"

His eyes met hers. Charlotte's heart beat faster. She shook her head vehemently. "No, sir."

Cosgrove picked up his hat and gloves. His gaze fell on the glazed bookcase. "It seems we need the glazier again." He strode into the corridor. "Fellowes!"

Charlotte remained where she was, clutching the key, holding Cosgrove's body heat in her hand. Her physical longing for him was so intense it was almost pain. She squeezed her eyes shut. *I must conquer this, before it conquers me.*

CHAPTER TWENTY-ONE

October 22nd, 1805
London

CHARLOTTE LAID DOWN the quill and flexed her fingers. The muscles in her chest and shoulders and arms ached from the flying she'd done yesterday. She glanced across at Lord Cosgrove. A week ago he'd interviewed her, had offered her this job, and she'd looked at the bruises on his face, the scabbed and healing cuts, and almost refused.

The marks of violence were gone from Cosgrove's face. And she knew she'd made the right choice. *There is nowhere else I'd rather be.*

She watched him for a moment—the brisk strokes of the quill as he wrote his next speech, the frown of concentration between the strong, black eyebrows. Her fingers curled into her palms. She craved to touch him, a visceral yearning that clenched in her chest, in her throat.

Scratch the itch, the earl had advised. But how?

Charlotte tore her gaze away and looked at the ebony and gold mantel clock, following the second hand with her eyes as it worked its way around the dial. "Sir? It's three o'clock."

The earl wrote a few words, read them back under his breath, crossed them out.

"Sir?" Charlotte said, more loudly. "It's three o'clock. You'll be late for Gentleman Jack."

"What?" Cosgrove glanced up, blinked, and then his gray eyes focused on her. "Three o'clock? So it is. Thank you, lad."

Charlotte fiddled with her quill while the earl gathered his notes together. "Sir . . . I've finished the Dorset accounts. May I take my belongings around to Chandlers Street?"

"Hmm? Yes, of course. You can start on the Somerset ledger when you get back."

Twenty minutes later, with her valise and portmanteau installed at Mrs. Stitchbury's, Charlotte hailed a hackney. "The Pig and Whistle," she said, with a sense of recklessness. "In Aldgate High Street."

NERVOUSNESS GREW INSIDE her while the hackney traversed London. Charlotte rehearsed what to say, muttering the words under her breath, as the earl had muttered his speech. The carriage was rattling down Aldgate High Street when it occurred to her that the Smiths might recognize her as Cosgrove's new secretary. Who was to say they hadn't been watching the earl's house, that they hadn't seen her in his company? Panic spurted in her chest—the hackney was slowing to a halt—before she remembered her magic. *I wish to have dark brown hair, straight, not curling, and a broad face.*

Insect legs crawled over her scalp for a second, over her cheeks and jaw.

The hackney lurched to a halt. Charlotte opened the door and jumped down. Across the street was the Pig and Whistle.

She took a deep breath. *I can do this.*

"Please wait here." Charlotte pulled her hat brim low, in case the jarvey noticed her change in appearance, but the man's attention was on the coins she was fishing from her pocket. "I'll be no more than ten minutes."

IT WAS DARK inside the Pig and Whistle, and the air was stale.

Charlotte inhaled shallowly. Her eyes slowly adjusted to the gloom. She was in a taproom with a low, beamed ceiling and a floor of bare timber. A dozen or so men sat at tables, drinking. She scanned their faces. None of them looked like the men from Tewkes Hollow.

One of the drinkers saw her. He nudged his companion, who turned and stared at her.

Charlotte resisted the urge to touch her cheeks and jaw and check that she had an ordinary man's face. It was her clothes they were staring at—the polished top boots and neatly tied neckcloth. *I'm too well-dressed.*

She inhaled another shallow breath and crossed to the tap.

"What d' y' want?" It was the same woman who'd shouted at her yesterday, wearing the same dirty apron. Her gown was faded and stained and straining at the seams.

Charlotte removed her hat and bowed. "Good afternoon, madam."

The woman tittered. "Madam!" she said. "Did y' hear that, boys? Them's manners for you."

One of the patrons replied. Charlotte didn't catch the words, but she understood the tone: derogatory.

Behind her, a guffaw went up.

A dull flush rose in the woman's plump cheeks. "Don't you pay no attention to 'em, sir. Ill-mannered louts as they are. What can I do you for?"

Charlotte took a shilling from her pocket. She slid it across the counter, but kept her finger on it. "I'm hoping, madam, that you may be able to help me in a matter."

The woman's eyes fastened on the coin. "And what matter might that be, sir?"

"I'm looking for two men who I believe are regular patrons of yours. Tall, heavyset men, a few years older than me."

The woman sniffed. "Ain't much of a description. Could be anyone."

"They may be going by the name of Smith."

The woman's eyes narrowed. "Smith?"

Charlotte felt her pulse quicken. "Do you know them, ma'am?"

"Mebbe, mebbe not." The woman took a filthy rag from her apron pocket and swiped it across the counter. "What's your int'rest in 'em?"

"My employer would like to hire them. They have been particularly recommended to him."

"Hire 'em?"

Charlotte nodded, holding her breath.

The woman pursed her lips. "It might be Abel and Jeremiah Smith. They does drink 'ere often enough."

Charlotte glanced over her shoulder at the men sitting, drinking. "Are they here now, madam?"

Her stomach tied itself in a knot while she waited for the reply.

"No."

The knot in her belly unraveled. "What do they look like, madam?"

"They's big men." The woman shrugged. "Ain't much to tell about 'em other 'n that."

"What is their trade?"

"Abel and Jeremiah?" She snorted a laugh. "They does whatever needs doin'. They ain't fussy."

"Do you know, madam, whether they ever undertake commissions out of town?"

"They was away from Lunnon the night before last, workin'."

And I know where: Tewkes Hollow. Charlotte tried not to let her excitement show. "Then, may I leave a message with you, madam?" She lifted her finger from the shilling.

The woman snatched it up.

"If you have a quill and paper—"

The woman snorted. "Abel and Jeremiah can't read. You tell me your message, an' I'll make sure they gets it."

Charlotte lowered her voice and leaned closer. "Can you please inform them that someone is desirous of offering them employment? There is a . . . a task that my master would like carried out that he believes to be well within their ability." She hoped her manner implied that the task was illegal. "They'll be generously paid for their efforts."

"I'll tell 'em." The woman wiped the counter again with her rag, then stuffed it back in her apron.

"If they are interested, they may reach me at . . ." Charlotte hesitated. She didn't want to give the Smiths her true address. "If they'd like to entrust their answer to you, I shall return to-morrow."

"As you like, sir."

"What's your name, madam?"

"Sally Westrup. *Mrs.* Sally Westrup." She emphasized the Mrs. as if it gave her respectability.

Charlotte bowed. "Thank you, Mrs. Westrup."

The woman's cheeks flushed a gratified pink. "Thank *you, sir.*"

CHARLOTTE SAT ON the squab seat of the hackney, almost bouncing like a child in her excitement. *I did it!* She had the men's names: Abel and Jeremiah Smith.

Alongside the excitement was a sense of pride, of achievement. She was growing into her role as a man, assertive and bold. Charlotte Appleby would never have dared venture into the Pig and Whistle by herself, but Christopher Albin had dared. Dared, and come away with valuable information.

A bubble of glee expanded in her chest as she imagined Cosgrove's reaction to her news—and then deflated. What exactly *was* she to tell him? She didn't want to lie to the earl, but she could hardly tell the truth.

She chewed on her lip as the hackney turned into High Holborn Street.

I'll tell him that I disobeyed him. That I went back to Whitechapel as Albin. That I asked questions that led me to Aldgate.

He'd be furious with her. Livid. But she wasn't afraid of Cosgrove's anger. He wouldn't slap her like Aunt Westcote. Wouldn't scream at her or send her to bed without dinner.

CHARLOTTE PAID OFF the hackney in Duke Street. She strode across Grosvenor Square and climbed the steps to Cosgrove's house two at a time, whistling under her breath.

"Good afternoon." She greeted the butler with a smile and took off her hat. "Is his lordship back yet?"

Fellowes looked down his nose at her. "And who might you be, sir?"

Charlotte stared at him blankly. "What?" And then she caught sight of herself in the pier mirror. Straight brown hair. Broad face.

I'm not Christopher Albin!

"I beg your pardon," she stammered. "Wrong house!" She wrenched the door open and fled outside, cramming her hat on her head.

Charlotte ran from the square, not halting until she was out of sight around a corner. Her heart hammered in her chest. How could she have forgotten she'd changed her appearance in Aldgate?

She wished her hair and face back to Albin's. Horror was cold on her skin, cold in her belly. It congealed in her lungs, making it difficult to inhale, difficult to exhale.

Fool, to be so careless!

Above the rooftops, dusk was falling, the color leaching from the sky. An icy wind blustered down the street. Charlotte hunched her shoulders and hugged her arms. She shrank from returning to Grosvenor Square. What if Fellowes noticed she wore the same clothes as the stranger who'd fled so precipitously? But she should be at her desk in Cosgrove's study, making a start on the Somerset accounts.

She shifted her weight from foot to foot, shivering. Cosgrove was likely still at Gentleman Jack's. Wouldn't a loyal secretary with exciting news to disclose follow him there?

Charlotte hailed a hackney cab. "Gentleman Jackson's, please."

SHE HAD HOPED for a long drive, for time to compose herself, but the hackney halted less than three minutes later.

Charlotte scrambled out. "Where—?"

The jarvey pointed across the street.

"Thank you."

Charlotte paid the man, and crossed the street. She tugged at her neckcloth, swallowed the nervous lump in her throat, and knocked.

After a moment, a bored servant opened the door. "We're closed for the winter."

"I'm Lord Cosgrove's secretary."

The servant shrugged and opened the door wider.

"He's here?"

"Sparring with the Gentleman."

Charlotte stepped inside. "Uh, where . . . ?"

She had a feeling the servant barely suppressed a yawn. He led her inside and gave a jerk of his thumb. "In there."

The door he'd indicated stood open. Charlotte heard the creak of floorboards, the scuff of feet, the puff of panted breaths.

She hesitated, then trod towards the door. She took a deep breath—*I'm excited, bursting with news*—and stepped into the room and halted, staring.

The two men sparring were stripped to the waist.

Charlotte's throat seemed to close, her lungs to drain of breath.

The man Cosgrove was fighting had to be Gentleman Jack, England's Champion, but she had no eyes for him. She was transfixed by sight of the earl.

He looked nothing like Phillip Langford—doughy, soft, plump. He was Heracles, magnificent of body. She saw the strong shapes of his bones, saw the lines of tendon and sinew, saw the lean slabs of muscle.

The men circled one another, moving lightly on their feet, punching with padded gloves. Cosgrove's hair was damp. A sheen of perspiration gleamed on his skin.

Neither man noticed her; their focus was wholly on each other.

A line of dark hair arrowed down Cosgrove's abdomen and disappeared into his breeches. The sight of it made her flush with embarrassment. It seemed such an intimate thing, so private—that line of hair disappearing from view.

On the heels of embarrassment came a wave of longing, intense and painful. She wanted Cosgrove so much that it *hurt*.

Sex, which had seemed so grotesque at Mrs. Henshaw's, wouldn't be repugnant with Cosgrove. It could only be exciting to explore that body. What would the texture of his skin be like beneath her fingers? Would that hair on his abdomen be soft or crisp and wiry?

Longing clenched in her chest, as if someone had taken hold of her heart and squeezed it.

She saw his muscles flex, saw the wings of his shoulder blades move beneath his skin, saw the corrugations of his ribs and the long line of vertebrae marching down his back.

I want to touch him.

No. It was more than mere want. It was craving, intense and uncontrollable.

Charlotte discovered that her pego was pressed against her breeches, hot and hard and aching, poking up the fabric. *I wish to have a soft pego,* she said urgently in her head. Her pego subsided.

Charlotte exhaled a shallow, horrified breath. What if Cosgrove had turned around and seen that?

It was all very well for the earl to tell her that if she scratched the itch, it would go away; but she had no way of doing that. Not as Christopher Albin. Not with Lord Cosgrove.

The idea crystallized between one heartbeat and the next. *I can do it as me. As Charlotte.*

She didn't see the blow that ended the contest. The earl stepped back with a laugh, clearly conceding defeat.

A servant she hadn't noticed came forward, unfastened Cosgrove's padded gloves and handed him a towel, then turned to remove the Champion's gloves. Cosgrove wiped his face. He turned and saw her. "Albin? What are you doing here?"

Charlotte had to swallow twice before she found her voice. "I have some news, sir."

"News?" He strode across to her. "What about?"

"The men from Tewkes Hollow."

Cosgrove's gaze sharpened. "What about them?"

Charlotte glanced behind him, to Gentleman Jack and the servant. "Should I tell you here, sir?"

"Perhaps not." Sweat trickled down his temple. He wiped it away. This close, she could see the pulse beating in the hollow of his throat. The impulse to reach out and touch it was so strong, so powerful, that her hands lifted a few inches.

Charlotte gripped the lapels of her coat tightly. *I wish to have a soft pego.*

Cosgrove turned towards the Champion. "Jackson," he said. "This is the lad I was telling you about." His hand closed on Charlotte's shoulder, urging her forward.

Charlotte walked into the center of the room.

Gentleman Jack looked her up and down. "Should strip well." He was a plain man in his mid-thirties, thicker in the torso than the earl.

Charlotte was acutely aware of Cosgrove's hand on her shoulder. The fresh, masculine scent of his sweat had a visceral effect, making the longing squeeze more tightly in her chest, making her throat close.

She wanted to turn her head and press her face to Cosgrove's chest. Wanted to inhale his scent deeply. Taste his skin with her tongue.

Heat gathered fiercely in her groin. *I wish to have a soft pego.*

"He needs to learn to defend himself."

The Gentleman nodded. "I'll give him some lessons. Starting next week?"

"Much obliged to you, Jackson." The earl released her shoulder.

Charlotte swallowed, found her breath, bowed to Gentleman Jack. "Thank you, sir."

"I shan't be long," Cosgrove told her. He strode across to a door. It opened into a chamber outfitted as a dressing room.

Charlotte walked the perimeter of the salon while she waited, but her attention wasn't on the pictures hanging on the walls, the scales and weights, the wooden staves.

Scratch the itch, Cosgrove had advised her.

Dare I?

She halted in front of a picture of a pugilist and stared at it unseeingly.

Charlotte Appleby no longer existed. She had no reputation to uphold, no virtue to guard. If she were ruined, no one would know or care.

Dare I?

Cosgrove hadn't shut the door to the dressing room. She slid her gaze sideways, watched him roughly towel his hair and face and torso dry.

The intense, visceral craving gripped her again, squeezing her throat, making breathing difficult.

Or perhaps the better question to ask was: *Dare I not?* Her lust for Cosgrove strengthened with each day that passed. If she was to continue as his secretary she had to conquer it. *Had* to.

Cosgrove pulled on his shirt and buttoned his waistcoat. He took a minute in front of the mirror to tie his neckcloth, then raked his fingers through his hair, tidying it.

Charlotte stared at him in helpless, aching longing. *I shall go mad if I don't touch him.*

And with that thought, the decision was made.

Cosgrove shrugged into his tailcoat. "Let's go, lad," he said, emerging into the main salon.

CHAPTER TWENTY-TWO

DARKNESS HAD FALLEN. The wind gusting along Old Bond Street had a damp, icy edge to it, as if sleet would soon follow. Marcus lengthened his stride, impatient to get back to Grosvenor Square. *What news? What news?* The question rang in his head with each step.

He strode faster. Berkeley Square. Mount Street. Charles Street. Albin was almost trotting to keep up. Mews opened like the mouths of caverns on either side of the street. Ahead, the lights of Grosvenor Square beckoned. *What news? What—*

A dark shape lunged at him, grabbed him, slammed him to the ground. The impact forced all the breath from his lungs.

"Sir!" Albin cried.

Instinct took over. Marcus snarled and kicked and fought to free himself from his attacker's grip, fought to breathe.

He was aware of movement in the darkness—a second assailant. Something whistled in the air and struck the cobblestones alongside him with a loud *thwack.*

He heard Albin yelling, heard the whistling sound again. Something smashed into the cobblestones a second time. Chips of stone flew up, stinging his face.

The ability to breathe returned. Marcus's lungs filled. His attacker's smell—sour sweat, ale—brought a rush of memory: St. James's Park.

A shout bellowed from his throat. Marcus broke free and surged to his feet, grabbing his assailant. *By God, you're not going to get away this time.* They swayed, wrestling, grunting.

Yells and running feet echoed in the mews. Bobbing lantern light splashed over them.

His attacker wrenched free and shoved him. Marcus lost his balance—a fraction of a second only, but it was enough. He fell to one knee. By the time he pushed upright, the man was gone.

Lantern light fell on two grappling figures—Albin and the second assailant. Marcus grabbed the man's arm, swinging him towards the light. An object rolled beneath his feet and he lost his balance for a second time, falling backwards, sprawling on the cobblestones.

A groom and a coachman in livery ran up, lanterns swinging in their hands.

Marcus sat up. "God *damn* it."

Albin crouched at his side. "Are you hurt, sir?" The lad's face was pale, his voice high with anxiety.

"Only my pride, Albin. Only my pride." He climbed to his feet.

"You're bleeding, sir."

"Am I?" Marcus put his hand to his brow, where something warm trickled. He turned to the coachman and groom. "Thank you. We're much obliged to you."

"Footpads!" the coachman said. "Here, and at such an hour!"

Marcus bent and picked up his hat. Something had flattened it.

Albin bent, too. "They had a cudgel." He held out a stout length of wood.

Marcus dug in his pocket and gave the coachman and groom each a golden guinea. "Thank you for your intervention."

"What's this city coming to?" he heard the coachman mutter as both men departed, leaving them in darkness.

"They could have killed you, sir," Albin said, worry trembling in his voice.

"Nonsense." Marcus pulled out his handkerchief and blotted the blood trickling on his brow.

"It's not nonsense, sir! They could have killed you!"

"I'm not so easily killed," Marcus said, but in his study five minutes later, with his flattened hat and the cudgel lying on his desk, he wasn't quite so certain. If that blow had caught his head . . .

"They weren't footpads, were they, sir?"

"I think they were two of the men from St. James's Park."

"Waiting for you."

"I walk that route back from Jackson's two or three times a week. Same time, same place." Marcus picked up the cudgel, noting the gouges where it had struck the cobblestones. "Did you wrest this from him?"

"Yes, sir."

"Thank you."

Albin didn't appear to hear the words. He leaned forward, his hands planted on the desk. "Sir, do you think it's coincidence you were attacked the day after Mr. Langford wished you dead?"

Marcus hefted the cudgel, feeling its weight, considering Albin's question.

"And do you think he needed money yesterday to pay whoever had burned down the conservatory?"

Marcus frowned, placing the events in order in his mind: the arson, Phillip's need for money, his refusal to give it to him, the attack. "It's possible."

But did Phillip hate him enough to engineer his death?

Of course not.

Marcus gave himself a mental shake. "No one's trying to kill me. Intimidation, that's all it is." He laid the cudgel down alongside his hat. "Now what's your news?"

"You need to have that cut dressed, sir."

Marcus sat on the corner of his desk, amused. "May I remind you, lad, that it's I who give the orders, not you?"

"But you're hurt, sir."

"A scratch. Nothing more." He pushed away from his desk, crossed to the decanters, and poured them both a brandy. "Now sit." He pointed to an armchair. "Tell me."

Albin obediently sat. He clutched the brandy glass and took a deep breath. "This afternoon, after I'd taken my belongings to Chandlers Street . . ." He gulped a mouthful of brandy. "I was approached by a lady who said she had some information for you. The names of the men who burned down the conservatory."

Marcus lowered his glass. "What?"

"She said she'd give you their names, sir. If you would meet with her face to face."

"Who is she?" Marcus demanded. "What's her name?"

Albin shook her head. "She wouldn't tell me, sir."

"What does she look like?"

Albin hesitated, then shook his head again. "She was veiled, sir."

"Young, old—"

"Young."

"What payment does she want? Did she say?"

Albin gulped another mouthful of brandy. He choked, coughed, cleared his throat. "She didn't say, sir."

"Where am I to speak with her? Here?"

Albin shook his head. "She said . . . if you're willing to meet her . . . she'll inform me of the time and location."

"She won't come here?"

"No, sir."

Marcus picked up his brandy again. "If I'm willing? How will she know that?"

"I'm to leave a message for her this evening, sir. At my lodgings."

"She'll go to Chandlers Street, but she won't come here?"

"That's correct, sir."

Marcus sipped his brandy, considering Albin's news from all angles. "It's a trap," he said finally.

Albin shook his head. "I don't believe so, sir. She wishes to help you. Her sincerity was most evident."

Marcus frowned at him. "You believe her?"

"Yes, sir."

Marcus turned his brandy glass in his hand. Then he shrugged. "Very well. Tell her I'll meet with her tonight."

"Tonight? But . . . but . . . but you're hurt, sir! Wouldn't tomorrow be—"

"Restrain your nursemaiding tendencies, lad. I'm fine." Marcus drained the brandy and stood. "And now you must excuse me." He needed to wash away the sweat and blood.

MARCUS CAME DOWNSTAIRS an hour later to find his study empty. He poured himself another glass of brandy and sat at his desk, turning the cudgel over in his hand. For the past six months he'd been trying to discover who was behind the vandalism—and in three days Albin had discovered three clues. The men in Tewkes Hollow. The trail leading to Cripple Lane. The mysterious veiled lady.

Marcus laid the cudgel on his desk. He sipped the brandy. Anticipation hissed in his blood. The answers were almost within reach. Soon they'd be close enough to touch. He'd know who. He'd know why.

Footsteps echoed in the corridor. Albin entered the study and closed the door.

Marcus lowered his glass. "Well? Will she meet with me tonight?"

"The Earnoch Hotel at eight o'clock, sir. The room will be in the name of Brown."

The hiss of anticipation became stronger, fizzing in Marcus's blood. "Is that her name? Brown?"

Albin nodded.

A LITTLE AFTER seven o'clock, Charlotte climbed the steps to the Earnoch Hotel, carrying a valise and wearing the face she'd worn in Aldgate. The hotel was in a backstreet off Piccadilly, an unassuming establishment for people of modest means and quiet habits. "I booked a room for Brown."

The landlord barely glanced at her. "Fred," he said, beckoning to a servant. "Show Mr. Brown to room seven."

"I requested that a bath be ready—"

"Water's already heated, sir. Ned'll bring it up for you."

Charlotte followed the servant up the staircase. Her heart thudded uncomfortably against her ribs.

The room was plainly furnished with a bed, a table and two chairs, and a washstand. A hip bath stood behind a screen. Once it was filled with steaming water, she locked the door and stripped out of Albin's clothes. Her hands trembled and her palms were damp with nervousness.

I want to be me. Charlotte.

The room became blurry, the edges of the furniture indistinct. *Me with good vision,* she amended, and everything came into focus.

Charlotte bathed quickly and dressed in the only gown she'd brought to London. Her best gown, the one she'd worn to church, of faded blue wool, with a high neckline and a narrow flounce at the hem. Then, she packed away Christopher Albin's clothes and pushed the valise well under the bed.

She stood in front of the mirror. Her face stared back at her. Brown hair, brown eyes, a scattering of freckles.

She needed to be pretty for Lord Cosgrove.

Charlotte closed her eyes, building an image in her mind of how she wanted to look. Nothing like the earl's dead wife. Raven-black locks. Green eyes. Lush rose-red lips. Ivory skin unblemished by freckles. As full a figure as her gown would allow.

The itch of magic crawled over her skin.

Charlotte opened her eyes. A stranger looked at her from the mirror.

She stared at her reflection, unsettled. The lustrous black hair and emerald-green eyes, the alabaster skin and rosy lips, the ripe breasts pressing against her bodice—it wasn't who she was. It was wrong. False.

But the earl would like it. He'd want to bed her.

She glanced at the clock. Fifteen minutes until Cosgrove arrived.

Charlotte paced the room, twisting her hands together, listening to the clock tick. Her lungs felt as if they were shrinking. With each minute that passed, it became harder to inhale, to exhale.

She *wanted* this—so why was she so afraid?

Because it was a terrifying intimacy. To be naked with a man. To have sex with him.

Footsteps came down the corridor. Was it Cosgrove? Was he early?

Panic squeezed the air from her lungs. *I can't do it.*

The footsteps passed.

Charlotte turned away from the bed and stared at the mirror, wringing her hands. Her outward beauty should give her courage. It was a mask, a barrier. The intimacy she was afraid of would be as false as the face she was wearing.

But somehow, that knowledge didn't make her feel better.

This encounter was a lie, a charade. Lord Cosgrove didn't deserve to be deceived like this.

A sense of wrongness swelled inside her. It pushed up her throat like bile.

Charlotte stared at her beautiful reflection and came to a decision: if she did this, she did it as herself. No false faces. As few lies as possible.

She changed back into herself. Her image in the mirror blurred.

Charlotte adjusted her eyes and looked at herself. Familiar. Ordinary. *He won't want to bed me.*

There was another alternative: she could give Lord Cosgrove the Smiths' names and not ask for anything in exchange. *And let my lust fester and grow until the earl notices—and dismisses me.*

Charlotte turned away from the mirror and stared at the bed, twisting her hands together.

No, she *would* conquer her lust for him. And she would do it as herself.

Charlotte fastened her hair at the back of her head. No sleek curtain of ebony-black hair—just plain brown hair in an ordinary chignon. She looked at herself again in the mirror and closed her eyes in despair. *He won't want me.*

She heard footsteps in the corridor.

Charlotte swung around. There was something wrong with her heartbeat: too high in her chest, too fast, too loud.

Someone knocked on the door.

CHAPTER TWENTY-THREE

MARCUS KNOCKED A second time. Perhaps he had the wrong room? The wrong time? Or perhaps Mrs. Brown had decided not to—

The door opened.

Marcus blinked. The young woman standing in the doorway was not what he'd imagined. She looked like a governess, respectable and dowdy, wearing a gown that had been cut for practicality, not beauty, her hair pulled back from her face. She needed only a cap on her head and a pair of spectacles to be the epitome of spinsterhood.

"Mrs. Brown?" he said, certain that he'd got the wrong room.

The woman stepped back, silently inviting him inside.

Marcus did as she bid. He felt off balance, as if the floor were on an angle. He'd expected a highflyer, an impure who'd seen a way to turn information gleaned between the sheets to good use, not this drab respectability. He turned to face his hostess, perplexed. "Mrs. Brown?" he said again.

"Miss Brown." The woman closed the door and stood with her back to it. Her face was pale. Freckles stood out clearly on her skin. "It's not my true name. Forgive me if I don't give you that, Lord Cosgrove."

Marcus removed his hat while he considered this answer. "Very well."

The woman gestured to the table, the chairs. "Please be seat-ed."

"After you, madam."

Miss Brown hesitated, then crossed to the table, smoothing her gown with nervous hands.

Marcus took his seat opposite her. He was aware of a bed out of the corner of his eye. Under the circumstances, it was oddly embarrassing. He kept his gaze firmly on Miss Brown's face. The soft glow of candlelight, the deep shadows in the corners of the room, the bed, made the moment seem too intimate, a lov-ers' rendezvous, not a meeting.

"My secretary says you have some information for me, mad-am."

"Yes." A candleholder and tinderbox lay on the table. Miss Brown straightened them, aligning them with one another. "I believe I know the names of the two men who razed your con-servatory."

His pulse gave a skip of excitement. "How did you come by this information?"

She met his eyes for a moment. "I cannot tell you," she said simply.

Her honesty was oddly refreshing. No lies, no evasions, just bluntness. Marcus decided to be blunt in his turn. "You'd like something from me in exchange."

"Yes." Color rose in Miss Brown's cheeks. She fixed her at-tention on the tinderbox, moving it so that it no longer lined up with the candleholder, then moved it back into place. "Before I give you their names, there is something I should like you to do for me."

The blush, the awkward embarrassment, the dowdiness of her gown told Marcus what she wanted. He reached into his pocket and pulled out banknotes.

Miss Brown's gaze jerked to him. She recoiled slightly in her chair. "Oh, no! I don't want your money."

Marcus replaced the banknotes in his pocket. He clasped his hands on the table, surveying her. "What then?"

Miss Brown's flush deepened. She bit her lip, as if holding words in. Her hands twisted together, white-knuckled.

"Tell me," he said gently.

Silence stretched between them, and then she inhaled a deep breath. "I'm a virgin," she blurted. "And I would like not to be."

Marcus blinked. *What?* He opened his mouth and then closed it again, at a loss for words. He stared at Miss Brown. She hadn't said what he thought she had. She *couldn't* have said it. And yet his ears told him she had. Her words reverberated in his head.

"I beg your pardon?" he said at last.

"I don't want to be a virgin anymore," Miss Brown said, her eyes fixed on his coat buttons, not on his face.

"And you want me to . . . to . . . ?" He couldn't articulate the words. There was no way in which to politely say, *You want me to bed you?*

Her gaze flicked to his face and then back to the buttons. Her cheeks became even rosier. "Yes."

Marcus stared at her while he processed this answer. His brain kept rejecting it. No respectable woman—and she was clearly respectable—would choose to lose her virginity under such circumstances. He tried to find a reason for her extraordinary request. "Do you wish to become a . . . a . . ." He groped for a polite word and failed to find one. "A prostitute?"

Miss Brown jerked back in another recoil. "No!" Her horror was too genuine to be feigned.

"Then why?" Marcus asked, at a loss to understand.

She met his eyes. Her expression was a mixture of embarrassment and defiance. "Because I wish to know what it's like."

Marcus shook his head, but even as his head moved, he knew

she spoke the truth. Her voice, her face, told him.

She wanted to know what sex was like.

This isn't real. I'm dreaming.

But it was real: the woman seated across from him, the bed in the corner, her request.

Marcus shook his head again. "I cannot. Of course I cannot! Your reputation, your virtue—"

"My reputation and my virtue are of no matter. I shall never marry."

The flat, matter-of-fact tone silenced him. He swallowed and tried again. "And if you fall pregnant?"

Her eyes fell to the objects on the table. She reached out and straightened the tinderbox a fraction. "I have taken the precaution of using a sea sponge."

Her manner struck him as evasive. Did she want a child? Did she intend to blackmail him into supporting her? "Forgive me if I disbelieve you, Miss Brown."

She looked up, meeting his eyes directly. "I can assure you, Lord Cosgrove, that if you agree to my request, I shall not fall pregnant." The sincerity in her voice, the certainty, was unmistakable; she meant what she said.

Marcus stared at her, perplexed.

Silence fell between them. Miss Brown's gaze dropped to the table again. She moved the candleholder an eighth of an inch, then straightened the tinderbox so that it was perfectly in line with it. "If . . . if it is too repugnant for you to consider, then of course you may decline."

Repugnant? Marcus blinked, and then examined her more closely. She wasn't as homely as he'd first thought. If she wore a more flattering gown, if her hair was dressed in a style that suited her, then she'd be . . . not beautiful or pretty, but attractive.

She was aware of his observation. The color in her cheeks

heightened. She looked up, met his eyes. "If it's repugnant—"

Marcus shook his head, silencing her. It wasn't repugnant. The emotion he was most aware of was . . . curiosity.

It was a long time since he'd lain with a woman and enjoyed it. He hadn't bedded Lavinia for many months before her death—he'd barely been able to look at her, let alone touch her. He'd visited a courtesan once since he'd been widowed, but the experience had been unsatisfactory; for all her beauty and skill, he hadn't been able to forget that the woman was having sex with him for money, that her eagerness—the kisses, the caresses, the sighing moans—was pretense, just as Lavinia's had been. He'd not repeated the visit.

If he had sex with Miss Brown, it would be an encounter utterly unlike anything he'd previously experienced. She wasn't a professional, she wasn't a bride he was besotted with, she was a stranger whose name he didn't even know. *I can do this, and then walk away and never see her again.*

His curiosity became sharper. The beginnings of arousal tingled in his blood. "Why me?"

The question seemed to disconcert Miss Brown. She frowned slightly as if searching for the right words. "Because you are a man who is honorable and . . . and kind. I don't believe you would deliberately harm me."

Kind? Where had she got that notion from? "Society generally credits me with hounding my wife to death," Marcus said dryly.

"Society is wrong."

Marcus studied her through narrowed eyes. "Do I know you from somewhere? Do you work on one of my estates?" A housemaid, perhaps. The servants had been well aware of the realities of his marriage and the events leading to Lavinia's death.

"No."

Kind and honorable. Marcus shook his head, not believing her. "That's your reason for choosing me?"

Miss Brown flushed. Her gaze fell. She straightened the tinderbox again. "And because I . . . I find you attractive," she said gruffly.

He couldn't doubt the veracity of that statement. Her blush told him it was true. "You've seen me before?"

She nodded, still not looking at him.

"Where?"

"In London."

It was an unsatisfactory answer. Marcus leaned back in his chair, baffled and intrigued. He examined Miss Brown again, noting the smoothness of her cheeks, the delicate curves of her earlobes, the soft tendrils of brown hair curling at her temple. The tingle of arousal in his blood became stronger. His gaze dropped to her breasts. What would she look like naked? Very different from Lavinia.

"All right," he said abruptly, hearing the words with a sense of shock. "I accept your terms."

Her gaze jerked to his face. "You do?"

He nodded and pulled off his gloves, laying them on the table. A tryst with a stranger. It should wipe away memory of Lavinia.

A flicker of emotion crossed her face; not excitement, but apprehension.

Marcus frowned. "Are you certain you wish to do this, Miss Brown?"

She nodded, her face as pale as it had previously been flushed.

"Forgive me, but . . . you look afraid."

She swallowed. "I have never done this before. It's somewhat alarming."

It was his turn to flush; shame warmed his cheeks. He'd been thinking only of himself, caught up in astonishment and curiosity. He'd forgotten that she'd never lain with a man before. This wasn't about his own pleasure; she was trusting him to deflower her.

Marcus almost balked as the full significance of what he'd agreed to do struck him. "You are aware that it's painful for a woman to, er . . . to relinquish her virginity?"

"Yes."

"Are you expecting a degree of pleasure? Because that may not be possible."

Miss Brown regarded him seriously for a moment, her eyes steady on his face, and then nodded. "I know."

The nod didn't completely reassure him. If he hurt her—

But it was what she wanted. Her choice, not his. Sex, and then she'd give him the names he was after.

Marcus stood, feeling awkward. After a second's hesitation, so did Miss Brown. She was taller than Lavinia had been, not as fragile, as slender. His curiosity surged again. The tingle of arousal returned. What would she look like unclothed?

I can't believe I'm going to do this.

Marcus removed his coat and laid it over the back of his chair. He cast his mind back to his own first sexual experience. How had the highflyer who'd done the honors made that encounter so pleasurable?

He unwound his neckcloth, recalling the way she'd teased him with her body, slowly undressing, giving him tantalizing glimpses of her breasts, her buttocks, the triangle of hair between her legs. Then she'd undressed him, skillfully touching him to heighten his arousal, and finally she'd guided his cock inside her and let him take her, a rough and clumsy coupling, during which she had squealed with pleasure.

And I actually believed she was enjoying it.

Marcus sat and took off his top boots. He regarded Miss

Brown dubiously across the table. He didn't want to titillate her by slowly removing his clothes.

Miss Brown undid the buttons at her cuffs. Her face was pale, her expression resolute.

"You look as if you're preparing to go to the scaffold."

He bit his tongue as soon as the words were out—now was not the time for clumsy jokes, however ill at ease he felt—but Miss Brown didn't appear to be offended. She glanced at him, a glimmer of amusement lighting her eyes. "I assure you, I don't consider it *quite* as terrible an ordeal as that."

Marcus was surprised into a small huff of laughter. Some of his discomfort eased. Perhaps this wouldn't be as awkward as he feared. If she had a sense of humor—

"Let me," he said, as she reached behind herself to undo the fastenings of her gown.

"Oh, no. I'm used to dressing without a maid."

Marcus ignored these words. He walked around the table and began unbuttoning her gown. The fabric was more faded than he'd thought. The gown had seen several years' wear. He tried to place her as he unfastened the buttons. She'd seen him in London. Was she governess to a family in Grosvenor Square?

It felt very intimate to be standing in shirt-sleeves and stock-inged feet, unbuttoning her gown. Strands of her hair brushed across his fingers, soft, tickling. Marcus worked lower, exposing the top of her chemise, then her stays. Warmth flushed beneath his skin and gathered in his groin.

He undid the final buttons and stepped back.

"Thank you."

Marcus cleared his throat. "You're welcome."

He retreated behind the table and took off his waistcoat and shirt. Yes, heat was definitely building in his loins.

Fabric rustled as Miss Brown stepped out of her gown. He glanced at her, then quickly away. His pulse began to beat a little faster. "Do you need help with your stays?"

"No, thank you." Her voice was as polite as his had been. "They fasten at the side."

Marcus nodded. He removed his breeches, his stockings. He kept his gaze on the table and the growing pile of his clothes, yet he was intensely aware of her—each quiet, rustling movement, each item of clothing she removed. She'd taken off her stays and her stockings. All she wore now was her chemise.

When he was naked except for his drawers, he halted and turned to her. Miss Brown hadn't removed her chemise—but she had let down her hair. It fell in soft waves over her shoulders and down her back. In the candlelight her skin was pale and luminous, her eyes dark. She looked mysterious, almost beautiful. The chemise hung loosely on her, concealing her figure. He saw the rise and fall of her breasts with each breath that she took. Beneath the hem, he glimpsed slim ankles and bare feet.

It was surreal to be standing in this shadowy, candlelit room: two strangers, almost naked, with the bed waiting behind them. *I don't even know her real name.*

Miss Brown's hands were clasped together, the fingers interlocked, nervously twisting. "I did bathe before you arrived."

For the first time, he noticed the hip bath half-hidden behind a screen. "Uh . . . thank you."

Lavinia had been apprehensive on their wedding night, but he'd soothed her fears with kisses and endearments. He didn't feel like doing either of those things with Miss Brown.

Marcus walked across and took her hands, stilling their twisting. "Relax."

For a moment she stood unmoving, unbreathing, as if his touch had turned her into a statue, then she uttered a faint, nervous laugh. "That is easier said than done, Lord Cosgrove."

Marcus gave what he hoped was a reassuring smile. He pulled her gently towards the bed. "Sit."

Miss Brown sat obediently on the edge of the bed, still tense, still resolute, still with the air that she was about to undergo an ordeal.

"You don't have to do this," he said. "If you don't want to."

"Yes, I do." Her expression became even more resolute. "I can't tell you why, but it's important. *Very* important."

Marcus stared at her, baffled, and then shrugged. He sat beside her on the bed. "Then, if we're going to do this, let's make it as . . . as enjoyable as possible."

She swallowed nervously. "How?"

"The tenser you are, the more difficult it will be." Experimentally, he stroked two fingers up the inside of her forearm. Her skin was warm and soft and smooth. Marcus's pulse began to beat slightly faster. This was what he enjoyed most about women's bodies: the warmth and the softness, the smoothness.

Miss Brown looked at him, her eyes wide and filled with trepidation.

Marcus smiled and offered her a compliment. "You have lovely hair."

Her expression changed for a fleeting moment, a twitch of her eyebrows, a twitch of her lips. She didn't say anything, but he heard her thoughts as clearly as if she'd spoken them aloud: *You don't need to lie to me.*

"It's true," Marcus said, stung into defending himself, and he raised a hand to stroke her hair and discovered that it *was* true. Her hair was soft, falling in loose waves. He let one long lock slide between his fingers. His imagination took off, telling him what her hair would feel like against his skin—tickling, teasing, pleasurable.

His arousal hitched up a notch. He wanted to tumble her back on the bed and strip off her chemise.

But not while she was so tense.

Marcus stroked the delicate skin inside her wrist, a feather-light caress. No other man had ever touched her. It was an oddly exciting thought. He trailed his fingers lightly up her arm until he reached the small, capped sleeve of the chemise. Did it make her skin tingle? Did it give her pleasure? He thought it did; a faint flush had risen in her cheeks.

He widened his exploration, stroking her throat, the nape of her neck. Minutes passed, while the flush in Miss Brown's cheeks deepened and his erection pressed insistently against his drawers.

It was time. Time to bare her body. Time to bed her.

CHAPTER TWENTY-FOUR

"I'M GOING TO take this off now," Marcus said, fingering the worn linen chemise.

Miss Brown tensed.

Was it fear or self-consciousness that drained the color from her cheeks?

"Would it make you feel better if I, er . . . took off my drawers first?"

The color flooded back into her face. She nodded shyly, a tiny movement of her head.

"Very well." Marcus stood and untied his drawers, stepping out of them to stand in front of her, entirely naked.

Miss Brown's eyes widened. She glanced at his cock, and then up at his face, as if asking for reassurance.

"It may hurt a bit," he admitted. "First times generally do." Uttering the words, hearing them in his ears, made him hesitate. *Should I be doing this?*

Miss Brown nodded and stole another glance at his erection. Was that apprehension or curiosity he saw on her face, or both? She stood, her jaw resolutely set, and undid the ribbons at the neck of her chemise and pulled the garment over her head.

Her figure wasn't lush, but neither was it as delicate as Lavinia's had been. Marcus's gaze rested on her breasts, on the curve of her waist and swell of her hips, on the dark triangle of hair at the junction of her thighs. The muscles in his groin tightened.

He cleared his throat, but could think of nothing to say; arousal had blanked his mind. Her skin was creamy in the candlelight, smooth and enticing. He wanted to touch it and learn its texture. He wanted to feel the weight of her breasts in his hands, wanted to slide his hands around her waist and cup her buttocks and pull her against him.

Remember she's a virgin. Take it slowly. Make this as pleasurable for her as possible.

Marcus cleared his throat again. This time he managed to speak: "Let me take that." He removed the chemise from her grip and draped it over a chair.

He turned to the bed and pulled the counterpane back, exposing the sheets. "Let's sit again." He matched movement to words, sitting, holding out his hand to her.

Miss Brown swallowed and gave him her hand and let him draw her down to sit beside him. She was tense, her breath coming shallowly.

Marcus touched her as he had before, stroking the inside of her wrist, trailing his fingers lightly up her arm. He was burningly aware of her exposed skin, the roundness of her breasts, the pink nipples.

Wrist and arm, throat and nape of neck, the same exploration as earlier, only this time they were naked . . . Then the line of her collarbone. Then lower, skimming across the slope of first one breast, then the other.

He felt Miss Brown tremble, watched color rise in her cheeks. She kept her gaze averted.

"Look at me," he said softly.

She did, her eyes wide and dark in the candlelight.

Marcus held her gaze, and let his hand slide down her hip, along her leg, and then up the inside of her thigh. Such soft skin, smoother than silk.

"I think it's time, don't you?"

She gave a tiny nod.

He patted the middle of the bed and gave what he hoped was a reassuring smile. "After you."

Miss Brown scrambled backwards on the bed and lay down, her movements awkward and self-conscious. Marcus lay down alongside her. He didn't feel self-conscious; it was months since he'd been so aware of his body, so aware of the blood rushing in his veins, the beating of his heart, the thrumming urgency of arousal.

Candlelight played across Miss Brown's skin, creating shadows between her legs, burnishing the smooth curves of her breasts. He'd not thought he'd want to touch her with his mouth, but he found himself kissing her throat, found himself tasting the pulse in the hollow of her collarbone with his tongue. She wore no perfume. Her delicate female scent acted on him like an aphrodisiac, heightening his arousal.

Marcus dipped his head lower and pressed his lips to one breast, so deliciously round, so deliciously warm. He closed his eyes and swallowed a groan of pleasure. It had been too long. Far too long.

He gently nipped one taut, pink nipple and felt Miss Brown tremble, heard her catch her breath. He nipped a second time. Was it his imagination, or was a *frisson* of anticipation building between them?

He slid his hand down her waist and over the curve of one hip. Her skin was impossibly soft, impossibly smooth. He felt her tremble again when he found the curls at the junction of her thighs.

Miss Brown flinched slightly as he slid one finger inside her.

Marcus lifted his mouth from her breast. "Relax," he whispered in her ear. He eased a second finger inside her, trying to gauge her readiness. She was warm, sleek, damp—and tighter than Lavinia had been. Much tighter.

He withdrew his fingers, slightly daunted. "This will likely cause you some pain."

"I know."

Her words should have made him feel better; they didn't. *Should I stop?*

This was what Miss Brown wanted, what she'd asked for. Sex, in exchange for information. But he wanted to give her pleasure, too . . . and he was uneasily aware that he might not be able to.

Marcus settled himself between her legs. Arousal rode him— and tempering the arousal was apprehension. She was so damned tight.

Miss Brown's eyes were wide, watching him. He could almost read her thoughts: *How much will this hurt?* Temptation flickered for a moment—temptation to kiss her soft mouth, to whisper tender reassurances. Marcus hesitated, and then pressed a light kiss to her temple. "I'll try to make it quick."

He took a deep breath, released it slowly, and entered her in one long thrust.

Miss Brown stiffened, every muscle in her body tensing. She uttered a strangled gasp of pain.

Marcus held himself still, his eyes squeezed shut in an effort to maintain control. "I'm sorry." His voice was a hoarse whisper. "I'll stop."

He began to withdraw, to push away from her, but Miss Brown halted him, her fingers digging into his arm. "No."

Marcus opened his eyes and stared down at her. "I'm hurting you." Far more than he'd hurt Lavinia.

"It doesn't matter."

It did. Even though she was a stranger, even though she'd asked for this—it mattered. It mattered a lot.

"Don't stop. Please."

Marcus inhaled a shaky breath.

"Please."

He surrendered to the entreaty, sliding his arms around her, gathering her to him, letting himself sink deeply into her again. He heard the breath catch in her throat, felt her tense, but she didn't try to stop him, didn't try to push him away.

Make this fast.

His body fell into an instinctive rhythm, rocking into her, withdrawing. Marcus bowed his head and squeezed his eyes shut. His breath came in gasps. Arousal spiraled inside him, becoming tighter, more urgent, until it almost felt like pain.

His control snapped in a moment that hovered between agony and ecstasy. A groan came from his throat as his seed spilled inside her. The contractions went on for a long, blissful moment. Marcus exhaled a deep, shuddering breath. The sensation of release, of fulfillment, was one he hadn't felt for a long time. Every inch of his skin tingled. His body felt sated, the sense of relaxation bone-deep.

Gradually his awareness expanded beyond himself. He became aware of Miss Brown again, lying soft and warm beneath him. He felt her heartbeat, heard each low breath that she took. She lay quietly, not pushing him away, letting him rest on her.

The sense of fulfillment vanished abruptly. Shame flooded him. *I gave her pain, not pleasure.*

Marcus rolled off her and sat up. "I'm sorry," he said, not meeting her eyes. Mortification was hot in his face. "I didn't mean to hurt you so much."

"Don't apologize, sir." Miss Brown sat up.

He glanced at her, and found his eyes caught by hers.

"You did precisely what I asked for."

He swallowed, his throat tight. "I hurt you."

She smiled suddenly. "I don't mind."

I do. "Are you bleeding?"

She blinked. "Should I be?"

Marcus got off the bed and found his handkerchief. He handed it to her.

He didn't watch as she wiped between her thighs. He began to dress. He'd not felt self-conscious while he was bedding her; he did now. *I hurt her.* His fingers fumbled as he pulled on his drawers, as he fastened his breeches. It wasn't the sweat of exertion that stuck his shirt to his skin, it was the sweat of shame.

Miss Brown had her chemise on by the time he'd buttoned his waistcoat and pulled on his boots. Marcus crossed to the mirror and tied his neckcloth. The knot was as lopsided and crooked as one of Albin's attempts. He watched Miss Brown's reflection as she laced her stays and pulled on her petticoat. When she reached for her gown he turned away from the mirror. "Let me help you."

Miss Brown gathered her hair and pulled it over her shoulder, out of the way. She was more relaxed than when he'd undressed her; the resoluteness, the tension, were gone. *It's I who feel awkward now.* He fumbled with the buttons. *I had sex with this woman. I took her virginity. I hurt her.*

"Their names are Jeremiah and Abel Smith," Miss Brown said.

"What?" For a moment Marcus had no idea what she was talking about—then understanding came. His fingers stilled at their task. "The men who burned down my conservatory?"

"I believe so, yes."

"How do you know this?"

"I'm sorry, I can't tell you that."

Marcus resumed the buttoning. Jeremiah and Abel Smith. It was useful information. With it, he might be able to find them—

"It's possible the Smiths will agree to meet with you this week."

His head jerked up. "What?"

"I left a message indicating the possibility of employment. If they agree to a meeting, I'll let you know. You do wish to speak with them, do you not?"

Marcus uttered a laugh. "Oh, yes." His teeth closed in a predatory smile. *Most definitely.*

"I hope to receive their answer tomorrow. I'll wait on your secretary in Chandlers Street, if you'll release him from his tasks between two and four o'clock."

"You don't wish to come to Grosvenor Square?"

"No."

Her answer made him certain she was employed in a household in the square. Whose?

Marcus silently fastened the rest of the buttons. Tendrils of soft hair brushed over his fingers when he reached the nape of her neck. Memories swept over him: the warm smoothness of her skin, the delicious curves of her breasts, and—indelibly— the memory of her body tensing in pain. He slowly fastened the last button. "Does it still hurt?"

"A little."

Marcus glanced at the bed, at the rumpled sheets, the crumpled handkerchief. Shame swamped him again. It sat in his belly, filled his lungs, clogged his throat.

He stepped away from Miss Brown, turning to the table, reaching for his gloves. "Mr. Albin will be at his lodgings between two and four tomorrow afternoon," he said, pulling on the gloves. He couldn't look at her; the shame was too intense.

He walked to the door, his hat clenched in his hands.

Miss Brown followed on stockinged feet. "Lord Cosgrove?"

Marcus swallowed, turned back to face her, forced himself to meet her eyes. "Yes?"

She looked younger than when he'd arrived, and far more attractive. Her eyes were dark, her skin creamy in the candlelight.

Her hair hung down her back in soft waves.

He opened his mouth to apologize once more, but Miss Brown stood on tiptoe and lightly kissed his cheek. "Thank you. I'm more grateful than you can imagine."

"Uh . . . you're welcome," Marcus managed to say. He groped for the door handle and escaped into the corridor and fled down the stairs, cramming his hat on his head. But he couldn't outrun shame; it followed at his heels.

Outside, on the street, he halted and touched his cheek where Miss Brown had kissed him. It burned, as if she'd branded him.

MARCUS WALKED BACK to Grosvenor Square, his feet blindly following the familiar route. The encounter with Miss Brown played in his head, awkward, erotic, shameful.

He kept coming back to her tightness, to the way every muscle in her body had clenched with pain when he'd entered her. Miss Brown had definitely been a virgin. No one could fake a response like that.

Marcus's thoughts slid even further back, to his wedding night. He remembered how anxious he'd been not to hurt Lavinia, remembered entering her for the first time, remembered how she'd stiffened and cried out. And then he placed that memory alongside the memory of tonight. The tension in Lavinia's muscles had been superficial, not deep and involuntary.

Marcus halted on the flagway. *Lavinia wasn't a virgin?*

He replayed his wedding night in his head, and came to the same conclusion: his penetration had been no painful invasion. Despite the blood on the handkerchief—her own handkerchief, that she'd displayed to him afterwards—Lavinia hadn't been a virgin.

"Sir?"

Marcus blinked, and focused on his surroundings: tall buildings with shuttered windows, torches burning in brackets, shadowy street, and a crossing-sweeper looking at him expectantly.

He fumbled a coin from his pocket, tossed it to the man, and crossed the street, striding grimly.

He'd learned a lot more than the Smiths' names from Miss Brown tonight.

CHAPTER TWENTY-FIVE

October 23rd, 1805
Grosvenor Square, London

CHARLOTTE WAS TALLYING a column in the Somerset ledger when she heard the earl's footsteps. Her shoulders tensed.

Breathe. Act as if you don't know what happened last night.

But she *did* know. She knew what Lord Cosgrove looked like naked and aroused, knew what it felt like to be bedded by him. Surely he'd see the knowledge on her face? He'd look at her and instantly know.

The earl entered the study.

Charlotte swallowed, made herself inhale, exhale. How would Albin behave? "Good morning, sir. How did your meeting with Miss Brown go?" Her voice sounded stilted, too high.

"What? Oh . . ." Cosgrove sat. He shuffled papers on his desk, not meeting her eyes. His cheeks reddened slightly. "It went well."

Charlotte gazed at him—the strong brow, the strong nose, the strong jaw—waiting for awareness of him to surge through her. The tingle. The heat. The physical yearning.

It didn't come.

Some of the tension she was holding in her shoulders eased. "What information did Miss Brown give you?" Her voice sounded more natural this time.

"The names of the men who set fire to the conservatory. Abel and Jeremiah Smith. Miss Brown believes she can arrange a meeting with them."

"That's excellent, sir!"

Cosgrove rubbed his forehead, as if trying to remove his frown, but it stayed there, a tight furrow between his eyebrows. "You're to go to Chandlers Street this afternoon between two and four and wait for a message from her."

"Yes, sir." Charlotte hesitated a moment, turning the quill over in her fingers. "Was there nothing more?"

Cosgrove's frown deepened, pulling at his mouth. He shuffled the papers on his desk again. "No."

SCRATCH THE ITCH and it usually goes away, the earl had said. And he'd been right. Last night's intimacies had conquered her lust for him. When Cosgrove leaned over her shoulder to explain a set of figures she didn't understand, when his hand accidentally brushed hers, she felt no flare of heat, no acute awareness of him. Her craving to touch him was gone, erased by the intense embarrassment of stripping in front of him, the intense embarrassment of lying down naked with him, erased by the pain of being bedded by him.

Relief bubbled inside her. Charlotte wanted to hum while she tallied the columns, to whistle under her breath as she wrote the totals neatly at the bottoms of the pages. She bit her tongue and stayed quiet, but still the relief bubbled in her chest.

Just before two o'clock, Charlotte closed the Somerset ledger. "I'll go and wait for Miss Brown's message, sir."

Cosgrove glanced up from his speech. His frown deepened. He didn't say anything, just nodded.

Charlotte almost skipped down the steps to Grosvenor Square. *I did it. I conquered it.* She made herself walk sedately.

Once out of sight of the tall windows of Lord Cosgrove's house, she hailed a hackney. "High Holborn Street. Is there an inn you can recommend? Something busy, but respectable."

THE HONEST SAILOR, where the hackney cab deposited her a quarter of an hour later, met her needs perfectly. Charlotte paid off the jarvey and went inside to negotiate the use of a private room tomorrow. Five minutes after that, she was back on the street. She changed her appearance while she adjusted the brim of her hat—broad face, brown hair—then waved down another hackney. "The Pig and Whistle, in Aldgate."

THE PIG AND Whistle's taproom was busier than it had been yesterday. The smell hadn't changed. Charlotte hesitated in the doorway, breathing shallowly, tasting the stale air on her tongue.

Nervousness squeezed her ribcage. Were the Smiths here? Would she have to speak with them?

She forced herself to take a deep breath, forced herself to tread across the stained floor to the tap.

"Good afternoon, Mrs. Westrup."

"Afternoon, sir." Mrs. Westrup mopped ale off the counter with the same filthy rag she'd used yesterday.

"Did you give the Smiths my message?"

"Indeed I did, sir."

"And . . . ?"

"Abel and Jeremiah will be pleased to do business w' you, sir."

"Excellent." Charlotte slid a shilling across the counter. "Are they here now?"

Mrs. Westrup snatched up the coin and shook her head. "If you was to come back tonight, sir, they'd be 'ere."

Her ribcage stopped squeezing so tightly around her lungs. Breathing became easier. "Unfortunately I have an engagement tonight." Charlotte reached into her pocket for another shilling. "Three o'clock tomorrow afternoon. At the Honest Sailor on High Holborn Street. Can you tell them that?"

"Tomorrer at three," Mrs. Westrup said, her eyes on the coin. "The Honest Sailor."

"My employer will be with me. He wishes to personally discuss the . . . er, task he has in mind for them. The room will be hired in his name. Mr. Black. Tell the Smiths they'll be compensated for their time whether they decide to accept the offer of employment or not."

She waited for Mrs. Westrup to nod before releasing the coin.

The shilling vanished into Mrs. Westrup's apron.

"Thank you." Charlotte turned away from the counter. The urge to skip was back again. *I did it! I am as indomitable as Lord Cosgrove.*

Chair legs scraped on the wooden floor. One of the patrons stood, a thickset man with a meaty, stubbled face. "Leavin'? After you just got 'ere?"

Charlotte's heart gave a panicked leap in her chest.

"Leave 'im alone, Sid," Mrs. Westrup called shrilly from the counter.

The man took a step towards Charlotte. "Too good for us, is you?"

I can become a bear if I have to. In the blink of an eye she'd be bigger than this man, stronger. He'd run screaming. Charlotte swallowed. She removed her hat and bowed politely. "Not at all, sir. This is a very fine establishment. It . . . it has a most pleasing ambience."

"Don't you be talking down t' me." The man lowered his head pugnaciously.

Charlotte clutched her hat tightly. Her hands were sweating.

"I assure you, sir, I was not. I . . . I have a prior commitment, otherwise I would happily remain here." If he took one more step, she'd change into a bear.

And Abel and Jeremiah Smith will hear of it; all of Aldgate will. And tomorrow's meeting won't take place.

She had to stay as she was. She had to fight.

Charlotte's mind went blank with panic.

"I knows talkin' down when I 'ears it." The man cleared his throat and spat. "And I don' like it."

Charlotte's mind jerked into motion and started working again. "I apologize if my manner has offended you." She groped in her pocket and slapped a handful of coins on the nearest table. "A drink for you and every man in this room," she said loudly.

There was a second of silence, and then noise surged in the taproom, chair legs scraping on the wooden floor as men scrambled to their feet.

Charlotte bowed to the man confronting her. "Good day, sir." She stepped around him, heading for the door with fast strides. Behind her, a chair tipped over.

At the door, she glanced back. The patrons were jostling for their share of the coins, shoving each other.

Charlotte hurried outside. As the door swung shut, she heard the crash of a table overturning.

She ran across the street to where the hackney waited. "Chandlers Street," she cried. "As fast as you can!"

CHARLOTTE PAID THE jarvey with the last of her coins. She changed back to Albin and tried to recapture her exhilaration. She'd made contact with the Smiths, had arranged a meeting between them and Cosgrove tomorrow. But the exhilaration refused to come. In its place was horror, echoing hollowly in her chest.

She blew out a breath. It hung in the air in front of her face.

Very well. If not exhilaration, then at least she could be brisk, pleased, enthusiastic.

She strode back to Grosvenor Square, strode up the steps, strode along the corridor to Lord Cosgrove's study. He looked up as she entered. "Well?"

"The Smiths will meet with us tomorrow," she said, crossing to her desk and pulling out her chair. "Or rather, with a Mr. Black and his secretary. Three o'clock, at the Honest Sailor on High Holborn Street."

"What?" Cosgrove laid down his quill abruptly. "She told you that?"

"Yes." Charlotte stared at him. Why did he look displeased? "What's wrong, sir?"

Cosgrove looked away. He shuffled the pages of his speech together, his movements almost agitated. "I had hoped to meet with her again."

He had? "Why?" Charlotte asked cautiously.

"I wish to speak with her." He stacked the pages jerkily, squaring the edges.

Charlotte looked down at the ledger on her desk and considered this reply. She didn't want to have sex with Cosgrove again; it had been an interesting experience, but not one she cared to repeat.

But perhaps he was telling the truth? Perhaps all he wanted was to speak with Miss Brown?

She glanced at Cosgrove. He was a gentleman; he'd not force her into anything she didn't want to do. She bit her lip, and then said, "Miss Brown did say that she'd be at the Earnoch Hotel tonight. If you had any questions for her."

Cosgrove looked up sharply. "She did?"

Charlotte hesitated. *He's a gentleman.* "Yes, sir. Seven o'clock."

IT WAS A different room tonight, but identical in its furnishings: bed, table, chairs, washstand.

Charlotte dressed in her own clothes, pinned her hair in a chignon, and sat down to wait. Nervousness took root as the minutes passed. She didn't want to be a woman with Lord Cosgrove. *I should have said no.*

But the earl had wanted to speak with her.

At seven o'clock, a knock sounded on the door.

Charlotte stood, smoothed her skirts, and opened the door. "Lord Cosgrove."

"Miss Brown." He removed his hat, bowed, and stepped into the room.

They sat one on either side of the table. The ease she'd had today with him as Albin was gone. Last night's embarrassment, last night's awkwardness, came flooding back. She rushed into speech: "Did your secretary tell you? The Smiths have agreed to meet with you. Tomorrow at three o'clock, at the Honest Sailor in High Holborn Street. I bespoke a room for you in the name of Black."

"Yes, he told me. Thank you. Er . . . would you like some form of payment?"

Was that what this was about? He felt the need to pay her? "No, thank you."

The earl didn't repeat his offer. He reached out and fidgeted with the brim of his hat, where it lay on the table.

An uncomfortable silence fell between them. Charlotte glanced at the clock on the mantelpiece. When thirty seconds had ticked by, she stood. "Thank you for coming, Lord Cosgrove. I hope your meeting with the Smiths is successful."

The earl didn't stand. "Miss Brown . . . last night wasn't a pleasurable experience for you."

No, not pleasurable. But it had worked. It had obliterated her physical attraction to him. "I don't mind," Charlotte said. *In fact, I'm deeply grateful to you.*

"I do." The earl remained seated. "I find that I mind a great deal."

Charlotte had a vivid flash of memory: Cosgrove's traveling carriage, dusk falling outside, the sound of the earl's voice: *A gentleman never hurts a woman he's bedding, even if she's a whore.*

She understood, suddenly, what was bothering Cosgrove.

"I would be grateful if you would allow me to . . . er, to do it over again."

Charlotte managed not to recoil. Again?

She admired Cosgrove, respected him, liked him—but she didn't want to have sex with him again. She shook her head. "Truly, sir, it's not necessary."

"I hurt you."

"I expected it to be painful."

"That much?"

"Well, no, but . . . it doesn't matter!"

Cosgrove fidgeted with the brim of his hat again. "Forgive me for asking, but do you intend to have intimacies with another man in the future?"

Charlotte shook her head. "No."

"So, last night will be your only, er . . . sexual experience?"

"Yes."

The earl stopped fiddling with the hat. He folded his hands on the table and looked at her directly. "Then please allow me to do it over. Without hurting you."

Charlotte tried to make a joke of it: "It bothers you that much?"

"Yes."

Charlotte bit her lip. Shame rose inside her. She took her seat and interlaced her fingers and looked down at them. *I used him—and he feels guilty.* "I'm sorry."

Silence lengthened between them, while the candles flickered and the fire gnawed at lumps of coal in the grate. "Miss Brown," Cosgrove said finally. "If thought of having sex with me again is abhorrent to you, I won't press you—"

She shook her head. It wasn't that it was abhorrent, it was that last night had been excruciatingly embarrassing, quite the hardest thing she'd ever done. Harder than leaving Westcote Hall. Harder than visiting Mrs. Henshaw's brothel. Harder than venturing into Whitechapel alone. She wasn't sure she could bear such acute embarrassment again.

He has already seen me naked. Will it be so mortifying a second time?

The tinderbox was on an angle. Charlotte straightened it, lining it up with the candleholder. *Well?*

She had used him. Cosgrove didn't owe her redress; she owed *him* redress.

Charlotte took a deep breath, lifted her head, and met his eyes. "Very well."

CHAPTER TWENTY-SIX

THE EARL INSISTED on unbuttoning her gown. "I brought a sheath with me," he said, his fingers working on the second to last button. "It's . . . it looks odd, but it will prevent you becoming pregnant."

A sheath? Dried sheep's intestines? Charlotte managed not to pull a face. "That won't be necessary, sir. The sponge . . ."

"You're still protected?"

"Yes." She bit the tip of her tongue. *Liar.* But it was only partly a falsehood; her magic would prevent her becoming pregnant.

The last button came free. Cosgrove retreated to the other side of the table.

Charlotte stepped out of her gown. She concentrated on folding it so it wouldn't crease. She was aware of the rustle of fabric as Cosgrove removed his clothes. Her embarrassment grew with each second that passed. It was quite as bad as last night—the tightness of her chest, the knot in her stomach, the heat in her cheeks, the icy prickling of her skin. She'd not realized until yesterday that embarrassment could be hot and cold at the same time.

Her fingers fumbled as she unlaced her stays. Her cheeks became hotter. *I don't want to do this.*

"It is embarrassing, is it not, to undress in front of a

stranger?"

Charlotte gave a choked laugh. "Yes." She risked a glance at him.

Cosgrove met her eyes, smiled at her. He had stripped to his shirt and breeches. "It's only natural."

"Yes," Charlotte said again, recognizing that he felt uncomfortable too, that he was trying to put her at ease.

She unlaced the stays and put them aside. Only her chemise remained. She stole another glance at the earl. He was naked except for his drawers.

Charlotte's throat tightened. Did he realize how magnificent he was? The strong shoulders, the muscled arms, the long, powerful thighs. She looked hastily away and started pulling out the pins that anchored her chignon.

Cosgrove came to stand behind her. For such a large man, he moved almost soundlessly.

Charlotte's fingers became clumsy. She closed her eyes and concentrated on the hairpins.

"May I touch you?" he asked.

Charlotte opened her eyes. Her heart beat faster. She swallowed. "Yes."

She expected him to take over the task of removing the hairpins. He didn't. He stepped closer, his arms circling her, his hands coming to lightly rest just below her breasts.

Charlotte froze with her arms upraised. Her throat closed, making breathing impossible. Even her heart seemed to stop beating. Cosgrove's hands burned through the thin linen of the chemise. She felt his thumbs, one on the outer curve of each breast.

Her heart began to beat again, a fast, fluttery rhythm, but her fingers were still frozen. She was acutely aware of his body pressed against her, his hands resting on her ribcage, his heat.

His thumbs moved, a light, stroking caress.

Charlotte closed her eyes tightly. She struggled to breathe, struggled to take out the last three hairpins.

Cosgrove's hands rose to lightly cup her breasts. "Need help with your hair?"

Charlotte swallowed. "No," she whispered, groping for the final hairpin.

He bent his head. She felt warm breath against the nape of her neck. Lips touched her skin and then teeth lightly nipped, sparking heat inside her. Charlotte squeezed her eyes more tightly shut. Her breath was shallow, her heartbeat rapid. She found the last hairpin and pulled it out. The chignon slowly uncurled, but there was no space for it to fall, not with him pressed against her. Cosgrove's hands moved, learning the shape of her breasts. His lips parted against her nape. She felt his tongue, tasting her.

Coherent thought fled. She was trembling, awash with heat.

Cosgrove lifted his head. "Finished?" His voice was low and intimate in her ear.

Charlotte nodded, unable to find the word *Yes*. The hairpins fell unheeded from her fingers.

He stepped back, releasing her.

Charlotte opened her eyes. She felt light-headed, feverish, burning inside.

Cosgrove took her hand and led her to the bed, three short steps, while her hair uncoiled down her back. "We can dispense with this, don't you think?" He touched the sleeve of her chemise.

Charlotte nodded again.

Cosgrove released her hand. He stripped off his drawers. His pego jutted from the black curls of hair at his groin.

Charlotte's throat tightened. She was unable to breathe again. *Cock,* she reminded herself dazedly. *He calls it his cock.*

Phillip Langford, naked, had been grotesque and disgusting. Cosgrove was anything but. The sight of his cock triggered a clenching sensation low in her belly. It wasn't fear, wasn't dread. *I want him.* The craving was deep and visceral.

Charlotte fumbled with her chemise, pulled it over her head, and let it fall to the floor.

Last night, being unclothed had been mortifying; tonight it wasn't embarrassment that made her heart beat so fast.

Cosgrove pulled back the counterpane and took her hand again. He drew her down to lie alongside him on the bed. The sheets were cool and his body hot, his skin scorching hers.

The world contracted, became just the bed, candlelight and shadows, and Cosgrove. He touched her as he had last night, stroking, caressing, laying trails of pleasure across her skin. Charlotte clenched her fingers around the sheet as he teased her nipples with his tongue, as he nipped lightly. She managed to stifle a sound of pleasure, managed not to beg him to do it again.

His hands roamed lower, across her belly, her waist, her hips. The feverish heat built in her body. She gripped the sheet more tightly, not bold enough to return his caresses. Even naked, he was still an earl, his status vastly superior to hers.

Cosgrove trailed his fingertips up her inner thigh, making her shiver. His fingers slid inside her.

Charlotte's body moved of its own accord, her hips lifting as if inviting him inside her, her inner muscles squeezing around his fingers. Cosgrove made a low sound of satisfaction. "No pain?"

"No," she said breathlessly.

Cosgrove withdrew his fingers. He settled himself between her legs. She was acutely aware of the heat of his skin, the solid weight of his body. His fingers were at her entrance again—and then she felt the head of his cock.

She tensed, bracing instinctively for pain.

He slid an inch inside her and halted. His body trembled, as if he held himself in check. "Does it hurt?"

"No."

Cosgrove took a breath as ragged as her own and thrust deeply.

Charlotte gasped, stiffened, clutched the sheet.

"It hurts?" His voice was strained.

"No." Having him inside her wasn't invasive tonight, wasn't painful. Instead, it touched off pleasure in every nerve in her body.

Cosgrove withdrew, and thrust back into her. Charlotte's body responded eagerly, her hips rising to meet him.

Cosgrove slid an arm around her waist, gathering her closer. Rhythm built between them. His heat was her heat, his ragged, panted breaths were her own. The rhythm became more insistent. Rising urgency consumed her. Her body was striving towards something. She didn't know what it was; she just knew she wanted it desperately.

The pleasure, when it came, was more intense than anything Charlotte had ever known. It spilled through her in waves. She cried out, a breathless sound, clutching Cosgrove's arm. He didn't halt; if anything, his movements intensified.

The pleasure went on for endless seconds, and then Cosgrove's body jerked in helpless spasms. She heard him groan as his seed spilled inside her.

They lay panting, entwined. Charlotte tentatively placed her hand on his back. His skin burned. His heartbeat reverberated inside her.

A surge of tenderness rose in her, so intense it closed her throat and brought tears to her eyes.

The earl pulled away. "Better that time?"

Charlotte nodded, not trusting her voice.

"Good." Cosgrove laid a kiss on her brow—not a formal salute, not a loving caress, but something in between—something *kind*—and rose from the bed and crossed to where his clothes

were piled on a chair. Perspiration gleamed on his skin. "Here."
He returned to the bed and handed her a handkerchief.

"Thank you."

Charlotte clutched the handkerchief tightly, watching as he
dressed. Drawers and breeches and stockings, shirt and waistcoat.

Cosgrove pulled on his boots and shrugged into his coat.
"You're not dressing?"

"I . . . I think I'll have a bath."

He nodded and raked a hand through his dark hair, glancing
at the door. He was already thinking of other things.

Charlotte scrambled off the bed and picked up her chemise,
holding it against her body, concealing herself. "I hope tomorrow goes well for you. With the Smiths."

Cosgrove's gaze snapped back to her. "Yes." He looked at
her, then past her, at the bed. "Would you, er . . . like to meet
again tomorrow evening? So I can tell you how it went?"

Would I?

Yes. Desperately.

Should I?

No.

"If you would like to," Charlotte said.

The earl smiled. His gaze on her was intent. Right now, he
was thinking of her; not the Smiths, not whatever other plans he
had for this evening. "Seven o'clock again?"

She nodded.

Lord Cosgrove picked up his hat. He bowed to her. "Good
night, Miss Brown."

"Good night."

The door shut after him.

Charlotte stood motionless by the bed, staring at the blank,
closed door. *I love you, sir.*

CHAPTER TWENTY-SEVEN

October 24ᵗʰ, 1805
Grosvenor Square, London

EIGHT WINDOWS WERE broken overnight and the contents of a nightman's cart deposited on the front steps, but these two events failed to ruffle Marcus's good mood. He worked on his speech, humming beneath his breath. The words were flowing this morning.

The longcase clock in the entrance hall chimed noon. Marcus laid down the quill. He was ravenous, hungrier than he'd been in a long while.

It occurred to him that Albin was rather subdued. "You all right, lad?" he asked, stretching his arms behind his head.

Albin glanced up from the ledger he was working on. "Perfectly, sir."

"Not anxious about this afternoon?" Anticipation tingled in his blood. In three hours he'd meet Abel and Jeremiah Smith—and discover who had hired them.

Albin frowned. "How do you plan to proceed, sir? Shall we take some footmen with us?"

"Footmen? Why?" Marcus lowered his arms. Every muscle in his body was marvelously relaxed. His thoughts slid to Miss Brown. Last night had been unexpectedly pleasurable.

"Because there are two of them, sir."

"And two of us."

"But I can't fight as well as you, sir."

"It won't come to a fight. I'll offer them money."

Albin's eyebrows quirked upward. "But . . . don't you want them arrested, sir?"

"Not today. Today I want the name of their employer."

"But . . . it was probably the Smiths who attacked you the night before last. They could have killed you! They should be arrested."

"We'll gain more information by appealing to their mercenary instincts than by violence or threats of arrest."

"But—"

"If they're the men from St. James's Park, I'll lay information against them." They'd half-killed Lionel. For that, they deserved whatever punishment the magistrate laid down. "But what I want today is the name of whoever hired them."

"Oh." Albin considered this, his brow furrowed in a frown. "But don't you think it would be wise to take some footmen, sir? Just in case? They might have cudgels."

"In daylight? No." Marcus leaned back in his chair, amused. "Afraid, lad?"

Albin flushed. "I don't want you to be hurt, sir."

"I'll take a pistol with me."

"And a footman?"

"No."

"But, sir, what if—"

"Do you always argue with your employers? Or is it just me?"

Albin's cheeks bloomed scarlet. He looked down at the ledger. "I beg your pardon, sir."

Marcus stood. His stomach was telling him it needed food. Lots of it. He crossed to Albin's desk and gripped the lad's shoulder. "I'll take two pistols. One for each of the Smiths. Will that set your mind at rest?"

THEY TOOK POSSESSION of the Honest Sailor's private parlor at two thirty. Marcus assessed the room. A table and four chairs. A winged armchair. A sideboard. He crossed to the window and peered down at High Holborn Street. "Does the door lock?"

"From the outside, sir. There's only a latch on this side."

"Is the key there?"

"No, sir."

It wasn't ideal—he'd feel better if he held the key—but with the door latched, no one except the landlord would be able to enter. Marcus shrugged. *It will do.* "Run downstairs, lad, and fetch up four tankards of ale."

He rearranged the furniture, dragging the armchair to the other side of the fireplace, so its back was to the door, placing two straight-backed chairs opposite. He sat in the armchair when Albin returned. "Can you see my face from the door?"

"No, sir. Just the top of your hat."

"Excellent." Marcus stood and examined the room again. It looked cozy and welcoming—the fire burning in the grate, the tankards of ale on the table. "Once they're inside, latch the door so no one else can enter. Offer them those seats—" he pointed, "and give us all an ale. Then sit at the table. Watch, but don't say anything."

"You have the pistols, sir?"

"Yes." Marcus glanced round the room one last time: chairs, ale . . . everything was in place.

"And you're sure they're loaded?"

"Yes."

Marcus sat in the armchair, crossed his legs, and steepled his hands. Anticipation hummed inside him. *Soon I'll know.* Albin didn't sit; he paced the room, fidgeting with his cuffs, with his neckcloth, with the buttons on his waistcoat, endlessly checking his pocket watch.

"Lad, will you *sit,*" Marcus said, finally.

Albin flushed and muttered an apology. He pulled out a chair at the table and sat. After a moment he began to straighten the tankards, lining them up neatly.

Marcus decided to ignore it. He glanced at his watch. Almost three o'clock. He fingered the banknotes in his pocket. Whose name would they buy him? Phillip? Monkwood? Brashdon and his cronies?

A knock sounded on the door.

The anticipation in his blood changed to exultation.

Albin stopped rearranging the tankards. He glanced at Marcus.

Marcus's smile felt as sharp-toothed as a wolf's. "Invite them in."

CHARLOTTE WIPED HER palms on her breeches, took a deep breath, and opened the door. Two men stood in the corridor, hulking shapes in Benjamin coats, with hats pulled low and mufflers wrapped around their lower faces.

She swallowed. Did those bulky coats conceal cudgels? Knives?

"Misters Abel and Jeremiah Smith?" Nervousness pitched her voice slightly high. "Come in and meet my employer."

The men entered. Charlotte caught a whiff of gin and old sweat. She gestured to the chairs opposite Cosgrove. "Please be seated." She latched the door; no one else could enter. "May I offer you some ale?"

"Thank'ee," one of the men said.

Cosgrove sat with his legs negligently crossed and one hand cupping his chin, his eyes shadowed by the brim of his hat.

The Smiths took their seats, moving with a slow animal wariness, loosening their mufflers, scanning the room, eyeing Cosgrove. Charlotte examined them as she crossed to the table. Were they the men she'd seen boarding the post-chaise in Tewkes Hollow?

It was difficult to be certain. There was nothing striking about either man's appearance. Eyes, nose, brow, jaw—all were unremarkable.

Charlotte picked up two tankards.

"Gentleman." The earl lowered the hand concealing his mouth and chin. "Thank you for coming." His voice was smooth, courteous. "Which of you is Abel?"

"I'm Abel," the man on the left said. His eyes narrowed. He pushed to his feet. "You're Cosgrove!"

Charlotte's heart kicked in her chest. Ale sloshed over the side of one tankard.

"I am." The earl seemed unconcerned that he'd been recognized. He pulled several banknotes from his pocket. "Allow me to thank you for razing my conservatory. It's something I've been wishing to do for a long time." He unfolded one of the banknotes. "In fact, I'm so grateful that I'd like to compensate you both for your efforts."

Abel Smith sank back in his chair. He exchanged a glance with his brother. "You would?"

"Yes." Cosgrove unfolded a second banknote, his movements unhurried. "And I'd like to offer you further compensation. In return for some information you possess."

"What information?" Jeremiah Smith demanded.

"A name." Cosgrove unfolded a third banknote, and a fourth. He held the notes carelessly between his fingers "Who hired you to burn down my conservatory?"

"How much is you willin' to pay?" Abel Smith asked.

Cosgrove smiled. "How much would you like?"

The two brothers exchanged a glance. Charlotte saw Jeremiah lift his eyebrows fractionally, a silent *Why not?* She remembered the tankards she clutched. "Your ale, gentlemen."

The two men seemed to recall her presence. Jeremiah scowled.

Charlotte crossed to the fireplace and handed them each a tankard. As she turned away she heard a low whisper: "—do it now? Or wait until—"

She walked back to the table, turning the half-heard question over in her head. *Do what now?* She picked up Cosgrove's tankard.

Abel Smith took a long swig of ale. He wiped his mouth on his sleeve.

"We'll give you 'is name," Jeremiah said.

"You will?" Cosgrove uncrossed his legs. "Excellent."

The Smiths erupted into movement, shoving up from their chairs. Jeremiah Smith lunged at Cosgrove, Abel Smith swung towards Charlotte, arms outstretched, coat flaring.

Terror squeaked in Charlotte's throat. She threw the tankard.

It hit Abel's shoulder, spraying ale, not slowing him. He caught her in a bear hug and knocked her to the floor, crushing the breath from her lungs.

Charlotte tried to buck him off, tried to kick, tried to draw enough breath to shout.

Abel's knee jabbed her groin.

Her body curled in on itself in helpless agony.

A fist struck her head, then Abel heaved off her. Through pain-slitted eyes she saw him turn towards the fireplace.

Cosgrove and Jeremiah wrestled on the floor, battling for dominance. She saw Cosgrove's face, his teeth bared in a snarl, saw the flash of a knife in Jeremiah's hand.

Terror flooded her. Charlotte struggled to her knees, wheezing.

Abel Smith reached beneath his coat and drew a knife.

They're going to kill him!

Charlotte tried to scream a warning, but there was no breath in her lungs. She lurched to her feet, holding onto the table.

Abel swung back to her. His expression hardened, intention stark on his face.

A bear! A bear! A bear! a voice shrieked in Charlotte's head.

Magic roared through her. She fell to hands and knees. Her skin seemed to split open, her bones to swell and shatter.

Charlotte lifted her head. She shrugged the table aside and charged at Abel Smith, her mouth open in a roar. He screamed, a high-pitched sound, and scrambled backwards, slashing with his knife.

Jeremiah and Cosgrove froze in their battle on the floor. Their heads turned towards her, mouths open, eyes stretching wide with disbelief.

Charlotte smelled blood. Cosgrove's blood. Rage surged through her. She swung at Abel Smith with a paw the size of a skillet. The blow lifted him off his feet. He hit the wall with enough force to shake the room.

Charlotte turned to Jeremiah Smith. The men broke apart as she advanced.

She swiped at Jeremiah.

He ducked, her claws slicing open his cheek, and scrambled backwards on hands and knees.

Charlotte followed, head lowered, herding him into a corner.

Trapped, Jeremiah held his knife out towards her. The blade trembled. Charlotte smelled his fear, as pungent as the blood streaming down his face, heard his panicked, almost sobbing, breaths.

I could kill him. It would be easy.

Charlotte clouted Jeremiah with her paw, knocking the knife spinning. She heard the crack of bones breaking in his arm. He gave a choked scream of pain, cowering from her, trying to cram himself further into the corner.

She turned back to the earl. How badly was he injured?

Cosgrove crouched beside the knocked-over armchair, grim-faced and disheveled, a pistol aimed at her, as if he expected her to attack him. But it wasn't the pistol that riveted her attention, it was the blood staining his neckcloth.

Charlotte changed back into Albin. "Sir! You're injured!"

CHAPTER TWENTY-EIGHT

MARCUS BLINKED AND shook his head. *I'm hallucinating.*

His secretary hurried towards him, stark naked.

Marcus leveled the pistol.

Albin brushed the weapon aside. "You're bleeding, sir!"

"I'm fine." His voice sounded normal, but nothing else was. What the hell had just happened?

"No, you're not." Albin ripped Marcus's neckcloth off. "Let me see how bad it is."

"I'm fine!" His view of the Smiths—one huddled whimpering in the corner, the other slumped half-dazed on the floor—was obscured by Albin's shoulder. Marcus rose to his knees, raising the pistol.

Albin pushed him down to sit and pressed the wadded-up neckcloth to Marcus's throat. "Hold this, sir."

"Damn it, I told you—"

Abel Smith crossed the room at a lumbering run. He wrestled with the latch, jerked the door open, and lurched out into the corridor. His brother followed, stumbling, cradling an arm to his chest, his face a scarlet mask of blood. The door slammed shut.

"God damn it!" Marcus shoved Albin aside. He scrambled over the tipped-up table and wrenched open the door, pistol in hand. The corridor was empty in both directions.

He ran left, plunging down the stairs to emerge in the busy

taproom. There was no sign of the Smiths, no stir as if two injured men had pushed their way through the patrons.

A dog yipped behind him.

He looked back.

A brown dog stood at the top of the stairs. It uttered another yip and trotted out of sight.

Marcus ran back up the stairs.

The dog was at the other end of the corridor. It scratched a door. *This one,* it seemed to say.

Marcus tightened his grip on the dueling pistol. He flung open the door. A flight of steep, uncarpeted stairs led downwards.

He took the stairs three at a time, thrust open the door at the bottom so hard it smacked the wall with a loud crack of sound, and emerged into the inn's backyard. The dog bounded past him, nose to the ground.

Marcus followed at a run—through the yard, along an alley, out into High Holborn Street. He saw pedestrians and street hawkers and carriages, but no Smiths.

The dog led him half a dozen yards along the street. It sniffed, cast around in a circle, then sat and looked up at him and whined.

Marcus halted. He knew the dog was Albin, and he knew what Albin was trying to tell him. The trail ended here. The Smiths had entered a carriage, most likely a hackney.

He hissed between his teeth. *God damn it.*

Marcus became aware of the sight he presented, wild-eyed and unkempt, clutching a pistol. He retreated, back along the alley, through the yard. Now that he wasn't running, he saw scarlet splashes on the ground. Jeremiah Smith's blood.

He climbed the back staircase, let the dog into the private parlor, and latched the door again. The overturned table lay in the middle of the room, one leg snapped off. His armchair was on its back by the fireplace. Banknotes littered the rug.

Alongside the table was a pile of shredded clothes and an up-turned hat.

"Albin."

The dog cringed at his tone and tucked its tail between its legs. It backed two steps away from him. Between the space of one heartbeat and the next, it became Albin.

Marcus blinked, and shook his head, and gripped the pistol more tightly.

Albin swallowed nervously, his Adam's apple bobbing in his throat. He picked up the torn remains of his coat and held it awkwardly in front of himself, hiding his nudity. "Sir."

"What the *devil* is going on?"

"I . . . uh . . ." Albin swallowed again, his expression slightly desperate, as if he hunted for a believable excuse. Marcus could have told him there was none. Nothing—*nothing*—could explain what he'd just witnessed.

The silence lengthened. Albin's expression became more desperate. He shifted his weight. Finally he blurted: "They were going to kill you, sir! I had to do something!"

"A bear?" Anger vibrated in his voice. "How?"

Albin's toes curled under, as if he wanted to dig himself a hole to hide in. "It's difficult to explain, sir. It's . . . it's to do with my mother."

"She could turn into animals too?" Marcus said, with heavy sarcasm.

Albin flushed. "No, sir. She, um . . . she could fly."

The absurdity of the answer made him even more furious. Marcus shoved the pistol into his pocket. Shards of wood crunched beneath his boots as he strode across to the armchair. He snatched up the banknotes.

"Sir," Albin said timidly. "You're bleeding."

Marcus looked down at himself. Blood soaked the front of

his shirt and waistcoat. No wonder he'd drawn so many stares on the street.

"Here." Albin offered his own torn neckcloth, a tentative gesture, as if he expected to be rebuffed. "There's a cut on your throat."

Marcus's anger evaporated, leaving him feeling ashamed of himself. "Thank you." He shoved the banknotes in his pocket and accepted the strip of muslin.

"Sir . . . you're cut here, too." Albin indicated his own chest.

"I am?"

The lad was correct. His shirt, waistcoat, and the left lapel of his coat had been sliced by Jeremiah Smith's knife. Marcus pulled the edges of fabric apart. A shallow cut ran from his collarbone to his ribs, passing over his heart.

"He almost killed you, sir."

"Yes." Marcus turned and surveyed the wreckage of the room. It made no sense. No sense at all. Why had the Smiths chosen to murder him rather than be bribed?

A knock sounded on the door. "Sir? Mr. Black?"

"Who is it?" Marcus asked loudly.

"Mr. Nutley, owner of this tavern."

Marcus glanced at Albin. The lad was as naked as the day he was born. "What do you want?" he called.

"I've had reports of a disturbance, sir. I must request admittance."

Marcus looked at Albin again. "Fuck."

Albin blinked, clearly not understanding the word. "Sir?"

"Half of London thinks I drove Lavinia to suicide. I'll be damned if I'll be known for a back door usher too!"

Albin's expression became bewildered. "A what?"

"He'll take you for my lover." And once arrested, he wouldn't be Mr. Black for long. His identity would be exposed. Lord Cosgrove, sodomite.

London would fall upon it with glee.

Albin's face cleared. "Oh. I'll leave." He hurried to the window and flung it open. One instant, he was standing naked, the next a sparrow hopped up on the windowsill and flew out.

Every hair on Marcus's body stood on end. He took an involuntary step backwards.

Fresh knocking came from the door. "Mr. Black?"

"One moment!" Marcus snatched up Albin's ruined clothes—coat and shirt, breeches, waistcoat, boots—crossed to the window in long strides and shoved them out. He heard the sound of a key in the lock. He slammed the window shut and swung round.

The door opened. A man stood framed in the doorway, an apron tied around his ample stomach. Behind him were two waiters.

Mr. Nutley stepped into the parlor. He surveyed the damage: the broken table, the upturned chairs, the puddles of spilled ale. His face reddened, swelling with rage. "Sir! This is a respectable establishment—"

"I apologize." Marcus pulled a banknote from his pocket. Five pounds. He crossed to the man. "This should cover the damage."

The landlord's eyes widened. His outrage abruptly vanished. He plucked the note from Marcus's fingers. "Yes. It will suffice."

Marcus glanced around for his hat. There, on the floor. He picked it up, brushed it off, put it on. Over by the broken table, was a second hat: Albin's. He picked that up, too. It was the only item of clothing that Albin's transformation hadn't destroyed.

A metallic gleam on the floor caught his eye. A silver pocket watch. Marcus picked it up and flipped open the lid. *Charles Appleby, Esq.* He frowned, trying to place the name.

Albin's former employer.

"Er . . . do you require the services of a doctor, Mr. Black?"

"No." Marcus slid the watch into his pocket. What he needed was to talk with Albin.

CHAPTER TWENTY-NINE

HE TOOK A hackney to Chandlers Street; he couldn't think where else Albin might have gone. Mrs. Stitchbury uttered a muffled shriek when she saw him. "Lord Cosgrove! You're bleeding dreadfully!"

"Mr. Albin said I might wait for him in his room." He displayed Albin's hat, as if that item of clothing could grant him admittance.

"Certainly, sir," Mrs. Stitchbury said, with an agitated curtsy. She led him upstairs and unlocked Albin's door. "But your poor throat! So much blood! I can bathe it for—"

"No, thank you, Mrs. Stitchbury." Marcus stepped into Albin's room and firmly closed the door.

He waited until he heard Mrs. Stitchbury depart, then crossed to the window and opened it. A sparrow flew in, landing on the rug beside the fireplace.

Marcus latched the window again. When he turned round, Albin stood naked on the rug.

Marcus's skin tightened in a shiver. What Albin did, changing the shape of his body, was impossible. *And yet I see it with my own eyes.*

"Are you all right, sir? Your throat—"

"Don't." His voice was flat, hard. "I've just endured your landlady's fussing and I'm not in the mood for any more." He crossed to the table and laid Albin's hat on it. "I want an explanation. No lies. And for heaven's sake, get dressed!"

"ON MY TWENTY-FIFTH birthday, a woman came to see me." Albin pulled on his drawers. "She wasn't human, sir. She said she was a Faerie." He blushed, as if aware how foolish it sounded, and hurried on. "She said an ancestor of mine had done her a favor, many centuries ago, and that I was due a gift. A wish." Breeches and stockings followed the drawers. "She said I could choose what I wanted. Invisibility or levitation or . . ." He paused part-way through pulling on the second stocking, his brow creasing in an effort of memory. "Longevity and translocation and . . . and foresight and . . . speech with animals."

Marcus shook his head, instinctively rejecting this as impossible. Albin didn't notice. He continued: "I chose metamorphosis, sir."

"Metamorphosis." The word felt strange on his tongue, as if the vowels didn't quite fit together. "That's what you did this afternoon?"

Albin nodded. He shrugged into a clean shirt and began doing up the buttons. "I thought it might be useful."

Marcus grunted. He touched the cut on his throat. Dried blood coated his skin, sticky and tight and uncomfortable.

"I didn't tell you, sir, because . . . because I haven't told anyone! How can I? It's too fantastical. Too . . . too unbelievable! I wouldn't have believed it myself if it hadn't happened to me." Albin's voice, his expression, were an appeal for understanding.

Marcus gazed at him stonily. *I am not a chawbacon to be won over by excuses.*

Albin's face fell. He picked up a waistcoat.

"Explain this to me." Marcus held out the pocket watch he'd found.

"What—? Oh!" Albin dropped the waistcoat. "You found it. Thank you, sir!"

"Charles Appleby was your former employer. Why is his watch in your possession?"

"He left it to me. If I'd lost it—" Albin took the pocket watch and held it in both hands, as if it were precious. "I can't thank you enough, sir."

"You were close to Mr. Appleby?"

"He was like a father to me." Albin picked up the waistcoat he'd dropped and carefully placed the watch in the pocket. "Uh . . . did you find a key, too, sir?"

Marcus shook his head.

Albin's expression became dismayed. "Mrs. Stitchbury won't be pleased with me."

Marcus couldn't care less. He was still furious. *You lied to me.* Except that Albin hadn't precisely lied; he'd merely concealed a fact about himself.

Lie or not, it felt like a breach of trust.

"Have you done it before today? Metamorphosed in my presence?"

Albin's gaze slid away from his.

Marcus's fury flared into rage. "You have."

Albin squeezed his eyes shut and nodded. "Yes, sir. At Hazelbrook. When I followed the Smiths." His eyes opened, beseeching. "I couldn't have run so far otherwise, sir."

"You were the dog I met in the woods."

"Yes, sir."

Marcus strode to the window, trying to control his rage. He clenched his fists on the sill and stared down at Chandlers Street. "The night you went into Whitechapel—you did that as a dog, didn't you?"

"Yes, sir."

"And I was worried for your safety!" He swung back to Albin. "More fool me!"

"I'm sorry, sir." Albin's face was pale, miserable. "I was only trying to help."

"You deceived me."

"Yes, sir." Albin looked ready to cry. He blinked and swallowed and looked at the floor.

"Tell me, Albin . . . how can I trust you?"

Albin's head jerked up. "But, sir, I did it for you!"

Some of Marcus's rage drained away. He turned back to the window and touched his throat, felt the dried blood. *I'd be dead, if not for Albin.*

"Sir . . . I heard them say something—the Smiths—just before they attacked you."

"What?"

"One of them said—I don't know which one—he said . . . he asked whether they should do it now, or wait. I think it means they were hired to kill you."

Marcus lowered his hand and turned to look at Albin. "Kill me?" Phillip might wish him dead, Monkwood might, Brashdon and Hyde might, but they'd hardly—

"Sir, you need to be extremely careful."

He stared at Albin, not really seeing him. The Smiths' attack was now comprehensible; not greed, not panic, but a question of business.

Someone wants me dead.

His mind rejected that statement, pushed it away, sought for something else to focus on. His attention latched on Albin's stockinged feet. He remembered the bundle of clothes he'd tossed from the inn window. "Do you have another pair of boots?"

Albin shook his head.

"Another tailcoat?"

Albin shook his head again.

Marcus took a banknote from his pocket and held it out. "Buy yourself new top boots and a tailcoat. And get yourself a greatcoat, while you're at it."

"I can't take your money, sir."

Marcus looked down at the banknote. Specks of his blood were dark on it. "You saved my life today." However angry he was with Albin, that fact was unmistakable.

Someone wants me dead.

His mind gave another automatic flinch, another rejection of the truth. He pushed away from the windowsill, laid the banknote on the table, and strode to the door.

"Sir? Am I still your secretary?"

Marcus halted. He turned and looked back at Albin, considering this question.

The lad's face was so pale it was almost bloodless. There was anxiety in his eyes, and mute entreaty.

Do I want you as my secretary?

He was angry with Albin, furious with him—and yet . . . despite the magic, he trusted the lad. Not as completely as he had before, but . . . enough.

"Yes," Marcus said. "You're still my secretary."

MARCUS PRESENTED HIMSELF for his meeting with Miss Brown at precisely seven o'clock. "Good evening," he said, aware of the weight of the dueling pistol in his pocket.

He examined the room while Miss Brown latched the door, satisfying himself that no one was concealed behind the folded screen, no one hiding beneath the bed.

They sat at the table with a candle burning between them. Marcus removed his hat and gloves. He ignored the invitation of the bed—clean sheets, soft mattress, plump pillows. It wasn't sex he wanted from Miss Brown tonight; it was answers.

"How did your meeting with the Smiths go, sir?"

Marcus resisted the urge to check that the bandage round his throat was hidden by his neckcloth. "Not as well as I had hoped."

"What happened?"

"A few questions first, Miss Brown, if you don't mind."

She moistened her lips. "Is . . . is something wrong, Lord Cosgrove?"

Marcus ignored the question. "Did you see the Smiths today, before my meeting with them?"

She shook her head. "No."

His eyes narrowed as he surveyed her. "How did you make contact with them? How did you arrange the meeting?"

"I left a message for them at a tavern, offering work."

"Did you mention my name at all?"

She shook her head again. "I called you Mr. Black. Sir . . . what's wrong?"

"What is your connection with the Smiths?"

"I have no connection with the Smiths. They wouldn't know me if they saw me."

Marcus frowned at her in baffled fury. "Then how do you know their names? How do you know how to contact them?"

"It was merely a . . . a lucky chance that I came by the information."

"What lucky chance?"

"I can't tell you," Miss Brown said, twisting her hands together. "I just . . . I just wanted to help you, sir! I've seen what they've done—the windows and . . . and the nightsoil. You don't deserve it, sir. You don't deserve any of it!"

"A philanthropist," he said, his voice flat with sarcasm.

She flushed at his tone.

Marcus scrutinized her. Was she telling the truth? Was she as genuine as she appeared to be? "The Smiths tried to kill me this afternoon, Miss Brown."

Miss Brown was silent for a long moment, her hands clutched together. "I don't understand," she said finally. "Why would they do that?"

"You tell me."

"Me?"

"You know more than I do."

Miss Brown shook her head.

"Where do they live?"

"I don't know. But I can try to find out."

"How?"

She bit her lip, then shook her head again. "I can't—"

"Can't tell me." Frustration flared inside him. If he took Miss Brown by the shoulders and shook her—

Marcus squeezed his eyes shut and pinched the bridge of his nose with hard fingers. *Control yourself, man.* How could he even *think* about offering violence to a woman?

"The Pig and Whistle in Aldgate. That's where I left a message for them."

Marcus lowered his hand, looked at her.

"I can't tell you how I know they drink there." Tears shone in her eyes. "If I could, I would tell you, sir. I give you my word of honor that I only wish to help you."

It was impossible to doubt Miss Brown's sincerity. She looked as tragic as Albin had. No one was that good an actress. Not even the celebrated Sarah Siddons.

Marcus's rage drained away, leaving tiredness in its place. He released his breath in a sigh. "I offered the Smiths money today, Miss Brown—quite a significant sum—in exchange for the name of their employer. But instead of accepting, they tried to kill me."

"Are you all right, sir?"

Marcus lifted one hand to his throat, feeling the layers of

bandage beneath his neckcloth. "We fought them off."

"You were hurt." It was a statement, not a question.

"A little." He let his hand fall. "But it begs the question—why? Why choose to kill me? Why turn down so much money?"

"Do you think . . . they've accepted a commission to kill you?"

"It's a possibility." Marcus leaned back in his chair. "You see why I'm eager to find them, Miss Brown?"

"Yes." Her fingers twisted tightly together, the knuckles whitening. "Sir, you need to be extremely careful. If they've accepted a commission to kill you—" She leaned across the table, her voice urgent: "Sir, you mustn't go anywhere alone!"

"The Smiths are in no position to harm me. Mr. Albin saw to that."

"But whoever hired them will hire new men!"

Probably. Tomorrow he'd have to start looking over his shoulder, but this evening he should be safe.

Marcus glanced at the bed. Last night, when he'd suggested this meeting, he'd been thinking of sex. Tonight . . .

He didn't want to return to Grosvenor Square, to a house that was empty except for servants. He didn't want to spend the evening thinking about his own mortality. A soft bed, a warm female body, sex—those were what he wanted.

But not with Miss Brown.

Tonight he wanted a woman who knew how to distract a man from his worries. A woman skilled in the art of giving pleasure.

He reached for his hat.

"You may stay if you wish."

Marcus looked at her. In the candlelight, Miss Brown wasn't beautiful, but she was undeniably attractive—smooth skin, clear eyes, soft lips. Behind her, the bed offered its silent invitation.

He could visit Madam Cecily's establishment, drink too much expensive brandy, pay for the services of the most talented of her girls. Or he could remain here.

Marcus turned his hat over in his hands, weighing up the options. Last night had been pleasurable, but an evening at Madam Cecily's would be even more so. Miss Brown was clean, he could catch no diseases from her, but she didn't have the skills of Madam Cecily's girls.

"Why?" he asked.

A blush mounted in her cheeks. "I thought . . . I thought it was why you asked to come tonight. But I perfectly understand if you don't want to. I'm not . . ." She bit her lip, and then blurted, "You can do much better than me, sir."

It was what he'd been thinking, but he tried not to show it. "Would you like me to stay, Miss Brown?"

Her blush became fiery. She lowered her gaze. "Last night was . . . nice."

Yes, last night had been surprisingly enjoyable.

Marcus turned his hat over in his hands again. A professional, or Miss Brown? *Or both,* a voice whispered in his head. He could visit Madam Cecily's afterwards.

"Are you still, er . . . protected?"

"There will be no child. I can promise you that, sir."

His gaze slid to the bed. Her body had welcomed him inside, last night. She'd been sleek and hot and deliciously tight. He'd climaxed hard inside her, harder than he had for a long time.

"Very well. I'll stay."

THERE WAS A familiarity to it tonight. This was the third time he'd stripped in front of Miss Brown, the third time he'd undone the buttons of her gown. Her breasts were familiar in his hands, the scent and taste of her skin was familiar, the softness of her hair—and the heat and tightness of her was familiar, too.

Marcus was less gentle than last night, more urgent. It wasn't a conscious choice; his body dictated it, demanded it. Sex. Affirmation of life at its most basic. Miss Brown seemed to feel his urgency—and to match it. She shuddered to a climax seconds before he reached his own release.

Marcus automatically gathered her in his arms afterwards. Was Albin prey to this elemental need to have sex after coming close to death? Was the lad even now in a brothel, losing his virginity?

He smoothed a hand over Miss Brown's hair, feeling an inexplicable tenderness towards her.

He pressed his lips to her shoulder, her throat, her cheek, inhaling the scent of her skin. His mouth found hers. He hadn't planned to kiss her properly, but it seemed natural—to tease her lips apart with his tongue, to gently explore her mouth.

That she'd never kissed anyone was blatantly obvious. Her response was hesitant, clumsy. Their teeth bumped.

"I'm sorry," she said, flustered, embarrassed, trying to draw back.

Marcus didn't let her. He held her close and laughed softly against her mouth. "The only way to learn is through practice." He kissed her again, lightly, gently.

Miss Brown hesitated—and then shyly returned the kiss, tasting his lips, learning the shape of his mouth.

Heat grew between them.

This time their lovemaking wasn't fast and urgent, but leisurely, intense. Marcus kissed her as he entered her, kissed her as he built a slow rhythm, kissed her as his arousal spiraled tighter. Long, exquisite minutes passed. Miss Brown climaxed, her sleek muscles clenching around his cock, and yet it wasn't over, wasn't over—

If anything, his climax was more intense this time. It felt as if his heart stopped beating for an instant.

Marcus floated slowly down to reality: a soft bed, Miss

Brown warm beneath him, the bandage tight and uncomfortable around his throat.

He gathered Miss Brown in his arms and held her while his heartbeat slowed and his skin cooled. Minutes passed. He didn't want to withdraw from her body, didn't want to climb out of the bed, didn't want to dress and leave.

Not Madam Cecily's. Not tonight. Not after this.

He stroked curling strands of hair back from Miss Brown's face, bent his head and kissed her. Small, feather-light kisses. No urgency, just gentleness, tenderness.

The way he'd kissed Lavinia after they'd made love.

Marcus released Miss Brown abruptly and rolled away from her. He didn't want tenderness. Tenderness was dangerous.

He climbed off the bed and dressed silently. When he was fully clothed, he looked at Miss Brown.

She had donned her chemise and stood barefooted beside the bed. Her hair was tousled, her lips rosy, her eyes dark.

Arousal stirred in his groin.

I want her again.

Marcus turned away, picking up his hat and gloves. "May I see you tomorrow evening?" he asked, not looking at her, as if by not meeting her eyes he wouldn't have to acknowledge how much he desired her.

"If you wish."

He did. Very much.

CHAPTER THIRTY

October 25ᵗʰ, 1805
Grosvenor Square, London

CHARLOTTE WAS WORKING on the Somerset ledger when Cosgrove entered the study. The earl walked across to her desk and stood staring down at her. He didn't smile, didn't offer a cheerful greeting. His gaze was cool and assessing.

As if he doesn't know whether he trusts Albin any longer.

Charlotte swallowed. "Good morning, sir. How are you?"

Cosgrove ignored the question. "Did you purchase new boots?"

"Yes, sir."

"And a greatcoat?"

She nodded.

"Then come along, lad. Let's be off."

Charlotte pushed back her chair. "Where to?"

"Aldgate. To find the Smiths."

THE PIG AND Whistle was empty of patrons so early in the morning. Mrs. Westrup was mopping the floor. She wheezed as she worked. Bedraggled blonde hair escaped from beneath her mobcap.

"Good morning, madam," Cosgrove said. "Can you tell me

where I can find Abel and Jeremiah Smith?" A silver shilling gleamed between his fingers.

Mrs. Westrup straightened. "They's gone, sir. Them and Hector and Ned. Left Lunnon yesterday."

"What?" Cosgrove's eyebrows drew together. "Nonsense."

"It's true, sir! Cross me 'eart. All over Aldgate, it is, sir."

"What is?"

"Well," Mrs. Westrup said, leaning on the mop. "The way I 'eard it, they'd been in a fight. Jeremiah was in a terrible way, bleedin' and groanin', and Abel 'ad broke all 'is ribs, but they wouldn't stay more'n a minute at their lodgin'. They reckoned the devil hisself was after 'em. They was all for gettin' out of Lunnon as fast as could be."

"Where did they go?"

Mrs. Westrup shrugged. "Dunno."

"You said they took someone with them?"

"Yes, sir. Hector and Ned."

"And who are they?"

"Hector's their cousin, sir. He broke 'is head in a fight a few weeks back and's been laid up in bed ever since. And Ned's 'is son."

"Skinny lad? Good runner?"

Mrs. Westrup nodded. "That's 'im."

Cosgrove handed her the shilling. "Would you be so good as to direct me to the Smiths' lodgings?"

Mrs. Westrup tucked the shilling into her bodice. "Abel and Jeremiah's been rentin' a room from ol' Martha Hill." She left her grimy mop and came out into the street to give directions to the coachman.

MRS. HILL LIVED in Buckle Street, above a dealer in pickled tongues and oxtails. She looked as old as Methuselah, her skin

folded into a thousand wrinkles, her mouth sunken and tooth-
less. She confirmed what Mrs. Westrup had told them: the
Smiths had left London, abandoning all but the most portable of
their possessions.

"Yesterday?" Cosgrove asked. "What time?"

"On dusk, it were."

"Did they say where they were going?"

Mrs. Hill shook her head. "Jus' that they wanted to put as
many miles between th'selves and Lunnon as they could. Right
scared, they was."

"Did they leave by stagecoach?"

Mrs. Hill shrugged. "I dunno, sir. They 'ad enough money.
The last few weeks they's been mighty flush in the pocket."

Cosgrove's expression sharpened. "Did you ever hear them
speak of their employer? Did they mention his name?"

Mrs. Hill considered this question for a moment, her wrinkles
deepening, her eyes almost lost in folds of skin. "They called
'im 'is nibs. Never 'eard no name other'n that."

"Did you ever see him? Did he come here?"

"They allus met in the city."

"Do you know where?"

Mrs. Hill shook her head.

For a shilling, Mrs. Hill gave them access to the room Abel
and Jeremiah had abandoned. It was furnished with a ramshackle collection of items: two mattresses, a lopsided table, chairs.
Bloodstains made a pattern on the bare floorboards.

The earl crouched and examined a pile of discarded clothing.
"They may have left something behind, instructions from their
employer, a note—"

"They couldn't read or write," Charlotte said, and then realized her mistake: Christopher Albin shouldn't know that. "At
least . . . I wouldn't think they could. Could they, Mrs. Hill?"

"Eddication?" The old woman shook her head. "Ain't none

of us got that. What'd we want it for?"

They searched, but found nothing to tell them where the Smiths had gone or who their employer had been. The earl swore under his breath, a muttered word Charlotte's ears didn't quite catch. "They have a cousin, I believe, Mrs. Hill. A man called Hector."

"Yes, sir, I knows 'im."

"Can you provide me with his address? Or the address of his son, Ned?"

Charlotte bit her tongue. She knew where Ned Smith lived. She'd been there as a dog. Crutch Street. She looked down at the floor and rubbed a stain with the toe of her boot, while Mrs. Hill gave directions.

"WHITECHAPEL?" CHARLOTTE SAID, once they were in the carriage. "Is that wise, sir? You said yourself it's not a safe place—"

"Worried?" the earl said, his tone sharp, sarcastic. "You can always change into a bear if we're threatened."

Charlotte flushed. She looked down at her hands.

Cosgrove sighed. "I beg your pardon, lad. That was uncalled for."

She glanced up, shook her head.

"We are *this* close—" Cosgrove showed her with thumb and forefinger. "This close." Frustration was fierce in his voice. "We won't find anything. I know that. They're gone. But damn it, I'm going to follow this trail to its end!"

He blew out a breath. With it, his anger seemed to deflate. He leaned back on the upholstered seat and grunted a laugh. "If I can without getting my throat cut again." His smile was wry. "I count on you to protect me, lad."

Her heart clenched in her chest. *With my life, sir.*

CRUTCH STREET WAS less frightening than it had been when she was a dog. It was still wretched and squalid and miserable, but no longer terrifying. The overflowing gutters, the dilapidated houses—those things were the same, but there were no knots of sullen, staring, dangerous men. The carriage lurched over potholes. Charlotte opened the window and peered out. The stench of the tanneries pushed into her mouth and nose. "I don't see many people, sir."

"Still abed, probably. Sleeping off last night's libations."

The carriage slowed. She heard the coachman ask a question, saw a barefooted boy point, saw a penny flipped down to the child. The carriage advanced three more houses and halted.

A footman opened the carriage door.

Cosgrove climbed down. "Which house, Howard?"

"That one, sir."

Yes, the warped, unpainted door was familiar. Ned Smith's scent had led her here four days ago. But even with her boots planted in filthy muck, it felt less dangerous than it had last time. *Because I'm a man, not a dog.* And because she wasn't alone. Cosgrove, the footmen, the coachman—they made her feel safe.

"Turn the carriage around," Cosgrove ordered. "We'll be as fast as we can."

AN ELDERLY MAN answered their knock. His face was whiskered, grimy. The odor of Crutch Street clung to him—sewage and tanneries—as if he hadn't washed in years.

For half a crown, he showed them the room Hector Smith and his son had rented. He also offered his name—Pa Hitching—and a swig from his gin bottle, an invitation the earl politely declined.

Hector and Ned Smith had lived in one room, filthy and dark, with broken floorboards. They'd abandoned their lodgings in haste. The bedding was turned back, as if someone had stepped out to use the outhouse and would be back any moment—except there was no outhouse here; a filthy bucket in the corner served that purpose.

"Hec's been laid up in bed with a broken 'ead," Pa Hitching said, and took a long swig from his gin bottle, the Adam's apple bobbing in his skinny throat.

"A broken head? When did that happen?"

"Couple o' weeks back. Mebbe three. I misremember exactly."

Cosgrove nodded. He surveyed the room. "What happened yesterday, Mr. Hitching?"

"Abel Smith come a runnin'. In a right state 'e were!" Pa Hitching cackled with laughter, showing brown stubs of teeth. "Said Satan hisself was after 'em all."

Cosgrove stirred a pile of discarded clothing with the toe of his boot. "I understand Hector and his son had been working for someone recently. Did either of them mention their employer's name?"

Pa Hitching squinted in an effort of memory, and shook his head. "Can't say as 'ow they did."

"Did Abel say where they were going yesterday?"

The old man shook his head again. "He jus' said they 'ad to get out of Lunnon as fast as could be."

"Do you know how they intended leaving? Stagecoach? Hired coach?"

Pa Hitching shrugged. "They left 'ere by 'ackney."

"Thank you."

They emerged to find a small crowd on the street. The mood—curiosity mingled with belligerence—made Charlotte's skin prickle. *This could turn ugly.* The horses had sensed it. Their ears were back, the whites of their eyes showing.

The glossy coach and liveried footmen looked unreal amid the squalor, as if a children's storybook had opened and shaken Cendrillon's golden carriage from its pages.

The coachman greeted them with relief. "Sir!"

"Let's go, Beaglehole. Drive slowly, mind! There are children about."

The carriage made its way back down Crutch Street, plowing through the potholes. Half a dozen ragged boys ran alongside, shouting shrilly, daring each other to touch the lacquered panels. Charlotte heard the slap of their hands on the door, heard the footmen shout, trying to scare them away from the scything wheels.

She glanced at Cosgrove. His face was hard-angled, his mouth grim.

He caught her glance. "No one should live like this."

"No, sir."

A stone hit the side of a carriage with a crack of sound like a gunshot. Charlotte flinched. Cosgrove's expression became grimmer.

They swung into Rosemary Lane. A second stone hit the carriage, a duller thud this time. The coach picked up pace. The shouting mob of boys fell behind.

At the end of Rosemary Lane, the earl rapped on the roof. The carriage slowed. He lowered the window and leaned out. "Anyone hurt? The horses?"

"Just the paintwork, sir."

The earl closed the window. He took off his hat and threw it on the seat. "Tell me, Albin . . . if you were born in Whitechapel, would you kill to leave it?"

Charlotte opened her mouth to reply *No,* and then closed it again. "I don't know, sir."

The earl touched his throat, where Jeremiah Smith had cut him. "I might."

Charlotte thought back to the dark, filthy room Hector and Ned had lived in, with its broken floorboards and foul air. The smell had been more than the tanneries, more than sewage. It had been the smell of poverty and violence and despair. *A more wretched existence than any creature—man or beast—deserves.*

Charlotte frowned. She looked down at her lap, and plucked at one of the buttons on her new greatcoat. Where had she read that phrase recently? *A more wretched existence than any creature deserves.*

The answer came: in one of Cosgrove's speeches.

She lifted her head. "Sir . . . the West Indies . . . is it worse than Whitechapel?" Surely nothing could be?

"For the slaves? Much worse." Cosgrove grimaced, his lips flattening against his teeth. He glanced out the window at the crooked line of roofs, at the coal smoke staining the sky. "One battle at a time, lad. One battle at a time." His grimace faded. He curled one hand into a fist, a slow, meditative gesture. "Hector Smith was the man who almost killed Lionel."

"You broke his head, sir?"

"I did." Cosgrove clenched his hand until the knuckles whitened, then relaxed his fingers. "Where the hell have they gone?"

"We could check the coaching inns, sir."

"Do you have any idea how many of them there are?" Cosgrove leaned his head back against the seat, closing his eyes.

Charlotte's heart squeezed in her chest. She wanted to reach over and smooth the frown from his brow. "They'd be memorable, sir. Three injured men. I'm sure if we tried—"

"It's of no matter." The earl opened his eyes. His gaze, gray and direct, seemed to pin her to her seat. Surely he could see inside her? Could see she was a woman, not a man. See that she loved him. "We don't need to find the Smiths to know who hired them. After yesterday there can be no question."

"Sir?"

"Don't be obtuse, lad. Who has the most to gain from my death?"

"But . . . Mr. Langford has no money to pay—"

"He must have promised payment upon his succession to the title."

Charlotte twisted the button on her coat. "Do you truly think he'd kill you, sir?"

Cosgrove rubbed his forehead, as if his frown hurt. "Do you truly think he wouldn't?"

Charlotte turned the button one way, then the other. "But . . . but he's your *family*."

"You think it's more likely to be Brashdon or Hyde?" The earl shook his head. "People don't murder over differences of political opinion."

"There's a lot of money at stake, sir. The plantations—"

"I'm not the only person fighting for abolition of the trade. If they got rid of me, they'd have to get rid of Grenville. Fox. Wilberforce. A dozen others."

"But what about Monkwood, sir? He hates you. If you were to die—"

"I've no doubt he'd be delighted—as would Brashdon and his set—but he's not so mad as to perpetrate it himself. No." The earl shook his head again. "Phillip is the only one with sufficient reason to wish me dead."

His flat, certain voice overruled any argument she might make.

Charlotte turned the button between her fingers while the carriage traversed Cheapside. "Will you let it go to trial, sir?" she asked, when they turned into Newgate Street. "If you find proof it's Mr. Langford?"

Cosgrove was silent until they reached Holborn. "I don't

know. Maybe he could be sent to the colonies. Australia." He rubbed his forehead again. "I don't know, Albin. I don't know."

AT GROSVENOR SQUARE, they climbed down from the carriage. In Whitechapel, it had gleamed, as bright as gold; here it looked bedraggled, the paintwork splashed with foul mud, smeared with handprints.

Cosgrove stood, watching the carriage rattle over the cobblestones on its way to the mews.

An icy wind tugged at Charlotte's clothes and slipped cold fingers beneath her hat, trying to flip it from her head. She clutched the hat brim and hunched her shoulders. Her toes were numb inside the new boots.

The carriage clattered out of sight. Still Cosgrove didn't move. He was frowning, his eyes narrowed in thought.

Wind gusted through the square again. The tall houses shivered, the trees behind the iron palings shivered, the gray clouds scudding across the sky shivered.

Cosgrove didn't notice. He stood motionless. Frowning. Thinking.

"Sir?"

The earl glanced at her. "You asked what I'll do once the slave trade is abolished. Do you remember?"

Charlotte nodded, clutching her hat, clenching her teeth to stop them chattering. She remembered the place—St. James's Street, on the way to Lord Brashdon's club—and the earl's reaction—the bemusement, the shrug.

"I think I've found it." He clapped her on the shoulder. "Inside with you, lad. You're freezing."

CHAPTER THIRTY-ONE

CHARLOTTE LOOKED UP from the columns of numbers in the Somerset ledger. The earl was muttering under his breath, trying out words on his tongue. As she watched, he scowled, scratched out a sentence, dipped his quill in ink, wrote fiercely.

Her heart did its familiar tightening in her chest.

She let her gaze rest on him—the strong-boned face, the scowling black eyebrows, the flawlessly folded neckcloth. Her awareness of Cosgrove was different from last week. It wasn't lust anymore. It was something she felt in her bones, in her blood, in each beat of her heart. *I love you, sir.*

She hugged the moment to herself—the fire mumbling in the grate, the clock striking two in the entrance hall, Cosgrove's quill making tiny scratching sounds as he wrote. This was what happiness was: moments like this, quiet companionship.

A footman knocked on the study door. "Baron Grenville to see you, sir."

"Grenville?" Cosgrove laid down his quill.

Charlotte knew the name. Baron Grenville was one of Cosgrove's political allies, a man dedicated to abolition of the slave trade. "Would you like to speak with him in here, sir? Shall I leave?"

"Please."

She gathered up the Somerset ledger and departed for the library, but she'd barely finished tallying another column before the door opened. It was the earl. "Albin. My study. Now!" Fury blazed in his eyes and vibrated in his voice.

"What is it, sir?"

Cosgrove made no answer. He strode back to the study.

Charlotte hurried after him.

Cosgrove shut the door, almost slamming it, and thrust a letter at her. "Read this."

The letter was dated two months earlier. "Philadelphia? That's in the colonies, sir?"

Cosgrove gave a curt nod.

Charlotte read swiftly. The writer claimed to have been in the West Indies both times Cosgrove had visited, but to only recently have become aware of the earl's abolitionary activities. *I put pen to paper, compelled by my duty to draw your attention to the true nature of this man. Countless times have I observed his violence towards the female slaves on his plantation. It was his habit—indeed, his delight—to force himself upon the women he owned.*

"What?" Charlotte's head jerked up. She stared at Cosgrove, her mouth open in shock.

"Keep reading," he said tightly.

Cosgrove took pleasure in inflicting pain. Sometimes he flogged the unfortunate females he'd chosen, sometimes he beat them with his fists, sometimes he throttled them half-senseless with his hands, before slaking his lusts on them.

Charlotte's eyes flinched from the words. She glanced at Cosgrove again.

"Keep reading." His voice was brittle, his face angular. The bones of cheek and jaw looked sharp enough to cut through his skin.

Cosgrove reserved the worst of his excesses for those females barely into womanhood, tender and fragile in their youth. It was his delight to break them with his foul pleasures, to make them beg for him to cease. To my knowledge, more than one poor creature killed herself afterwards.

Horror grew inside Charlotte, swelling like a tumor in her stomach. She closed her eyes briefly, not wanting to read further, knowing she had to.

I write, the letter-writer concluded, *because I feel it is my God-given duty to expose Lord Cosgrove for what he is: the worst kind of monster, an abuser of helpless women, obscene and violent in his lusts, a man without morals or conscience. That he should embrace the cause of Abolition is hypocrisy at its greatest. He does not deserve a place in the House of Lords; he deserves a place in the fires of Hell.*

Yours faithfully, etc.

Reverend Jonathan L. Banks

Charlotte lowered the letter. "Sir . . ." She searched for words, but found none. The accusations were too shocking. "It's not true."

"Of course it's not true! No one who knows you could possibly think so! Baron Grenville didn't . . . did he?"

"No. But men all over town received copies today." The earl's voice was thick, as if choked by rage. "Grenville knows of at least a dozen!" He strode to the window and stared out, his fists clenched on the windowsill. His silhouette was sharp-angled, sharp-edged.

Charlotte clutched the letter, feeling helpless. She could protect the earl from physical attack, but how could she protect him from this? How did one fight such accusations, prove them baseless and unjust?

She looked at the sender's address. Philadelphia. "Reverend Jonathan L. Banks. Who's he, sir?"

"I doubt he exists." Cosgrove turned to face her. "It's the work of someone here. Someone who's trying to destroy my political career."

Charlotte looked closely at the writing. "You think it was written in England and sent out to Philadelphia to be posted back?"

"I do." Cosgrove pushed away from the windowsill. "The Smiths, the attack yesterday—Phillip was behind that. But this—" He took the letter from her and clenched it in his fist. "This isn't Phillip's work. It can only be Brashdon or Hyde."

Charlotte frowned. "You think it's unconnected to everything else?"

"Of course! Phillip wants the earldom; Brashdon and Hyde want me discredited." Cosgrove's grip tightened on the letter, white-knuckled. His nostrils flared. His lips pulled back from his teeth. "By God, I'll kill them for this."

The violence in his face, in his voice, scared her. "Sir, it's not—"

"Not what? Not important? Not of any consequence?" His rage seemed to heat the air. "This is worse than anything that's happened yet!"

"But the Smiths tried to kill you!"

"That, I can fight. This, I can't. This is my *name*. My reputation!"

Charlotte heard the weight of the words, heard the silence they created in the study.

Cosgrove valued his name as highly as he valued his life.

"What did Baron Grenville recommend, sir?"

"That I ignore it. That I laugh it off. Dismiss it as a prank." Cosgrove tossed the crumpled letter on the desk. His laugh was harsh. "A *prank*!"

Charlotte picked up the letter and smoothed it.

The earl strode back to the window. "The less attention I'm seen to pay to it, the less attention it will draw—or so Grenville believes. And I am not—*not*—to lose my temper publicly over it." He raised one fist, as if to smash a pane of glass, and then lowered it. "Fuck," he said, in a low voice. "Fuck, fuck, *fuck.*"

Charlotte didn't know what the word meant, but his rage was palpable. "Someone may recognize the writing—"

"It'll be disguised. Whoever wrote it's no fool."

Charlotte looked down at the creased paper, the spiky letters in black ink, the ugly words. "If you write to the West Indies, ask for reputable people there to vouch for you—"

"Of course I'll do that." Cosgrove's voice was impatient. "But it'll take months before any replies reach London."

Charlotte bit her lip. A sentence caught her eye: *It was his habit—indeed, his delight—to force himself upon the women he owned.* She grimaced and folded the letter, hiding the words. She examined the writer's address. Philadelphia.

It told her nothing.

Charlotte turned the letter over in her hand. There were no clues to the writer's identity that her eyes could see. "Sir . . ." She hesitated, uncertain of what Cosgrove's reaction might be. "If I change into a dog, I may be able to smell the writer's scent."

There was a moment of utter silence—the ticking of the ebony and gold clock on the mantelpiece was loud—then Cosgrove swung to face her. "What?" His gaze was so fierce she almost stepped back a pace.

"I may be able to smell something."

"Do it!"

MARCUS TURNED THE key, locking the study door. He tried not to pace while Albin undressed. "It may not work," the lad said, when he was down to his drawers. "I may not be able to smell anything."

Marcus nodded. "I understand." He turned away to give Albin some privacy. He heard the lad strip out of the drawers; then came silence.

He glanced over his shoulder. A brown dog stood in the middle of the study.

The skin on the back of Marcus's neck, the skin down his spine, prickled in an involuntary shiver, as if he, too, were a dog and his hackles had risen.

The letter lay on his desk. He unfolded it, placed it on the floor, and stepped back a pace.

Albin padded over and touched his nose to the paper, breathing deeply, as if inhaling the ink itself. He sniffed every inch of the letter and then pawed at it.

Marcus turned the letter over, exposing the address and postmark, and watched as Albin sniffed thoroughly.

Faerie magic. It was ludicrous. Preposterous. Impossible. *And yet I see it with my own eyes.*

But . . . Faeries? Magic? He shook his head in instinctive rejection.

Albin stepped away from the letter. Marcus managed to close his eyes in time not to witness the unsettling transformation. When he opened them, his secretary stood before him, naked and human.

"Well?"

"The outside is covered in smells, sir." Albin reached for his drawers. "Inside, I could smell you and me, sir, and I think . . . two others."

"You think?"

Albin fastened his drawers. "One was strong, sir. Baron Grenville, I'd guess. But the other . . ." His expression was apologetic. "It's very faint, sir. I couldn't quite catch it."

Marcus tried not to let his disappointment show on his face. "The letter must have been written several months ago," he said turning away. "Not your fault, lad."

"I might recognize who wrote it, if I smelled him, but . . . I might not."

Marcus swung back to face him. "Recognize?"

"Maybe." Albin shrugged, a diffident gesture.

"You're willing to try?"

Albin nodded.

Marcus tried to quash the excitement that flared in his chest. *He's not promising anything.*

"We could go for a walk, sir. To their houses. Brashdon and Hyde and Keynes. And Monkwood. And even Mr. Langford, sir. I can see whether I recognize that smell—" Albin gestured at the letter lying on the floor, "—or the Smiths."

"When? Now?"

Albin nodded.

Marcus bared his teeth in a smile. "Let's go for a walk."

Albin obediently removed his drawers again.

"Can you be any breed of dog? Or just that one?"

"Anything you like, sir."

"How about a . . ." He needed something a gentleman might have. "A spaniel."

"Yes, sir."

Marcus bent and picked up the letter. Rage surged through him at sight of the spiky writing. *By God, I'll bring you down, if it's the last thing I do.* He folded the letter and thrust it into his pocket. When he next looked, Albin was a black spaniel. "Excellent."

He bundled up Albin's clothes and hid them in a cupboard, then crossed to the window and opened it. "Meet me outside." He turned back to the spaniel, but it was no longer there. A sparrow winged past him.

Marcus watched the sparrow swoop across the square. The back of his neck prickled again, but alongside that sensation was a twinge of envy. To be able to fly . . .

He shook off the envy and slammed the window shut.
Time to go hunting.

CHAPTER THIRTY-TWO

MARCUS STRODE DOWN Curzon Street, the black spaniel at his heels. "Hyde's house is the one on the corner," he said in a low voice. "Would you like to smell the letter again?"

The dog nodded.

Marcus unfolded the letter and glanced over his shoulder. There was no one nearby. He crouched to let Albin sniff it.

Albin inhaled the scents, snuffling, then trotted ahead, his tail wagging.

Marcus replaced the letter in his pocket and strolled after him. The black spaniel looked like any other dog. He almost expected Albin to cock a leg and pee.

Albin sniffed the four steps leading up to Hyde's door, then as much of the door as he could reach, standing up on hind legs to smell the keyhole and knocker. He came back down the steps and shook his head.

Marcus tried not to feel disappointed. "Keynes is around the corner, in Halfmoon Street."

He'd only gone half a dozen paces when the door to Hyde's house opened. He looked back and saw Hyde and Keynes emerge.

Marcus halted. "Gentlemen," he said politely. "Good afternoon."

Hyde didn't return the greeting. His chin pushed out slightly, making him look even more like a bulldog.

"Afternoon." Keynes smiled genially. "What a handsome dog. Is he yours?"

Albin sniffed the proffered hand.

"Aren't you a fine-looking spaniel?" Keynes said, patting Albin on the head.

Albin growled, pulling his lips back, showing his teeth.

Keynes removed his hand hastily.

"He's an excellent judge of character," Marcus said.

Keynes gave him a sour look. "Come along, Hyde. We'll be late."

Marcus stayed where he was. "Was it Keynes?" he asked, when the men had turned the corner into Halfmoon Street. "Is that why you growled?"

The spaniel shook its head.

Marcus was relieved. He wanted it to be Brashdon. He *knew* it was Brashdon.

"Little King Street next. That's where Brashdon lives."

They walked down Halfmoon Street, following Keynes and Hyde, crossed Piccadilly, and headed down St. James's Street. Keynes and Hyde turned into their club. "Probably meeting Brashdon," Marcus said in an undertone, as they passed the entrance. "If we're lucky, we'll run into him." He turned into Little King Street. "Ah, speak of the devil. You see him?"

Brashdon was half a block away, a thin, precise figure.

Marcus strolled to meet him. A grin wanted to spread across his face, fierce. *I've got you.* "Afternoon," he said, as Albin sniffed Brashdon's boots.

Brashdon stepped back, his mouth pursing in distaste. "Is it yours, Cosgrove? Keep it away from me. I can't abide dogs. Filthy creatures."

Marcus snapped his fingers. "Here, Trojan."

Albin didn't obey. He reared up and planted his paws on

Brashdon's breeches, his tail wagging.

Brashdon recoiled. "Ugh! Disgusting creature! Away with you!"

Albin's tail wagged harder. He scrabbled at Brashdon's breeches, leaping up as if trying to lick the man's face.

Brashdon batted with his hands, like a girl. "Get off me!"

Marcus gave a contemptuous snort of laughter. "Trojan. Heel!"

Albin stopped harassing Brashdon. He came and sat at Marcus's feet, his tongue hanging out, grinning.

Brashdon brushed fastidiously at his breeches. The look he gave Marcus was venomous. "Someone showed me a letter this morning. About you."

You wrote it. Marcus shrugged lightly, as if he didn't care. "Half of London got one."

Brashdon stepped past him. "I shall enjoy watching your fall."

Marcus clenched his jaw, clenched his hands. He watched Brashdon turn the corner into St. James's Street. "Tell me it was him," he said tightly.

The spaniel shook its head.

Marcus hissed between his teeth. The letters *had* to be from Brashdon. He was cunning enough, conscienceless enough.

He inhaled a deep breath and unclenched his hands. "Come along, lad."

At Brashdon's house Albin sniffed the steps thoroughly. "Anything?" Marcus asked, and was unsurprised when the spaniel shook its head. "He must have had someone else write the letters. A clerk, perhaps."

Unless it wasn't Brashdon.

Marcus kicked the bottom step. He *wanted* it to be Brashdon. "Come on," he told Albin. "Monkwood next."

THE BLACK SPANIEL ran ahead once they reached Hanover Square. A cold wind whipped smoke from the tall chimneys, smearing it across a gray sky. Marcus crossed the square, watching Albin sniff Monkwood's steps, sniff the door, stand up on hind legs and sniff the knocker and keyhole.

The spaniel ran back to meet him when he was two-thirds of the way across the square. "Well?" Marcus asked, already knowing the answer. But instead of shaking his head, Albin uttered a small bark and pawed at Marcus's pocket. "What? You want to smell the letter again?"

Albin sat back on his haunches and nodded.

Marcus unfolded the letter and let the spaniel sniff it. He resisted the urge to see whether anyone was watching; he was merely a man with his dog.

The spaniel bounded away again and investigated Monkwood's front door with his nose.

"Well?" Marcus asked, when he reached the steps.

Albin didn't come down to meet him; instead, he lay down on the top step.

"What?" Marcus said in disbelief. "You're not telling me it's Monkwood?"

The black spaniel made an odd movement—a ducking of his head, a hunching of his shoulders. It took Marcus a few seconds to realize it was a shrug.

"It might be Monkwood, but you're not certain? Is that what you're saying?"

The spaniel sat up and nodded.

Marcus shook his head. *I don't believe it.* The letter *had* to be political. "Why on earth would Monkwood—"

The door opened. The butler stood there, his face long and lugubrious. "Sir?"

"Uh . . . hello, Sprott. I was just taking Trojan here for a walk and, uh . . ."

The butler glanced down at the spaniel. His expression became even more mournful. "Do you wish to come in, Lord Cosgrove?"

Albin cocked his head and looked at Marcus.

Marcus shrugged. "Why not? Since we're passing."

ALBIN'S CLAWS MADE delicate clacking sounds on the marble floor as they entered. Marcus handed Sprott his hat and gloves.

"And the dog, sir?"

"Oh, Trojan's very well behaved," Marcus said. "Aren't you, Trojan?"

Albin wagged his tail.

The butler gave a doleful sniff and set off down the corridor. Marcus followed, Albin trotting at his heels. He glanced down at the spaniel. Albin *had* to be mistaken. There was no earthly reason for Monkwood to send the letters.

Sprott ushered them into the library. Monkwood stood at the window, looking out at the square. He turned. "Cosgrove. Thought it was you out there. New dog?"

"Yes."

As always, sight of Monkwood brought memory of Lavinia flooding back. Gerald was a coarser version of his sister, his curls not as angelically golden, his eyes not as vividly blue, his face not as fine-boned. Lavinia had been slender, but if she'd lived to thirty, perhaps she'd have grown soft and plump, like her brother.

Monkwood strolled to the fireplace. "Have a seat. Sprott will bring us some claret."

The butler withdrew.

Marcus sat across from Monkwood. The friendly welcome was disconcerting. He was used to animosity, not smiling hospitality.

Albin lay down on the rug between them.

"I hear the Hazelbrook conservatory burned down. Such a terrible thing to happen. You must be devastated." There was an undertone of ill-concealed glee beneath the sympathy. Monkwood's lips twitched at the corners, as if he couldn't quite hide a smile.

"On the contrary. I'm pleased to have it gone."

"What? Nonsense! It was a jewel."

Marcus shrugged. "I didn't like it. With it gone, I can sell Hazelbrook."

"Sell?" Monkwood stiffened, and uncrossed his legs. "You can't sell Hazelbrook!"

"The conservatory's gone. My pledge to my mother no longer stands."

"But Lavinia died there!"

Marcus felt an unexpected pity for the man. "You think I should keep Hazelbrook as a monument to her?" He shook his head. "I'm sorry, Monkwood."

Monkwood's face flushed with rage, with distress, with hatred. "You never loved her!"

Marcus's own temper stirred. "Of course I did. I wouldn't have married her otherwise."

"It's your fault she's dead!"

"It was an *accident,*" Marcus said, keeping a grip on his temper. "She fell."

"Fell?" Monkwood spat the word. "Lavinia didn't fall."

Cold rage washed through him. "What exactly are you implying, Monkwood? That I drove her to suicide? Or that I pushed her myself?"

Monkwood pressed his lips together, not answering. Silence stretched between them, taut, brittle.

I shouldn't have come here. Monkwood loved her too much.

Marcus's rage drained away. "It was an accident," he said. "Lavinia didn't jump, I didn't push her; she *fell*. Five gardeners and three house servants saw it happen. Didn't you pay any attention at the inquest?"

Monkwood lifted his lip in a sneer. "Servants? They'd lie for you if you paid them enough."

"Oh, for heaven's sake!" Marcus stood. "For the last time, it was an *accident*."

Monkwood pushed to his feet. Albin uttered a low growl. Monkwood didn't so much as glance at the dog. "I received a letter about you today."

"So did a lot of people. It's someone's idea of a prank. Throw it in the fire."

"It's about time society saw you for what you are."

"What?"

"Accusations of rape. A young wife so afraid of her husband that she jumped—"

"I never harmed Lavinia," Marcus said, rage choking his voice. "Not once. Ask the servants if you don't believe me."

"They'd lie—"

"If I paid them enough?" It took all his willpower not to punch the sneer off Monkwood's mouth. "If you think that, you're a bigger fool than I took you for!"

MARCUS WALKED BACK along Brook Street, striding fast, driven by fury. How many people would jump to the same conclusion Monkwood had? That he'd abused Lavinia?

The servants had been privy to the details of his marriage. They'd seen Lavinia in violent rages, smashing ornaments. They'd seen her pull books from the library shelves and hurl them across the room. Seen her storm, shrieking, through the house. And they'd seen that he'd never struck her. Not once.

Even though it had been within his rights as a husband.

When I next choose a bride, I shall interview her servants.
Servants saw things, heard things. They knew their employers'
true faces, not merely the masks they showed the world.

They emerged into Grosvenor Square. Above the rooftops,
the sky was darkening. Marcus blew out a breath. He didn't feel
up to facing Phillip today. He'd had as much hatred as he could
stomach.

He glanced at his watch. In a couple of hours he'd meet with
Miss Brown.

His black mood eased fractionally. "Wait here," he told the
spaniel. "I'll open the window."

CHARLOTTE DRESSED IN Albin's clothes—stockings, breeches,
shirt. The earl poured two glasses of brandy and brought her
one. "Well? What did you smell?"

"The scent on the letter isn't Hyde or Keynes or Brashdon,"
Charlotte said, buttoning the waistcoat.

Cosgrove leaned against the mantelpiece, his glass in one
hand. "And Monkwood?"

"It might be him."

"Or it might not."

"The scent on the letter's too faint. I just . . . I can't be certain, sir."

Cosgrove pushed away from the mantelpiece. "I don't think
it's Monkwood. I think Brashdon hired someone to write them.
A clerk."

Charlotte pulled on one boot. It wasn't her place to disagree
with him, but . . . "I think it's Monkwood, sir."

Cosgrove sat on one corner of his desk. "You do? Why?"

"He hates you, sir." She reached for the other boot. "More
than you realize."

"I think it's fairly obvious how much he hates me," Cosgrove said dryly. He took a long swallow of brandy.

"No, sir, before that! I felt it from the moment we entered the library." She gripped the boot. How to verbalize what she'd sensed? She wasn't even sure what it had been—a scent, something in Monkwood's voice, something in the way he'd turned to greet the earl. He wanted Cosgrove dead. Of that, she was absolutely certain. His desire to kill the earl had come off him in waves, as if exuded from his skin, as if he breathed it out with each exhalation. "If you want my opinion, sir, it was Monkwood who sent the letter." She pulled on the second boot. "He wants you ruined. And he wants you dead."

Cosgrove didn't believe her—she saw it on his face—but he didn't scoff or dismiss her words. He merely said, "Thank you, lad. I shall bear it in mind."

Charlotte picked up her neckcloth and looked for a mirror. There was none. She looped the length of muslin around her neck, squinting down as she tried to tie it.

"Let me do that," Cosgrove said, putting down his glass. "You're making a mess."

Charlotte relinquished the neckcloth. "I didn't smell the Smiths anywhere, sir."

"If you smell them, it'll be at Phillip's." Cosgrove tied the knot, a slight frown of concentration on his brow.

The last time he'd done this, she'd been painfully conscious of his closeness, his maleness. This time, there was no awkwardness, just a quiet hum of contentment in her chest. When Cosgrove's knuckles touched the underside of her chin, blood didn't rush to her cheeks. Her pego didn't stir. Her tongue didn't tie itself in knots when she spoke: "What about Mr. Langford, sir?"

"We'll deal with him tomorrow. I have an appointment this evening."

With me.

Soon she'd be as close to him as one human being could be to another.

The earl tightened the knot. "That'll do."

"Thank you, sir." Charlotte picked up her coat and shrugged into it. She straightened her cuffs, then picked up the brandy glass and took a sip. It filled her mouth with heat.

Cosgrove returned to his desk. He glanced at the clock. "It's five o'clock. Off you go, lad. Have a good evening."

"Yes, sir." *I shall.* But it wasn't Cosgrove's lovemaking she craved as much as what came afterwards, when he held her close and she listened to his breathing, heard his heart beat, felt him still inside her. Those were the moments that took her breath away: the quiet, still, precious moments that came afterwards.

Charlotte swallowed the last of the brandy and placed the glass on the sideboard. "Sir . . . if you're going out, you'll be careful? Take the carriage and footmen?"

"You're a mother hen, aren't you, lad?"

"Yesterday—"

"Yes, the Smiths." Cosgrove lost his smile. "I'll be careful. I promise." He sketched a salute with his glass, as if she were the one who gave the orders, not he. "Now, away with you!"

CHAPTER THIRTY-THREE

MARCUS TOOK A bottle of champagne and two crystal glasses to the Earnoch Hotel.

"Are you celebrating something, sir?" Miss Brown asked as he opened the bottle.

Marcus shook his head. "Today has been . . . a trial." And he needed a drink. Several drinks.

"Did you have any luck finding the Smiths, sir?"

"No. They've left London." The Smiths and Phillip were minor problems; the letters were his most pressing concern. His hand paused in its pouring. "You've heard about the letters? Did your employer receive one?"

"I heard about them. I'm sorry, sir."

His grip on the champagne bottle tightened. "Do you know the details of what I'm supposed to have done?" Did Miss Brown think him a rapist?

"I do. And I know it's untrue."

Marcus finished pouring. Rage was building in him again—and he didn't want to be angry tonight. He wanted to be relaxed. He handed Miss Brown a glass. "To your health."

"To yours, sir."

He swallowed a mouthful of champagne. It was cool, the bubbles popping and fizzing on his tongue. It wouldn't dull his rage as fast as brandy would, but if he drank another couple of glasses, it should do the trick.

A hip bath stood half-hidden behind a screen. The water steamed faintly.

Miss Brown's skin would be warm, clean, soft, smooth.

Marcus transferred his gaze to her, standing in her faded blue gown, with her hair pulled back from her face. He'd thought her plain the first time he'd set eyes on her, dowdy and drab. *How could I have been so blind?* Miss Brown wasn't as beautiful as Lavinia, but she was more attractive than Lavinia had ever been. It was the freckles, he decided, and the candid brown of her eyes. Lavinia had looked like an angel; Miss Brown looked like a real woman. He wanted to kiss her mouth, unpin her hair, strip off her clothes and bare her skin.

The lingering remnants of rage evaporated, and with it, his need for alcohol. Arousal stirred in his blood. Marcus put down the glass. He stepped closer to Miss Brown, tilted up her chin, and laid his lips on hers.

Miss Brown shyly kissed him back. She tasted of champagne.

Marcus unpinned her hair. It tumbled down her back, just as he'd imagined. He gathered her closer, deepening the kiss, burying his hands in warm, silky hair.

Long, heated minutes passed. His arousal built, his body demanding that he do more than merely kiss Miss Brown. Reluctantly, he released her. They were both breathing raggedly.

Marcus set to work unfastening her gown. He kissed Miss Brown's cheek as he undid the buttons, kissed the curve of her jaw, kissed her throat as the gown fell away from her shoulders. Petticoat and stays rapidly followed the gown. When she was dressed only in her chemise, he halted.

He stripped off his own clothes until he was naked except for the bandage at his throat. She glanced at his erection, not boldly as a whore would, but shyly.

Marcus took her hand and drew her to the bed. *Slow,* he told himself as he lifted the chemise over her head. *Don't hurry.*

But even so, it went quickly. Her body welcomed him eagerly inside and once he'd started he couldn't stop, couldn't slow down. Their lovemaking was rushed and intense, his orgasm a brief, savage release of tension. "I apologize," Marcus said afterwards, ashamed of his lack of control. He eased himself off her. "Did I hurt you?"

Miss Brown shook her head and smiled at him. "No." She lifted a hand, as if to stroke the hair back from his brow, and then hesitated, her fingers curling into her palm. "May I touch you, sir?"

The words were like a slap across his face. Did she feel she needed to ask permission to touch him?

Marcus frowned and thought back over the times they'd lain together. Had she never stroked his skin? Never caressed him?

No. He'd done the touching, not her.

His sense of shame deepened. He'd taken Miss Brown's virginity, bedded her four nights running—and yet she didn't feel free to touch him.

"Of course you may." Their positions in society might be poles apart, but while they lay naked together, they were equals. He took her hand and placed it on his chest, looked her in the eyes. "Touch me as much as you like."

"Are you certain, sir?"

Marcus found himself unable to look away, unable to speak, almost unable to breathe. Her hand was warm on his skin, but it wasn't her touch that held him frozen, it was the directness of her eyes, that searching gaze, as if she looked inside him, as if there were no need for words because she could see his answer before he uttered it. *Yes, I'm certain.*

Silence stretched between them—her hand on his chest, her eyes holding his, his tongue frozen in his mouth—and then perhaps she truly did see his answer, because she looked away.

Marcus dragged a deep breath into his lungs, feeling winded. What the devil had just happened? And then his attention was caught by what Miss Brown was doing, the path she traced across his torso with her fingertips.

Her touch was light, skimming over his skin—down his ribcage, across his abdomen, and up again. She outlined the faint, pink line Jeremiah Smith's knife had made across his heart. The blade had cut through coat and waistcoat and shirt, but barely marked his skin.

Her gaze lifted, her eyes catching his again. "Your throat, how bad is it?"

"Shallow. No stitches. This—" he touched the bandage, "is at my valet's insistence." To preserve the whiteness of his neck-cloths, should the cut leak blood. Another day or two and he'd stop wearing it, however much Leggatt fussed.

Miss Brown nodded. Her gaze lowered. She stroked the faint, scored line across his chest again—from collarbone to ribcage— then her fingers slid sideways. She outlined his pectoral muscle. The path she made was hot and tingling on his skin.

Her fingertip traced decreasing circles. Marcus's skin tightened, became hotter. His breath was shallow, his pulse quickening, arousal rising inside him.

Miss Brown circled his nipple, light, tickling. Anticipation shivered through him. "Pinch it," Marcus said. His voice was low, almost a whisper.

Their eyes locked for another long, breathless moment, and then she did as he bid, her fingers closing around his nipple, pinching.

Arousal spiked through him. He couldn't control the twitch of his body.

A smile lit Miss Brown's eyes. She turned her attention to his right nipple, repeating the light, teasing circles, the pinch, and his body gave another helpless twitch.

From his nipple, she moved higher, tracing the line of his collarbone, then the muscles of his shoulder and arm. Her shy curiosity was oddly arousing. Wherever her fingers moved, heat followed.

Miss Brown's exploration grew bolder. She returned to his torso, moving lower, circling his belly button with tiny, tickling circles, stroking down his abdomen. She halted at the crisp black curls at his groin, at the semi-erect length of his cock.

"You may touch me there, too. If you wish." Marcus gently took her hand, let her cup his testicles in her palm, let her feel their weight and heat, and then curved her fingers around his cock. Arousal pulsed through him.

Miss Brown's gaze jerked to his face.

It felt incredibly intimate: her hand on him, his gaze holding hers. "Like this," he whispered, guiding her hand, letting her stroke him. Pleasure shivered over his skin, ran like quicksilver through his veins, pooled in his groin, stiffened his cock.

It would be easy to let her continue, easy to let himself come to completion—but that wasn't what he wanted with her. Marcus removed her hand. "Now it's my turn." He sat up and pointed to where he'd been reclining. "Lie down."

After a moment's hesitation, Miss Brown obeyed.

Marcus gazed at her. Candlelight gilded the pale curves of her breasts and made shadows pool between her legs. Anticipation gathered inside him. Where to touch her first? His gaze rose to her dark eyes, her soft mouth. A blush colored her cheeks; she was embarrassed by his perusal.

Marcus leaned down and kissed her. "Relax," he whispered against her lips, and then he bent his head and kissed her jaw, her throat, the beating pulse at the hollow of her collarbone.

Slow, delicious minutes passed as he moved down Miss Brown's body, kissing, tasting her skin with his tongue, nipping lightly with his teeth, teasing. She was soft, womanly, beautiful.

He explored her breasts, her belly, the silken skin of her inner thighs.

Her feminine scent came to him, a light, erotic fragrance that seemed to reach inside him and wrap itself around his bones, to pulse in his veins.

Marcus stroked his fingers up her inner thigh, drawing shivers of response from her, then parted the curls of hair and slid a finger inside her. She was hot and slick and tempting.

He wanted to taste her.

For a long moment he hesitated—and then he gave in to temptation, parting the soft folds with his fingers, bending his head, licking her.

Arousal jolted through him.

Miss Brown inhaled sharply.

Marcus explored, caressing with his tongue, teasing with his teeth, learning what made her tremble, what made the breath catch in her throat. Her scent and taste were intoxicating, heightening his arousal. His cock grew harder, hotter.

Miss Brown's body began to shift helplessly. Marcus held her hips down as she climaxed. Satisfaction surged inside him. He lifted his head and laughed, a soft, triumphant sound.

Miss Brown was flushed and breathless.

Marcus laughed again. He rose to hands and knees and kissed her, tasting her mouth as he'd tasted her body. Miss Brown clutched him, her fingers digging into his arms, and kissed him back deeply. He almost groaned aloud when she broke the kiss.

Sex. Now.

He shifted his weight, ready to bed her, ready to sink himself into her.

"Sir . . . may I touch you again?"

Marcus hesitated, the word *No* on his tongue. He wanted sex, not titillation. But what happened in this bed was as much about Miss Brown as it was about him. He dragged a breath into his lungs. "If you wish." He could wait a few more minutes for his release.

He let her sit up, let her place her hand on his chest and push him back onto the pillows. Her face was shadowed by the fall of her hair.

Two minutes, he told himself. He could wait that long.

Miss Brown bent forward and pressed her mouth to his shoulder.

Marcus closed his eyes. Heat and pleasure rose in him as she traced his collarbone with light kisses, as she tasted the pulse at the base of his throat with her tongue. Soft hair spilled over his chest, tickling.

Miss Brown took his nipple between her teeth, nipping lightly, making his body shiver. She licked his belly. Her mouth moved lower, lower . . .

Marcus opened his eyes and stared up at the shadowy ceiling. Was she going to taste his cock? Anticipation tied itself into a tight knot in his belly. She wasn't a whore, he couldn't expect it of her—

Her fingers lightly touched his erection, halting his ability to think for a moment. "May I?"

His throat was so tight he could barely speak. "If you wish."

He squeezed his eyes shut, clenched the sheet in his hands, willed his body not to move.

Her lips touched the head of his cock. Marcus stopped breathing. He lay motionless, trembling. And then, he felt her tongue. A groan came from his throat.

Miss Brown explored with her tongue, hesitantly at first, and then more boldly, learning his shape. Arousal pulsed through Marcus, growing more urgent. When she took him into her mouth it took all his self-control to hold still, to stop his hips from bucking off the bed.

Marcus inhaled a shuddering breath. Women had pleasured

him like this before. The expensive courtesans whose services he'd used before his marriage had sucked him expertly, had brought him to climax—but it had never felt so intimate as it did now, so erotic.

Finally, Marcus could bear it no longer. The heat of Miss Brown's mouth, the caress of her tongue, were driving him wild. His cock ached to be inside her. "Enough," he said, hoarsely.

He rolled her beneath him, settled between her legs, bent his head to kiss her, and thrust deeply into her.

He'd needed to be inside her so much that he closed his eyes and held on to the moment, motionless, drinking in the sensations: the heat, the delicious tightness, the beginnings of an orgasm rippling through her—and then he opened his eyes and took hold of her hips and eased into a slow rhythm. Miss Brown climaxed almost immediately, her fingers gripping his arms, a cry coming from her lips. Marcus gritted his teeth and held on to his self-control; he wanted this to last.

Time slowed. Reality faded. He was unaware of the hotel room, unaware of the bed. His universe narrowed to Miss Brown and the exquisite pleasure of being inside her, the exquisite pleasure of each deep thrust, the exquisite pleasure of her body moving beneath him as she climaxed again. His arousal spiraled tighter and tighter until it felt as if his skin would burst from the pressure—then the orgasm engulfed him, pulsing through him in vast, endless waves.

Reality slowly returned: the bed with its plain hangings, the folded screen in the corner, his clothes piled on the table. He gathered Miss Brown in his arms and rolled onto his side, but he didn't withdraw from her body; he wanted to stay inside her as long as possible. He felt her warm breath against his skin, felt her heartbeat.

Miss Brown didn't try to pull away. She lay relaxed in his embrace. *She trusts me. She feels safe with me.* The thought made his throat tighten.

His skin gradually cooled. Miss Brown shivered when he released her, when he withdrew from her body. Marcus pulled the
covers up over her shoulders. He was as hungry as he'd been
that morning. Ravenous. "Shall I send for food?"

Miss Brown's expression became anxious. "I'd rather not,
sir. If you don't mind."

"Of course." He mentally kicked himself. Miss Brown had a
position in a respectable household. She wouldn't want anyone—even a servant—to witness what was clearly a sexual
liaison.

They dressed in front of the small fireplace. Marcus fastened
Miss Brown's gown. The nape of her neck tempted him. He
wanted to press his lips to her skin, inhale her scent, taste her.

His fingers slowed as he did up the buttons. He'd been more
intimate with Miss Brown than he'd been with any other woman, but he didn't know her name. She'd held his cock in her
mouth, he'd tasted her with his tongue—and yet they were still
Lord Cosgrove and Miss Brown to each other.

A sense of wrongness grew inside him as he pulled on his
boots. He and Miss Brown were too intimate for *Sir* and *Miss*.

But knowing her name would alter their relationship, take it
from tryst with a stranger to something more personal. Did he
want personal? While she was Miss Brown, he could walk
away, never see her again, forget about her.

Marcus uttered a silent snort. Who was he trying to fool? He
couldn't walk away from Miss Brown. He wanted to visit her
again. Wanted to kiss her again. Taste her. Bed her.

Marcus cleared his throat, and took a deep breath. "Miss
Brown . . . will you please tell me your Christian name?"

Miss Brown's eyes lost their smile, became wary. "My
name?"

"Yes." He felt gauche and awkward, a callow youth, not a

man of thirty-one. "Mine is Marcus. I'd like it if you used it."

Miss Brown hesitated. She moistened her lips. "My name is Charlotte."

"Your real name?"

She nodded.

It felt significant to know her name, as if they were no longer strangers, but lovers. Significant—and disconcerting.

Marcus picked up his coat and shrugged into it. Had he done the right thing, asking for her name, giving his? "May I see you tomorrow evening?"

"If you wish."

I do. He didn't want to leave now. If he weren't so hungry he'd take her back to bed and spend the evening with her.

"Tomorrow I'll bring a picnic," he said. "Would you like that?"

A smile lit her face. "Yes."

Marcus picked up his hat and gloves from the table. He wanted to kiss her, to lay a tender goodnight upon her lips.

The tenderness disturbed him. Lust, he was fine with. Desire, he was fine with. But tenderness was dangerous. Tenderness was a precursor to love, and he didn't want to love her. He took a step back, away from her. "Good night, Charlotte."

"Good night."

He walked to the door.

"Sir . . . Marcus, please be careful. Don't walk home. Take a hackney."

Reality impinged. From the moment he'd first kissed her this evening, he'd not thought of the Smiths, or Phillip, or the letters. "I'll be fine."

Miss Brown crossed to him, anxiety creasing her brow. "It's not safe for you to walk alone." She laid her hand lightly on his arm. "Please."

Marcus grunted a laugh. She reminded him of Albin. "I'll

take a hackney. I promise."

Her face relaxed. "Thank you, sir."

"Marcus."

She bit her lip and lowered her gaze, blushed. "Marcus."

He gave in to temptation, took her chin in his hand, and kissed her. Her lips were soft, warm, sweet.

Tenderness is dangerous.

Marcus released her. He jammed his hat on his head and opened the door. "Good night."

CHAPTER THIRTY-FOUR

October 26th, 1805
Grosvenor Square, London

ALBIN WAS SLIDING a ledger from the bookcase when Marcus entered the study. "Put that back. We're heading out."

"Where to, sir?"

"Phillip's." Marcus glanced at the clock. A few minutes past eight. Phillip wouldn't be sober at this hour of the morning, but he might still be awake.

The lad shoved the ledger back. "Shall I be a dog again, sir? I might smell the Smiths. It would prove he had dealings with them."

I don't need proof; I know it was him. Marcus shrugged. "If you wish. But I should warn you, I intend to walk there."

Albin bent to pull off his top boots. "Perhaps it would be wise to take a pistol, sir."

Marcus patted his pocket. "Ahead of you, lad."

IT WAS THE better part of a mile to Upper Rathbone Place, where Phillip had his lodgings. The sky was an ominous pewter gray, promising snow.

Marcus tried to plan as he walked. Phillip first. Then, the letters.

Brashdon was behind the letters. If he could gain entry to Brashdon's house and search the place, he knew he'd find proof.

But with his reputation so badly damaged, was searching Brashdon's a risk he dared take? If he were caught . . .

He turned into Rathbone Place, the black spaniel trotting at his heels. The street narrowed, the tall houses funneling the wind. Marcus turned up the collar of his greatcoat.

Phillip lodged opposite the small, dark-stoned Percy Chapel. Albin set to work sniffing the steps, sniffing the door.

A knife grinder was making a circuit of Upper Rathbone Place. "Knives or scissors to grind today?" he cried.

Marcus watched the man broodingly. How to gain entry to Brashdon's house?

"Do you smell the Smiths?" he asked, turning back to Albin. He blinked. The spaniel was now a large brindled mastiff. He didn't need to wonder why: *To protect me.*

The mastiff shook its head.

"I have a pistol." *I'm not helpless.* "Change back."

Albin didn't obey. He stayed as he was, a mastiff.

"Fuck," Marcus said, under his breath. He scowled at Albin, climbed the steps, and rapped sharply on the door.

The middle-aged maid who opened the door recognized him, but she didn't bob a curtsy and invite him inside. Her eyebrows pinched together in a frown. "Mr. Langford is behind with his rent, sir. Master wants him out by tomorrow."

Marcus looked down his nose at her. "I beg your pardon?"

A flush mounted in the woman's cheeks. "Mr. Langford ain't paid—"

"That will do, Jenny!" Honeymay, the retired valet who owned the building, hurried up behind her. "Enough! Cook needs you in the kitchen."

The maid pressed her lips together. "Don't let that dog in the house," she said, and departed, a flounce in her step.

"I beg your pardon, Lord Cosgrove. Please come in. Please come in." Honeymay punctuated each sentence with an agitated bow.

Marcus held on to his anger a moment longer—sharp, hot—and then made a conscious effort to let it go, leaving it on the doorstep as he stepped inside. Honeymay didn't deserve his anger. Even Albin, despite his disobedience, didn't.

"I beg your pardon for Jenny's behavior, sir," Honeymay said, pink-cheeked, flustered. "She's got it into her head that I need looking after and she sometimes steps above herself. But she means no harm, sir."

Marcus glanced sourly at the mastiff. *I have the same problem.* He removed his hat. "Mr. Langford is giving you trouble?"

"You could say so, sir," Honeymay said. He looked at the mastiff, but made no protest.

"He hasn't paid his rent?"

"No, sir. Not for several weeks now."

"Did he tell you I'd pay it?"

"No, sir. He said you'd . . ." Mr. Honeymay became even pinker. "What he said isn't for repeating, sir."

"I'm sure it isn't. Is he in? I'd like a word with him."

"Yes, sir. Mr. Langford didn't go out last night. Or the night before."

"He didn't?" That was unusual.

They climbed the stairs, Honeymay, himself, the mastiff. Honeymay knocked on Phillip's door. After a moment he knocked a second time, more loudly.

"Where's his man?"

"He left several days ago, sir." Honeymay took a bunch of keys from his pocket and inserted one into the lock. "Said he hadn't been paid and he wasn't about to give his service for free." He knocked once more and swung the door open.

The room released a foul exhalation of air. Marcus recoiled

from the stink of gin, the stink of vomit, the stink of shit.

"Oh, dear me," Honeymay said faintly.

Marcus pulled a handkerchief from his pocket and pressed it to his nose. The mastiff pushed past him, entering the darkened room.

Marcus followed. He threw open the curtains and heaved up the window, letting cold air gust in, and then turned and surveyed the room, the handkerchief still pressed to his nose.

In the absence of his manservant, Phillip hadn't bothered to tidy up after himself. Clothing littered the room—hats, gloves, a greatcoat, neckcloths. A half-eaten meal sat on the table. The tankard alongside had tipped over.

Phillip had clearly spent some time drinking beside the fireplace; several gin bottles lay on the floor. There was vomit on the rug, vomit on the armchair, even vomit in the grate.

Marcus crossed to the open doorway to the bedchamber. The stench emanating from it was even worse. Behind him, Honeymay articulated his dismay: "Oh, dear me. Dear me."

Marcus pressed the handkerchief more firmly to his nose and entered, jerked the curtains wide, flung the window open.

There were gin bottles here, too, and vomit, and several days' worth of clothing on the floor. The chamber pot was full. Phillip hadn't bothered to empty it; he'd let it overflow.

The bed was a filthy nest of twisted sheets. Phillip lay on it, half-naked and unshaven. His snores were snuffling, grunting. A pig in his sty.

"Phillip."

Phillip kept snoring.

Marcus reached down and gripped his shoulder, shook him. "Phillip!"

It took almost a minute to rouse him. At last, Phillip squinted open his eyes. "Wha'?"

The slurred voice, the bloodshot eyes, the gin fumes, told him

Phillip was still drunk. *Good. I may get an honest answer.* "I've come about the Smiths."

"Wha'?" Phillip blinked and focused. "You." His face twisted into an expression of loathing.

"Yes, me," Marcus said grimly. "You and I need to talk. About the Smiths."

"Smiths? What Smiths?"

"The Smiths you hired."

"Hired? I haven't hired anyone." Phillip fumbled among the sheets and found a gin bottle. "Norton left me. Took my watch and all my fobs, damn his eyes. And my best coat. Said I owed him."

"I imagine you did."

Phillip opened the bottle and emptied what gin was left down his throat. "Go away. Leave me alone."

"With pleasure."

Marcus retreated to the sitting room, where Honeymay stood wringing his hands. "I apologize for Mr. Langford." He pulled several folded banknotes from his pocket. "I'll be back shortly to remove him. If you could have someone clean up the vomit and the chamber pot, I would be extremely grateful, but please don't touch anything else until my secretary and I have gone through Mr. Langford's papers." He unfolded a banknote. "How much does he owe you in rent?"

Marcus trebled the amount Mr. Honeymay stated; cleaning the rooms, making them habitable again, wouldn't be cheap. He was conscious of Albin exploring the sitting room, sniffing the furniture. From the bedroom came the sound of snoring. "I apologize," he said again. "I didn't realize matters had come to such a pass."

"Thank you, sir," Honeymay said, clutching the banknotes. "You're most generous." He escorted Marcus downstairs. As the door closed, Marcus heard him call for the maid, Jenny.

Marcus grimaced; she had a foul task ahead of her.

"ARE YOU GOING to bring Mr. Langford here?" Albin asked, pulling on his breeches.

"Heaven forbid." Marcus crossed to the brandy decanter, reached for a glass—and hesitated. Memory of Phillip intruded: the stench, the squalor.

He'd been drinking more heavily the past year and a half. Nowhere near as heavily as Phillip, but even so . . .

Marcus put the glass down. "I'll send him to his mother until I decide what to do with him. He can't stay in London. He's incapable of looking after himself, the state he's in."

Albin shrugged into his shirt. "I don't think the Smiths had been there, sir . . . but it was hard to smell anything." His nose wrinkled.

Marcus grunted. He leaned against the sideboard. "Let that be a lesson to you, lad; drink too much and it'll ruin you."

Albin buttoned his waistcoat. He reached for his neckcloth. "What now, sir?"

"Now? Now we go back to Rathbone Place, pack Phillip off to Derbyshire, and search his rooms." Marcus straightened away from the sideboard. "Give me that neckcloth. I'll tie it."

SHORTLY BEFORE ELEVEN o'clock, Phillip was carried from his room in a snoring stupor. Tiny snowflakes drifted from a gray sky. The water in the puddles was congealing into ice.

"He'll likely kick up a fuss when he wakes," Marcus told the two footmen he'd chosen to accompany Phillip. "If it helps to keep him half-sprung, do it—but make sure he's sober by the time you reach Derbyshire."

"Yes, sir."

"You'll need to clean him up before his mother sees him. There's a change of clothing in the valise, and more in the trunk. Mrs. Langford will undoubtedly be upset. Give her my message and tell her I'll be up as soon as I can."

"Yes, sir."

"Keep your wits about you . . . and if he should mention anything about anyone named Smith, make note of it."

Marcus watched the post-chaise depart. The footmen hadn't a pleasant journey ahead of them. *It should be me taking him home.* He owed Phillip's mother that courtesy.

The carriage turned the corner and disappeared from sight.

Marcus climbed the stairs to Phillip's rooms two at a time. Once he'd exposed the letter-writer, he'd post up to Derbyshire, talk with Mrs. Langford, see if anything could be retrieved from this mess.

Albin was where he'd left him, going through the drawers of Phillip's escritoire, putting everything in a leather satchel.

"Honeymay?"

Albin nodded in the direction of the bedroom.

He found Honeymay staring dolefully at the soiled bed. "Please direct anyone who wants payment from Mr. Langford to Grosvenor Square." He handed the man his card. "Mr. Albin will settle any outstanding bills."

"Yes, sir."

The vomit and the overflowing chamber pot were gone, but their stench remained, filling his nose and mouth with each breath. "Have I reimbursed you sufficiently, Mr. Honeymay?"

"Oh, yes, sir," Honeymay said, a smile wreathing his face. "You're been most generous."

Marcus nodded. "My apologies once again for the trouble Mr. Langford has caused you." He strode back into the sitting room. "Do you have everything, lad?"

"Yes, sir."

"Let's be off."

On the doorstop, Marcus inhaled deeply, clearing the stink from his lungs. Specks of snow drifted down, stingingly cold on his face, stingingly cold on his tongue.

One problem dealt with.

No, only part of one problem. The fact that Phillip had attempted to murder him still remained.

Marcus trod down the steps to the street. Percy Chapel drew his gaze—small, built of dark stone, reminding him that the first anniversary of Lavinia's death was only a few days away. How did one mark such an event?

Marcus's footsteps slowed.

How could he be relieved that Lavinia was gone from his life when it meant she was in her grave?

"Sir?"

Marcus blinked, and saw Albin with the satchel of Phillip's bills and letters.

"Did we forget something, sir?"

He shook himself. "No. Nothing."

CHAPTER THIRTY-FIVE

THE EARL POURED himself a glass of brandy, tipped it back into the decanter without drinking, and rang for a pot of tea.

Charlotte emptied the satchel onto her desk. She sorted through the papers—bills, dunning notices, a handful of letters.

The pot of tea arrived. Cosgrove drank a cup, frowning.

"There's nothing here that links Mr. Langford to the Smiths, sir."

Cosgrove grunted. His frown deepened. He poured himself another cup of tea.

Charlotte shuffled the dunning notices. Bootmaker. Tailor. Hatter. She glanced at Cosgrove. That dark hair, those gray eyes, that tired face. Her heart did its familiar tightening in her chest. "Sir . . . is something wrong?" And then she bit her tongue at the stupidity of her question. Of course something was wrong. The earl's heir was trying to kill him and his political enemies were intent on destroying his reputation.

Cosgrove lowered his teacup. "The anniversary of Lavinia's death is in two days. How would you suggest I mark it? Putting flowers on her grave seems hypocritical, given the state of our relationship."

Charlotte opened her mouth, and then closed it again. She shook her head. "I don't know, sir."

"Neither do I." The earl placed his teacup in its saucer. He

raked his fingers through his hair. "I must discover who wrote
that letter. Until my reputation is restored, I can't remarry—and
I *have* to remarry. I *have* to sire an heir. If anything were to happen to me—" He grimaced. "I have over five thousand acres of
land, hundreds of employees and tenants. It's *my* responsibility
to see that the estates prosper, *my* responsibility to ensure that
everyone's welfare is taken care of. If Phillip were to succeed to
the earldom . . ." He shoved the teacup away, making it rattle in
its saucer. "It doesn't bear thinking of!"

"We'll find the letter-writer, sir."

"How?" Cosgrove pushed to his feet, strode to the window,
and looked out at the square. "I can think of only one way, and
that requires someone to enter Brashdon's house and search it."

Charlotte nodded. She'd come to the same conclusion herself.
"I'll do it, sir."

"No." Cosgrove swung around. "I can't ask that of you."

"I don't mind, sir."

"Well, I do! If you're caught—"

"I won't be caught, sir. No one will see me. I have a . . . an
advantage."

"An advantage." Cosgrove grunted a laugh. "Yes. You do."
His eyes squeezed shut for a moment. "God, I hate this."

Her heart clenched again. *I'll discover who did it, sir. I promise.*

Cosgrove returned to his desk and poured himself another
cup of tea. "It'll be harder to find a wife, after this—even once
I've cleared my name. No smoke without a fire." His voice held
a bitter inflection.

Charlotte looked down at the bill she held. She folded it in
half. Unfolded it. *I don't want him to marry anyone.*

But Cosgrove had to remarry. For the sake of his tenants. For
the sake of his estates.

She folded the bill. Unfolded it. *He'll do it soon.* His wife had been dead almost a year. Once that anniversary was past, he could remarry without censure.

Dead. A year.

She looked up. "Sir, what date did your wife die on?"

"October twenty-eighth."

"And what date was your marriage?"

"April twenty-second, the year before last," Cosgrove said. "Why?"

Excitement prickled through her. "Let me check something, sir . . ." Charlotte hurried to where the ledgers were shelved and took down the latest London accounts. She turned the pages hastily. "The windows were first broken on April twenty-second!"

Cosgrove frowned. "So?"

"So, the Smiths started harassing you on the anniversary of your marriage."

"Coincidence."

She heard whispered words in her ears: . . . *do it now, or wait until* . . .

"Sir, I think they were hired to kill you—not now, but soon—and the anniversary of your wife's death is in a few days."

"Coincidence," Cosgrove said again.

Charlotte closed the ledger. "The twentieth of October, when the conservatory was burned down . . . was that date at all significant in your marriage?"

Cosgrove opened his mouth—and paused, his lips shaped to say *No*. His eyes narrowed.

"It was significant, wasn't it, sir?"

"I asked Lavinia to marry me on October twentieth, three years ago. In the Hazelbrook conservatory."

"They're connected, sir! Your marriage and the vandalism, the attacks. It's not Phillip who hired the Smiths; it's Monkwood!"

The earl's eyes narrowed still further. He was silent for almost a minute. Finally he shrugged, with his eyebrows, with his shoulders. "You could be right."

Charlotte shoved the ledger back into the bookcase. "And the letters? Do you think they could be Monkwood too?"

Cosgrove shook his head. "No."

I do. Charlotte returned to her desk. It wasn't human reasoning that made her think Monkwood was behind the letters; it was what she'd sensed as a dog. Monkwood's hatred. The faint scent on the letter.

But why would Monkwood do such a thing?

She stared at Phillip's bills, turning pieces of information over in her head, trying to make a pattern . . .

"People knew you were divorcing your wife?" She glanced at the earl.

"A few." Cosgrove leaned back in his chair. "I came up to London the day after I found out about the affair, to speak to the Upper House. While I was here, I met with my lawyer, set things in motion for both church and court divorces. I told Grenville and Fox and a few others. They needed to know; it was going to be a scandal, in all the newspapers. If it got too bad, I'd have to step down from the campaign for a while." He grimaced. "When I got back to Hazelbrook, I told Lavinia I was divorcing her."

"And she ran up to the roof and fell off?"

"There were a couple of weeks while she tried to make me change my mind. Tears. Sex. Tantrums." His expression altered, as if he tasted something rancid in his mouth. "When they didn't work . . . the roof."

"Monkwood knew about the divorce?"

"He knew." The earl snorted, a contemptuous sound. "He came down to Hazelbrook for a few days. To support her."

"Were there rumors in London? About the divorce?"

"Grenville said it was all people were talking of."

The pieces fitted together in her head. Lady Cosgrove had been facing social ruin. No longer a countess, but a divorced adulteress, her standing in Society lost. And then, she'd died.

"Sir . . ." Charlotte leaned forward. "Sir, I think Monkwood's trying to punish you for what happened to his sister. He wrote the letters."

"What? Nonsense."

"Public disgrace. And then, death. That's what happened to Lady Cosgrove. That's what's happening to you."

The earl's lips pinched together. He shook his head.

"Think about it, sir."

Cosgrove's lips tightened still further. He thrust to his feet, walked to the window, and stared out at the square.

The ebony and gold clock on the mantelpiece ticked a minute away. Cosgrove was rigid, motionless, a statue silhouetted against the falling snow.

Another minute ticked away. The hour hand crept closer to twelve.

Cosgrove turned and looked at her. His face was sharp-edged and angular, jawbone and cheekbones pushing through his skin. "I *want* it to be Brashdon!"

"I know, sir. But I think it isn't. I think it's Monkwood."

She saw emotions on his face—anger, frustration, denial—then he exhaled, a sharp and hissing sound. The lines of his face became weary, not angry. He leaned against the windowsill. "Very well, Monkwood's house first. If you find no proof he wrote the letters, we'll move on to Brashdon."

"Today?"

Cosgrove's gaze flicked to the clock. "Tomorrow morning. Monkwood's a late riser, takes a good hour to dress, doesn't leave his bedchamber until noon. His study will be empty all morning." He pushed away from the windowsill. "Here, I'll draw a plan of the house."

A footman knocked. "Message from Baron Grenville, sir."

The angularity returned to Cosgrove's face. He took the note, tore it open, read it. "His man's waiting for a reply?"

"Yes, sir."

Cosgrove refolded the note, creasing the lines sharply between his fingers. "Tell him yes."

The footman bowed and withdrew.

Cosgrove met her glance, and answered her unspoken question: "Lunch with Grenville and a number of others. At his club. A public show of solidarity. As long as I can keep my temper."

"Can you, sir?"

His mouth twisted in another grimace. "I've had plenty of practice the last year and a half." He screwed up the note and threw it in the fire. "I'm a cuckold—and impotent, because why else would a young wife have an affair?" His voice was tight, flat. "And depending on what gossip you listen to, I'm either the man who drove his wife to suicide—or murdered her. And now I'm a rapist." The bones of his face were sharp again, pushing through his skin. "Yes, I can keep my temper in public."

Charlotte's ribcage did its familiar squeezing around her heart. The earl didn't deserve this. Any of this. *I'll discover who sent the letters, sir. I promise.*

The longcase clock in the entrance hall struck noon. A second later, the clock on the mantelpiece chimed, too.

Cosgrove glanced down at his clothes. "I need to change." He took two steps towards the door, halted, and turned back. "While I'm gone, can you write out these notes for me?" He opened a drawer in his desk, took out a handful of pages, and spread them for her to see. It was the speech he'd been working on the past few days. The pages were covered in scrawled writing, crossed-out words, slanted annotations. "The paragraphs are a bit out of order. I've numbered them, see? If you could copy them out in the order I want, that would be helpful."

"Of course, sir."

"Good lad." Cosgrove clapped her shoulder and strode from the study.

CHARLOTTE READ THE speech once she'd copied it. It was logical and concise and to the point. No meandering waffle, no extraneous words, no straying arguments. But more than that, it was passionate, powerful. There was fire in the words.

I'd love to see him give this in the Upper House.

But could Cosgrove give it? Would he be listened to—or heckled?

Just after four she heard the earl's voice in the corridor, heard his footsteps. He didn't enter the study.

A housemaid bustled in, lit the candles, closed the shutters, and departed. A while later, the study door opened again. Charlotte looked up. Cosgrove stood in the doorway, a towel in his hand. He'd taken off his coat and neckcloth and waistcoat. His shirt was rolled up at the sleeves, unbuttoned at the neck. The bandage was white around his throat.

"How was your lunch, sir?"

Cosgrove shrugged. He wiped his face with the towel. "Not too bad."

But he'd still needed to use his punching bag.

The earl walked across to his desk. "Excellent, you copied it. What did you think?"

Charlotte blinked. Did he truly want her opinion?

It seemed he did. He was looking at her, waiting for her reply.

"Very good, sir."

Cosgrove shook his head. "Does my argument make sense? Are there places where I can make it stronger?"

Oh. Charlotte blinked again. It wasn't praise he wanted, it was criticism.

"Uh . . . well, there was one place. Let me show you . . ." She crossed to his desk and sorted through the pages. "Here, sir. I think it would be stronger if you combined these two paragraphs. Cut out these sentences and put this one first, followed by these."

Cosgrove read the paragraphs under his breath. Charlotte smelled his sweat, his maleness. The muscles in her stomach tightened. This was how he smelled when he had sex with her.

She wanted to step closer, wanted to push the plackets of his shirt apart and press her face to his chest, inhale his scent, taste the salt on his skin.

Charlotte curled her fingers into her palms and held herself motionless, willed her pego not to stiffen.

"You're right, lad. Thank you."

"You're welcome, sir."

Cosgrove glanced at her, the corners of his eyes creasing in a smile. "You've made more work for yourself. Copy out this page again, please, with those changes."

"Yes, sir." Charlotte took the page and went back to her desk, sat, picked up the quill—and hesitated. "Sir . . ."

"Yes?" Cosgrove rubbed his hair with the towel.

"Your father saw nothing wrong with owning a plantation and having slaves. How is it that your views are so different from his?"

Cosgrove lowered the towel. His hair was damp with sweat, spiky.

"If . . . if it's not too forward a question?"

Cosgrove shook his head. He leaned against his desk. His eyes narrowed, not in anger, but as if he was turning over old memories, sorting through them. "It was that essay," he said after a moment. "The one I asked you to read. By Clarkson. It was originally written in Latin, when he was up at Cambridge. I found a copy in the school library and translated it for the practice." He shrugged. "I was at an impressionable age; it had a strong effect on me."

Not strong: profound.

Cosgrove resumed drying his hair. "In a way, you could say it was my father's fault. I translated that essay because I wanted to win the Latin prize."

Charlotte frowned, not following the logic.

Cosgrove caught the frown. "I was trying to make him notice me."

"Oh." She turned the quill over in her fingers. What did that statement tell her about Cosgrove's relationship with his father? Had the old earl not spent time with his son? Not praised him? Not given him affection? "Did you win the prize, sir?"

"Yes."

"Was your father pleased?"

Cosgrove shrugged again. "Not that he said."

A footman appeared at the door. "Your bath is ready, sir."

"Thank you." Cosgrove pushed away from the desk. "I'll see you tomorrow, lad. Have a good evening."

CHAPTER THIRTY-SIX

MARCUS BROUGHT A covered basket to the Earnoch Hotel. He placed it on the table in the room Miss Brown had hired. Anticipation was taut inside him. He took off his hat, stripped off his gloves. Would tonight's sex be as good as last night's? Or not? He shrugged out of his greatcoat, preparing himself for disappointment. Of course it wouldn't be as good. Nothing could be.

He shook snowflakes from the coat, draped it over the back of a chair, and looked at her.

Miss Brown's gaze had the same impact it had had last night, driving the air from his lungs. He couldn't look away.

Charlotte, he told himself. *Her name's Charlotte.*

The room seemed to hold its breath.

Charlotte took a step towards him.

He met her halfway, captured her face in his hands, kissed her. Her mouth was soft and sweet and eager.

Minutes slipped away while they kissed, while they undressed. Their lovemaking was unhurried—touching, tasting, drawing pleasure from each other's bodies. Marcus's climax was as intense as it had been yesterday evening.

He rolled so that Charlotte lay on top of him, her head pillowed on his shoulder. He smoothed a hand down her back and over the curve of one buttock, delighting in the softness of her skin, the beautiful womanliness of her shape. Each time they made love she was a little less shy, a little more confident. In a few days, he'd suggest they try making love like this: her on top of him.

He stroked his fingers down her back again. The connection that had been forged between them last night, the trust and the intimacy, was still there. *I could grow used to this.* Charlotte in his bed every night.

Sex with her was better than sex with Lavinia had been. She didn't have Lavinia's slender fragility. He didn't have to hold himself in check, didn't have to fear he might accidentally hurt her. And after yesterday, he wasn't afraid he might shock her. He'd been more intimate with Charlotte than he'd dared be with any woman.

And yet, I know nothing about her.

Marcus's hand stilled in its stroking. His contentment wavered slightly.

"I brought a picnic," he said. "Are you hungry?"

THEY SAT ON the rug in front of the fireplace, cross-legged like Turks, wrapped in sheets. Outside it was cold and dark, snowing; inside was warmth, firelight and candlelight, quiet intimacy. Marcus unpacked the basket. Game pie, faintly warm, with a flaking golden crust. Sweet pastries sprinkled with sugar crystals. Plump grapes from his succession houses, their skins glossily black, ripe almost to bursting. A cool, fizzing bottle of champagne. Gilt-edged plates and silver cutlery and crystal glasses.

"And they feasted like kings," Charlotte said.

Marcus grunted a laugh, and then blinked. Had she said that in Latin? "Where's that from? Virgil?"

She nodded.

They talked of Greek philosophers and Roman poets while

they ate. Charlotte was far better educated than he'd expected. The breadth of her knowledge astonished him.

Marcus sipped his champagne and watched as she ate a grape. Her hair hung down her back. She reached for her glass, the sheet slipping off one smooth shoulder.

I want this every night. The intimacy, the companionship.

"Charlotte . . ."

She glanced at him, her eyebrows lifted in question.

"Would you . . ." How to phrase his question without destroying the fragile trust between them? "Please, will you tell me a little about yourself?"

Charlotte didn't move on the rug, but it seemed as if she drew back, as if there was suddenly more distance between them.

"Not your surname," Marcus said hastily. "Or who your employer is, but . . ." *I need to know more about you.* "Please. I know nothing about you."

Charlotte was silent for a long moment, her eyes on his face. "What would you like to know?"

Everything. "Where are you from? Which county?"

A long pause. "I grew up in Yorkshire."

And? He bit his tongue to keep the word in his mouth.

The silence between them lengthened. Charlotte put the glass down on the hearth. "My father was a scholar. He was meant to be a soldier—my grandfather was in the army, and his father before him—but he had an accident when he was fourteen, fell off his horse, broke his leg badly. It took him years to recover." She was talking to the fireplace, not him; her gaze was on the flames, on the glowing coals. "After that, it was decided the army wouldn't be suitable for him."

A military family. Marcus filed away the information.

"Father always said study suited him better than soldiering ever would have. He loved to wrestle with Greek translations. He said it stretched his mind."

"Where did he study?"

"Cambridge. He took two Firsts."

Marcus filed that information away, too. "And your mother?"

Charlotte's gaze moved to him. She bit her lip, clearly considering how much to tell him. "She was a baronet's daughter," she said finally. "They had to wait until she was twenty-one to marry; her father wouldn't give consent."

Charlotte was a baronet's granddaughter? Marcus managed to conceal his surprise. "Why?" he asked. "Because your father wasn't well-born enough?"

She shook her head. "His breeding was well enough; he was the son of a general."

Marcus blinked. "A general? Which one?"

Her expression told him that he'd asked too close a question.

"I beg your pardon," Marcus said, trying to retrieve his position. "Er . . . why did her father disapprove of the match?"

"Because my grandfather wasn't wealthy. Generals may be good at strategy and tactics, but they're not always prudent with money."

"Ah, money."

"Yes." Her mouth twisted. "Money."

"But they married?"

"Yes."

"And moved to Yorkshire?"

"Father wanted somewhere quiet to work on his translation of the *Iliad*, so they took the lease on a house on the edge of the moors." She reached for her glass, as if that was the end of the conversation.

Marcus searched hurriedly for another question to keep her talking. "Do you have brothers and sisters?"

Charlotte shook her head.

"You must have been lonely." Marcus thought back to his own childhood. Without Barnaby, he'd have been wretchedly miserable.

"Oh, no!" A smile lit her face. "Mother said that Father could stretch his mind all morning if he wished, but he had to stretch his lungs and his legs in the afternoon. We went all over the moors. And if the weather was bad, we stayed indoors and played at theatrics." Charlotte paused, as if listening to what she'd said. Her brow creased slightly. "It must sound very dull to you, but I assure you it wasn't. We had fun, we laughed a lot."

"Your parents schooled you?"

"Father taught me Latin and Greek and mathematics, Mother taught me French and music."

There was a flat, slightly bitter taste on Marcus's tongue: envy. Charlotte's childhood had been very different from his. Her parents had been her companions, her teachers, her friends. They'd had fun together. Laughed together.

Fun. Laughter.

His relationship with his parents had been too formal for fun and laughter, too distant. He'd been brought up by nursemaids and tutors, sent away to school as soon as he was judged old enough.

The taste of envy became stronger on his tongue. Marcus drank some champagne to wash it away.

When I have children, I'll laugh with them, play with them. I'll give them the kind of childhood Charlotte had. The words had the weight of a vow, an oath. Marcus drank another mouthful of champagne to seal the promise. His glass clinked slightly when he placed it on the hearth. "Did your father publish his translation of the *Iliad*?" The words were out of his mouth before he realized it was too probing a question. If she said yes, it would be easy to discover her father's name, to learn her true identity.

Charlotte shook her head. "He died before it was completed."

"I'm sorry."

She looked away from him and shrugged lightly. "It was eight years ago." But her tone didn't quite match that light shrug. Her father's death still hurt.

"Your mother . . . ?"

"She died when I was twelve."

"Ah." So Charlotte had been an orphan for some time. Alone in the world. "You had relatives? People to take you in?"

"My uncle's family." Charlotte's voice flattened slightly.

Marcus picked up his glass and sipped from it. Questions rose on his tongue. Should he be blunt? Delicate? Circuitously roundabout?

He decided to be blunt. "You don't like them. Your uncle's family."

She glanced at him. Her mouth was rueful. "Is it so obvious, sir?"

He let the *sir* slide; now wasn't the time to interrupt the reminiscent mood. "What did they do?" They had to have done something, or Charlotte wouldn't be in London earning her living.

"Oh . . ." She shrugged. "It was several things."

"Such as?"

Charlotte looked down at the grapes on her plate. He saw a hint of a frown on her brow.

Marcus waited.

Charlotte removed the grapes from their stems. "They did one thing that I couldn't forgive them for. Well, two things—" She pulled a face. "But one in particular. It . . . poisoned how I felt about them."

"What was it?"

Charlotte arranged the grapes in a straight line, not looking at him. "My mother had a small annuity. She saved money from it every year and put it aside for my coming out." A grape rolled on the plate. Charlotte captured it, returning it to its place. "My parents met during my mother's first Season and they always said that if I had a Season, I should meet someone." She shrugged, still not looking at him.

"But you never had a Season," Marcus guessed.

She glanced up at him. "My aunt said I would. She made that promise to Father, when he was dying."

"But she didn't keep it?"

Charlotte shook her head. "No. First she said I should wait until my cousin came out, that it made sense to combine both, but then she said it wasn't fair on my cousin to share her début, that I should wait, and then . . . then she said that the cost of having me in the household had used up all the money my parents had put aside." Her eyebrows pinched together. "But I tutored the boys before they went to Rugby. I was the girls' governess until they came out. If I hadn't been there, my uncle would have had to pay for a tutor *and* a governess. How could it have cost my aunt all my coming-out money to keep me at the Hall?"

"It didn't," Marcus said. Anger simmered beneath his breastbone. "They sound like despicable, nipcheese people!"

"Nipcheese?" Charlotte's frown vanished. She laughed. "No. My uncle isn't nipcheese. He's very wealthy."

"Wealthy? Then why—"

"Because there was ill-feeling between him and Father." She looked down at the grapes again and began to rearrange them. "My uncle bought a plantation in the West Indies many years ago and Father told him that owning slaves was immoral and that he ought to be ashamed of himself. They had a dreadful row. When Mother died, my uncle wouldn't even come to her funeral." The line of grapes had become a lopsided circle. "So it's only natural that my uncle and aunt weren't happy that they had to take me in."

"Their argument with your father doesn't excuse their breaking their promise to him!"

"I know." Charlotte examined the crooked circle of grapes on her plate and moved one slightly with a fingertip. "But I also know that if I'd had a Season I probably wouldn't have contracted a match. My looks are ordinary and my dowry extremely modest." She shrugged, as if this was a fact she'd accepted long ago. "I wouldn't be upset about not having a début, except . . ." Her lips pressed together. She met his eyes. "It was what my parents wanted. It was their dream. They *saved* for it. And my aunt and uncle took their money and just . . ." She made a gesture with her hand, as if throwing something away. "I can't forgive them for that, which is ungrateful of me; they gave me a home when Father died."

Marcus shook his head. "You owe them no gratitude." He swallowed the last of his champagne in a gulp. It didn't douse the anger smoldering in his chest.

Charlotte smiled slightly, and shrugged again. "That's debatable. I think I probably do."

"And the second thing?"

"Second thing?"

"You said there were two things you couldn't forgive them for."

"Oh." She pulled a face. "They called me Charity, not Charlotte."

"They what?" Marcus put his glass down on the hearth with a sharp *clunk*. "No wonder you left them!"

"Finally, yes." She looked at her plate and moved another grape. The circle was almost perfect. "For years I was too afraid to. My uncle said that if I left, he'd wash his hands of me, I wouldn't be welcome back." Charlotte pushed away the plate. The grapes rolled, the circle was broken. "I knew I could find a position as a governess, but I was worried something would happen—I'd become ill or be turned off, and end up dying in a poorhouse. So I stayed at West—" She flicked a glance at him. "At my uncle's."

Her uncle's seat started with *West*. Marcus tucked that information away, too. "What made you change your mind?"

"My twenty-fifth birthday. I couldn't face living the rest of my life there. So . . . I left."

Marcus studied her face, trying to imagine how she'd felt. "You have a lot of courage."

Charlotte shook her head. "I'm not brave."

You're very brave. "You found a good position?"

"Yes." A smile lit her face again, shone in her eyes. "Better than I ever hoped for. A thousand times better!"

Marcus laughed at this exaggeration. Some of his rage slipped away, but the rest of it still smoldered in his belly. "You have a good employer?"

She nodded. "My employer is very kind. Very generous."

"A paragon," he said, allowing himself to be amused.

Charlotte shook her head. "Definitely not a paragon. But kind and patient and good-hearted."

Marcus sipped his champagne, mentally reviewing the residents of Grosvenor Square. Who among them could be described as kind, generous, patient, and good-hearted?

"I know I made the right decision leaving my aunt and uncle. Even if something should happen . . . if I should lose my position—"

"I promise you'll never end up in the poorhouse." Marcus lowered his glass. "Never."

Charlotte smiled. "Thank you, sir, but no one can know—"

"I can," Marcus said, his voice emphatic. "Charlotte, I'm extremely wealthy. Believe me when I say that you will *never* end up in the poorhouse."

She lost her smile. "I don't want your money, sir."

"Marcus."

A faint flush rose in her cheeks. "Thank you, Marcus, but I don't want your money." The set of her chin, the set of her mouth, were stubborn.

"I won't even notice it's gone," he said, exasperated. Lavinia had always coaxed him for money; Charlotte was refusing it. The irony should have made him laugh. Instead, he wanted to shake her.

"I still don't want it."

Marcus closed his eyes for a moment. He didn't want to argue with Charlotte. What he wanted was to give her things. Money. Security. A safe home.

He opened his eyes and gazed at her. The brown hair. The freckles across her nose and cheeks. The shadowed hollow at the base of her throat where her pulse beat.

He felt the same need to protect her, the same need to make her world safe, that he'd had with Lavinia. It was visceral, in his organs, in his blood, something he had no control over.

For a brief moment, Marcus considered marriage—and just as swiftly rejected it. He didn't want to marry Charlotte. Of course he didn't. He'd only spent a few hours in her company. She stirred strong emotions in him, but she was little more than a stranger.

And besides, marriage wasn't the only way he could protect Charlotte.

Marcus reached out and took hold of her hand. "What would you say if I bought a house in your name? You could live there. We wouldn't have to meet at a hotel."

Charlotte became very still, like a doe caught grazing in clearing. She didn't seem to breathe, didn't seem to blink. After a moment, she swallowed. "Sir . . . Marcus . . . are you asking me to be your mistress?"

Am I?

He enjoyed bedding her, but what he felt for Charlotte went beyond that. There was the dangerous tenderness. The protectiveness. He hovered on the brink of loving her—and if he wasn't careful, he'd fall over the edge.

But would it be so terrible? To have a mistress he loved? Someone whose company smoothed the sharp edges of each day. A woman he could relax with, could talk and laugh with, not merely have sex with.

Marcus took a deep breath. "Yes. I am."

CHAPTER THIRTY-SEVEN

COSGROVE'S MISTRESS. CHARLOTTE'S imagination took flight, telling her what that would be like. Not just a few stolen hours in a hired room, but whole evenings, whole nights, in a house that was theirs alone.

But only on the evenings Cosgrove was free, only the nights he wasn't engaged elsewhere. Perhaps there'd be the occasional lazy morning, the occasional snatched afternoon, but never full days. The earl had a busy life, and she'd be separate from it. He'd visit when it was convenient, when he felt the need for her. Otherwise, she'd be alone. Waiting for him.

I'd be Ophelia. Slowly going mad.

But it was tempting. So very tempting.

Charlotte stared at him. The black hair, the gray eyes, the strong face. A man of staunch principles, who wasn't afraid to fight for what he believed was right. A man who made her laugh. Who made her love him.

What should I choose?

If she accepted Cosgrove's offer, she could no longer be Albin. The earl would expect to find her home whenever he visited: day or night. She could be his secretary, or his mistress, but not both.

Which did she want? Working with Cosgrove, helping him fight his battles? Or the intense pleasure of sharing his bed,

when the world retreated and it was just the two of them—
candlelight and shadows and intimacy?

I want both.

She tried to swallow, but the muscles in her throat were too
tight. "And when you marry again?"

"It will be a marriage of convenience. It wouldn't alter our
arrangement."

Perhaps not for you, but for me it would.

She couldn't share Cosgrove's bed if he had a wife.

The decision became clearer. This wasn't a choice between
mistress or secretary; it was a choice between mistress for a
short time, or secretary for a long time.

Put like that, it was easy to choose.

Charlotte removed her hand from his clasp. "Thank you, sir.
Marcus. But I . . ." She searched for an excuse. "I can't leave my
position."

His eyebrows drew together. "Your job means that much to
you?"

My employer does. "I came to London to earn my living. I
don't wish to be dependent on anyone ever again."

"You wouldn't be dependent on me. The house would be in
your name. It would be yours should we decide to terminate our
relationship."

Charlotte shook her head.

"You wouldn't need to work again."

That's what I'm afraid of. She shook her head again. "I'm
sorry, sir."

Cosgrove stared at her, his mouth tight, as if her refusal was
more important than she'd thought.

"If . . . if we could just continue as we are? Until you marry?"

"No," he said. "From now on I'll pay. You can't tell me you
earn enough to hire a hotel room each night."

Charlotte bit her lip. She looked down at the rug, plucked at a tuft of wool. Five nights had considerably eaten into the money Cosgrove had advanced her.

"I'll hire a set of rooms. Will you accept that much?"

She glanced at him, and nodded.

His mouth was still tight, his cheekbones and jaw sharp. *He's displeased. He wanted me as his mistress.*

"I'm sorry," Charlotte said. "I've made you angry."

Cosgrove's face lost its angularity. "No. Don't apologize. It was presumptuous of me. It's I who should be begging your pardon. Forgive me." He took her hand again and pressed his mouth to her palm.

Charlotte's heart seemed to turn upside down in her chest, like a carriage tipping over.

His eyes caught hers. "Shall we?"

Charlotte let him pull her to her feet, let him lead her to the bed.

The earl smoothed strands of hair back from her face, and bent his head and kissed her. The tenderness of his mouth made her close her eyes, made her want to change her mind and accept his offer.

Charlotte opened her eyes. Cosgrove's face filled her vision, strong-boned, beloved. *I love you, sir, but I can't be your mistress.*

She'd made her choice. Albin, not Charlotte.

CHAPTER THIRTY-EIGHT

October 27th, 1805
Grosvenor Square, London

ALBIN LEANED OVER the desk, studying the sketch of Monk-wood's house.

"Well?"

"The study looks easy to find, sir."

Marcus glanced at the ebony and gold clock on the mantel-piece. Half past eight. Monkwood would still be abed. "Let's do it."

He locked the door and went to look out the window, giving the lad privacy while he stripped. The rustle of clothes being removed, the knowledge that Albin was preparing to change shape, didn't make his skin crawl today. It seemed almost normal.

How quickly we accustom ourselves to the extraordinary.

Outside, snow drifted gently down. Marcus's thoughts slid to Charlotte. His hands clenched on the windowsill.

What would her answer have been if he'd offered marriage instead of a *carte-blanche*? Would she have accepted? Or refused?

He had to remarry. It was his duty. He wanted a marriage of convenience this time, more friendly than his parents' cold, formal marriage had been, but businesslike nonetheless. A cordial relationship with a woman for whom he felt a degree of respect and affection. A sensible woman. A woman who wouldn't indulge in histrionics or *affaires*. A woman with whom he'd have careful, amicable sex.

That was what he wanted—what he *knew* he wanted—and yet part of him wished for more. Wished for laughter and friendship and love. Wished for the kind of sex he'd been having with Charlotte. Passionate sex. Intimate sex.

If I asked Charlotte to marry me, would she say yes?

The expression in her eyes when they lay together . . . He could almost believe she loved him.

Marcus scowled at the snowy square. He wanted to protect Charlotte, wanted to give her a home and financial security. But marry her? He barely knew her. A few hours' acquaintance, a few orgasms. It wasn't enough to base so important a decision on.

Damn it. He didn't want to lose Charlotte. If only she'd agree to—

"I'm ready, sir."

He half-turned. "Let's be off, then."

"You don't need to come, sir."

"I'm coming."

"But it's snowing, sir—"

"I'm coming," Marcus said again, an edge of irritation in his voice. He wasn't going to sit in his study, safe and warm, while Albin risked his neck for him.

He opened the window. The sill was an inch deep in snow. "Out you go."

A SHAGGY WHITE dog met him in the middle of Grosvenor Square. "Are you warm enough?" Marcus asked. He wore top boots, a greatcoat, gloves, a muffler, a hat, whereas Albin was essentially naked.

The dog wagged its plumy tail. Marcus took that to mean *Yes*.

Grosvenor Square was shrouded in white. It felt as if the tall houses had emptied overnight and he was the last person left. Marcus strode through the square and along Brook Street. The only sound was the *squick squick* of his boots in the snow, the only other creature the white dog loping alongside him. Snowflakes spun gently in the air, landing on his face like light, stingingly cold kisses.

At Hanover Square, he halted. "You remember which is his study?"

The dog nodded.

Marcus looked across at Monkwood's house. His eyes fastened on the second row of windows, scanned to the right—one, two, three—and halted. Monkwood's study. Where he and Monkwood had discussed marriage settlements.

He looked away, and focused on the dog.

"I'll come through the square every five minutes." Marcus dug in his pocket for the stone he'd brought. It was almondlike in his hand, small and oval. "Here."

Albin took the stone gently in his mouth.

"Be careful."

Albin wagged his tail.

Marcus watched the dog trot purposefully across the square. Frustration surged inside him. *It should be me.* Instead, he was letting Albin take the risks.

He scowled down at the snow, kicked it. When he looked up, he couldn't see the dog.

Marcus walked briskly around the square, his gaze on Monkwood's house. Was that a bird flying up from the snow-covered ground? Was that a monkey crouched on the windowsill, breaking a pane of glass?

The ghost of a breeze blew snowflakes into his face. By the time he'd blinked them away, the shape on the windowsill was gone.

Marcus quickened his pace, his gaze riveted on the study window. He was fifty yards away now, thirty yards, twenty . . . Close enough to see that the lowest pane of glass was missing.

Albin was inside.

CHARLOTTE ARRANGED THE glass on the floor so that it looked like an act of vandalism: a stone thrown from the square, a broken windowpane. She rose from her crouch and glanced around. Desk. Fireplace. Armchairs. Bookcases, some of them glazed, reflecting Albin's naked image back at her. The study didn't have the lived-in feel Cosgrove's did. There were no papers on the desk, no ledgers lying open, no ink-stained quills.

Charlotte tiptoed to the desk, aware that servants were busy in the house even if Monkwood still slept. She eased open the top left-hand drawer and rifled through its contents—receipts—while her ears strained to hear footsteps in the corridor. *A mouse,* she told herself. *If anyone comes, I become a mouse.* But the only sound was the ticking of the clock on the mantelpiece.

An icy breeze crept in through the broken window. Charlotte shivered and opened the next two drawers, finding sheets of paper, unused quills and a penknife for trimming them, bottles of ink, sealing wax, red ribbon.

She moved to the right-hand side. The topmost drawer held letters. She went through them quickly. Business and personal correspondence. None of them mentioned Cosgrove, or the Reverend Banks and Philadelphia. Charlotte replaced them and glanced at the clock. She'd been inside ten minutes. Cosgrove would be walking through the square a second time.

The next drawer held letters, too, dozens of them, in bundles bound with red ribbon. A flowerlike scent wafted up.

Charlotte took out a bundle and examined the top letter. The address was written in a round, girlish hand. The letters were franked. She recognized the scrawled signature: Cosgrove's.

The feminine handwriting, the perfume, the frank, told her the letters were written by the earl's dead wife.

Charlotte hesitated, shivering, her bare skin covered in goose bumps. *Should I look at them?*

There was no reason except curiosity to read the dead countess's letters. She put the bundle back.

The bottom drawer contained more letters bound in red ribbon. Charlotte checked them. The handwriting was the same on them all: Lady Cosgrove's.

Charlotte closed the drawer. Monkwood had kept his sister's letters—but nothing pertaining to the Smiths, nothing that connected him to the slanderous Reverend Banks. *Was I wrong?*

She scanned the study. One of the bookcases drew her attention. Behind its glazed doors were shelves of small leather-bound volumes.

Charlotte tiptoed to the bookcase. She tried the doors. They were locked.

She peered through the tiny diamond-shaped panes of glass. Through Albin's reflection she saw dozens of slim books that looked like diaries. They filled four and a half shelves.

The latch was simple. If she broke one of the panes she could reach inside and lift it with a fingertip.

But Monkwood would know someone had opened the bookcase.

Unless she made it look as if a maid had accidentally elbowed the glass while dusting . . .

Charlotte glanced at the clock. Twenty minutes had passed. *I must hurry.*

She worked quickly—breaking a corner pane, changing into

a sparrow, flying up and hopping inside. Another change and she was a small monkey. Smells enveloped her: leather, paper, ink—and a scent she recognized as Monkwood's.

Her nose twitched. Wasn't it the same smell as on the letter from Philadelphia?

Her monkey fingers made swift work of the latch. Charlotte leapt down to the floor and changed back into Albin. She plucked the last book from the half-empty shelf. It was small enough to fit into the pocket of a man's coat, the red calfskin soft and well-worn beneath her fingers.

She opened it. *April 5th, 1805 to October 14th, 1805* was written inside the cover.

The pages were filled with writing. Charlotte turned to the last one.

October 14th. Woke at 10.23 a.m. Clothes: yellow pantaloons, cream-and-gold Marcella waistcoat, single-breasted port-red tailcoat, Hessians. Neckcloth: Waterfall, with ruby pin. Cane: gold-topped ebony. The handwriting was nothing like the Reverend Banks's—rounder, less spiky. She skimmed the page, looking for references to Cosgrove, to the Smiths.

Monkwood had meticulously recorded everything he'd eaten on the fourteenth, the number of pages he'd read of a novel, details of two letters he'd written, his changes of clothing—but there was no mention of Cosgrove or the Smiths.

Charlotte thumbed back several pages. When had the earl been attacked in St. James's Park?

On October eleventh, below a list of the clothes Monkwood had donned that morning and the food he'd eaten for breakfast, he'd written: *Success! Cosgrove injured! Hector Smith injured too, but that is of no consequence.*

"Yes." The *s* hissed between her teeth, triumphant. She snapped the diary shut.

Charlotte selected the six latest volumes, rearranged the others to look as if none were missing, then reversed the steps she'd taken—monkey, sparrow, Albin. The breeze from the broken window settled on her skin like ice. Her bones seemed to shiver inside her.

She wrapped the diaries with paper from Monkwood's desk and tied the bundle with red ribbon. Her fingers were clumsy with cold, clumsy with anxiety. If a servant came now, if someone opened the door and discovered her—

Hurry. Hurry.

Charlotte shoved open the window. Snowflakes swirled into the study.

Was that Cosgrove on the far side of the square, heading this way?

She leaned out and dropped the diaries, closed the window, changed into a sparrow. *Hurry. Hurry.* Up onto the windowsill, a careful hop through the broken pane, a swift glide down, another itching change and she was a dog.

Snow engulfed her paws.

Charlotte bent her head and took the knot of red ribbon between her teeth. Was that distant pedestrian Cosgrove?

Yes. The height, the way he held his head, the long strides, were unmistakable.

She trotted across the square towards him, tail wagging, the bundle banging against her muzzle.

CHAPTER THIRTY-NINE

FIFTEEN MINUTES LATER Charlotte was in Cosgrove's study, soaking up heat from the fire.

The earl handed her a glass of brandy. "Warmer?"

"Yes, sir." Charlotte gulped a mouthful of brandy, felt it burn down her throat, felt it heat her belly.

Cosgrove walked to his desk. "I didn't know Monkwood kept diaries."

"I'd say he's been keeping them since childhood, sir." Sensation was returning to her fingers; they stung as she buttoned her shirt. "You're in there. And the Smiths."

"Anything about the letters?" Cosgrove unknotted the ribbon, tore off the paper, and laid the diaries out on the desk.

"I only read a couple of pages, sir."

Cosgrove pulled out his chair and sat. He opened a diary. "Good Lord. Such detail. Listen to this: *Woke at 10.36 a.m. Clothes: cream pantaloons, pale-green-and-cream Valencia waistcoat, double-breasted dark green tailcoat, Hessians. Neckcloth: an Oriental, with the emerald pin.*" From Cosgrove's expression, he didn't know whether to be amused or appalled. He thumbed through the pages. "You say you found reference to the Smiths?"

"In the latest one, sir. On October eleventh, the day after you were attacked in St. James's Park." Charlotte drank another mouthful of brandy. The warmth in her belly spread.

The earl sorted through the diaries, checking dates, then selected one and began to read.

Charlotte buttoned her waistcoat and picked up her neckcloth. The earl didn't offer to tie it for her; he was engrossed in the diary.

She tied the neckcloth by guess and pulled on her tailcoat. "Shall I read, too, sir?"

Cosgrove grunted without looking up. Charlotte took the sound to mean *Yes.* She chose a diary, one of the less recent ones, starting in 1803.

I stole this. I am a thief. But she didn't feel that she'd done anything terrible. Not if Gerald Monkwood was planning to kill the earl.

They read in silence. Charlotte sipped the last of the brandy, turning pages, skipping over lists of clothes, details of meals eaten. Monkwood had a lover whom he regularly visited, a woman he called his beautiful Helen. Other than that, there was nothing of interest.

"Here!" Cosgrove said, his voice so loud she started in her seat. "May seventeenth. He talks of writing a letter to discredit me. There's a complete transcript of it. Word for word!" He grinned at her like a schoolboy. "This is what I need. This is proof!"

Charlotte grinned back at him.

"You are a jewel of a secretary, Albin. An absolute jewel! I'm doubling your salary."

Charlotte lost her grin. "Oh, no, sir. It's not necess—"

"What price is a man's reputation, Albin? Tell me that."

There was no answer to that question. Charlotte shook her head.

"You were correct about it being Monkwood. Much more objective than I was. I still *want* it to be Brashdon." Cosgrove laid down the diary. "You did well, lad. Very well."

The praise made Charlotte blush. She shook her head again and changed the subject. "Does Monkwood say why he did it, sir?"

"I'll read it to you." Cosgrove picked up the diary, flicked back a few pages, and read aloud: "*Cosgrove shall know what it's like to suffer the agonies of public humiliation. He ruined my darling and made her last days a misery, and I shall do the same for him.*"

"Revenge."

The earl pulled his mouth into a grimace and nodded.

"Does he write about hiring men to kill you, sir?"

"Not yet."

Charlotte went back to the diary she was reading. The study was silent but for the sigh of coals shifting in the fireplace and the sound of pages turning. A few minutes later, Cosgrove said, "Here. April twelfth. He went to a cockfight. Listen to this. *I found the perfect candidates. Two brothers and a cousin, rough, brutish men who are quite happy to kill in exchange for payment. I shall meet with them again tomorrow.*" Cosgrove turned a page. "And then this: *Their names are Abel, Jeremiah, and Hector Smith, and they profess themselves most happy with the sequence of events I outlined. Everything is now in place. I shall begin on April 22nd, as planned.*"

"Does he say what his plan is, sir?"

"Plan? We know what it is." Cosgrove lowered the diary. "Vandalism. Arson. Public disgrace. Death."

"And the attacks."

Cosgrove grunted. "And the attacks." He turned his frowning attention back to the diary.

Charlotte read through March 1803 and into April. Monkwood wrote about his clothes, his menus, his mistress. *April 21st. Today my beloved Helen and I took our pleasure together for* *the last time under this roof. Tomorrow she goes to Cosgrove. From now on, I will share her kisses and the sweet treasures of her body with him. How shall I bear it?*

Charlotte frowned and reread the sentences. Did they mean what she thought?

No. Impossible.

She turned the page. It was dated April 22nd, 1803. The day the earl had married Lavinia Monkwood.

I couldn't eat this morning. How can I, when I lose my darling today? Then followed a meticulous list of his wedding attire. *My Helen has never been more beautiful than she is today. It makes me ill to think of Cosgrove touching her, but my darling is in high spirits. Cosgrove is a husband worthy of her. His status and wealth are what my sweet Helen deserves. She will lead Society. I would endure worse agonies than this for her sake.*

At the bottom of the entry, Monkwood had penned: *I have given my darling a handkerchief marked with chicken's blood, that she may prove her virginity tonight. That treasure, of course, was mine, many years ago.*

Charlotte stared at the page for a long time. "Sir . . . did Monkwood have a pet name for his sister?"

The earl glanced up. "What?"

"What did Monkwood call his sister? Did he have a pet name for her?"

Cosgrove leaned back in his chair. His eyes narrowed slightly. "He called her . . . let me think . . . His angel. His jewel. His diamond."

"He never called her Helen?"

"Helen of Troy, the most beautiful woman in the world." Cosgrove snorted. "Yes, he called her Helen. Lavinia liked it. It pandered to her vanity."

Charlotte looked down at the diary. *Today my beloved Helen*

and I took our pleasure together for the last time under this roof.
"Sir . . . either Monkwood is writing nonsense or . . ."

"Or what?"

She looked up. "Or . . . he had a sexual relationship with his sister." The words left an unpleasant taste on her tongue.

Cosgrove didn't scoff; he frowned and pushed to his feet. "Let me see."

Charlotte held the diary out, open to April 21st. She watched as he read—quick, frowning—and turned the page and read again.

"It can't possibly be true," she said, when he lowered the diary.

"I think . . . it might be." Cosgrove said the words slowly, as if trying them out.

Charlotte shook her head, rejecting this. "No."

"Lavinia wasn't a virgin on our wedding night. I didn't realize at the time, but recently . . . I became certain of it."

Because of me? Charlotte looked down at the desk. She traced a knot in the wood with one fingertip.

"I wondered who it might have been, but I never . . . Not Monkwood!" The tone in Cosgrove's voice wasn't rage; it was revulsion.

She looked up and watched as he reread the pages, his brow knotted, his concentration fierce. "What does this mean?" He pointed to a line. "Many years ago. When did it start? How old *was* she?"

Charlotte shook her head.

"Was she a child?" The earl looked as if he tasted bile in his mouth. "Dear God. This is . . . I know Monkwood covets beautiful objects, but his own sister!" He swallowed. "Can you tell from this how often . . . ?" He thrust the diary at her as if he couldn't bear to look himself.

"Several times a week, sir." Charlotte took the diary. "He

called her Helen, so I didn't realize . . . I thought he was writing about a mistress."

"God!" Cosgrove said. The word was an explosive, savage sound. He strode to the decanters and poured himself a large glass of brandy. "Make a note of the dates. All of them."

"Will you make it public, sir?" Charlotte asked, clutching the diary. "The incest?"

Cosgrove shook his head. "No. But by God I'll make him pay for what he did to her!" His face twisted; not rage, but distress.

Charlotte's throat tightened. However his marriage had ended, the earl had once loved his wife deeply.

Cosgrove walked to his desk, his grip on the glass white-knuckled. He jerked out the chair, sat, and reached for the diary he'd been reading.

Charlotte opened the red calfskin volume and started taking notes, glancing up every few minutes to check on the earl. His expression was bleak as he turned the pages, the bones angular beneath his skin. When he'd finished, he tossed the diary aside.

"Anything more?"

"He talks about the Smiths, the windows, the shit, St. James's Park. It's all there. Towards the end, he's worrying about where the letters are. See . . ." He picked up the diary and turned to the final pages. "*Still nothing from Philadelphia. Time is growing short. If they don't arrive soon, it will be too late.*" He closed it with a snap.

Too late because Cosgrove would be dead? Charlotte repressed a shiver. "Anything about what he plans for your death?" That final word—*death*—was difficult to say. It stuck in her throat. She almost had to spit it out.

Cosgrove shook his head.

"We need his current diary, sir. The anniversary of your wife's death is tomorrow!"

"I know."

"He could have hired new men to—"

"Enough." Cosgrove's voice held an edge of irritation.

Charlotte closed her mouth. She looked down at her desk.

The earl released his breath in a sigh. "I beg your pardon. I'm in a foul mood."

Charlotte glanced up and shook her head. *I will kill Monkwood myself before I let him kill you, sir.* The words echoed in her ears, as if she'd spoken them aloud.

Cosgrove reached for another diary, opened it at the first page, and began to read.

Charlotte watched him for a moment, then returned to her own task. The clock ticked its way towards noon. "October eleventh, 1804," Cosgrove said suddenly. "He's received a letter from Lavinia saying I beat her." His voice held disbelief and indignation in equal measure. "I never beat her. Not once!"

"Why would she lie about such a thing, sir?"

The question earned her a savage glare. "You don't believe me?"

"Of course I do." Without hesitation. "But why would she lie? What did she hope to gain from it?"

"I don't know. Unless . . ." Cosgrove lowered the diary. "It was just after I'd told Lavinia I was divorcing her. Perhaps she thought Monkwood would support her, if she painted herself as a victim?" His eyebrows drew suddenly together. He cast aside the diary and picked up another one, thumbed swiftly through the pages. "I wondered what this meant. Listen: *October 10th, 1805. Today Cosgrove will learn what it's like to receive a beating. Blood for blood, on the day it was shed.*" Cosgrove's head lifted. His eyes skewered her, fierce. "St. James's Park. It was retribution. For a beating I never gave Lavinia." He threw the diary down on his desk, a slapping sound, and hissed between his teeth.

"And the attack in Charles Street, sir? Was that also an anniversary?"

"Charles Street?" Cosgrove's scowl deepened. He reached for a diary, opened the cover and read the date, tossed it aside, picked up another red calfskin volume, flicked rapidly through the pages, paused, and read, tight lines bracketing his mouth.

Charlotte discovered she was holding her breath. She made herself inhale, exhale, made herself wait patiently, listening to the *tick tick tick* of the clock on the mantelpiece.

"October twenty-third, 1804. He's received a letter from Lavinia saying I beat her black and blue." Outrage was vivid on Cosgrove's face. "How dared she write such lies about me!"

Charlotte shook her head.

"And there's a comment here I don't understand, mention of something they'd discussed. A plan." Cosgrove thumbed back through the diary. "I remember Monkwood came down to Hazelbrook . . . Here. October twelfth. The day after she first wrote to him saying I beat her." He fell silent, reading.

Charlotte watched as he read to the bottom, turned the page, read again. He raised his head and looked at her, his lips parted, apparently speechless.

"What, sir?"

Cosgrove closed the diary and laid it on the desk. "Lavinia confessed to her involvement with Barnaby. She said I was a brutal husband. That she'd turned to Barnaby for consolation."

"An excuse? So Monkwood wouldn't be jealous?"

The earl didn't appear to hear her. "Monkwood says . . . He says . . ." He closed his eyes and rubbed his forehead, pressing so hard she saw his fingertips whiten.

"What, sir?"

Cosgrove opened his eyes. "He says he offered to arrange my death. And Lavinia agreed to it."

CHAPTER FORTY

CHARLOTTE OPENED HER mouth, but no sound came out.

Her shock, her silence, made the earl laugh harshly again. "Yes, that's how I feel." He shoved the diary away, a violent gesture.

Charlotte closed her mouth, and shook her head.

Cosgrove pushed to his feet, as if he had too much rage to stay seated. He strode to the window.

Charlotte found her voice. "Why would she—?"

"Think about it." Cosgrove stared out the window, his hands fisted on the sill. "Would you rather be a widow with a handsome jointure, or a divorced adulteress?"

Charlotte weighed the dead countess's choices. As Cosgrove's widow, whispers of adultery would have clung to her, but she'd have kept her title, her jointure, her position in Society. Only the highest sticklers would have closed their doors to her.

As a divorced adulteress who'd been at the center of a very public scandal, she would have existed at the fringes of Society, no longer respectable.

Charlotte pressed her lips together. *Lady Cosgrove made her own bed; she should have been prepared to lie in it.*

The earl turned around. "Lavinia wanted me dead." His face wasn't angular, wasn't angry. Her father had worn that look—

pale, bewildered—after he'd been widowed.

He's devastated.

Charlotte's throat closed. Tears stung her eyes. It took all her willpower not to go to Cosgrove, not to put her arms around him and hug him.

She blinked the tears back. What would Albin say at this point? Not Charlotte, who wanted to comfort him, but Albin, the practical, competent secretary. She cleared her throat. "Monkwood loved his sister more than was natural. If he believed her lies . . . No wonder he hates you, sir. No wonder he wants you dead."

"Yes." The emotion seemed to drain from Cosgrove. He leaned against the windowsill, his face settling into lines of exhaustion.

"Sir . . . we need his current diary. We need to know what he's planning! I can search his bedchamber—"

Cosgrove shook his head. "No. The time's come to confront him."

Charlotte pushed to her feet. "It's too dangerous!"

"Dangerous?" Cosgrove snorted, a contemptuous sound. "Gerald Monkwood might hire someone to kill me, but he wouldn't do it himself. He's *soft.* All wind, no mettle."

"But, sir—"

A knock sounded on the door. A footman entered. "Luncheon is served, sir."

MARCUS STARED DOWN at his plate. The mingled scents of beef and pastry made his stomach shift queasily. Monkwood had been Lavinia's brother and guardian. He should have protected her; instead, he'd seduced her. How old had Lavinia been? *Not a child,* he prayed. *Let her not have been a child.* It was too sickening to imagine—

No. Marcus shook his head sharply. He wouldn't imagine it, wouldn't allow himself to envisage so grotesque a coupling.

He stared down at the pie, at the flaking golden pastry and glistening juices and tender lumps of meat. Lavinia had lied to him, betrayed him, wished him dead—but she had also been a victim: an orphan, innocent and vulnerable, seduced by her own brother.

Marcus picked up his fork and stirred the food on his plate. If Monkwood had never touched her, who might Lavinia have been? Would her heart have been less fickle? Her sweetness not just a veneer? Her disposition kinder and less covetous? Less deceitful?

Perhaps she could have truly loved me. Perhaps our marriage would have survived.

Marcus put down the fork with a clatter of silver on china. "How could Monkwood have done such a thing?" He shoved his hands through his hair. "God! How old was she when it started?"

"I could take some of the earlier diaries," Albin said diffidently. "If you truly want to know."

Do I?

Marcus thrust his plate away.

A faint frown puckered Albin's brow. "You should eat, sir."

If I do, I'll vomit. Marcus shook his head.

Albin laid down his own fork. "Sir . . . Monkwood has two drawers in his desk full of letters from his sister. Would you like to see what she wrote to him? Would it help?"

Marcus pushed to his feet and walked to the window. Did he want to read Lavinia's letters? Read her lies about him?

What I want is to destroy Monkwood.

His hands clenched on the windowsill. He imagined throttling Monkwood. Imagined squeezing the life from him. He heard the frantic wheeze of Monkwood's breath, saw Monkwood's face swell and grow purple—and then his eyes focused on the scene outside.

Snow blew in thick, fierce flurries, blotting out Grosvenor Square.

Marcus unclenched his hands and turned back to Albin. The lad was anxiously watching him.

"We won't be visiting Monkwood this afternoon. It's blowing a blizzard."

Albin's anxiety seemed to ease slightly.

He's relieved we can't go. He's afraid Monkwood will attack me.

Marcus suppressed a snarl of temper. Words rose on his tongue: *You should be a nursery maid, not a secretary.* He swallowed them, went back to the table, and sat. He pulled his plate towards him, picked up his fork, and forced himself to spear a piece of beef, to lift it to his mouth, to chew, to swallow.

After a moment's hesitation, Albin resumed eating.

Marcus ate a dozen mouthfuls, then pushed the plate away again. The silver bowl of fruit was tempting. He reached for a grape and bit into it. The flavor brought back memories: sitting on a rug in front of a fire dressed only in a sheet, Charlotte refusing to be his mistress.

The grape suddenly tasted sour in his mouth.

Think of something else.

He fastened his gaze on Albin. Less than two weeks ago he'd hired the lad—and wondered whether he was making a mistake. *One of the best decisions I ever made.*

Although Albin was certainly unusual.

"What's it like to fly?"

"To fly?" Albin blinked, then laid his knife and fork neatly on his plate and pushed it away. "Flying is . . . Exhilarating. But also terrifying." He broke off a small bunch of grapes. "It's . . . I don't know quite how to explain it, sir, but when I'm a bird I feel *exposed*. Like there's a cat I haven't seen, or a hawk waiting to swoop on me." He pulled the grapes off their stems. "I feel much safer as a person."

"You said your mother could fly. Did she teach you?"

Albin shook his head. "She died when I was young. I suppose she was planning to tell me when I was older." He looked down at the grapes and arranged them in a circle on his side plate. "I didn't know about the magic until a few weeks ago. I don't think my father knew either. He had enough time to tell me before he died." Albin frowned and pushed the last grape into place with a fingertip. "My mother must have kept it a secret from him."

The circle of grapes was oddly familiar. Marcus stared at it. Where had he seen it before? Recollection teased at him.

Grapes. Arranged in a lopsided circle . . .

The recollection clicked into place. Last night. Charlotte had made a circle with grapes while she talked.

The room tilted and seemed to swing around him. Marcus squeezed his eyes shut against dizziness. Fragments of memory whirled in his head: things Albin had done, things Charlotte had said.

"Sir?"

He opened his eyes and stared at the grapes, stared at Albin.

The fragments settled into place in his head and made a whole picture.

Albin is Charlotte.

CHAPTER FORTY-ONE

RAGE SURGED THROUGH him, contracting his muscles and heating his blood, clogging his throat. Flesh, blood, bone, breath—all was rage.

Marcus pushed to his feet so abruptly that his chair fell over. "Sir? What's wrong?"

I've been making love to a man. He'd kissed Albin. He'd fucked him.

"Sir?" Albin said again. "What—"

"You're Charlotte."

Albin froze with his mouth partly open. Silence was loud in the room—it roared in Marcus's ears—and beneath it was the bellow of fury in his blood, the violent thump of his heart.

Albin closed his mouth. He swallowed. "I . . . I don't know what you mean, sir."

"Don't lie to me!" Marcus's voice was a shout. This was worse than Lavinia's adultery, a greater violation of trust than Barnaby's betrayal. Albin had tricked him into having sex with him. Sex. With a man.

Marcus seized the tablecloth and ripped it off the table. The sound of china and glass smashing fueled his rage. "*You* are Charlotte." He balled the tablecloth in his fists. "Charlotte is a *man*."

Albin scrambled to his feet. "No, sir. You've got it wrong."

Rage consumed him. He shook with it. Burned with it. "Get out!"

"It's Albin who's not real." Albin's words fell over themselves. "I'm not a man. My name is Charlotte Christina Albinia—"

"Get out!" Marcus roared.

Albin closed his mouth. He swallowed. He was starkly pale. Tears stood in his eyes. He turned and walked to the door.

"Don't you *dare* set foot in this house again—in *any* shape or form." Marcus's voice was rough with fury, rough with loathing. "Stay away from me. Otherwise I swear to God I'll kill you!"

Albin stepped out into the corridor and closed the door.

Marcus's breathing was loud and harsh in the silence. Rage bellowed inside him. He wanted to upend the table and smash the chairs and rip the curtains from their rails. And most of all, he wanted to draw blood. Albin's blood.

The door opened cautiously, revealing the butler. "Sir?"

Marcus clenched his hands around the balled-up tablecloth. "Mr. Albin is not to be admitted to this house ever again, under *any* circumstances. If . . ." How to explain Albin's ability to change shape? Fellowes would think he was as mad as King George. "If anyone you don't know asks to see me, deny them entrance."

"Yes, sir."

Marcus threw the tablecloth aside and strode to the door. The butler stepped hastily out of his way.

"I'll be down in the cellar. Don't let anyone disturb me."

HE SPENT THE rest of the afternoon punching the sawdust-filled bag in the cellar. Rage and fury spilled out of him, filling the room with a smoky, crackling heat.

I fucked a man. It was a chant in his head. *I. Fucked. A man*.

Thirst burned in his throat. Sweat soaked his hair, ran down his face, dripped off his chin. There was blood on the bag now, each blow brought a spurt of pain, but he didn't put on the padded gloves. His rage needed pain, needed blood. *I. Fucked. A man*.

"SIR!" HIS VALET said, aghast, when he entered his bedchamber. "What happened?"

Marcus ignored the question. "A bath." He stripped off his shirt and used it to wipe his face.

"Yes, sir. The tub's almost full. Mr. Fellowes said you were in the cellar so I took the liberty of ordering up hot water . . . Your hands, sir. They're bleeding!"

"Almost full?" Marcus headed for his dressing room. Yes, a steaming brass tub stood in the center of the rug. He bent and tried to prize off his boots.

"Allow me, sir." Leggatt knelt, removing the boots with swift expertise.

Marcus grunted his thanks. He stripped out of his clothes. They were soaked with sweat, flecked with blood. "Throw them away," he said, and stepped into the steaming water.

"Your hands, sir—"

"Don't fuss." Albin had fussed. Had tried to protect him. Tried to seduce him. "And bring me a glass of brandy. A big one."

THE BRANDY HELPED. His rage receded slightly. Marcus rested the glass on the edge of the tub, leaned his head back, and closed his eyes. He heard Leggatt moving in the bedroom, laying out clothes for the evening. He heard the shutters rattle, heard wind snarl in the chimney. Heard Albin's voice: *It's Albin who's not real. My name is Charlotte Christina Albinia—*

Marcus opened his eyes. Fury rekindled in his chest. How dared Albin try to lie? Try to make his deceit less than it was?

He gulped another mouthful of brandy.

Memory teased at the edges of his mind. He remembered Albin's nervousness at Mrs. Henshaw's brothel. Remembered his appalled expression when they'd walked in on Phillip and the whores. Remembered his question: *Was she trying to play a tune on his cock?*

Marcus sipped the brandy, scowling, sifting through the memories, examining them. The moment of insight didn't come suddenly, as it had at luncheon; it crept up on him slowly, one piece of evidence laid upon another.

Albin hadn't known how to punch, or ride a horse, or tie a neckcloth. He hadn't known the slang names for a cock. He hadn't known what a sheath was.

Marcus's scowl deepened. He heard Albin's voice again: *Was she trying to play a tune?* Only someone with complete ignorance of male anatomy could have asked such a question.

The fragments of information settled into place again in his head—but this time, they made a different pattern.

Albin wasn't a man. He was Charlotte. No, *she* was Charlotte.

Charlotte Christina Albinia. Christopher Albin.

Marcus swallowed the last of the brandy, almost choking on it. His rage built.

Albin had been a woman.

He'd sworn in front of her. Used words like cock and shit and fuck. He'd discussed sex with her. Taught her to punch. Taken her to a brothel.

Marcus hissed between his teeth. He put the glass on the floor and stood, shedding water. He grabbed the towel and dried himself roughly, fury smoldering in his chest.

Lavinia. Barnaby. Albin. Charlotte. People he'd trusted. People who had betrayed him.

Four times a fool.

Albin hadn't been his best friend, Charlotte hadn't been his wife—but this betrayal hurt just as badly. He'd been on the brink of friendship with Albin. On the brink of loving Charlotte.

Marcus hissed between his teeth a second time. His hands clenched around the blood-smeared towel. He wanted to go downstairs and take his rage out on the punching bag again.

"Sir, allow me to dress your hands." Leggatt stood in the doorway.

Charlotte wasn't worth so much emotion. She wasn't worth even one drop of his blood.

Marcus unclenched his hands. He laid down the towel. "Do your best, Leggatt."

HE WAS DRY, clothed, and on his third glass of brandy when a footman knocked on the bedroom door. "A message for you, sir. Marked urgent."

Marcus scowled. It would be from Charlotte. "Throw it in the fire."

The footman blinked. "Sir?"

Or it could be from Grenville or Fox. "Give it here."

The Earl of Cosgrove. Urgent. The handwriting was in block letters, disguised. Not Grenville or Fox.

Marcus ripped open the letter.

Dear Lord Cosgrove,

I have come into the possession of some information that I believe may interest you, namely, the identity of the person who commissioned the scurrilous letter about you. If you will do me the honor of meeting with me at the monument of Britannia in

Hyde Park at half past nine tomorrow morning, I shall be pleased to share my knowledge with you.

Yours sincerely,

A Friend.

Marcus grunted. Did Monkwood believe he'd fall into so obvious a trap?

He reread the lines. Nine thirty. An early hour for Monkwood. *So I won't think it's him.*

Marcus folded the letter. The Britannia monument was an isolated spot. Had Monkwood hired replacements for the Smiths? Would those replacements be waiting for him? Would Monkwood be watching?

How am I to die? Cudgels? Or knives?

CHARLOTTE HAD CRIED when her mother died, when her father died, but she'd never cried this deeply, this despairingly. She'd never felt as alone as she did now.

My own fault.

She had deceived the earl, abused his trust, hurt him. *Just like his dead wife.*

And like the dead countess, she'd engineered her own downfall.

Except that hurting the earl hadn't been deliberate, any more than falling in love with him had been.

She huddled in front of the fire, shivering, aching with grief, aching with loss and despair.

Eleven days. That's all it had taken. To meet Cosgrove. To love him. To lose him.

Charlotte bowed her head and wept more tears. The future stretched in front of her, bleak and barren. To never see Cosgrove again. Never talk with him. Never see his face light up with laughter, never see him scowl in concentration. *How will I survive?*

The question answered itself: She could be a footman. A housemaid. She could watch Cosgrove from a distance. Perhaps even exchange a few words with him from time to time.

Charlotte raised her head and stared into the flames. What kind of existence would that be? Surviving on glimpses of him, on scraps of overheard conversations. Watching his life unfold—career, family—but having no part in it.

The answer was easy: Such an existence would eat away at her sanity and make her as mad as an inmate of Bedlam. Instead of independence, she would create a prison for herself.

And I'd be deceiving him, pretending to be someone I'm not.

No. She had made her own bed. Unlike the countess, she would lie in it. She would leave London, leave Cosgrove.

But first, I must apologize to him.

She owed him an explanation—but no excuses. No pleas for forgiveness. What she'd done was inexcusable. Unforgivable.

THE LETTER TOOK three hours to write. When it was finished, Charlotte looked at the pages, the smudged ink, the words crossed out and rewritten. *And so it ends.*

She washed her face, washed her ink-stained fingers, and copied the letter neatly—no smudges, no mistakes, no splotches from tears—and signed her name and sealed it.

Charlotte shrugged into her greatcoat, put on her hat and gloves, and let herself out. Darkness had fallen. The streets were almost a foot deep in snow. A few flakes drifted lightly down.

She walked to Grosvenor Square. The curtains were drawn at the earl's residence, but a few slivers of light laid themselves across the snow.

Charlotte stood in the darkness, in the snow, shivering, staring up at the house. She'd wanted independence; instead, she was bound more tightly to Cosgrove than she'd ever been bound to the Westcotes.

She made herself climb the steps and knock on the door. Fellowes opened it. His face gathered into disapproving folds when he recognized her. "You are not allowed admittance, Mr. Albin."

"I know." Charlotte held out the letter. "Can you please give this to the earl? It needn't be tonight. Perhaps . . . perhaps tomorrow?"

Fellowes hesitated, then took the letter.

"Thank you, Fell—"

The door closed.

Charlotte leaned her forehead against the icy door and squeezed her eyes shut against tears. *I love you, sir.*

Tomorrow was the anniversary of his wife's death. A dangerous date. Whether Cosgrove wanted her help or not, she would give it. But after tomorrow . . .

I must go. I must start again.

Happiness she would leave behind in London, but independence was something she could still strive for.

CHAPTER FORTY-TWO

October 28th, 1805
Grosvenor Square, London

MARCUS READ HIS mail while he ate breakfast. His hands ached each time he wielded the knife and fork or unfolded a letter, the scabs across his knuckles threatening to split open. His head ached too; from last night's brandy, from last night's rage.

The third letter was thick, addressed in familiar handwriting. He started to break the seal—then recognition came. Albin. Charlotte.

Rage thundered in his chest. Marcus screwed the letter into a ball and threw it at the fireplace. It hit the grate and bounced off, coming to rest on the hearth.

Fellowes entered the breakfast parlor. "The carriage will be round in half an hour, sir."

Marcus thrust back his chair. "I'll need two—no, make it three—footmen. Howard and Felix and . . ." Who else among the footmen was young and strong? "Arthur." He crossed to the fireplace and threw the crumpled letter into the grate. "Tell them to dress warmly, they may be standing outside for some time. And Fellowes . . . tell them they may need to use their fists."

The letter flared alight and burned swiftly into ashes.

"I'll see to it at once," Fellowes said.

CHARLOTTE CROUCHED IN the corridor outside Monkwood's bedroom, a mouse. Smells invaded her nose: furniture polish and candle wax, coal dust, bacon and coffee, a chamber pot stink.

It was barely eight thirty, yet light came from beneath the bedroom door and her ears caught the low murmur of voices. Was Monkwood awake?

The crack beneath the door was too narrow for a mouse. Charlotte changed into a lizard. The smells became duller, the colors brighter, the sounds harder to hear.

She eased beneath the door.

Yes, Monkwood was awake. Candles blazed in sconces and candelabra.

An ocean of carpet stretched before her. A bed reared up from it, an immense island draped in crimson and gold hangings. Someone moved on the other side of the bed; she felt the vibration of footsteps.

"A black waistcoat, sir?" The voice was muffled, as if something blocked her ears.

"Yes, yes. Everything black today."

Charlotte scuttled across the carpet and beneath the tasseled hem of the valance. She crept to the other side of the bed and peered out. Chair legs, cabinet legs, table legs.

The floor quivered again. "Single-breasted or double-breasted, sir?"

"Double, with the mother-of-pearl buttons." Monkwood's voice came from above her.

Charlotte hesitated, uncertain what to do. She'd expected Monkwood to be asleep. Had expected to be able to explore the room without fear of being observed.

I need a vantage point.

On the far side of the expanse of carpet were tall curtains.

Charlotte took a deep breath, slipped out from under the valance, and scuttled around the perimeter of the room, pressing close to the skirting board. The floor quivered to the rhythmic tread of the valet walking back and forth.

Monkwood's curtains were brocade, crimson heavily ridged with golden thread. Charlotte scaled them cautiously, hidden in the shadow of a fold. When she judged herself halfway up, she paused and looked out across the bedchamber. Her stomach gave a sickening swoop. Her claws dug into the fabric. *So high.*

Gerald Monkwood sat in his bed, a tray across his lap, writing in a diary. A nightcap perched on his head. Stubble glinted on his soft cheeks. On the bedside table were the remains of a breakfast. The bacon she'd smelled, and the coffee.

Charlotte stared at Monkwood. The first time she'd seen him, she'd thought he looked like Cupid. She still thought it. The plump cheeks were cherubic, as were the soft feminine mouth and the golden curls escaping from beneath the nightcap.

How could so benign an exterior hide such darkness, such ugliness?

The valet emerged from what she thought must be the dressing room. "Are you ready to be shaved, sir?"

"Yes." Monkwood closed the diary, placed it on his bedside table, and climbed out of bed.

Charlotte inched her way back down the terrifying precipice of the curtain.

At the washstand, the valet dipped a small towel in a basin of steaming water, wrung it out, and dampened Monkwood's face.

Charlotte scrambled over the hem of the curtain, her breath coming short and fast.

The valet picked up the shaving brush.

Now. While Monkwood had his eyes closed. While the valet lathered his master's cheeks—

Charlotte crossed the carpet as swiftly as her lizard legs could carry her. She changed into a monkey and reached for the diary. Every hair on her body stood on end. Her pulse echoed deafeningly in her ears. Surely the valet would notice her? Surely Monkwood would open his eyes and see?

No shout came.

Charlotte crouched, clutching the diary. Now what? With Monkwood awake, her plans were awry. She couldn't cross to the door and slink out. The valet would see her.

She *had* to get out of this room. Had to get back to the spare bedchamber, back to the window she'd broken. Back to Chandlers Street.

Her gaze fastened on the dressing room door. It was ajar.

Charlotte crept across to it. She eased through the gap between doorframe and door.

Candles were lit in the sconces. She saw crisp white shirts and gleaming boots, satin and brocade waistcoats, tailcoats in olive brown, emerald green, claret, and a dozen shades of blue. Each breath she inhaled smelled of linen and leather and wool. And Monkwood.

On the far side of the dressing room was another door.

Charlotte opened it with deft monkey fingers and peered out. An empty corridor stretched in both directions.

CHAPTER FORTY-THREE

CHARLOTTE GLIDED IN through her open window, skimmed over the writing desk, and hovered on hawk's wings above the armchair. She dropped the diary on the upholstered seat, landed alongside, and changed into Albin. She didn't bother closing the window, didn't bother dressing, just snatched up the diary and opened it.

October 28th. Today Cosgrove dies! Monkwood had underlined that sentence three times. Beneath it, he'd written the time he'd woken—7.45 a.m.—the food he'd eaten for breakfast, and the garments he intended to wear. *Black breeches, black waistcoat, black tailcoat.*

Charlotte turned back a page. *Still no word from the Smiths, but I shall do it myself. It's better that Cosgrove die at my hands. My beloved Helen would prefer it so.* She skipped over several paragraphs of anguish about the snowstorm. *It must be done tomorrow.* "Must" had been underlined so deeply the paper was torn. At the bottom of the page Monkwood had written: *8 p.m. The snow has stopped. God is on my side.*

She turned back another page, almost ripping the paper in her haste. Here was the text of a letter.

Dear Lord Cosgrove,

I have come into the possession of some information that I believe may interest you, namely, the identity of the person who commissioned the scurrilous letter about you. If you will do me the honor of meeting with me at the monument of Britannia in Hyde Park at half past nine tomorrow morning, I shall be pleased to share my knowledge with you.

Yours sincerely,

A Friend.

Charlotte's heart lurched in her chest. Half past nine?

The church bells were ringing nine o'clock now.

Charlotte dressed faster than she'd ever dressed in her life—shirt, breeches, boots—her fingers clumsy with haste. She flung aside such time-consuming items as waistcoat and neckcloth and stockings, didn't even bother with her tailcoat. She snatched up the diary and the last of her coins and ran down to the street, dragging on her greatcoat. A scattering of snowflakes drifted from the low, gray sky.

Where was Hyde Park from here? Where was the Britannia monument?

She needed a hackney, but Chandlers Street was empty apart from tracks in the snow.

A hundred yards away, on Oxford Street, a hackney trotted slowly past. Charlotte started running. "Hie! Jarvey! Wait!"

THE HACKNEY DEPOSITED her in Hyde Park. Snow was now falling steadily. "You can just see the top o' it through them yews," the jarvey said, pointing through the haze of snowflakes. Bells tolled distantly, ringing the half hour. "There's a carriageway on t'other side. I can take you round—"

Charlotte thrust some coins at him. "No, thank you."

She ran, her boots churning the snow. Panic drove her. *Faster.* Cold air whistled in her throat. Snowflakes struck her face and stung her eyes. *Faster.*

The yews had been planted in concentric rings. Prickly

branches slapped her, grabbing at her coat, trying to slow her down. *Faster.* Don't let her be too late. Don't let Cosgrove be dead. *Faster. Faster.*

Charlotte burst out of the trees, gasping, her breath pluming white in front of her face.

The monument towered high—a marble Britannia with trident and shield and centurion's helmet, a lion at her side like a dog. Two figures stood on the snow-covered steps, half a dozen yards distant from each other. One was the earl. The other was Monkwood.

"It's a trap, sir!" she shouted.

Both men swung to face her. Snowflakes spun in the air.

"He's planning to kill you," Charlotte cried, panting, plowing through the snow towards them.

"Nonsense." Monkwood's face twisted in a contemptuous sneer. "Your secretary is delusional, Cosgrove."

"He's not my secretary." The earl's voice was hard, clipped. He looked through Charlotte as if she didn't exist.

"Sir," she said desperately, pulling the diary from her pocket, holding it out to him. "It's all in here."

The earl made no move to take the diary. "I may be a fool," he said coldly. "But I'm not so much of a fool that I came alone. Of course I knew it was a trap."

Monkwood's sneer turned into a snarl, his teeth bared like the marble lion. "You—" He lunged at Cosgrove, one fist raised to strike.

Charlotte flung herself forward, taking the blow on her right shoulder. The impact knocked her off her feet. She grabbed Monkwood as she fell, taking him with her, tumbling in the snow, hanging on to him with all her strength. *I won't let you kill him.*

Monkwood fought like an animal, scratching, snapping his teeth. A mad keening came from his throat.

Someone tore them apart, lifting Monkwood off her.

Charlotte lay where she'd fallen, panting, and watched two of Cosgrove's footmen haul Monkwood to his feet and hold him restrained. Snowflakes settled on her face.

"Get up," the earl said. His eyes met hers for a fleeting second before he turned away, shoving a dueling pistol into his pocket.

Charlotte stayed where she was a moment longer, catching her breath, blinking snow from her eyes, then slowly pushed to her feet. Her shoulder ached, as if Monkwood had hit it with a sledgehammer.

The diary lay where she'd dropped it, red against the churned-up snow. She bent and picked it up, but her mind wasn't on the diary, wasn't on Monkwood and the curses he was hurling at Cosgrove; it was on what she'd seen in the earl's gray eyes.

Her fingers trembled as she brushed snow off the calfskin cover. *He hates me.*

It was what she deserved. What she'd earned.

The earl was speaking, his voice overriding Monkwood's curses. "—sue for slander. I'll win; we both know it. Your diaries contain more than enough evidence."

"You son of a bitch!" Monkwood screamed, high-voiced, his face engorged with rage. Breath billowed from his mouth like smoke. "Son of a bitch! Son of a bitch!"

The earl didn't move. He looked as if he were hewn from stone, like the Britannia towering above them; his body didn't stir, no muscle in his face twitched. He waited until Monkwood drew breath and continued: "You hired men to kill me, and then you tried to do the job yourself. Do you know what the penalty for murder is?"

"You killed Lavinia! What's the penalty for that?" The footmen wrestled Monkwood back as he tried to lunge at Cosgrove.

"I didn't kill Lavinia," Cosgrove said. "Nor did I ever beat her or rape her. You shouldn't have believed everything she told you."

"You bastard!" Monkwood lunged again, red-faced with fury.

"Do you know what else I learned from your diaries, Monkwood? Can you possibly guess?"

Monkwood's face contorted. His sobbing, panted breaths were loud.

"Guess!" Cosgrove's voice was like the crack of a whip.

Monkwood shook his head, tears running down his face.

"Incest."

The word brought with it silence, as if the world held its breath. Charlotte saw the footmen's shock through the spinning snow—the flinching of the muscles around their eyes, the flaring of their nostrils.

The silence grew, widening around them like ripples spreading in a pool. She could almost hear the snowflakes floating in the air. Then, Monkwood spoke: "It wasn't like that. We loved each other. It was special—"

"She was your ward! She was your *sister!*" The earl roared the last word, making Monkwood cringe. "I should kill you for that. And God knows I want to." She heard how much he did. It trembled in his voice. His body vibrated with rage. "But for Lavinia's sake, I shall give you a choice. You can sail for Australia and never set foot in England again. Or you can stay and face the courts. Your choice, Monkwood. Do you want it public? Your *special* relationship with your sister?"

Monkwood shook his head. He no longer strained to be free of the footmen; he sagged, his face mottled. Tear tracks gleamed on his plump cheeks. Snow dusted his black hat, his black coat.

"Leave England. If you're quick, you might even make it before I lay charges for slander. I'll give you one week." The earl stepped back. "Let him go."

The footmen obeyed.

Monkwood stood swaying between them. Even beaten, even weeping, he made the hairs on the back of Charlotte's neck lift. *He's still dangerous.*

Monkwood turned and walked down the snowy path to the carriageway, his gait shambling, as if he were drunk.

"Sir . . ."

"Stay away from me," the earl said, not looking at her.

"His diary, sir. It could be useful as evidence."

Cosgrove turned his head and looked at her. His hatred wasn't like Monkwood's, hot and mad; it was cold, implacable. His eyes were a flat, hard gray, his face angular.

Charlotte held out the diary.

Cosgrove's lips thinned. He took half a dozen steps and snatched the diary from her hand. "Stay away from me." The words were hissed through his teeth.

Charlotte's throat was too tight for speech, too tight for breath. She nodded.

The earl's face became even more angular, his eyes even harder. He turned from her.

Charlotte watched him go, striding with his footmen into the haze of falling snow. *I love you, sir.* Tears burned in her eyes. Her right shoulder ached with each beat of her heart.

When Cosgrove was gone from sight, she turned and stumbled back the way she'd come, hugging her shoulder, shivering. Her fingers tingled as if she had pins and needles.

My fault. I made this bed; now I must lie in it.

How *dared* Charlotte think he needed her help? How *dared* she think he was fool enough to fall into Monkwood's trap? Marcus's anger increased with each stride. He wasn't helpless.

He didn't need protecting.

His carriage came into sight, waiting where he'd left it—the horses with blankets over them, haloes of breath surrounding their heads.

Marcus halted. He turned to the two footmen. "Monkwood's relationship with Lavinia . . ."

"We won't say nothing, sir," the elder of the footmen, Howard, said. He grimaced. "Stuff like that ain't to be bandied about in public."

No. Marcus suppressed his own grimace. "Thank you."

The third footman hurried up, puffing, as they reached the carriage. "Monkwood's coach has just left, sir."

Marcus nodded. "Good. You did well. All of you." But he didn't feel triumphant; rage simmered in his chest. How *dared* she turn up today? How *dared* she think he needed her help?

He climbed into the carriage and tossed the diary on the seat. It slid, leaving a dark smear on the upholstery.

Marcus frowned. Was that blood?

He picked up the diary. Yes, blood, all over the red calfskin cover, and blood all over his right glove.

Where the devil had it come from?

The door swung shut. The carriage swayed as the footmen climbed aboard.

Marcus pictured the scene at the monument: Albin standing in the snow, blond head uncovered, holding the diary.

But he hadn't seen any blood on Charlotte.

Someone had been bleeding, and Charlotte was the only person other than himself who'd touched the diary.

The carriage lurched forward.

Marcus swung open the door and jumped out. "Stop! I need to check something."

He ran back through the snow to the monument, cursing himself with each step. Charlotte had deceived him, betrayed his trust. What did he care if she was injured?

He didn't.

She could die for all he cared.

The ground where she'd wrestled with Monkwood was a mess of boot prints and churned snow. Where the boot prints were deepest, where she'd stood and watched him confront Monkwood, were a dozen scarlet spots. Blood.

His heart seemed to stop beating for a moment—and then to speed up. *She's hurt.*

A dark object protruded from the snow. The end of a twig?

Marcus bent and pulled it out.

It wasn't a twig; it was the hilt of a weapon. The blade was six inches long, thin and wickedly sharp, more skewer than knife. Tarnished with age. Red with blood.

The footmen came up, panting. "Sir?" one of them said.

Marcus held the weapon out. "Stiletto," he said in disbelief, and then the disbelief fell away and the full weight of realization caught up with him. His ribcage seemed to clench around his heart. "Mr. Albin's been stabbed."

Stabbed. Charlotte.

CHAPTER FORTY-FOUR

MARCUS RAN, FOLLOWING the tracks Charlotte had made—boot prints, bright splotches of blood. He plunged into the yews and burst out the other side. The park stretched in front of him. Dimly, through the falling snow, he saw the carriageway, saw trees, saw the Grosvenor Gate, saw the tall buildings of London beyond. But no Charlotte.

Where was she?

He ran, his boots squeaking in the snow, his breath pluming from his mouth. Behind him the footmen crashed through the trees. *Stabbed. Charlotte.* Her trail was easy to follow: churned-up snow, scarlet blood.

The trail stopped at the carriageway. She'd entered a vehicle, most likely a hackney.

What do I care? Marcus asked himself, panting, dashing snow from his face. But he did care, damn it. There was a feeling close to panic to his chest.

A hackney trundled along the carriageway, the horses picking their way through the snow. Marcus ran towards it. The stiletto was still in his fist. He shoved it into his pocket. "Hie! Driver!"

"Sorry, guv'nor," the jarvey called down from his box. He jerked a thumb back at the carriage. "Passenger."

Marcus dug in his pocket and pulled out several golden guineas. "These are for you if you get me to Chandlers Street as quickly as possible."

The hackney halted.

Marcus wrenched open the carriage door. "I beg your pardon," he said to the startled occupant, a stout man with a moustache. "My business is urgent."

The man bristled. "I hired this hackney—"

Marcus thrust some guineas in the man's direction. "Here."

"Sir!" someone cried behind him.

Marcus jerked a glance back. Two of his footmen, red-faced and puffing, had reached the carriageway. The third trailed halfway across the snow. "Howard, come with me. Arthur, bring the carriage to Chandlers Street. And hurry!"

A HACKNEY CARRIAGE was drawn up outside Mrs. Stitchbury's house in Chandlers Street. Snow drifted gently down. Mrs. Stitchbury was on her doorstep, arguing with the jarvey. Everything about her was agitated: the gesticulating hands, the shapes her mouth made as she spoke, the hectic flush in her cheeks. Even the pleats of her gown and the ruffles on her lace cap were agitated.

The door of the hackney was open. The jarvey stood in front of it, a pugnacious jut to his chin.

Of Albin, there was no sign.

"Pay the driver," Marcus said, shoving money at his footman. He wrenched open the carriage door and jumped down.

"Sir!" Mrs. Stitchbury cried. "Mr. Albin's dead!"

His heart kicked in his chest. Dead?

Marcus thrust the jarvey aside and looked into the hackney. He saw Albin slumped in one corner, eyes closed, his skin corpse-pale. He saw blood. Blood on the squab seat. Blood on the floor.

Marcus scrambled into the carriage. *Don't let her be dead.*

Don't let her be dead. Was she breathing? Was her heart still beating?

"Jus' look at the mess," the jarvey said behind him, aggrieved.

If Charlotte was breathing, he couldn't hear it. If her chest was rising and falling, he couldn't see it. Marcus ripped off a glove and felt at the base of her jaw with trembling fingers.

She had a faint pulse.

"She's—he's alive." He turned to the door, where the jarvey and his footman peered in. "Howard, fetch Dr. Baillie to my house. Make it fast! You know where he lives?"

"Yes, sir." The footman departed at a run.

"You, take us to Grosvenor Square."

The jarvey stepped back, shaking his head. "I ain't taking 'im nowhere."

"Damn it, man! Do it now! Before he dies!"

The jarvey shook his head again, mulish. "I'll be fined if I 'ave a dead man in me carriage. I ain't doin' it."

"For God's sake!" Marcus shouted. He dragged the last guinea from his pocket and threw it at the man. "Get us to Grosvenor Square!"

"WELL?" MARCUS ASKED, when Dr. Baillie had examined the puncture wound in Albin's shoulder. "He'll live, won't he?"

"How much blood has he lost?"

"Uh . . . three or four pints. Maybe more."

Dr. Baillie pursed his lips. "I won't bleed him." He bent over the wound again. "A couple of stitches . . . If you could hold him down, Lord Cosgrove, in case he rouses."

Marcus leaned over the bed and gripped Albin's upper arms, pinning him to the mattress. Albin didn't stir when the needle pierced his skin. He was deathly pale, breathing so shallowly his chest seemed barely to move.

Marcus stared down at him. It was Albin's face, Albin's body—but Charlotte was inside that. *Live, damn it.*

"You may let go now, sir."

Marcus released his grip, but he didn't step back. He stayed beside the bed, looking down at Albin.

Dr. Baillie bandaged the shoulder, his movements neat and precise. "That's all I can do, sir. Now we must wait."

"He will live, won't he?"

Dr. Baillie pursed his lips again. "I can't say that for certain, sir. If the wound is infected, if he becomes feverish or develops lockjaw . . . But Mr. Albin is young and healthy—that's in his favor."

Marcus stayed at Albin's bedside once the doctor had gone, trying to understand his emotions. Why did he care so much whether she lived or died?

Because Charlotte had taken a blow meant for him, a blow meant to kill—and he'd turned his back and walked away.

"Sir?"

He glanced up. Leggatt stood in the doorway, and behind him, one of the footmen.

"Your clothes are bloody, sir."

Marcus looked down at Albin. "He shouldn't be left alone."

"Howard can stay with him, sir."

"He needs to be kept warm."

"Yes, sir." It was Howard's voice this time. "I'll keep the fire high."

Marcus reached down and pulled the coverings up around Albin's throat. *Live, damn it.*

MARCUS WASHED THE blood from his skin, dressed in clean clothes, and returned to the Blue Bedchamber. "Any change?

The footman shook his head.

"I'm going out for half an hour, to Chandlers Street. If anything should change . . ."

"I'll send for you, sir."

Marcus strode round to Chandlers Street. Mrs. Stitchbury was in bed with the vapors. One of her housemaids let him into Albin's rooms. "How's poor Mr. Albin, sir?"

"Still alive."

"Ma'am will be pleased. Right overset she is. We all is! We ain't had nothing like this happen before. Terrible, it is, sir. Terrible!"

Marcus nodded politely and shut Albin's door on her. He turned, surveying the room. *Why am I here?*

Because he needed to understand.

Why had Charlotte gone to Hyde Park? Why had she stepped between him and Monkwood?

His breath hung in the air in front of his face. The window stood open. Marcus closed it, then looked at the room once more, trying to get a sense of who Charlotte was.

The room didn't look any different from when he'd first visited a week ago. Table and chairs, writing desk, bookcase, two armchairs on the rug beside the fireplace. A bachelor's sitting room.

He walked through into the bedchamber. Clothes were flung on the bed: waistcoat, neckcloth, stockings. The items Charlotte hadn't been wearing when she'd come to Hyde Park.

She was in a hurry. To save me.

The bed, the washstand, the dressing table, the chest of drawers, the wardrobe—they were generic. A hundred bachelors slept in rooms like this. A thousand. They told him nothing about her.

Marcus stripped off his gloves and searched methodically. Under the bed was a valise containing women's clothing. Gown and petticoat and chemise, all neatly folded, stockings and stays and shoes. They were familiar. Miss Brown had worn them.

The wardrobe and chest of drawers held men's clothes. A couple of shirts, a couple of neckcloths, a couple of pairs of stockings. Marcus frowned. Even his footmen had more clothes than these. *Could she not afford more?*

She had a comb and hairbrush, but no shaving brush or razor. Marcus studied the washstand, perplexed. How did Albin shave?

Tucked into the corner of the mirror was a square of folded paper. Marcus removed it, unfolded it, and scowled. It was a sketch of a young man wearing a toga and carrying a lyre. He knew where the sketch had come from—Swiffen's *Cyclopaedia*—and he knew why Albin looked so like Orpheus.

Marcus screwed up the sketch and tossed it into the cold grate.

On the nightstand lay a silver pocket watch and a pair of spectacles. The watch was the one he'd rescued from the Honest Sailor. Marcus picked up the spectacles and turned them over in his hand. Albin didn't wear spectacles. Miss Brown didn't wear spectacles.

So why does she have them?

He crouched and opened the nightstand. Inside was a clean chamber pot, nothing more.

Marcus moved into the sitting room. There were no personal items on the table, no personal items on the mantelpiece, but in the bookcase were half a dozen books.

He examined them carefully. A battered three-volume set of the *Iliad* in the original Greek, heavily annotated, with the name Charles Appleby scrawled inside the covers. One tome from the *Aeneid* in Latin, ditto battered and annotated and inscribed. A slender volume of French poetry with marbled endpapers that had been owned by a woman. Albinia West-something, 1776.

Marcus frowned and tried to decipher the surname.

Westcole? Westcott? Westcolt?

The last book was also in French, a sturdy edition of Perrault's *Fairy Tales*. He could read its owner's name easily. Charlotte Appleby. The handwriting was careful, childish.

Charlotte Appleby. Daughter of Charles and Albinia?

Marcus closed the book and put it back in its place on the bookshelf. He crossed to the writing desk and opened the left-hand drawer.

Here were more things that told him about Charlotte. A man's signet ring, heavy and silver. A coiled necklace of red coral beads, inexpensive, but clearly treasured, folded carefully into a scrap of muslin. Two silhouette portraits, each no larger than his palm, one a man, one a woman. Were they her parents?

Marcus studied the silhouettes, trying to discover a likeness to Charlotte. Perhaps the woman's chin? The angle of the man's nose?

He replaced them in the drawer, and closed it.

The middle drawer held two one-pound notes. Marcus frowned at them. Were these all the funds Charlotte had? Two pounds, and the few pennies that had been in her greatcoat pocket?

The right-hand drawer held paper, ink, quills. Nothing personal. No letters or notes or calling cards. It seemed that she'd had no contact with anyone since arriving in London.

Marcus lowered the drop-flap. A dozen sheets of paper lay inside, covered with writing.

He picked up the topmost one. The ink was smudged, but the handwriting was familiar. Albin's handwriting. Charlotte's handwriting.

Dear Sir, I owe you an apology and an explanation.

Marcus pulled out the chair and sat down to read.

CHARLOTTE TOLD HER tale chronologically, starting with her twenty-fifth birthday and ending with his dismissal of her yesterday. What she'd done. Why she'd done it.

Marcus read to the end. It was disconcerting to see the past two weeks through someone else's eyes. It made him feel slightly off-balance, as if he wore spectacles and the focus wasn't quite right. So much that he'd been unaware of, so much he hadn't noticed. *Am I so blind?*

When he'd finished, he folded the pages carefully. This must be the letter Charlotte had sent him. The letter he'd thrown in the fire. It wasn't what he'd expected. No excuses, no pleas for forgiveness. The language was plain and starkly honest, unemotional—but emotion permeated the pages. He felt it through his fingertips, as if the paper had soaked up more than just ink.

Grief. Despair.

He cleared his throat and placed the letter in his breast pocket. Charlotte's betrayal, her deceit, no longer seemed as unforgivable as it had this morning.

If she tells the truth.

But he couldn't doubt that she did. She'd crossed out words because they were misspelled, because they lacked specificity, not because she was trying out different versions of the truth.

Marcus glanced at his watch. He'd been gone almost an hour. Too long.

He crossed the room with long strides and opened the door— and looked back. He'd come here to discover who Charlotte was. What had he learned?

That she lived on the edge of poverty.

That she was alone.

That her motivations hadn't been what he'd thought.

Marcus touched his breast pocket, feeling the thick wad of folded paper. *That she loves me.*

He closed the door and walked back to Grosvenor Square

through the silent, drifting snow and climbed the stairs to the Blue Bedchamber and stood for a long time looking down at Albin. He wanted to be angry, to feel the same rage he had yesterday—but it wouldn't come.

CHAPTER FORTY-FIVE

MARCUS PASSED THE night in the armchair beside Albin's bed. Twice he thought she stopped breathing, twice he jerked to his feet and bent over her, and twice he discovered a pulse, heard a faint exhalation, and sat back in the chair, his heart thudding in his chest.

He read her letter again, skipping the beginning, concentrating on her reasons for becoming Miss Brown. *You thought me bashful, but that wasn't why I blushed and grew tongue-tied whenever you were close. It was a physical response that I had no control over. Each day it grew worse, and I knew that soon you would recognize it for what it was and dismiss me.*

Marcus lowered the letter and looked at the motionless figure in the bed. Charlotte had rated his powers of observation too high.

He found his place again. *. . . and dismiss me. I was most anxious to avoid that; working for you was better than anything I had dared hope for. I cannot imagine having an employer I liked and admired and respected more than you.*

Marcus grimaced, and rubbed his brow. She placed him on a pedestal that he was ill-fitted to stand on. God knew he had enough flaws.

When I saw you at Gentleman Jackson's my physical reaction to you almost overmastered me. I was desperate to be rid of it, so I decided to take your advice. I know it's not advice you would have given to a female, but it was good advice. It worked.

He had a flash of memory: Miss Brown's nervousness, her tension, her resolute expression, her voice saying, "It's *very* important."

He'd wondered what reason could be so imperative, so pressing, that she would put herself through such an ordeal. *Me. I was her reason.* Marcus grimaced again, rubbed his forehead again.

He turned the page, skimmed over Charlotte's description of visiting the Pig and Whistle, the fight she'd narrowly avoided, and focused on her account of his second meeting with her.

I should have refused your request. That was my downfall. But how could I refuse when my actions had caused you distress? I could not be that selfish. And afterwards—after you'd been so kind and so gentle—how could I not love you?

Marcus lifted his gaze to her. Albin lay as still as a waxwork figure.

Had her breathing become irregular?

He jerked out of the armchair and leaned over her. Albin's breath fluttered against his cheek, so faint he barely felt it, barely heard it. Inhalation. Exhalation. Even and regular.

Marcus sat again, his heart hammering against his sternum. He poured himself a cup of lukewarm tea and sipped, while his heartbeat slowed.

He picked up the letter and continued reading, seeing events unfold through Charlotte's eyes—the Smiths' attack at the Honest Sailor, the visit to Whitechapel, the growing sexual intimacy between himself and her. He halted when he came to why Charlotte had refused his *carte-blanche* and read the paragraph three times. *I wanted to spend my life with you. As your secretary, I could do that. As your mistress, I couldn't. You'll marry again, and I will not be an adulteress.*

The words made him feel shame—and they answered the

question he'd asked himself two days ago. If he'd offered marriage instead of a *carte-blanche*, Charlotte would have said yes.

Marcus went back to the first page and reread the encounter with the Faerie, reread what the woman had said about metamorphosis. *I asked her what the dangers were, and there was only one: I'll miscarry if I change shape while pregnant. She did say that if I die, I'll change back into my own shape, but I count that an awkward inconvenience, not a danger. Inconvenient for whoever finds me, that is. It won't matter to me; I'll be dead.*

He grunted. Inconvenient, yes. He lifted his head and gazed at the motionless figure in the bed. What would he do if she died? If Albin became Charlotte? How did one explain the presence of a dead woman in one's house?

Marcus read the letter through to its end again, caught between anger at her many deceptions and admiration for her courage. *I'm sorry for the harm I have done you,* she concluded. *For pretending to be someone I was not, for lying to you, for abusing your trust. You need not worry that I shall take another person's shape and try to enter your life again. I give you my word that I won't—if you can bring yourself to believe it.*

He could. He did.

Marcus refolded the letter and placed it in his breast pocket and looked at Albin. At Charlotte. He didn't agree with all the choices she'd made, but he understood them. He could forgive them. As it had been with Barnaby, it wasn't a conscious decision, wasn't something he had control over. It was a choice his heart made: forgiveness.

He placed more coal on the fire and turned his attention to the seven diaries Charlotte had stolen for him. Reading them elicited quite different emotions. Revulsion. Fury. Guilt. He'd failed Lavinia. Failed to notice that Monkwood's brotherly affection was in fact something warped and foul. Failed to rescue her.

Such ugliness, under his nose, and he'd been oblivious to it.

Marcus grimaced and turned a page. A paragraph jumped out at him: *Today I received a letter from my beautiful Helen, asking for more sponges. She wants to reign for another Season, not grow fat with Cosgrove's child. I shall purchase them tomorrow and take them down to Hazelbrook next week.*

Rage flared in his chest. He might have had an heir if not for Lavinia's vanity, if not for Monkwood's connivance.

But some of the rage was directed at himself. A blind fool. That's what he'd been: a blind fool. Too deeply in love to notice that his bride was taking precautions not to have his child.

Why had he not realized?

Why had Lavinia's maid not realized?

Marcus lowered the diary. Lavinia's maid must have known about the sponges, just as she must have been aware of the incest. For years, she must have known—and been complicit.

I should have spoken to Monkwood's servants before I offered for Lavinia.

He glanced at Albin. What would the servants at Westcote Hall tell him about Charlotte? Was she the person he thought he knew—Albin, Miss Brown, the Charlotte of her letter—or did she have another face? A face he hadn't yet seen.

A HOUSEMAID KNOCKED before dawn. She smelled of furniture polish and coal dust. "Sir, Mr. Plaistow's arrived from Hazelbrook. He says he needs to speak with you."

"Plaistow?" What was his bailiff doing here? "Are you certain?"

"Yes, sir. He says it's some'ut to do with Mr. Monkwood, sir."

"Monkwood?" Marcus pushed to his feet. "Stay with Mr. Albin, please, Lucy."

He took the stairs two at a time and found Mr. Plaistow in the study, huddled over a newly lit fire.

"Plaistow? What's wrong?"

"Sir!" The bailiff wore travel-stained riding clothes and a distraught expression. "Something's happened at Hazelbrook. Right terrible, it is."

"Monkwood?"

"Yes, sir. He . . . He . . ." Plaistow's face twisted. "He's killed himself!"

"Ah . . ." It wasn't distress Marcus felt unfurling in his chest. It was satisfaction. Satisfaction—and a prick of disappointment. *I would have liked to have been the one to kill him.*

He crossed to the decanters, poured a glass of brandy, and gave it to the bailiff. "Tell me."

Plaistow took a large gulp. "Mr. Monkwood arrived yesterday, sir. Almost at dusk. He asked to be taken up to the roof, where her ladyship had fallen. Mr. Gough didn't see no reason not to let him—he was her la'ship's brother!"

"He jumped?"

"He jumped, sir. Right at the very spot her la'ship fell. Killed himself dead!"

"Did someone inform the magistrate?"

"Immediately, sir. And then I came straight here. I'd have got here sooner, sir, but the roads—"

"You did well."

Plaistow turned the glass in his hands. His face twisted again. "Mr. Gough is right cut up about it—"

"No blame attaches to him," Marcus said firmly. "Absolutely none."

The only person to blame for Monkwood's death was Monkwood himself. He'd seduced his own sister, and everything had spread outwards from that act.

DR. BAILLIE VISITED at ten o'clock. "Good, good," he said, clucking his tongue as he examined the wound. "No more bleeding, no infection, no fever. He's doing well, sir. Very well."

"But he hasn't woken."

"Give it time, sir. Give it time." Baillie cast him a shrewd glance. "You look as if you could do with some rest."

Marcus dismissed this with a shake of his head. "You think he'll live?"

"I can't say that, sir. Not categorically. But it looks hopeful. Very hopeful." Baillie rebandaged the wound, his fingers deft. "Rest, Lord Cosgrove. Let someone else watch over him."

Marcus rubbed eyes that were gritty with tiredness. "That injury was meant for me."

Baillie pulled the covers up to Albin's chin. "Depriving yourself of sleep won't keep him alive, sir. Or make him heal any faster."

I know.

But he didn't take Baillie's advice, didn't send for one of the footmen to take his place, didn't go to his bedchamber and strip off his clothes and crawl into bed.

If Charlotte died, if she changed back into herself . . . He couldn't leave a footman to cope with that.

But that wasn't the only reason that kept him here at her side, unable to sleep.

Charlotte loved him. And she might die. And he couldn't leave her.

DR. BAILLIE RETURNED at six o'clock that evening. "Didn't take my advice, I see, sir."

Marcus grunted. He pushed up out of the armchair. His joints seemed to creak, as if he'd aged thirty years in the course of the day.

Baillie examined Albin. "No fever. No infection. I'd say he's out of danger."

"But he still hasn't woken."

"He will." Baillie pulled the bedcovers up, smoothed them, then turned to face Marcus. He crossed his arms over his chest. "Do I have to get your servants to slip you some laudanum?"

Marcus's lips twitched in a smile. "I'd like to see you try."

Baillie laughed, a small *harrumph* of sound. "Sleep, or I will." He turned towards the door.

"Mr. Albin will live?"

Baillie halted and looked back. "In my professional opinion, yes."

Marcus stood motionless for several minutes after the doctor had left. Relief made him feel light-headed, or maybe it was exhaustion. He rang for Fellowes. "A trestle bed, set up in here."

"For one of the footmen, sir?"

"For me."

MARCUS HAD INTENDED to check on Charlotte every hour, but he fell asleep within seconds of his head touching the pillow and didn't wake until the shutters were opened. Weak daylight streamed into the room.

He yawned and rubbed his face. Stubble rasped beneath his hands. "What's the time?"

"Nine o'clock, sir." The voice was Leggatt's.

"Nine!" Marcus threw back the covers and hurried to the four-poster bed.

Albin had moved in the night. He no longer lay like a corpse, arms and legs straight. His head was turned to the side, one leg was bent, his left hand curled by his cheek. His breathing was even, peaceful.

Leggatt came to stand alongside him. "Looks like he'll wake

today, sir."

"Yes." And once Charlotte woke, what then?

MARCUS REREAD CHARLOTTE'S letter while he ate breakfast. When he'd finished, he was no closer to knowing what to do. Charlotte had deceived him, but her deceptions had been nothing like Lavinia's, her motivations not vanity and greed and a desire to hurt him. On the contrary, she'd tried to protect him. Had risked her life for him more than once.

And she claimed to love him.

But so had Lavinia.

He rubbed his forehead, pressing skin against bone. What to do? The faces Charlotte had shown him were remarkably congruent with one another, but how could he know—truly *know*— that they were real and not an enticing façade?

A footman entered the breakfast parlor, carrying a silver teapot. "More tea, sir?"

"Thank you."

Marcus watched the man pour, and thought about servants, and then took his steaming teacup to the library and looked up the Westcote baronetcy in Debrett's *Baronetage, Knightage, and Companionage*. Near the village of Halstead, in Essex. He found Halstead on the map, and rang for Fellowes.

"Sir?"

"I'm going into Essex. To Halstead. Have my traveling carriage ready in an hour—no, make it a post-chaise." He didn't want to arrive at Halstead in a carriage with his arms blazoned on the door. "Someone is to stay with Mr. Albin every minute I'm away. If he takes a turn for the worse, send for Dr. Baillie and inform me *immediately*. I'll be putting up at whatever inn Halstead has, under the name of Langford."

"Yes, sir." If Fellowes was surprised by this sudden journey, he didn't show it.

"I expect to be gone three days. When Mr. Albin wakes, don't let him leave this house. He's to stay until I return."

Marcus repeated the instructions to his valet, with one additional command: "Look after Mr. Albin as you would myself."

"Of course, sir." Leggatt briskly placed folded shirts in a valise, starched neckcloths, a change of collars. "Don't worry about Mr. Albin. We'll take good care of him."

CHAPTER FORTY-SIX

November 2nd, 1805
Grosvenor Square, London

MARCUS LEFT LONDON pristine beneath a mantle of snow, and returned to find the city wet and filthy. Gray piles of snow lay melting in the middle of Grosvenor Square, icy sludge filled the gutters, and water dripped steadily from the eaves.

He took the steps two at a time to his front door. "Mr. Albin?" he asked, stripping off his gloves in the entrance hall. "How is he?"

"Weak as a kitten, sir," Fellowes said. "But Mr. Leggatt had him sitting up today."

"Excellent." Some of the tension he'd been carrying in his shoulders eased.

"Frederick and Oliver arrived back from Derbyshire not two hours ago, sir," Fellowes said, taking his hat. "I'm afraid I gave them the rest of the day off, as I didn't expect you back so early, but if you'd like to talk with them—"

"Tomorrow's fine." Marcus shrugged out of his greatcoat. So many things to deal with: retrieving his political reputation, Monkwood's suicide, Phillip—but those could all wait. "I'll see Mr. Albin now."

"I believe he's asleep, sir."

Damnation.

"Would you like luncheon, sir?"

What he wanted was to speak with Charlotte. The urgency that had driven him to travel through the night hadn't lessened now that he was home. If anything, it was stronger.

"Sir? Would you like luncheon?"

Damn it. "Yes."

LEGGATT FUSSED OVER her. She was washed and combed and shaved, her teeth cleaned, her nails trimmed, as pampered and polished as if she were Cosgrove himself. "There," the valet said, with a final flourish of the comb.

"Thank you."

"Not at all, Mr. Albin. We're all very happy to see you recovered."

Leggatt helped her dress—freshly laundered nightshirt, brocade dressing gown, slippers—carefully tied her right arm in a sling and supported her to the winged armchair beside the fire. He spread a large cashmere shawl over her knees, then positioned a second armchair across from her. "I'll fetch his lordship."

Charlotte's stomach clenched. *I'd rather you didn't.* But she had to face the earl before she left, had to thank him for his care of her.

She stared down at the shawl. It was woven in shades of brown and gold, with a tasseled fringe.

None of the servants who'd looked after her the past three days had mentioned her falling-out with the earl, but they must all be wondering. Cosgrove had dismissed her from his service, banned her from his house—and then brought her back and looked after her.

Why had he brought her to Grosvenor Square?

Why had he stayed at her bedside for two days and nights?

How easily one's mind leapt to foolish conclusions. If the earl had brought her back to Grosvenor Square, if he'd stayed at her bedside, he'd done it out of a sense of duty.

Charlotte squeezed her eyes shut against memory of Hyde Park: the angularity of Cosgrove's face, the hatred in his eyes, the cold and implacable anger in his voice.

Footsteps sounded in the corridor.

She opened her eyes and watched the earl step into the doorway. Her stomach contracted into a tighter knot.

There was no emotion in Cosgrove's eyes as he examined her. His face was expressionless, remote.

Charlotte tried to swallow, but her throat was too tight. "Good afternoon, sir."

"Good afternoon." Cosgrove closed the door. "You're looking much better. How do you feel?"

"Fine, sir," Charlotte said, ignoring the exhaustion, the ache in her shoulder.

Cosgrove crossed to the second armchair. "A sling, I see."

"Yes, sir. Dr. Baillie says I can go back to Chandlers Street in a day or two." The words were stilted in her mouth. This—being in the same room as the earl, making meaningless conversation—was almost as excruciating as her first meeting with him as Miss Brown.

We're both pretending.

Her deception, Cosgrove's fury—those things lay just below the surface, politely ignored.

"You'll stay until you're properly on your feet again. Whether you realize it or not, you came within a hair's breadth of dying." Cosgrove crossed his legs. His pose was casual, but he didn't look relaxed. There was a stiffness in his limbs, a stiffness in his face.

An awkward silence fell. Charlotte looked down at her lap, counting the seconds as they lumbered past. Four. Five. Six.

Cosgrove spoke: "I must thank you for your actions on Monday. I had anticipated an ambush, but not . . . what happened. I didn't think Monkwood personally capable of violence. It's possible you saved my life."

Charlotte glanced up, and shook her head. "You would have knocked him down."

"Perhaps. Perhaps not." Cosgrove tugged at his neckcloth, as if it was too tight. "And I must apologize for my behavior at Hyde Park. It was unpardonably rude."

She shook her head again. "You treated me as I deserved, sir. It was I who behaved unpardonably."

His eyebrows pinched together. "You were injured—"

"You didn't know that, sir. I didn't even know."

Cosgrove's frown didn't ease. His face had a familiar angularity to it, but she didn't think it was rage he felt. Guilt? Did he blame himself for her injury?

Charlotte looked down at her lap. She wound her fingers in the shawl's fringe.

"Charlotte?"

She looked up.

"Will you please change into yourself?"

She shrank back in the armchair. "I'd prefer not to, sir, if . . . if you don't mind." Albin's face was a mask, a barrier between herself and the earl. If she wore her own face he'd be able to see her much more clearly.

Cosgrove's mouth tightened fractionally. She couldn't quite read his expression. Discomfort?

He crossed his legs the other way and tugged at his neckcloth again. "Did Leggatt tell you where I've been?"

Charlotte shook her head.

"Essex. Westcote Hall."

For a moment, she couldn't breathe. It wasn't shock that choked her lungs; it was horror. Charlotte forced herself to inhale, forced herself to speak: "Did you ask my uncle to take me back?"

"I didn't meet with him. I talked to some of the servants."

She blinked. "The servants? Why?"

"To ask them about you."

"Me?" *Why?*

Cosgrove must have read the question on her face, because he answered it: "To see if you're who I think you are."

"Oh." Charlotte looked down at the cashmere shawl and smoothed the fringe with the palm of her hand. *Do I want to know what the servants thought of me?*

Pity. They'd pitied her. And perhaps—

"I spoke with the housekeeper, the butler, and two of the maids. They were relieved to hear you're safe in London. The housekeeper cried."

Charlotte glanced up. "Cried? Mrs. Heslop?"

"She's been extremely worried about you. She wanted to send you some money to tide you over."

"Money?" Charlotte said, horrified. "From her savings? I couldn't accept that!"

"I persuaded her that you had sufficient funds."

"Thank you." The horror subsided. In its place was shame. "I'll write to her at once."

"Do that." The earl shifted in the armchair, as if he was uncomfortable. He uncrossed his legs, then crossed them again. "Charlotte, will you please change into yourself? I . . . I have something I wish to say to you."

Charlotte cringed inwardly. If she showed Cosgrove her real face, it would be like stripping naked in front of him. "One of the servants might see me."

"I gave orders we weren't to be disturbed."

Charlotte looked down at her lap again. She twisted the shawl's fringe between her fingers.

Cosgrove stood. He walked to her armchair, placed a hand on each upholstered arm, and leaned over her. There was nothing threatening about his stance; if anything, it was suppliant. "Charlotte . . . please. I'm begging you."

Charlotte closed her eyes tightly. How could she deny his request when he spoke like that, his voice low and pleading?

The cringing sensation in her chest grew stronger.

Charlotte inhaled a shallow breath and wished herself back into her own shape. Magic itched over her skin. When she opened her eyes, her vision was blurred. She didn't correct it; she didn't want to see the earl clearly. She kept her head bowed, her gaze lowered.

"Thank you." Cosgrove smoothed a strand of hair back from her brow, his touch light, as if she were fragile, breakable. His fingers stroked down her cheek, then tilted her chin upward. He bent his head and laid his mouth on hers for a moment, softly, gently.

The world seemed to lurch sideways. "But . . . but you hate me, sir."

"No." The earl kissed her again, then straightened and felt in his pocket. "Here, I forgot you need these." He held out her spectacles.

Charlotte put them on clumsily with her left hand. Thoughts spun in her head in a confused, jerky dance. Cosgrove didn't hate her? He'd kissed her?

The room came into focus. The earl's face came into focus. Gray eyes, strong nose, black eyebrows. He lowered to a crouch in front of her. "Charlotte . . . you were extremely honest in your letter. I shall try to be as honest." He took her left hand in both of his. "I liked Christopher Albin a lot. And . . . I liked Miss Brown a lot, too. The reason I asked you to be my mistress was because I wanted you in my life." Color crept along his cheekbones, as if the admission embarrassed him. "I think I know who you are, as a person, and . . . I like that person. And so . . ." He swallowed, and took a deep breath. "Will you please marry me?"

Charlotte stared at him. Cosgrove wasn't offering her a choice between secretary or mistress; he was offering her marriage.

Impossible.

"You want to marry *me*?" The words were awkward on her tongue, oddly shaped.

Cosgrove nodded, his gaze fixed on her face. "We'd be happy together, don't you think?"

"But, sir—"

"Marcus."

"But I'm not well-born enough for you! You're an earl and I'm . . . I'm nobody."

"The granddaughter of a baronet and of a general is not nobody. Your birth is perfectly respectable."

Charlotte bit her lip. Perhaps she'd misunderstood his offer. "You're proposing a . . . a marriage of convenience?"

Cosgrove's face relaxed into a smile. "No, you goose. A love match."

"But . . . you don't love me."

The earl's smile faded. His grip on her hand tightened until it almost hurt. "I do. That's what I'm trying to tell you."

The world lurched sideways again. *He loves me?* "But I deceived you, sir."

"Marcus. My name is Marcus, not sir."

Charlotte flushed. "I deceived you . . . Marcus."

"You did. But I find I still trust you." His gaze was so intense she could scarcely breathe. It was as if those gray eyes looked into her soul. "Am I wrong to do so?"

Tears blurred her vision. Charlotte blinked them back. "No."

"Then . . . you'll marry me?"

She saw how much her answer mattered to him—the painful intensity of his gaze, the tension in his body, the way he held his breath. *He truly wants to marry me.*

Charlotte's throat was too tight for speech. She nodded.

Cosgrove released his breath. "Thank you."

The world still hadn't quite settled back into place. She felt as if everything was tilted fractionally. Charlotte looked down at their linked hands. Marriage. To Cosgrove. It was a dream, as unreal as finding a Faerie in one's bedchamber. *And yet that was real. And so is this.*

Scabs ridged the earl's knuckles. The skin was gray with bruises.

"Your hands, what happened?"

"The punching bag. Charlotte . . ." Cosgrove leaned closer, his face suddenly serious. "I must ask that you don't use your magic until I have an heir. I'm sorry, but I can't risk the earldom."

"I'll never use my magic again. Ever. I promise." And then she remembered Monkwood. "Except to protect you. Sir—I mean, Marcus—Gerald Monkwood is dangerous! Even if he leaves for Australia he could hire someone—"

"Monkwood's dead. He jumped from the roof at Hazelbrook. Did no one tell you?"

"No." Charlotte blinked, and turned this unexpected fact over in her mind, examining it. "Do you think he may have hired someone to murder you?"

Cosgrove shook his head. "He killed himself on Monday, at dusk. He must have left London immediately after our altercation. He had no time to hire anyone."

"Oh." Charlotte calculated the distances in her head. Cosgrove was correct. Relief surged through her. "I'm glad he's dead."

"So am I." The earl's grip tightened on her hand. "He almost killed you."

His gaze—intense, fierce—caught hers. Charlotte found herself unable to look away, unable to think clearly. She blinked,
and swallowed, and tried to find coherency. "I give you my
word I'll never use magic again."

His fierceness eased. "Don't say that. I confess . . . I envy
you. I should very much like to be able to fly."

Cosgrove was telling the truth; she heard it in his voice, saw
it in his wry smile. He wished he could fly.

"Perhaps I'll use it one day," Charlotte conceded. "But I
promise I'll never do it without your knowledge. And not until
we've had children. Lots of children."

"Thank you." Cosgrove lifted her hand to his lips, kissed it,
and then sat back on his heels and studied her, his head tilted
slightly to one side. "You look charming in those spectacles."

Heat rose in Charlotte's face. She shook her head.

The earl grinned. He reached out and tapped her cheek lightly
with a fingertip. "You'll stay here until you have your strength
back, and then Christopher Albin ceases to exist. All right?"

Charlotte nodded.

"And then I'll visit Ramsgate or Brighton or wherever you
choose, and while I'm there I'll meet a young lady called Charlotte Appleby. And I shall marry her. What do you think?"

I think I must be dreaming.

She'd come to London to earn her independence, to forge a
career as a man, but this—what Cosgrove offered her—was
more magical than anything she'd envisaged.

Not his secretary, not his mistress, but his wife.

The future shone so brightly it was almost blinding. She'd
share Cosgrove's life. Help him fight his battles. Build a family
with him. Laugh with him. Love him.

"I think it will serve perfectly, sir."

"My name is Marcus, not sir." The earl reached out and gently pinched her chin, his eyes smiling. "Say it."

"Marcus." The world settled into place again, firmly, solidly, with a sense of permanence. "It will serve perfectly, Marcus. And we shall have *dozens* of children and live happily ever after."

He grinned. "Indeed, we shall."

AFTERWARDS

ON NOVEMBER SIXTH, 1805, news of England's decisive victory in the Battle of Trafalgar reached London. In the ensuing frenzy of excitement—and public grief at the death of Lord Nelson in battle—Christopher Albin quietly departed from Grosvenor Square.

The earl relocated to the seaside town of Ramsgate for the winter, where his whirlwind romance and marriage put all thought of vanished secretaries out of his servants' heads.

The new countess was proved correct in her prediction: she and Cosgrove lived happily, their home filled with laughter and children.

The earl was also successful at foretelling the future. He predicted that the slave trade would be abolished in the British Empire, and on March 25th, 1807, it was.

AUTHOR'S NOTE

AN ESSAY ON the Slavery and Commerce of the Human Species, Particularly the African, was written by Thomas Clarkson in 1785, while he was a student at Cambridge University. Originally written in Latin, the essay was subsequently published in English. Thomas Clarkson became a leading campaigner against the slave trade.

Other notable abolitionists mentioned in this novel are William Wilberforce, William Grenville (1st Baron Grenville), and the Honorable Charles Fox. Of course, many more men and women were involved in the battle for abolition of the slave trade. Thankfully, they prevailed.

THANK YOU

Thanks for reading *Unmasking Miss Appleby*. I hope you enjoyed it!

If you'd like to be notified when I release new books, please join my Readers' Group (www.emilylarkin.com/newsletter).

I welcome all honest reviews. Reviews and word of mouth help other readers to find books, so please consider taking a few moments to leave a review on Goodreads or elsewhere.

Unmasking Miss Appleby is the first book in the Baleful Godmother series. The next books are *Resisting Miss Merryweather, Trusting Miss Trentham, Claiming Mister Kemp, Ruining Miss Wrotham,* and *Discovering Miss Dalrymple,* with more to follow. I hope you enjoy them all!

Those of you who like to start a series at its absolute beginning may wish to read the series prequel—the Fey Quartet—a quartet of novellas that tell the tales of a widow, her three daughters, and one baleful Faerie. Their titles are *Maythorn's Wish, Hazel's Promise, Ivy's Choice,* and *Larkspur's Quest.* A free digital copy of *The Fey Quartet* is available to anyone who joins my Readers' Group. Visit www.emilylarkin.com/starter-library.

If you'd like to read the first chapter of *Resisting Miss Merryweather,* the novella that comes next in the Baleful Godmother series, please turn the page.

CHAPTER ONE

April 6ᵗʰ, 1807
Devonshire

BARNABY WARE LET the curricle slow to a halt. He gazed past the horses' ears at the high-banked Devon lane that opened like a tunnel on his left. The knot of dread that had been sitting in his belly all morning tied itself even tighter. *Picturesque,* a voice noted in his head. The tall banks were clothed in grass and wildflowers and shaded by overhanging trees.

"This'll be the lane to Woodhuish Abbey, sir," his groom, Catton, said, with a nod at the lightning-struck oak on the far bank.

I know. But Barnaby didn't lift the reins, didn't urge the horses into motion.

Four days it had taken to get here, each day traveling more slowly. Today, he'd practically let the horses walk. And now, with less than a mile left of his journey, all he wanted to do was turn the curricle around and head back to Berkshire.

"No mistaking that oak," Catton said, after a moment's silence. "Split right in half, just like the innkeeper said."

I know. The dread was expanding in his belly, and growing apace with it was a bone-deep certainty that he shouldn't be here. So what if the invitation had been in Marcus's handwriting? *I shouldn't have come.*

Barnaby glanced over his shoulder. The road was empty. And there was plenty of space to turn the curricle.

Catton would think him a coward, but what did he care what the groom thought? What did he care what *anyone* thought anymore?

"Sir Barnaby Ware?" a female voice said.

Barnaby's head snapped around. He searched the shadows and found a young girl in a dark-colored redingote, up on the nearest bank, in the deep green gloom of the trees.

"Er . . . hello?" he said.

The girl descended the bank nimbly. She wore sturdy kid leather boots and a straw bonnet tied under her chin with a bow. How old was she? Twelve? Fourteen?

"Sir Barnaby Ware?" she asked again, stepping up to the curricle and tilting her head back to look at him.

Sunlight fell on her face, showing him sky-blue eyes and flaxen ringlets.

Barnaby blinked. Not a girl; a woman in her twenties, trim and petite. "Yes."

Was this Marcus's new wife? Surely not. The gossip was that the new Lady Cosgrove was a plain woman, and this woman was definitely not plain.

"I'm Anne Merryweather," the woman said, with a friendly smile. "Lady Cosgrove's cousin. May I possibly beg a ride to the abbey?"

"Of course," Barnaby said automatically, and then his brain caught up with his mouth. *Damnation.* He managed a stiff smile. "It would be my pleasure, Miss, er, Mrs.—?"

"Miss Merryweather," she said cheerfully. "But most people call me Merry. It's less of a mouthful!"

Half a minute later, Miss Merryweather was seated alongside him and Catton was perched behind in the tiger's seat. Barnaby reluctantly lifted the reins. It appeared he was going to face

Marcus after all.

His stomach clenched as they entered the shady lane.

"I saw you once at Vauxhall," Miss Merryweather said. "Several years ago."

Barnaby wrenched his thoughts back to his companion. "Er . . . you did?"

"At one of the ridottos."

Barnaby looked more closely at her—the heart-shaped face, the dimples, the full, sweet mouth. Did she expect him to recognize her? "I'm afraid I don't recall meeting you," he said apologetically.

"Oh, we weren't introduced. I was there with my fiancé, and you were with Lord Cosgrove and his fiancée."

"Oh." His face stiffened. The familiar emotions surged through him: guilt, shame, remorse.

Barnaby looked away, and gripped the reins tightly. God, to be able to go back to the person he'd been then. To be able to relive his life and not make the same dreadful mistake.

"I noticed you most particularly. You were the best dancer there."

It took a few seconds for the words to penetrate the fog of shame and regret. When they did, Barnaby blinked. "Me?"

"Marcus dances fairly well," Miss Merryweather said. "He's a natural athlete, but he's a pugilist. He's trained his body for strength, not grace. You, I'd hazard a guess, are a better fencer and horseman than Marcus."

"Not by much," Barnaby said, staring at her. What an unusual female.

"It takes a number of qualities to make a truly excellent dancer. Not merely precision and grace and stamina, but a musical ear as well, and of course one must *enjoy* dancing. You have all of those qualities, Sir Barnaby. You're one of the best dancers I've ever seen."

Barnaby felt himself blush. "Thank you." He refrained from glancing back at Catton. The groom was doubtless smirking.

"Marcus's neighbors are holding a ball tomorrow night. I know it's terribly forward of me, but I hope we can dance at least one set together?"

"Of course." And then he remembered Marcus. The blush drained from Barnaby's face. Dread congealed in his belly. "If I'm still here."

Miss Merryweather's eyebrows lifted slightly. "You're staying for two weeks, aren't you?"

"Perhaps not." Perhaps not even one night. It depended on Marcus. Depended on whether Marcus could bear to be in the same room as him. Could bear to even look at him.

Barnaby's stomach twisted in on itself. *This is a mistake. I shouldn't have come.* Some errors could never be atoned for. His hands tightened on the reins. The horses obediently slowed.

"Marcus expects you to stay for a fortnight, you know. He's been looking forward to your visit."

Barnaby felt even sicker. He glanced at Miss Merryweather. Her gaze was astonishingly astute. *Oh, God, how much does she know?*

He halted the curricle. "Miss Merryweather, I—"

She laid her gloved hand on his arm, cutting off his words. "Don't make any decisions now, Sir Barnaby. Wait until you've talked with Marcus."

She knows I'm about to turn around and run.

Miss Merryweather removed her hand and gave him a warm, sympathetic smile. "He says you're his best friend."

To Barnaby's horror, the words brought a rush of moisture to his eyes. He turned his head away and blinked fiercely, flicked the reins, urged the horses into a brisk trot. He concentrated on the shade-dappled lane, on the horses, on the reins, on his breathing—anything but Miss Merryweather's words.

The lane swung right, the grassy banks lowered, and a view opened out: woodland, meadow, a sweeping drive leading to a large stone building that must be Woodhuish Abbey. The abbey was a sprawling, whimsical structure, with gracefully arched windows and a crenellated roof parapet. Ivy climbed the stone walls.

"Beautiful, isn't it?" Miss Merryweather said.

Barnaby's brain was frozen in a state between dismay and panic. It took him several seconds to find a response. "Very gothic."

The curricle swung into the driveway. Gravel crunched beneath the wheels. Dread climbed his throat like bile. *Oh, God, I can't face Marcus again.* The last time had almost crucified him. But it was too late to turn back now. Far too late. They were within sight of the windows. Another minute and they'd be in front of the great, arched doorway.

Barnaby sat in numb horror while the horses trotted down the driveway.

"It was a monastery for more than three hundred years—Augustinian—they built the most *marvelous* walled gardens—but it's been in private hands since Henry the Eighth. Marcus says the previous owner remodeled it in the Strawberry Hill style. Are you familiar with Strawberry Hill, Sir Barnaby?"

Barnaby managed to unstick his tongue. "Walpole's place. Gothic."

He brought the curricle to a halt at the foot of the steps. Catton leapt down and ran to the horses' heads.

"Thank you for the ride, Sir Barnaby," Miss Merryweather said.

Barnaby's throat was too dry for a response. He managed a stiff nod. His fingers didn't want to release the reins.

The door swung open. A butler emerged into the sunlight. Behind him was another man, taller, younger, darker. Marcus.

Barnaby's stomach folded in on itself. *Oh, God.*

Like to read the rest?
Resisting Miss Merryweather is available now.

ACKNOWLEDGMENTS

A NUMBER OF people helped to make this book what it is. I would like to thank my editors, Laura Cifelli Stibich and Bev Katz Rosenbaum, my copyeditor, Maria Fairchild, and my proofreader, Martin O'Hearn.

The cover and the series logo are both the work of the talented Kim Killion, of The Killion Group. Thank you, Kim!

And last—but definitely not least—my thanks go to my parents, without whose support this book would not have been published.

EMILY LARKIN GREW up in a house full of books—her mother was a librarian and her father a novelist—so perhaps it's not surprising that she became a writer.

Emily has studied a number of subjects, including geology and geophysics, canine behavior, and ancient Greek. Her varied career includes stints as a field assistant in Antarctica and a waitress on the Isle of Skye, as well as five vintages in New Zealand's wine industry.

She loves to travel and has lived in Sweden, backpacked in Europe and North America, and traveled overland in the Middle East, China, and North Africa. She enjoys climbing hills, yoga workouts, watching reruns of *Buffy the Vampire Slayer* and *Firefly,* and reading.

Emily writes historical romances as Emily Larkin and fantasy novels as Emily Gee. Her websites are www.emilylarkin.com and www.emilygee.com.

Never miss a new Emily Larkin book! Join her Readers' Group at www.emilylarkin.com/newsletter and receive free digital copies of *The Fey Quartet* and *Unmasking Miss Appleby.*

Made in the USA
Middletown, DE
01 January 2018